Mary's Vision

Mary's Vision

Mary Magdalene and the
Quest for Gender Equality

Philip R. Pryde

"So there is no difference between … men and women;
you are all one in union with Christ Jesus."
(Galatians 3:28)

PrydeBooks
SAN DIEGO, CALIFORNIA

PrydeBooks™
San Diego, California

10 9 8 7 6 5 4 3 2
First Edition 2022
Printed in the United States of America

ISBN-13: 978-0-578-37345-4

Library of Congress Catalog Card Number: 2022910115

Cover & book design by CenterPointe Media
www.CenterPointeMedia.com

DEDICATION

To everyone I have encountered in life who helped teach me the
wisdom of truth, equality, honor, justice, and understanding,
I dedicate this book.

To all who throughout history
Tried hard, but sadly failed,
Yet still inspired new dreamers
Who, seeking truth, prevailed.
– PRP

MARY'S VISION

ACKNOWLEDGMENTS

This work was difficult to prepare, given that so little is known about its central character. Also, the story is necessarily set in unfamiliar places and at a time from the distant past. As a result, it involved considerable research from a wide variety of sources. A complete list of the sources consulted is presented in Appendix E, with the ones found to be most helpful indicated by an asterisk.

Particularly informative, besides the Bible itself, were *Daily Life in Biblical Times* by Borowski, *Secrets of Mary Magdelene* by Burstein and de Keijzer, *Peter, Paul, and Mary Magdalene* by Ehrman, *Guideposts Family Topical Concordance to the Bible, Mary Magdalen: Myth and Metaphor* by Haskins, *The Story of Christianity* by Isbouts, *The Gospel of Mary of Magdala: Jesus and the First Woman Apostle* by King, *The Gospel of Mary Magdalene* by Leloup, *Women in Scripture* by Meyers, *The Women Around Jesus* by Moltmann-Wendell, *The Gnostic Gospels* by Pagels, and *The Resurrection of Mary Magdalene Understood* by Schaberg. Any and all of the foregoing works are recommended to anyone who is interested in gaining a better knowledge of Mary Magdalene.

Of major assistance were the several persons who read the manuscript and offered helpful suggestions for its improvement. Among those were Holly Lorincz, Terrin Irwin, Peggy Ellis, Thomas Owen-Towle and Romney O'Connell. Their detailed and insightful commentary on the work at various stages in its evolution is especially appreciated.

A particular word of heartfelt thanks goes to Matthew Greenblatt and CenterPointe Media for their considerable assistance in preparing the manuscript for publication and its ensuing promotion. I greatly appreciate how much time and effort their knowledge saved me.

Also to be thanked for their assistance in various forms are Chip MacGregor, George Christakos, Diana Richardson, Aurie Kryzuda, Marcia Buompensiero, Penn Wallace, and David Waters.

This work is unusual for a novel in that its contents are supported by over one hundred footnotes. Most of these are references to the passages in the Bible that were the source of quotations or situations that were needed by the author in order to create a plausible life for this most important of the female disciples. Further, the footnotes allow readers to examine more of the contexts that surrounded these situations and the interpretation given to them by various authors and reviewers.

Special appreciation is extended to my life partner Alison Cummings, whose encouragement, recommendations, and patience were much appreciated during the twelve years the book was in preparation.

TABLE OF CONTENTS

Part One: Galilee

Part Two: Gaul

Part Three: Fugitives

Epilogue

INTRODUCTION

The purpose, background, and storyline of this book is unusual. Its goal is to offer a new perspective, and an enhanced appreciation, of one of the most intriguing but enigmatic women who ever lived – the disciple Mary Magdalene. Sadly, we know almost nothing factual about her. For this reason, readers may wish to familiarize themselves with her via this introduction.

The task of writing about Mary Magdalene is challenging. Since so little is known about her, writers can invent anything they want, and they have. This often results in contrived stories which lack both justification and credibility.

This doesn't mean they're bad stories. At least three successful motion pictures – *Jesus Christ Superstar*, *The Last Temptation of Christ*, and *The Da Vinci Code* – have been made with Mary Magdalene as a central figure. While these films are entertaining, it's widely agreed that Mary Magdalene's depiction in them is unsupported by anything in the Bible.

Indeed, only twelve passages in the Gospels make any reference to Mary Magdalene. In them, Mary says only one word to Jesus: "Rabboni!" ["Teacher!"] (John 20:16). After the four Gospels, there is no further mention of Mary Magdalene.[1]

Other sources exist, however, most notably several second-century writings known as the Gnostic Gospels. Time caused some to be partially destroyed, and it's unknown who wrote them or their sources. None of them were accepted at the Council (Synod) of Carthage in 397 c.e. to be part of the official (canonical) Bible.[2] For those who reject the Gnostic Gospels, all that's left are the four canonical Gospels which, as noted, reveal almost nothing about Mary Magdalene.

Or is it not much? Two days after the crucifixion, Mary suddenly becomes the most prominent disciple. She is the only person reported in all four Gospels as being present at both the crucifixion and resurrection (none of the Apostles are). Further, in three of the four Gospels, she is described as the first person to whom the risen Christ appeared. It seems clear that Mary Magdalene was far more than just another dedicated follower of Jesus.

Writers have speculated about her for centuries. The most common image of her is that of a repentant prostitute. The problem here is that nothing in the Bible supports this. Indeed, the Catholic Church itself, in 1969, admitted that she was not a prostitute, ending an undeserved guilty sentence of almost fourteen hundred years (see Appendix B).

Other writers believe Mary was the opposite, a wealthy woman who helped support Jesus' ministries out of her own resources, but no facts are offered that would support this. Yet another depiction of Mary Magdalene is as an African, possibly from Egypt or Ethiopia, sometimes being referred to as the Black Madonna. There are also multiple traditions of Mary Magdalene's post-resurrection life in France.

Thus, despite a lack of supporting evidence, various stories about Mary Magdalene have flourished. During the Renaissance, many paintings of her appeared as the repentant prostitute. This view of her was exploited in the play and film, *Jesus Christ Superstar*.

The real fantasizing, though, began earlier when books appeared hypothesizing that Jesus and Mary Magdalene were married and may have had children. This was the theme of Dan Brown's hugely popular *The Da Vinci Code*. Again, nothing in the Bible supports this. All of these images of Mary Magdalene intrigued me and peaked with *The Da Vinci Code*. The thought wouldn't go away that if none of these images of Mary Magdalene's life were correct, then what *was* her life like? That persistent question motivated this book.

I believe it's possible to make some assumptions. First, she's called Mary Magdalene, meaning she was from the small town of Magdala, located on the shore of the Sea of Galilee. Magdala was a small farming and fishing community, so it's unlikely Mary's family would have had sufficient wealth to support Jesus' ministry. Further, if they were wealthy, her father would be well known, and she'd probably be known as "Mary, daughter of [her father's name]."

More likely, I feel, she was an average woman of the time and place. It's assumed that Mary, like Jesus, was Jewish, although there's no specific mention of this. Magdala was near Capernaum, a larger town where Jesus preached, and Mary might have met Jesus there. However, nothing in the New Testament tells us how Mary first met Jesus.

In my portrayal of Mary of Magdala, I relied on Jesus' teachings as put forth in the four gospels. Since they give us just one word spoken to Jesus, I had to imagine what conversations between Mary and Jesus might have been like. I used little from the Gnostic Gospels, as their content is often both esoteric and controversial. When I do, it is noted via a footnote.

What did Mary do after the resurrection? I believe she would have wanted to spread Jesus' words. But where? It would have been unsafe for her to teach in the Palestine region. The societal morals of the time would have placed Mary in constant danger of her life.

The main French tradition has her spending the rest of her life in Gaul (France). This French tradition has her residing near the present city of St. Maximin. I believe it is reasonable that she might have gone to Gaul, as it would have been a safe place to relocate. Therefore, in this book, I have her remain in what today is known as the Provence region. The French tradition also has Mary living in a cave for a great many years, so I paid homage to this belief by having her hide in a cave for a few days to avoid arrest.

I endeavored to craft the story by using the guidelines of plausibility and credibility. My goal was for readers, when they finished the book, to think, "You know, it really could have happened that way." I feel that should be the critical plausibility test.

A few other underlying considerations that I used to guide the plot are worth noting. I felt it was important to show Mary absorbing and reacting to the key teachings of Jesus, and two chapters are devoted to this. I assume that Mary met Jesus early in his ministry, was profoundly impressed by his words, and would have wanted to teach about Jesus herself.

In general, I felt the storyline should not rely too much on miracles. The two exceptions are the story of Lazarus being raised from the tomb, and Jesus' curing Mary Magdalene of her purported afflictions. I believe the plot will clarify why these two were included.

Rather than relying on miracles, it seemed better to have Mary work her way out of difficulties on her own. The tenacity she showed in the Bible by staying with Jesus at his crucifixion, burial, and resurrection suggests Mary was determined, courageous, and capable. That is how I wished to portray her as well.

Another guiding principle was to conform to the historic timeline of events as much as possible. For example, several key events in Judeo-Christian history occurred in the period 65 to 70 c.e. I wanted Mary to remain alive to learn of these events as an elderly woman, rather than have her hear about them in the novel decades before they actually happened.

Many readers might like to learn more about the Biblical passages used in the book. For this reason, and to document other aspects of the times and cultures being depicted, I took the unusual step (for a novel) of providing footnotes to the sources I used. These footnotes are in the first appendix following the end of the novel. I hope readers will find them informative.

There are many versions of the Bible in use today. I made frequent reference to three: the *King James Version*, the *Good News Bible*, and the *New Revised Standard Version*. It was instructive to see how the translation of certain passages varied. I used wording from each of them as seemed appropriate, or because one particular wording was most familiar.

Finally, some additional words about the goals of this book. Although its setting is religious in nature, the story I present is not primarily about religion. Its main focus is on how the societal mores of the times affected one ordinary person's desire for personal fulfillment and gender equality in the patriarchal first century. Its goal is to suggest a credible answer to the book's primary question: Who, really, was Mary Magdalene?

Sadly, the main themes of the book could have been set in the present century. In many countries, little has improved regarding gender equality. In 2016, though, a major change occurred in the Vatican's view of Mary Magdalene[3]. This and other events relating to Mary Magdalene, and to gender equality in general, are chronicled in Appendix B.

So please enjoy this search for a plausible life story for Mary Magdalene at your leisure. Imagine yourself born two thousand years ago, living in a small town near the Sea of Galilee, bound to your routine but boring life, when one day rumors arise about a charismatic young preacher in the area. You believe it would be interesting to listen to him, and so …

Additional information about the book and its
author can be found at: marymagdalenebook.com

PART ONE

Galilee

CHAPTER 1

The trial soon to begin was no ordinary event. This was the trial of Mary of Magdala, also known as Mary Magdalene. The year was 71 c.e.[1]

The emptiness of the assembly hall stage was broken as the door at its rear sprung open. Through it emerged an imposing sergeant-at-arms, muscles bulging, sharpened spear at the ready. He had been consigned from the local Roman military garrison in Aix to ensure order.

Behind him limped an elderly woman with hands bound, struggling to match his pace but with head held high. Her wrinkled face, impassive but not submissive, displayed no fear. Her ragged brown robe was tattered and soiled, but as a prisoner she had no other garments.

The sergeant-at-arms pointed to a small wooden chair and snarled, "Sit." Once she complied, her hands were freed. In Mary's seventy-five years she had learned there are things in life a person cannot control. She accepted this trial as one of them.

Her appearance caused an eruption from the perspiring male bodies assembled in the fetid chamber. She studied their angry faces, more out of curiosity than dread, as they bellowed furious threats. "She's guilty! Send her to prison!" From nearby, "Jail isn't good enough! Stone her!" A sweaty red-faced man bellowed, "Just turn her over to us! We know what to do with her!" The outcries came from all parts of the hall, except the rear.

The women present, a minority of the audience, sat quietly in the back of the room. Their faces were obscured by head coverings, but their eyes, Mary noted, reflected confusion and foreboding. Nonetheless, they remained silent.

They had no choice. Expressions of opinion by women in public were unthinkable.

The door behind Mary opened again, and through it walked a slender, stern-faced figure in an elegant robe, a cross around his neck. The Bishop of Aix was a domineering man who expected, and received, unquestioned deference and respect. His confidence this day reflected the fact that he was about to act as both judge and jury for these proceedings.

Furthermore, he already knew the outcome.

As he surveyed the crowd with an intimidating glare, their clamor subsided. The sergeant-at-arms stood beside Mary, towering over her. She took no notice of either man.

Having stared down the audience, the bishop gestured to the sergeant-at-arms, whose booming voice and imposing spear garnered immediate attention. "Silence! The trial will now begin! His Grace here, the Bishop of Aix, is in charge. You will all be silent. Anyone who does not will be arrested. These are the bishop's orders!" With a resounding smash of his lance upon the floor he stepped back, and the bishop strode forward.

As the bishop began speaking, Mary studied his face and words, hoping for fairness.

"We are here today to determine whether the defendant, Mary of Magdala, is guilty of heresy by willfully violating the rules of our sacred church. The defendant will attempt to explain her odd claim that she was a companion and confidant of our Savior, Jesus of Nazareth, and why she feels Church strictures forbidding women to preach the word of God do not apply to her."

With a disdainful glare at his prisoner, he summarized, "Mary of Magdala, you were warned of the serious consequences of your heretical actions, yet you ignored all pleas to save yourself. Despite my doubts regarding your claims, I will allow you to defend them in such detail as you wish. You shall tell us, with God as your witness, why you believe that you alone among all Christian women have the right to engage in the prohibited act of instructing men in matters of the church. You may proceed."

Mary Magdalene arose and directed a faint bow to the crowd before her. Her face reflected the hope that she might convince them of her truthfulness and innocence. Above all, she wanted them to know why it was not a sin for her to convey the words of Jesus to others. After all, he had said she could, hadn't he?

She knew, though, that no one's opinion mattered except the bishop's.

Her voice was calm, strong.

"The story of my association with Jesus of Nazareth began many years ago … ."

CHAPTER 2

More precisely, the relationship between Mary of Magdala and Jesus of Nazareth had begun forty-two years earlier in the province of Galilee, the region within northern Palestine where the towns of Magdala and Nazareth were located. Mary lived with her mother in a small village on the outskirts of Magdala.

Hot weather was common in Magdala, and this spring day in 28 c.e. was no exception. The exhausting heat and relentless flies notwithstanding, Mary and her mother, Rachel, were busy in the yard attending to the morning chores.

Mary, in her early thirties, was attractive in a simple, unadorned way. She was average in height, of slim build, with a gentle and comforting countenance. In the right light, her long, dark hair could appear to have a reddish tint. Her soft eyes, which seemed to take in and understand everything around her, could extend either a sympathetic smile or a steely determination in equal measure. In recent years, though, her face more often reflected inner sadness and turmoil. Her temper had grown as well, both in magnitude and in the ease with which it could be aroused.

Mary entered their small, barren yard through its rustic wooden gate, carrying water from a nearby well. Her mood this day was not pleasant, being deteriorated by the sticky heat, the flies, and the onset of one of her periodic headaches.

An olive tree she had helped plant many years ago needed attention, and keeping it healthy was Mary's responsibility. It offered a seasonal supply of nutritious olives but also had symbolic value; it was one of the few trees in the neighborhood, and its growth and recurring gift of savory fruit extended a metaphorical hope for the future. Of more importance, in its early years, the rest of Mary's family had been alive to enjoy it with her.

Part of the water was for her mother who was weeding a small vegetable garden, her most pleasant diversion. As Mary set the water by Rachel, an unsuccessful slap at a thirsty sandfly on her forehead produced a scowl and audible curse.

Rachel, used to Mary's quickened temper, sighed but responded with a patient smile, "I appreciate your helping, Mary. We rarely have visitors; it makes me happy to have the house looking nice when we do."

Rachel pushed her dark hair to the side. Its increasing grayness reminded Mary of her mother's years and the hardships she had endured. She knew some of the grey was her fault, caused by her mood swings and easy anger, but this was not the only reason. Both women bore faces weighted with grief, a sorrow caused by events Mary sorely wanted to forget. To forget about the death of her father. And her husband. And her small son. All in one frightful night.

Mary wiped her brow and searched for a suitable sarcastic reply, "The visitor is only Uncle David. I doubt he'll care how clean the house is."

"Perhaps, but I'm grateful for your help with the cooking and baking. Men always enjoy special little treats, you know."

"Mother, please! Haven't I made it clear I have no interest in getting married again? Your annoying hints won't change that."

"I know. You often say that. I merely meant I'm trying to make things pleasant for my brother. I'd like to see you enjoy life again. Socialize more, meet new people."

"There's no one here for me!" Mary retorted. "I feel my life is wasting away. I'd like to do something worthwhile, but what can anyone accomplish in Magdala? The world is large, but I've never been farther away than Nazareth and Capernaum. The thought of dying a lonely, pitiable widow in Magdala terrifies me."

"What do you have in mind, Mary? Fancy plans only lead to disappointment and heartache. Try to find happiness where you are. Do you think you're someone special? Magdala is just a small, ordinary town; no one special has ever come from here."

"If no one special can come from Magdala, then why were you and father so insistent I learn to read and write? That's not a common skill of women here."

"You know Jewish people have always valued education."

"Yes, for men. But why for me? Perhaps you *did* want me to have the skills to become someone special."

Rachel avoided answering by asking, "What kind of a special person do you have in mind for yourself?"

"I don't know what I want to do with my life, Mother, but I know it's more than I can achieve in Magdala. I intend to keep looking. You only find those things you search for."

She thought a moment. "Why not make use of my education? Maybe I could teach. I think I might be a good teacher."

"A teacher! Mary, that's impossible. You know women are forbidden to teach in public. Only men can become teachers."

"Here that might be true, but what about elsewhere?"

"Stop dreaming. You'll receive the same answer everywhere. No!"

Mary's voice rose again. "There's a huge world outside Magdala, Mother. I can dream about a better life, can't I? My future is my decision to make, not yours. I love you, Mother, but I'm no longer a child. I must decide my own life. And I will!"

Her voice low and worried, Rachel replied, "You know I would dread losing you, Mary. It's my worst fear. Please try to find happiness here. Magdala is a wonderful little town."

"No! For me, Magdala's a jail! I can't live in a jail. I'm tired of this debate; I need a walk." As she strode through the door she mumbled, *Sometimes I wish God had taken me, too.*

Mary hurried to get home before the darkening sky thrust its fury upon her. As the wind got stronger, she began to run, but it was no use. The screeching maelstrom thrusted her upward and whirled her like a rag doll at its will. Her family was swept up as well, powerless to escape. She tried to grab her son's hand but it was just beyond her reach, and he disappeared into the dire blackness of the cloud. In an instant her husband and then her father also vanished into the ominous unknown. Only her mother remained behind her, tossed helplessly by the wind. The shrieking cloud was entirely black, except for huge orange eyes glaring out of it that embodied every evil imaginable. Mary could only scream in terror, but the cloud screamed back twice as loud. Suddenly an invisible hand grabbed her shoulder, and her whole body trembled. She screamed even louder. Now the hand was shaking her, shouting at her … .

"Mary, wake up! You're having that awful dream again! It's the third time this month!"

Mary, still shaking, stared at her mother. She was barely able to mutter, "It's at least the fourth. Is there no way to make the nightmares stop?

Rachel wiped the cold sweat from Mary's face and cradled her quivering daughter in her arms. "I wish I could, Mary. I wish so much I could."

CHAPTER 3

Mary's home in Magdala was near the Sea of Galilee,[1] a region that had been settled for thousands of years. Despite the arid climate, the Jordan River conveyed fresh water from the Mt. Hermon range down to the waiting Sea, fulfilling an essential need of crops and livestock. The Sea, for its part, provided a reliable fishing industry for those along its shores.

The town of Magdala nestled between Capernaum to the north and the new political center of Tiberias to the south. These towns benefited by being on a main Roman trade route, the Via Maris, which connected the larger cities of Damascus to the north and Jerusalem to the south. The Galilean region enjoyed a dry but benign Mediterranean climate. In peaceful times, Galilee was a pleasant place to live and work. The region, however, was under Roman rule, and times were rarely peaceful.

Those who lived there were a diverse group, especially linguistically. Most Jews in Galilee spoke Aramaic, a language resulting from the long exile of the Palestinian Jews in Babylon.[2] The Greeks, who controlled the area prior to the Roman arrival, also left a legacy of their tongue and customs. The Greek language was still widely spoken, even in the region around Jerusalem known as Judea. For the politically ambitious, Latin, the language of the Roman-imposed government, could be useful.

The only monotheistic religion in Galilee was Judaism, which had existed there for many centuries. Even small towns like Magdala had a synagogue. Many, however, were not Jewish. Some families revered the entertaining assemblage of either Greek or Roman gods, or maybe just lived the simpler life of worshiping nature. Many chose to ignore religion altogether.

Magdala was similar to other small towns in the region, except that it had a large tower in its center.[3] Nearby was a central plaza where those with goods to sell could gather to tempt customers. A thriving fish market, which included the preparation of salted fish for export, was the main commercial activity. An amphitheater, a remnant of the region's Greek heritage, was available for public activities. Productive agricultural fields surrounded the town.

Individual homes were usually square, one-story, and white-washed, with flat roofs sloped to capture rainwater in cisterns. Wealthier families might enjoy a two-story house. Further out in the countryside, houses were similar but often clustered within a fenced area, or built over an open area at ground level, to provide a safe haven for domestic animals.

It was in a simple house of this type that Mary Magdalene grew up, about a ten-minute walk from the center of Magdala. Everyone in a Magdala household worked to keep the family supplied with the necessities of daily life. Many had a family specialty, such as a food product or handicraft, which they could sell or barter to obtain other needed staples. There was little free time, but most families lived comfortably.

Following the nightmare, Rachel had remained with Mary until the eastern sky brought the first welcoming light of dawn. Mary had said little since awakening, a blank stare on her face, as she performed her early morning chores. She knew David would arrive today, and they needed to finish preparations.

Rachel tried to take her daughter's mind off the terrible dream. "I'm sorry, Mary, that we quarreled yesterday. I should let you plan your own future."

"It was my fault too. I seem to get upset at the smallest things.

Maybe the nightmares are to blame. And the next day the headaches return. I dread them."

"I know. Ever since that horrible night you've been unhappy and depressed, and you have few friends. You rarely go to the synagogue anymore."

"What do I have to be happy about? There's no need to mention 'that horrible night.' What happened, happened. It can't be changed or forgotten. Unless you have some way to bring back the dead."

Rachel sighed at the sarcastic outburst. "Losing our family was hard on both of us; let's think of more pleasant things." She smiled at Mary. "Your uncle will be here this afternoon. I'll look for some flowers for the table. We'll need more water. Could you draw another bucket?"

Mary wandered toward the well, her listless gait reflecting both her troubled mind and the gnawing absence of any goal in life.

◠

The village well was not merely a source of water, it was the lifeblood of any community in an arid world. This particular well had been there for generations, and was centrally located among the local village homes. It offered a convenient social center to chat with friends and catch up on local gossip. Early morning was best, as many village women would be there drawing the day's water supply.

A neighbor, Esther, was the first to greet her. "Good morning, Mary. You seem a bit glum on such a sunny day."

"Maybe it's because my pointless life in this stifling little town depresses me. Why doesn't anything exciting ever happen around here?"

Her neighbor smiled. "You can't expect Magdala to rival Jerusalem."

Sarah, a friend of Rachel's but closer to Mary's age, joined in. Sarah was taller than most villagers, broad-shouldered and strong from work in her family's orchard, which provided a variety of fruits and nuts for local consumption. She was of gentle demeanor, with kind eyes and a pleasing smile, seeking to be a peacemaker whenever she could.

"I have an idea," Sarah offered. "If you are seeking something different, you could go hear this preacher who travels around Galilee. They say he's quite a speaker; sometimes entire villages come out to hear him. My husband said he talks about God and sin and forgiveness, how to achieve happiness, things like that."

The word "husband" set Mary off again. "Yes, it's easy for you to be happy; you have a husband to talk to. Not everyone does, you know."

Tamar, the sharp-tongued village curmudgeon, was quick to seize the opportunity. "Yes, they say this preacher even cures people of things. Maybe he can cure Mary's churlish little tongue and superior attitude."

With a derisive laugh, she added, "And if Mary's lonely, maybe he can cure that too!"

"That was rude, Tamar, not funny." *Still, it might be intriguing to listen to this person, whoever he is. If whole towns turn out to hear him, he must be saying something impressive. At least it would be better than sitting at home doing nothing.*

Turning to Sarah, she asked, "Where is he now?"

"I'm not sure," Sarah replied. "Somewhere in Galilee is all I know."

Interesting. Mary cast a wistful gaze towards the gentle hills in the distance that suddenly seemed to be beckoning her. *Quite interesting.*

CHAPTER 4

Rachel's modest home was clean and ready for David, her favorite guest. The kitchen, which also served as the social center, contained little other than a small wooden table and four well-worn chairs. On a shelf behind the table was a menorah, several earthenware cups and four mismatched plates. Across the room was Rachel's most important possession, a small iron oven for baking. Any other cooking took place outside.

A splendid dinner lovingly prepared by Rachel and Mary was spread out on the simple table. In addition to the first carrots of the year from Rachel's garden, it included a rare treat – a small piece of veal for which she had bartered two loaves of bread.

David arrived in late afternoon, tired from his long trip from the coast but eager to see what little was left of his family. He was younger than Rachel and only twelve years older than his niece, who thought of him more as an older brother. He was healthy and fit, a sailor by trade, with a dark beard. The elaborate trim on his tunic suggested his maritime trade was rewarding his hard work and ambitions.

"I must return home more often. My meals aboard ship are feeble compared to this. I hope your baking business is doing well. Do your neighbors still come by when they want something special?"

"They do. The baking provides sufficient income for my daily needs."

"It should. Everyone knows you're the best cook in Magdala."

"You exaggerate, but people do seem to like my sweet cakes. I barter with Ezekiel, the beekeeper – my cakes for his honey. We both benefit, and the sweetened cakes sell well."

Looking embarrassed, Rachel added, "I ought to keep this secret, but I sometimes neglect to tell Herod's tax collectors about *every* sale I make. I know I should."

David, normally imperturbable, roared back across the table, "What do you mean? Don't even think of apologizing. Good for you! Herod Antipas is nothing but a vile thief! He stuffs tax money into his own pocket so he can buy more slaves! Since when is it wrong to withhold your money from a common thief?"

Mary hastened to change the topic. "Tell me, David, what's the name of your ship?"

"Ah, the *Ikaría!*" he replied, also happy to discuss something different. "It was built in Greece, so the owner named it after his favorite Greek island. He told me Ikaría is a beautiful place. I should go there some day; it's only a short sail from Ephesus."

"You mentioned you're now some kind of assistant to the captain. That sounds impressive! What is it you do?"

"I serve as the ship's Master," he replied. "I handle the business matters on our trips. I make sure everything is loaded on the boat properly, collect the payments when we get to our destination, buy provisions we need, pay the crew, and so forth. The captain pays me well."

"I'm impressed," Rachel replied. "I had no idea you were that good with money."

"He chose me for the job because I'm educated, honest, and keep accurate records. Our captain's a fine sailor but poor at business. A dishonest Master could cost him a lot of money."

"You go to so many different ports. How do you know all those languages?"

"There's no need," David responded between bites. "Greek is the international language of commerce. Alexander the Great traveled to many places around the Great Sea besides Alexandria,[1] and left his legacy in all of them."

He laughed. "I've learned a little Greek. I can say, 'You owe me more money.' "

"Is your boat big?"

"The captain had it made for speed, not size. The Romans have boats that can carry huge loads, but ours is no lumbering Roman galleon. It was built to be fast by a master shipwright in Corinth. We specialize in getting goods to customers quickly; it helps keep their business. The main purpose of this trip is to see some merchants in Tiberias. I'll bet I can persuade them to ship their wares on the *Ikaría*."

"You'd bet on two flies crossing the table." Rachel knew her brother.

Feigning annoyance, he chuckled, "Never! How could you accuse me of such a thing?" Another laugh. "It takes at least three flies to make a good race!"

"Well, it pleases me to know you're doing well."

"I try hard to earn money, maybe even get rich. Nothing wrong with that."

Mary broached a new subject. "By the way, David, on your way here from Caesarea, did you happen to hear anything about a preacher who travels around Galilee?"

"I did. They spoke of a young man who claims to be teaching the word of God. He talks about bringing peace to the world, how people should lead their lives, that sort of thing. They said hundreds of people show up to hear him."

David had Mary's full attention. "Really! How interesting. Sarah said the same thing. What else do you know about him?"

"Not much. His name is Joseph, or James, or something like that. No, wait, it was Jesus. Yes, that's it, Jesus. I think they said he's preaching in Nazareth now."

Mary's eyes radiated excitement. "Really! Nazareth! That's not far."

Rachel cast a nervous look at her daughter. "Why is this of any interest to you? A wandering preacher is of no concern to us."

"How do you know? If hundreds attend his talks he must be saying something important. Nothing like this has happened here in years! What would be wrong with listening to him?"

Rachel looked at her brother for support, who seemed deep in thought. After a pause David replied, "You know, this reminds me of something from years ago when Mary was just a little girl. She insisted on going to see some important men who had traveled to Magdala. I think there was a whole caravan involved. Do you remember, Mary?"

⟍⟍

The image of that long-ago day was still vivid in Mary's mind as well. At the time, she was just four years old, and often played with her handmade doll in the courtyard. It was her only plaything. The sole bit of landscaping was the small olive tree she had helped plant a few weeks before. Mary saw it as *her* little tree, and she loved it.

Her mother, then a happy, attractive woman of twenty-four, was working in the house. She glanced outside at her daughter, who was busy teaching her doll to dance in the dirt.

"Mary, please come in and put on clean clothes; Uncle David will arrive soon. Your father won't be home from fishing until later, so I need you to help me in here." Mary tossed aside a leaf she had just discovered, picked up her tattered dance partner, and ran into the house. A visit by her favorite relative was all the incentive she needed.

As the sun lowered in the winter sky, Rachel picked up little Mary and both peered out the window. Mary was the first to spot the distant figure. "Mommy, look! Someone's coming!"

"I think you're right. Come here, your hair's a mess! Bring a comb."

Mary, ignoring the request, ran out to greet her uncle.

An energetic young man of about sixteen, muscular and enthusiastic, greeted them with open arms and his customary big smile.

"Seeing you two again is like a sunny day after a storm at sea! I knew my sister was home; I could smell your fantastic biscuits a mile away!"[2]

"Really? Even though they're not in the oven yet? You have talent! The men are still out on the Sea fishing, so we're here by ourselves. You look wonderful!"

Mary was jumping up and down. "What did you bring me? Let me see!" Mary knew he always had something in his bag for her. Sure enough, out came a pretty yellow hair ribbon.

Following a bountiful dinner, Rachel asked, "David, tell us more about being an apprentice seaman. I've never even seen the Great Sea."

"The captain keeps me busy. I do little jobs no one else wants. Sometimes he lets me help adjust the sails. I enjoy that most, unless a storm is approaching. Not so much fun then."

As he finished off the last of Rachel's biscuits, he thought of something else. "I almost forgot – have you heard the gossip in town? About the strange caravan?"

"We hear nothing way out here."

"The rumor in town is that a camel caravan bearing some important men is heading towards Magdala. They may have arrived today."

Mary's eyes were wide with excitement. "What kind of men? Kings and princes?"

"I have no idea, but they might be in town by now."

Rachel observed the dark sky. "All I know is, it's Mary's bedtime. Run along, little girl."

The next morning Rachel and Mary were up early, while Mary's exhausted father and David were still asleep. As Rachel was preparing porridge, an impatient knocking at the door interrupted breakfast. It was a neighbor, excited and panting.

"Rachel, have you heard? Right in town! The fanciest caravan you ever saw! Princes, and porters, and camels! You must see it! Come!" Not wanting to wait for Rachel, she rushed off.

Mary, wide-eyed, shouted, "Camels, and princes! I want to go! Right now!"

"Mary, I'm too busy to take you to see smelly camels. You've seen camels before."

"Not these camels! And princes too. Maybe I can go see them by myself!"

"No, you cannot! You stay right here! David might take you later."

Rachel headed for the bedroom to see if David was awake. Once she rounded the corner, an impatient little girl bolted out the door and headed into town as fast as her legs would permit.

"Can you get dressed, David? Mary really wants to see those camels."

On re-entering the kitchen, Rachel found it devoid of anyone named Mary, but could see her from the window, advancing rapidly toward Magdala. Mild panic set in. Her frenzied voice completed the task of waking her brother.

"David! Mary has run off to see the camels! Please, help me get her back home!"

David smiled from the bedside. "That little girl certainly has a mind of her own! I'd also like to see what's going on. I'll bring her back right away."

Mary approached the camp as everyone was preparing to depart. Servants were folding tents while porters lifted crates and bags onto camels. Mary was fascinated, but her eyes soon spotted a well-dressed elderly gentleman not far away.

"Mister! Mister! Who are you? Where are you going?"

He cast an annoyed glance at his tiny interrogator, but Mary's innocent smile won him over. "Hello, little girl. Did you come here by yourself? My name is Melchior. What's yours?"

"Mary. Where did you come from?"

"I live far to the east. I'm one of our king's Magi. I serve as one of his advisors."[3]

At this point David arrived, smiled at Melchior, and hugged his eager niece. "Please excuse little Mary, here. She always wants to know everything that's happening."

On cue, Mary asked, "Why did you come here? Did your king send you?"

Melchior raised his eyes and pointed upward. "Tell me, Mary, have you noticed the very bright star in the sky? Look, it's daytime, but you can still see it."

"I see it! I can see the star!"

David had noticed this brilliant star, but he hadn't given it any serious thought.

"We've been told if we follow that star, we'll find a baby, a new king who will bring peace to the world. We want to see this child, so we can tell our people about him." He resumed packing. "We think we're close to the place where he'll be born, so we're anxious to depart."

Mary could hardly contain her excitement; she had never seen anything like this. "I want to go with you and follow the star! I want to see the baby king!"

David laughed and bent down towards Mary. "These Magi are much too busy to worry about taking care of a little girl like you. It would be best if we head home. Here, take my hand. You'll have plenty of time for adventures when you grow older."

Mary looked up at her uncle, wondering if he somehow knew that would be true.

They started home, but Mary kept glancing back over her shoulder, her wide eyes and curious mind easily imagining she was seeing something of great importance.

CHAPTER 5

Mary smiled at her uncle. Her memory of the exotic travelers she had encountered as a child was as sharp as his. "I do remember them, David, even after twenty-eight years! I can still see the camels and tents, and the curious Magi!"

"Yes, and as I recall you wanted to run away with them. Even as a little girl you liked excitement. It sounds like you're much the same today."

"I'm not looking for excitement. I'd simply like to hear this Jesus that Sarah talked about. He might say something that would inspire me."

Rachel stared at her daughter. "Oh, Mary, such an imagination! This man sounds like just another wandering storyteller, a fancy talker after your money, I'd guess."

"You've no reason to say that, Mother. First of all, I have no money. Second, he draws huge crowds; even the village women have heard of him. I just want to meet him, listen to him. Perhaps he could suggest some new goals for my life. What's wrong with that?"

Mary awaited an encouraging response, but Rachel said nothing. Seeking support, she turned to David. "You said he's preaching in Nazareth? That's not far away!"

Rachel's mouth dropped. "Mary, what are you thinking? You know a woman can't travel around by herself. Even if others went with you, when you got to Nazareth he would be in some other town."

"I understand your concerns, but try to look at it through my eyes. I see this as an opportunity. If whole villages come to hear him, he must be saying something worthwhile. Maybe he could open a door for me to the world beyond Magdala."

Sensing the extent of Rachel's concern, Mary assumed a more serious tone. "You are right, though, about not traveling alone. Perhaps there are others in our village who would like to hear him. Maybe some of their husbands as well. Nazareth is close by. Even if we walked, we could get there in a day." [1]

Rachel knelt in front of Mary and grabbed her arm. "Please, Mary, think about this more. How would you get there? Where would you stay? You have no money, and you know no one in Nazareth. Think of all that might happen! This is crazy!"

Mary was outwardly calm, but inside her mind was whirring as she planned each step. "I'll inquire at the synagogue in Nazareth if someone can let me stay with them ..."

"Mary, you have no idea if there even *is* a synagogue in Nazareth! What if it has no synagogue?"

"Then I'd inquire in nearby Sepphoris; it's a larger city."

Mary looked at David, hoping he was nodding agreement, but instead saw concern.

"Mary, Rachel is right. The trip could be dangerous, especially around Tiberias.[2] I've been there on business; it's a Roman center of power, infested with crime. I think you should avoid Tiberias altogether. This needs more thought."

Mary kept her eyes on David as he pondered the situation, hoping he would support her. She could also sense Rachel desperately hoping the opposite.

"I may know a way to keep you safe. I leave for Tiberias tomorrow on business, and have contracted with a nearby farmer, an old friend, to have his son, Joel, take me there in one of their farm wagons. For an extra compensation, which I'd be happy to provide, I'm sure he would allow Joel to take you on to Nazareth."

"David! What are you doing? You should talk her out of this, not help her!"

"Mother, let him continue. He's only trying to keep me safe. Keep going, David."

"Here's my suggestion. Avoid the main roads, especially the one from Magdala to Nazareth that goes through Tiberias. I know a route to Nazareth on the plateau that bypasses Tiberias. This junction is only an hour from Tiberias, so I can bid you farewell there and walk the rest of the way into the city. Joel will then take you on to Nazareth."

Mary was ecstatic, but Rachel's alarm just kept rising. "David, I know nothing of this Joel. Is this safe?"

"Joel is quite reliable. I've known him since he was a child, and his father even longer. They're good, honest people. I would never suggest this if I had doubts."

"This side road I would be taking – what is it like?" Mary asked.

"It's simple but serviceable. There are no towns on the plateau, and few people travel that way. There might be some shepherds, but they keep to themselves and pose no danger. If anyone sees your wagon, they'll think you and Joel are also shepherds, or maybe merchants. Joel should have you in Nazareth before sunset."

"That sounds reasonable, if you stay with me until we get to where the road splits. This can work!"

Rachel was no longer just worried, she was now wide-eyed and scared. "Mary, I beg you, please forgo this. How will you get back here? Think of all the possible dangers! If anything should happen I might never see you again!"

Mary had been trying to restrain her temper, and she did not wish to be rude, but her mind was made up. "This is my life we're talking about, Mother, and I must decide for myself how I'll lead it. Right now, my life involves going to Nazareth." She arose from her seat and ended the conversation. "Now, if you'll excuse me, I need to pack a few things."

Mary felt David touch her arm as he attempted to reassure both her and his sister. "Rachel, you know how much I love my niece, and I assure you I'll make certain she's safe." Hugging his sister, he added, "The same applies to you as well. As the only remaining man in our family, I feel a duty to look after both of you. I promise you I will do this."

He immediately realized he had made a promise he had no ability to keep. How often was he even in Galilee? But there was no way to retract what he just said.

◦

The sunrise adorned the fleecy clouds in hues of gold and coral, and the birds' dawn concert beckoned all to enjoy the show. The low morning sun directed David and Mary's shadows symbolically southwest towards Nazareth. Mary, whose smile concealed her nervousness, clutched a small bag packed with travel essentials. David had a fancier goatskin case, as befitted a ship's Master. A distraught Rachel stood beside them, the first tear set to begin its journey down her cheek. Joel was already seated in the wagon, waiting to convey them to the trail juncture.

Despite hidden qualms, Mary was fueled with excitement. She had chosen to wear her best tunic, the one in her favorite Venetian red color. "I'm ready, David. Please try not to worry, Mother. I'll return home in a few days; I can find someone with a cart. I'll be fine."

Rachel reached into her pocket. "Mary, please take this. My mother gave it to me many years ago. It's not at all fancy, but I'd like you to have it. For good luck."

Rachel handed Mary a simple metal necklace. It was of modest design and attached to the most basic of chains, but it was one of the few accessories she possessed.

"It's an amulet for your journey. Keep it with you as you travel, as a remembrance of how much I love you. God bless you, Mary."

Mary threw her arms around her mother. "Thank you! I will treasure it always. I love you too, and I understand your concerns, but this is something I must do."

Rachel could only feign a slight smile of acceptance. "Godspeed, Mary."

After prolonged final embraces, David helped Mary into the wagon. Rachel, hands clasped and eyes moist, watched the little wagon, and her only relatives, as they set off down the road and slowly became mere specks against the horizon.

And then disappeared.

She had never felt so alone.

Figure 1:   *Palestine in the First Century c.e.*

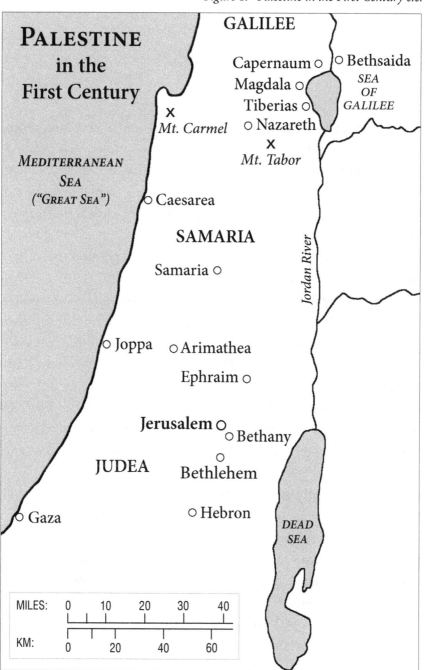

CHAPTER 6

In a similar small town a thousand miles west of Magdala, another household dispute was underway. This one was between a mother and her son, Maurice, an intelligent youth of slender build with blond hair offset by dark eyebrows. He was about twelve years old, ambitious, energetic, and very certain of himself. He was deliberately dawdling over the remains of his breakfast.

"Maurice, will you please finish eating and get dressed? You're going to be late for your Greek lesson."

Maurice made no effort to eat faster and cast an annoyed look in his mother's direction. "You know I hate Greek. Why do you insist on making me study it? It's boring and pointless; no one speaks it around here. We both know I'll never use it. I want to learn Latin instead."

"You will learn Greek because I say so! I'm your mother. I've lived a lot longer than you have, and I know what's best for you. Greek is the language of literature, art, and the sciences. You have to learn a second language. Why wouldn't you want to be well-educated?"

Maurice silently made what he felt to be an important correction: *You are not my mother; you are merely my stepmother. You have no right to tell me anything.*

With an almost paternalistic air, he explained once again what he thought should have been obvious. "Mother, you know I'm smarter than all my classmates. I'll be somebody important when I grow up, maybe even go to Rome. Greek is the dead language of ancient history. Latin is the language of the future, of wealth and power; it's what they speak in Rome. That's why I want to study it. I want to go to Rome someday. If you want to be somebody famous, you must know Latin."

"Why on earth would you want to go to Rome? It's the most corrupt city in the world!"

"No, it's the most important city in the world. It's where rich and influential people live. It is where you go if you want to be a success in life." *But what would you know about being successful?*

His stepmother hated Rome, and so pressed her maternal prerogatives.

"If you want to be successful, you need to be well-educated, and if you want to be well-educated, you need to know Greek. As your mother, I am responsible for your education. What language you study is my decision to make, not yours. I have provided you with the best instructor of Greek in the province. You will do what I decide is best for you, and that's the final word on this matter! So be on your way. Monsieur Stavros is waiting for you."

Maurice reluctantly got up, avoided eye contact with his stepmother, sighed, and gathered up his lessons.

"That's a good boy."

Maurice gave his tormentor a sideways glare as he headed towards the door. *You think you know what's best for me? You know nothing! Do you think you can keep me from learning Latin? You have no such power; I can and will learn Latin on my own! What right do you have to tell me what to do? You're not even related to me; a stepmother can't issue orders. Next you'll want to order grown men around! I'll be somebody important one day, and no bossy woman will stop me.*

As he reached the door, he repeated in a more audible mutter, "I *will* be famous someday. And I won't let anything or anybody stop me!"

☙

Not far from Jerusalem was a large rock quarry. It didn't contain high-value minerals, such as marble, but it had a large deposit of good quality building stone. Its economic value was recognized long ago, and it had been worked for decades.

Working in the quarry was not only physically demanding, it was also dangerous. The men who toiled there were aware of this, but the lure of guaranteed employment and steady income, no matter how small, trumped the danger. Good building rock was in high demand.

The workers at the mine came from Jerusalem and surrounding towns, such as Emmaus, Bethany, Eleph, and Gibeon. They were of all ages, and most were the head of their respective families. Their meager compensation was often all the family had to live on, so they worked not only hard, but also carefully. Most days any accidents that occurred were minor, and serious injuries were rare.

Today, however, would be the exception. A large piece of rock had been loosened, and in keeping with normal practice would be allowed to roll downslope to the floor of the mine. From there it would be hauled on roller logs out the open side of the mine to a nearby work area, where it would be fabricated into the desired size and shape for construction uses.

The foreman scanned the slope and pointed to a likely path for the rock to take. He then signaled the workers above and below as to his decision and warned them to be alert. The men below moved further to the sides. A team of workers approached the rock, and with a few determined pushes started it on its way down the selected slope to the bottom of the pit.

Fate, however, intervened. Partway down the slope the future building stone tumbled against a protruding rock ledge that was not visible from higher in the mine. The collision knocked it from its intended path onto a slightly different trajectory, one that curved to the left and had it descending into an area where workers were still present. Urgent, panicky shouts alerted the workers below that something had gone wrong, and the frantic men began to scatter.

One of them, intent to keep his eye on the rock that was approaching him from behind and getting larger every second, failed to notice a pickax that was lying on the ground. His foot hit it as he ran and he lost his balance and fell, fell onto a space that only seconds later would be occupied by a huge cascading rock.

It was sadly, tragically, a fatal mistake. One that would keep him from ever seeing his three children again.

CHAPTER 7

Mary and David were enjoying their bumpy wagon ride, talking, reminiscing, and appreciating this rare opportunity to spend time together. Other than her mother, David was the only family Mary had left, and the chance to be with him, even for a short while, had lifted her spirits. It occurred to her that what she thought was boredom back in Magdala might really have been loneliness, the result of her missing husband and son.

They had reached the top of a low plateau and were taking a welcome break from their bone-jarring seats on the wagon. The stop had a more poignant aspect, though – this was where their paths would diverge. The city of Tiberias, shrouded in a veil of dust, was spread out below them on the coastal plain to the east. Beyond Tiberias, the sunlit sparkles of the Sea of Galilee faded into the distant haze.

"As promised, Mary, there's Tiberias, safely out of your way. You needn't worry about that now. From here, Joel will follow the sheep trails heading west. If he can maintain a steady pace you should be in Nazareth before sunset."

Mary turned and examined the pathway ahead. Its packed-clay surface wound its way through low vegetation and past an occasional thirsty tree or lichen-covered rock, until it disappeared beyond a distant arm of the hillside. She could imagine the town that was her destination coming into view just beyond the horizon.

"Don't worry, David, I'll be fine. In Nazareth, I'll ask at the synagogue where I can stay. At the least, I'm sure they'd let me spend the night there. Thank you so much for your help and understanding."

David looked at Mary with a twinkle in his eyes. "I doubt you know this, but I never had my parents' permission to become a sailor. They felt it was much too dangerous. One day, I just walked out the door and headed for the harbor. You see, we're much alike. I understand your need to create your own life. However, I don't think you have adequate resources."

He dropped his arms and reached into his travel case to pull out a small leather bag. "Here, this is a little something to help you along your way."

"Oh, David, thank you! But this is too generous. I doubt I'll need half this much money."

"You may want to stay in Nazareth an extra day or two. You will also need to hire a wagon to bring you back to Magdala. I know you're prudent, so use it as you see best."

Mary couldn't resist a little kidding. "You know, for a ruthless businessman, you're truly a wonderful friend. Good-bye, David, until we meet again."

David laughed. "What have I done? I'm too soft-hearted! My reputation is ruined!"

More seriously, he said "Mary, may fate smile upon you, and may you find what you're searching for in Nazareth. I feel we'll see each other again before too long."

They exchanged one last embrace, reflecting a mutual admiration that made their parting even harder. With a sad smile and final wave, David turned left and began walking to Tiberias.

Mary watched him for a few minutes, then climbed back into the wagon and instructed Joel to follow the trail to the right. A tap on the horse started them moving westward, towards the unknown future that was Nazareth.

☙

The trail was easy to follow; centuries of shepherds and thousands of sheep had etched its sinuous course. For the most part it was smooth, but with an occasional rock to avoid. The plateau around them consisted of gentle hills dressed with course grasses and small scrubs. The sparse landscape was randomly accented by an occasional struggling oak tree.

David was right, except for sporadic flocks of sheep the plateau was empty. The only people they had seen were two shepherds tending their flock in the distance. Even the sky contained only a solitary black vulture, circling around in search of a carrion breakfast.

They had been making good time along the trail, and by noon were more than halfway to Nazareth. Since the scenery had become familiar, both Mary and Joel were preoccupied by various trains of thought and paying little attention to the monotonous trail beneath them. Neither noticed the dust-covered rock that was directly in the path of the wagon's right front wheel. The resulting jolt sent them flying off their seats and propelled the wagon into the air. The wagon crashed back down with an even greater jolt and came to rest at an alarming angle.

"Are you all right, Mary?" Joel asked.

"Just a bruise and a scrape. What about the wagon?"

Joel climbed down to assess the problem. When he looked back at Mary, his was not a happy face.

"The right front wheel is listing at quite an angle away from the axel, and the axel itself looks like it might be damaged. It may be cracked or even partially broken. I worry about how long it will be usable."

"Can we keep going?"

Joel tugged on both the wheel and the axel. Mary could see the wheel wiggle.

"I'm sorry to say, Mary, but I think the wagon may be dangerous to ride in. If we keep going, the wobble in the wheel will get worse, and either it or the axel could break, maybe before we get to Nazareth. This is our only wagon, we need it on the farm. I can't risk abandoning it way out here."

"What should we do?"

"The only choice I see is to lead the horse and wagon back along the trail to Magdala, with the wagon empty. You and I will have to walk along beside it."

Mary stared at Joel. What he was proposing meant forsaking her goal of seeking Jesus in Nazareth. It meant going back to her meaningless life in Magdala and listening to Tamar taunt her failure every time she went to the well.

"No! I'm so close to Nazareth, I must continue on. I can walk to Nazareth from here while it's still light. Once I reach the edge of the town, the fact that I'm alone won't matter."

"Are you sure?"

"Yes. When you get back to Magdala tell your father, and Rachel as well, that you dropped me off in Nazareth, that the accident happened later. Say that it happened on the way back home. I don't want them to worry."

Joel looked quizzically at Mary. Asking him to lie for her proved how determined she was to achieve her goal. They had encountered no one along the trail, and he agreed she should make it to Nazareth before sunset. He could make it back to Magdala faster without her along, but even so it would be dark before he arrived.

"Very well, if you're sure that's what you wish to do. I wish you a safe trip."

Mary thanked Joel and watched as he rotated the crippled wagon back towards the east, then began leading his horse on the long journey back to Magdala.

Mary turned the other way and began walking westward, but with a worried look. It was impossible for her not to wonder about the wisdom of her decision. *What if mother was right? What if there's no synagogue in Nazareth?*

She walked faster.

❧

About an hour later she came to a small hill, and as she began to descend the trail became steeper. Small pebbles made the footing precarious. In her hurry, she failed to notice a root protruding from the path. Her foot caught on it, thrusting her forward.

Gravity prevailed, and Mary hit the ground hard, one leg under the other. The impact twisted her left foot, followed by a sharp pain.

Oh, no. Damn! She grabbed her ankle. It was hurting. A lot.

Mary got up with difficulty and tried to walk, but could not put much weight on the injured foot and was able to walk only with an awkward limp. She collapsed back onto the ground. A tear appeared, but she soon realized the futility of crying. Her confused mind wondered how long it would take to reach Nazareth if she had to crawl there.

Get back to reality, Mary. You need a crutch. Looking around, she could see only one tree that was reasonably close. With discomfort she hobbled to it and began searching for a sturdy fallen branch, eventually spotting a dead limb that might suffice. Using a small table knife from her bag, she began trimming it to resemble a crutch. The effort was only marginally successful.

"Curses! This stupid knife is for peeling apples, not carving wood!" The work was tedious, frustrating, and used up much valuable time, but eventually the task was completed. Mary tried out her primitive crutch. "Not great," she concluded after a few limps. With a sigh, she added the obvious, "Regardless, it will have to do."

She arose and staggered back to the sheep trail. The hand-made crutch was a clumsy contrivance but proved sturdy enough. With discomfort and at a much slower pace, she resumed her journey towards Nazareth, with frequent pauses to rest. The sun began to descend towards the western horizon faster than her painful limping could match.

After a few hours, she looked up at the low sun angle and muttered, "This wretched ankle … I'll never make it to Nazareth before dark. Damn! Of all the things I dreaded – I'll have to camp out here tonight!" She tried humor: "That vulture might be more interested in me now!"

She found a spot under an oak tree not far from the trail that might serve as a rough bed. Mary then realized it would be chilly before dawn, and she had no bed coverings. She used her small knife to dig a shallow trench, and gathered dead leaves to serve as a cover. As the sky grew dark, she ate her remaining bread supply and settled down under her leafy blanket.

While trying to arrange herself so as to have a little comfort, something poked into her neck. *Mother's necklace.* Mary took it off, stared at it, and mumbled, "She thought you would bring me good luck. Some amulet you are!" She stared at it again, wondering if she even wanted to keep it. With a dismissive look and a shake of her head, she tossed it to the ground.

"Good luck? Hah! You were wrong about that, mother."

Still, she couldn't help thinking that maybe Rachel's worrying had some basis. The thought was discomforting, but not enough to alter her resolve to get to Nazareth.

To take her mind off her ankle, she gazed upwards towards the heavens. The stars and planets had always fascinated her and tonight, prolific against a moonless sky, they seemed unusually bright, especially Venus. That led her thoughts to the very bright star she had seen so long ago as a child. *What was his name? Melchior – he said they were looking for a baby who would bring peace to the world. If this preacher I'm looking for lives in Galilee, I wonder if he saw the Magi too? Maybe he even saw the famous baby king they were looking for!*

As Mary's mind revisited the aged Magi and the crush of porters and camels, her weary body gave in to the physical punishment of the day, and sleep replaced her pain.

CHAPTER 8

Mary's exhaustion produced a sleep so sound that even the most terrifying of her nightmares couldn't invade it. Nonetheless, her welcome rest was interrupted after only a few hours by the unsettling sound of raucous laughter and incoherent shouting not far away, and coming closer.

What? Someone is out there – two men, coming down the path. Lie low, Mary, do not move. Mary did her best to resemble a rock and blend in with the leaves, hoping that, since the moon had dropped below the horizon, the two men might pass by without noticing her.

The men, clearly inebriated, approached along the trail. As they got closer Mary could make out their features. The older man was thin, shifty-eyed, slovenly, and mean looking. His companion was pudgy, round-eyed, insecure and dim-witted. He walked a little behind the older man like a dog that had been trained to heel.

The pudgy one, peering through bloodshot eyes at the unfamiliar surroundings, cast his gaze for a moment in the direction of the oak tree. His senses were functioning just enough to notice a slight movement under it.

"Erascus, wait … I think I saw something move, over there, by that tree. Prob'ly just a dumb animal."

Erascus was always imaginative, especially if some redistribution of assets might be possible. "Or maybe, Phlegian, it's a drunk with some money on him he might be willing to share. You know, drunks shouldn't travel at night!" He snickered at his inane joke.

"Yeah. Maybe it'll be lucky we got lost and wound up on this hill. Wherever we are."

"Then let's see what good fortune awaits us."

The two men staggered toward the tree, not quite sure what to expect. Phlegian kicked the motionless Mary, who moved enough that her face became partially visible.

"C'mon, wake up, you drunken bum. Wait a minute …" Phlegian grabbed her head and turned it. "Erascus, it looks like a woman!"

Erascus bent over to see for himself. "What? It is! Who are you? What are you doing here? Speak!"

Mary tried to stay calm, but her eyes were wide and her pulse was racing as she stared at the two disheveled drunkards. "I was sleeping here, that is all. I was just on my way to … to visit a friend in Nazareth, but I twisted my ankle and had to spend the night here."

"Hah! A likely story," snorted Phlegian.

Erascus concocted a more insulting version. "You lie! No one will ever believe your stupid story. Everybody knows the only women who travel by themselves at night are harlots or worse. You're even wearing a bright red tunic. That's the favorite color of prostitutes. Admit it!"

"No! That isn't true!" Mary pleaded. "I'm on my way to Nazareth to find someone named Jesus, who they say teaches the word of God. I swear that is all."

Phlegian had no trouble improving on Erascus' version. "What? Talks with God? She sounds crazy! A crazy prostitute!"

The expression on Erascus' dirt-smudged face now turned more calculating and sinister. With narrow, menacing eyes he said, "You know, Phlegian, she might not be crazy; she might just be confused and tired from walking so far. Maybe we can help this unfortunate lady of the night. You know me, I always like to help people. Maybe she could sleep better if she practiced her trade. What do you think?"

Mary had no difficulty realizing the seriousness of what was happening. "No! Stop talking like that! I swear to you I'm an honorable woman who has hurt her ankle. Please, go away. Let me be!"

They had no intention of letting her be, and both men grabbed at her. To their surprise, Mary did something most unexpected – she fought back. An uneven struggle ensued, with Mary doing her best to resist. Erascus was astonished that a woman would put up such a fight.

"Why do you struggle? We merely want to provide a lady of your profession with some pleasant entertainment."

His repugnant euphemism was rewarded with the heel of her hand hitting him squarely in the eye. "You filthy dogs! You will do no such thing!"

Erascus knelt over her, attempting to pin her arms to the ground. Mary thought about her paring knife, but it was tucked away in her travel bag. Lacking any other weapons, instinct led Mary to send a knee to his groin.

"Aaaah! Why you … that was a serious mistake! You'll pay dearly for that, you stupid whore!"

Mary's efforts at resisting could last only so long. She continued to kick, bite, punch, and scratch, but a lone woman with only one usable leg was no match for two men, not even two pathetic specimens such as these. They soon succeeded in pinning their exhausted victim to the ground. As Phlegian sat on Mary, Erascus grabbed a cord from his cloak and used it to tie her arms to the tree.

Erascus gave Mary a vicious look and snarled, "There! Now you better lie still, whore. You hurt me a little, but one more move out of you and I promise I'll hurt you a whole lot. If you try to resist any more, your twisted ankle will be joined by two broken knees!"

Phlegian's low self-esteem induced him to sound even tougher than Erascus. "Yeah, an' then we'll entertain you and then tie you to a tree and then maybe break some more bones and then leave you for breakfast for the wild dogs. So you better behave!"

When you have no other options, prayer is all that remains. Mary's desperate plea was audible only to herself.

Oh, please, God, help me. Someone, anyone, help! Jesus, if you're in Nazareth, can you hear me? Can you help me? Please, please …

Mary realized there was no way to escape her fate. Her anguished, tear-stained face reflected the pain, helplessness, and humiliation of her situation.

Chapter 9

A brilliant sun thrust itself over the ridge and awakened the two groggy and disheveled drunks. Phlegian's brain tried to function. "Where are … ahh, my head! Damn sun!"

After his eyes focused, he noticed Mary. "What? Who is this …? Oh, right, we had a little entertainment last night. I guess we did anyway; my memory's sort of poor."

"Your brain is useless even when you're sober. Yeah, we had fun. I did anyway." Erascus rubbed his bloodshot eyes. "She fought a lot for a prostitute. Must have been her day off!" They laughed at the infantile humor.

Mary, though awake, remained motionless and silent. She was in pain, frightened, angry, and wanted to avoid further interaction with her attackers for as long as possible.

A more serious thought entered Erascus' soggy brain. "We slept late. We better get back to Tiberias or we'll get another idiotic lecture from the goddamned magistrate."

Phlegian looked at the motionless figure in the leaves. "What do we do with her?"

An evil grin curled across Erascus' face as he pointed at Mary. "You know, maybe we can get more use out of the lying whore. We caught a criminal, right? Then let's take her back to Tiberias, have her arrested for prostitution and anything else we can think of, and the magistrate rewards us for being such good, law-abiding citizens. Brilliant!"

Phlegian chortled. "Yes, and I have an even better idea. We can demand she gets stoned. That would be exciting."

"Good thinking! For you, anyway. Wake the stupid harlot; we need to get on our way."

Mary paled. *Oh, my God, is this really going to be the end?*

Phlegian untied Mary from the tree and gave her a kick to the thigh. "Come on, you lazy whore. Move! You're going to Tiberias to get the punishment you deserve."

Mary propped herself up on one elbow and winced; almost every part of her body was aching. Another troubling thought came to mind, just in case she should get out of this alive. She looked inside the travel bag she had used as a pillow and blanched. *David's gift is gone!*

She whirled around to look at Erascus, who had been watching her. "Looking for this?" he asked with a contemptuous sneer as he held up the small leather bag. Phlegian broke out sniggering. "Don't you remember? This is merely the tip you gave us for providing you with such a good time last night. Thank you so much, we appreciate your generosity!"

Mary could only stare at the ground, drained and demoralized. Not only was her search for Jesus ended, now it seemed her life might be as well. As she painfully arose, something caught her eye. Barely visible in the leaf litter was the necklace she had tossed away. Erascus saw this and yelled at Phlegian, "Grab that necklace; it might be valuable."

He did so, but even he could see it had no value. "It's just junk." He threw it back down.

Mary seized it, and glared at Phlegian. *It is not junk!* After a pause, she looked at it again, and thought of her mother. *It was her gift to me. I said I would treasure it always. If my fate is to die in Tiberias, I want to be wearing it. Mother, I do love you! None of this is your fault.* She picked it up and fastened it around her neck.

☙

The magistrate for Tiberias sat in his immaculate toga behind an elevated desk, glancing through bored, squinty eyes at various bureaucratic documents. His was a high political position, and his stuffy, arrogant demeanor suggested he was aware of this and was duly impressed with his status and generous salary. He wanted more of both, of course.

A knock at the door startled him. "Who is there? I have no time for trivial matters."

Erascus and Phlegian entered, one in front and one behind the bound but unbowed Mary. Her foot was so swollen she could barely move. She had learned to ignore the pain.

Erascus spoke first. "Your most noble Honor, we your devoted servants have captured this wanton prostitute. Not only is she the worst kind of depraved criminal, but she's crazy too." He rolled his eyes upward. "She thinks she hears people talking to some kind of god."

Phlegian hastened to add with an eager smile, "Of course, the customary penalty of a public stoning will need to be administered."

Mary, feeling she had nothing to lose, counter-attacked. "Sir, I was simply on my way to Nazareth, to hear a preacher named Jesus, when I hurt my ankle. Because of that, I had to rest overnight along the path. The despicable ones before you are these two filthy drunks, who accosted me in my sleep and bound and raped me. You should jail *them!*"

Erascus then displayed his prime "evidence", Mary's gift from David. "Your nobleness, here's proof she's a prostitute. Who but a woman of the night would be traveling alone with this much money?"

The magistrate squinted at the beggarly men who were smiling at him like two puppy dogs expecting a treat.

"Give me that money, you fool. That's state evidence!" He hid the bag under his desk. "Erascus, I sent you to Nazareth on business. Might you have been drinking last evening?"

"Umm, maybe a little wine with supper."

"Ha! Knowing you, a "little" means a magnum. No doubt you've disgraced me in public once again. However, it's possible what she said is true. Her ankle is swollen, and I've heard a man named Jesus is in the Nazareth area, talking nonsense and confusing the gullible."

Mary's hopes rose. "Yes! I swear I'm telling the truth!"

The magistrate pondered a bit, then beckoned Mary to approach him. He leaned forward over his desk and spoke to her in a barely audible voice.

"We might settle this, you know, without a trial. For example, we could discuss this evening how to minimize, maybe even eliminate, your sentence. Just us two, enjoying a pleasant evening, over some nice wine. And half of whatever is in that bag would be yours as well!"

Mary's reaction was at first confusion. *Is he merely testing me? To see if I really am a prostitute?*

Then a second thought occurred to her, and anger and defiance set in. *Did he say, "half of what is in the bag"? Everything in that bag is mine! This despicable reprobate is nothing more than a common thief!*

She blurted out, "Despite what these thugs have said, I have never been a disreputable person. I have always been a woman of honor. And I assure you, I will die, if necessary, a woman of honor."

The magistrate didn't flinch or bother to look up. He pretended to be writing something and simply mumbled, "Oh well, always worth a try."

He then turned and addressed his two eager errand boys at full voice. "Let me explain the situation. The only evidence I see here is the questionable word of two drunks who may well have accosted and raped this injured woman."

Phlegian whined, "Oh, no sir, I assure you we would never do anything …"

"Silence, you imbecile! In case you have forgotten, I am being considered for the position of Assistant to the Regional Procurator. The Romans pay me well to keep the local population peaceful and subservient. I don't need you two idiots upsetting my well-deserved promotion. There can be no scandals, no people asking why employees of mine are getting drunk and raping women. Rather than a stoning, I think it best that no word of this incident leaves this room."

"But sir ..."

"I said silence! Are you deaf as well as useless? My promotion is of foremost importance. This whole event never happened. You, madam, will be out of Tiberias by tomorrow morning, and will never set foot here again. If you do, you will be arrested and jailed for prostitution. Do you understand?"

He then glared at his two henchmen. "You two incompetents have made my life difficult once too often. You are both unreliable drunkards, and I will no longer entrust you with delivering important documents for me. Running simple errands is all you two are good for. And your salaries will be reduced accordingly."

Glowering at his two underlings, the magistrate pointed to the door. "Your last official duty will be to escort this miserable woman to the city limits. Lock her in the storeroom for the night, and have her on the road out of town first thing in the morning. With no further incidents! While you still have a job at all! Now get out of here, all of you."

Mary was expressionless on the outside, but inwardly hugely relieved. She would not be stoned; she would live another day. Even her foot felt better. *Maybe I could make it to Nazareth after all,* she thought. Mary bowed her head and said a prayer of thanks, just as she used to do in the Magdala synagogue.

❧

Shortly after sunrise the three of them reached the edge of town. Erascus untied Mary's wrists, brusquely turned her around, and gave her a threatening glare.

"All right, whore. We have no choice but to obey the magistrate, but we'll never forget you cost us our jobs! You will pay for that! Beware for your health if we ever set eyes on you again. If we do, Phlegian will enjoy watching you get the stoning a slut like you deserves! And I'll be delighted to personally arrange it."

He stepped closer to Mary, the smell from his rotting teeth further deteriorating her morning. "As additional punishment, we'll inform everyone in Galilee that this Mary from Magdala is indeed an infamous prostitute. That will be our revenge for you costing us our jobs. And it will also be your reputation from now on. We'll see to it, whore!"

Mary, dazed and weak but thankful to be alive, said nothing. She was too numb, weary, and hungry to worry about their threats. Her only goal was to get as far from Tiberias as possible, as fast as possible. The fact that she was now penniless hadn't fully impressed itself on her. She began to limp down the road to Nazareth on her makeshift crutch, which at this point was one of her few possessions.

To make up for being deprived of his stoning, Phlegian picked up a small rock and threw it at Mary. As bad luck would have it, his aim on this occasion was better than normal. His projectile hit Mary on the cheek, cutting her and drawing blood. The new pain was only a minor addition to that emanating from her foot.

❧

In a small town called Bethany, not far from Jerusalem, a burial service had just been completed. At the center of the service, nearest the sepulcher, were three heartbroken young people, two barely in their twenties, the third, just a teenager. As they departed the cemetery the two young adults tried to be stoic, but the younger girl could not be as brave. She fell to her knees, tears flowing, and could only blurt out, "Why? Why? What possible reason is there for this?"

She looked with pleading eyes at her older sister. "Martha, what will we do? Mother died only a year ago, but she had been sick, and

I told myself I had to accept that. Now we have no father, either, and no money! How are we to live?"

Now she let it all out. "It's so stupid! I mean, to be killed by a falling rock! It makes no sense! Why should that happen to an honest, hard-working man like our father?" She collapsed onto the ground, sobbing. "It's so unfair. We're a good family; we worship God. A falling rock! Why is this happening to us?"

Her older brother, named Lazarus, responded. "If it was God's will, it is not for us to question. There was a reason, but only God knows why. Maybe in time we will understand."

Martha knelt beside her sister and put her arm around her, thinking that perhaps a few comforting words might be therapeutic for her as well.

"God will take care of us. I enjoy working with glass and tiles; maybe I can make decorative mosaics and sell them. Your brother is too ill to work in the quarry, but he writes well and could help the rabbi in exchange for food. Our aunt in Jerusalem could also assist us. And we still have a house in Bethany to live in. We'll be fine."

Martha had to wonder if it was really going to be that simple. Would her young sister have to work as well? At that moment all her sister could offer was, "I will try to help too."

The young girl got up, attempted to dry her eyes, and took Martha's hand. They resumed the doleful walk home.

Martha smiled at her younger sister. It was a good, reassuring speech she just gave. She almost convinced herself.

CHAPTER 10

The going was slow and difficult for Mary. Her ankle was severely swollen, and she couldn't put her full weight on it. The crutch was not that much help. The cut on her face was no longer bleeding, but her cheek was swollen, discolored, and painful. She had not eaten all day, and had no money to buy anything. It was impossible not to feel angry and pessimistic. Above her, rain clouds were starting to form, depressing her spirits still more.

Her discharge from Tiberias had Mary on the main road to the Great Sea, one crowded with people, wagons, and animals. Those who looked her way at all gave her crutch a curious glance, then resumed staring straight ahead. Her own mood was bleak, with a surly resentment towards people who could move easily down the road. Still, the crowd provided a certain comfort. *Ironic. I may be safe on this busy road than on the deserted sheep trail.*

Her progress along the road was slow, the ankle was not improving, and she realized it might be necessary to walk all night to be in Nazareth by morning. That was a painful prospect in many respects, as hobbling along the rutted road into a cold wind combined with the lack of food had given her another severe headache. She could only pray the rain would hold off.

After a few hours of forcing herself onward, Mary was having second thoughts. *I could turn around. Magdala is still closer than Nazareth.* She paused and looked wistfully behind her. The path back towards Magdala, towards home and her mother, was seductive and appealing.

She turned, faced the western horizon again, and slowly began moving forward, saying sternly to herself, *I will not be a quitter!* Realistically, though, she knew the injury could not be ignored. *Nazareth is still a long journey; am I physically able to do this?*

As she debated with herself, she took little notice of the people, carts, and wagons passing her. That indifference ended when she observed that one nearby farm wagon, which had been about to pass by, had slowed down, and its driver was looking at her.

Both fear and anger welled up with in her. "Please, sir, I have an injured ankle, and I have no money. Please leave me be." But the man on the wagon was elderly, did not look at all threatening, and seemed to be extending a faint smile in her direction.

"Good afternoon, young lady. You looked like you were having trouble walking. If you wish, you can hop on the wagon. I could take you a few miles down the road."

Mary could hardly believe her ears. She looked at his creased but benign face for a few seconds, and realized she ought to be accepting this merciful offer.

"Sir, that is most kind. If it's not too much trouble, I would indeed appreciate a ride."

Getting up the rickety wooden ladder on the side of the wagon was a painful challenge, but the driver offered her his hand. Mary tumbled over the railing and collapsed onto an empty crate. A hard, splintery seat had never felt so good.

She looked more closely at his tanned wrinkled face and calloused hands, and concluded he might be a local farmer. "Thank you so much, sir. My name is Mary. From Magdala. Do you live near here?"

"Barsabas is my name. Me and my wife, we've got a small farm down the road a bit. I go to Tiberias now and then to sell things, get some money to live on. I hate Tiberias, would never want to live there. People just seem crazy about money and status and power. False gods is what those things are, if you ask me. I like the farm. A lot of work, but a more pleasant life." He gave his mare a gentle tap, which didn't improve its speed at all. "Sales were slow today, but we should be all right 'til the end of the month."

"It pleases me to hear that. I appreciate your offering me a ride. No one else stopped." She paused for a moment. "Could I ask why you stopped for me?"

"A few days ago, I was selling some goods in Nazareth. I was in no hurry, so I spent a little time listening to this preacher fellow who was talking in town. He was saying we should be helpful to others, because some day we might need help too. Things like that. Made sense to me. You looked like you could use a ride."

Mary, amazed, asked, "Do you happen to recall this preacher's name?"

"I think they called him Jesus. Seemed like a nice young man. Lots of people there."

"Really! I hope I might be able to listen to him as well."

They continued down the road. The click-clop of the horse's hooves was the sweetest music Mary had ever heard. Every step the horse took were three painful ones she could avoid.

After a few hours they came to a narrow side road, at which point the farmer turned the cart onto it and stopped. Mary prepared for the effort of getting out of the cart, but the farmer saw her struggling and made a second offer.

"Hard to imagine you want to be out walking at night. Those dark clouds look like rain. Good, we could use it. Now, if you want, you could stay at the farm tonight. I think my wife would be all right with that. We've no guest room, but we have a good supply of hay out in the barn you could bed down on."

This time there was not the slightest hesitation. "Oh, hay would be wonderful. Thank you so much, you're most thoughtful."

"It's like that preacher fellow said, someday I might need a helping hand too."

"What he said is true. Sooner or later, we all do."

As they approached the farmhouse, Barsabas pointed to the barn and said, "When you get settled, come on in. We can find an extra plate so you can have some supper."

"That's most kind. I'll be there shortly."

Mary was fully aware she had not eaten for two days. Although her stomach was empty, her spirits were soaring. Earlier, she believed the human race was loathsome, but Barsabas had changed her mind. *I have to find this preacher and hear what he has to say.*

Following a simple but most welcome dinner, sleep came easily to Mary that night, aided by the pleasant patter of rain on the barn's roof.

As the eastern sky began to lighten, Mary gathered her things, brushed the hay from her robe, and prepared to continue on to Nazareth, praying her ankle would hold up. But once again the farmer intercepted her.

"Hey, where you going? An egg and some bread are inside waiting for you. Come on in."

Remembering that she was penniless, Mary readily accepted. Not only did a little more to eat sound good, she also realized she needed to know how far it was from the farm to Nazareth.

"How far? Only about five miles. I can take you there; hate to think about you walking so far with that miserable crutch. Maybe I can sell a few things in town after I drop you off."

The farmer's kindness had now restored Mary's hope and optimism. As they headed towards Nazareth, for the first time she felt confident her search would be successful.

CHAPTER 11

Nazareth was a small town, smaller in population than Magdala. It was home to a mix of skilled craftsmen and hardworking farmers. Barsabas dropped Mary off near the end of the main street and received more fervent thanks. Mary apologized for having nothing tangible to offer him, but didn't elaborate as she wanted to avoid explaining why she was penniless. She limped down the cobblestone street and approached the first woman she saw.

"Excuse me. I'm seeking a man called Jesus, and I was told he might be somewhere in Nazareth. Would you happen to know where I might find him?"

The woman, heavyset and humorless, sneered, "Another unfortunate wanting a miracle." She pointed down the road. "You'll have no trouble finding him, maybe in the area around the synagogue."

"Thank you so much."

Mary hobbled on down the road until, as she rounded a bend, a synagogue appeared just ahead. The woman was right; there was a sizable crowd in the courtyard, and all eyes were focused on the charismatic young man addressing them.

As she scanned the crowd she noticed something odd. It appeared that some of the townspeople were scowling, as if doubting his credibility. A few were making dismissive hand gestures as they walked away. Why, she wondered, were they not accepting him?[1]

Mary joined the rear of the group, her eyes wide with anticipation. Along with joy and excitement, a feeling of calm came over her. Her quest was over.

She had found Jesus.

For a while, Mary was not so much listening to Jesus as just looking at this man she had endured so much to find. He was not remarkable in height or build or general appearance, it was his face that was so compelling. It was a face that could simultaneously reflect joy, empathy, and sadness, and from which could come simple words that nonetheless conveyed a message both enduring and profound. She found herself captivated by him.

His attire also intrigued her. She had imagined he would be wearing a fancy robe, something that would reflect a position of authority. To the contrary, his robe appeared even plainer than what his followers wore. *It's as if he wants to say, "I'm not seeking power, and I don't think of myself as better than those around me."*

After a few minutes Jesus concluded his comments. "... I know many of you are troubled, or sick, or crippled. Do not despair. Remember, help is nearby if you place your faith in God. Now, go in peace and, if you can, please join us here again tomorrow."

All of Jesus' words reverberated in Mary's mind. She limped over to where a few of the group had come forward following his sermon to talk with him. She stayed in the rear, wanting to remain half hidden. She couldn't muster the courage to approach any closer. Nor did she have the slightest idea what she would say if she did find the courage.

An older woman close to Mary noticed her obvious discomfort and asked, "Have you ever seen such a marvelous speaker?"

"No, this is the first time I've heard him."

"You look tired. It's a pity you have to walk with such an awful crutch. Your family must be poor."

"I have little money, but I manage to survive."

"You should go and meet Jesus. He might be able to help you. He's helped others."

Mary glanced at Jesus. "I don't know, I'm not deserving ..."

"Go!" she insisted. "Just say hello to him. What do you have to lose?"

Mary pondered this. *She's right, what is there to lose? Isn't that the reason I came here?*

As people departed, she cautiously made her way to the second row of those crowding around Jesus. Still nervous, she peeked over the shoulders of the two men in front of her, trying to remain inconspicuous. She had never felt her heart beat so fast before.

Jesus finished talking to one of the group, and glanced around to see who else might have a question. He paused when he observed Mary's inquisitive eyes peering at him between the two broad shoulders.

"Good morning. What is your name? I cannot recall seeing you here before."

"Ah, no sir. My name is Mary. I just now arrived in Nazareth."

The two men in front of Mary stepped aside to observe this new person who had gained Jesus' attention. He could now see what she had under her left arm.

"Tell me, why do you require such a crudely made crutch?"

"I was walking here from Magdala, hoping to hear you, but I fell along the trail, and twisted my ankle."

"Magdala! That's a long journey, especially with an injured foot. Tell me, Mary from Magdala, do you have other things that trouble you?"

"Oh, no, I feel fine, I ..."

Mary's impulse to internalize her problems faded as she realized that lying to Jesus was a poor strategy, not to mention the obvious cut on her cheek. A slight smile on Jesus' face encouraged her to be more forthcoming.

"Well, yes, I seem to have a quick temper. Maybe the headaches cause this; they can be intense. And I have awful nightmares. I wish more than anything they would go away. I curse at the worst ones.

Also, I envy women with families. I know it's wrong, but I do. Sometimes I act very rude to my dear mother, a wonderful person, who I truly love. I wish I could stop." She lowered her eyes. "There are times I think I'm not a kind and caring person."

"And anything else?" His angled head, the nature of the question, and his quieter voice made it seem he already knew the answer.

Mary looked around her, then approached closer to Jesus, and in a low voice summarized the events of the last two days into his ear. "… and so, I worry that I may be with child. Please, it would be horrid to have a child by those terrible men!"

Jesus likewise replied in a tone only Mary could hear. "Do not despair, Mary. I assure you, you are not with child. Nor need you curse any longer at headaches or nightmares."

Jesus then resumed speaking in a more audible voice. "But I ask you, Mary, why do you carry that crutch with you? You have no need for it."

Mary's face reflected her confusion. "My ankle …"

Jesus interrupted her. "Have you tried to walk without it?"

Mary was still confused, but after a moment let go of the crutch. She took a hesitant step, deliberately limping. Then she tried another, without limping. She looked at Jesus in amazement; she sensed no pain. She put her full weight on the foot, and took a couple of small steps. Still no pain, and the swelling was gone.

She looked up at Jesus, beaming with delight and gratitude. "I can't believe it! My ankle is healed! I … I can walk normal, with no pain!"

With a puzzled expression she asked, "Why have you helped me? I'm no one special."

"Do you not remember, Mary? When you were most in need of help, you called out to me, asking if I could help you, and you did not even know me. That made you special to me. Your faith has made you whole,[2] and your belief in me will help you believe in yourself."

Mary was astonished that he would know this.[3] How could he? She was at a loss for words and could only stare in wonder at him. She fell to the ground in front of Jesus, tears of joy hitting his feet. She touched the hem of his garment and dried the fallen tears with her hair.

Jesus motioned for Mary to rise and spoke directly to her. "My time here in Nazareth is finished, and I will depart tomorrow. If you wish, you would be welcome to join our group."

Mary looked up at him, her eyes filled with awe and wonder. Her face reflected the realization that she was about to make a life-altering decision.

But there was not the slightest hesitation.

"I would be honored to join you."

CHAPTER 12

Traveling around Galilee with Jesus was an exhilarating experience for Mary. In addition to his inspiring sermons, she was experiencing for the first time the sounds and subtle beauty of the Galilean landscape. Her door to the larger world had opened.

In the months that Mary had been with Jesus, today's crowd was by far the largest she had seen. Thousands of people, including families with children, had gathered on a Galilean hillside near the town of Tabgha to hear his message.

All eyes were on Jesus as he made his way through the crowd and ascended to a prominent knoll on the hillside.[1] Behind him were his twelve Apostles, led by an older man named Peter, a fisherman from the town of Capernaum. The Apostles seated themselves around Jesus, and Mary chose a place just behind them. She not only wished to hear his words, she also wanted to observe him and learn why he was such a compelling speaker.

Jesus spoke in a strong, clear voice. "Blessed are the merciful, for they shall obtain mercy. Blessed are the peacemakers, for they shall be called the children of God. Blessed are the humble, for they shall inherit the earth."

Jesus turned and faced Mary. "Blessed are the pure in heart, for they shall find God." Mary, not seeking recognition, lowered her eyes.

At the end of his talk, an eager mother urged her two young children to go forward and meet Jesus. Mary smiled at them and said, "Yes, go. Jesus loves little children."

Peter was quick to overrule her. "Please, people want to talk with

Jesus about his teachings. Small children shouldn't be interrupting them."

As the embarrassed mother pulled her children back, Jesus made clear his own priorities. "Let the children come unto me. They are God's gift. His kingdom belongs to such as these. Whoever does not approach the kingdom of God as would a child shall not enter it himself."[2] He placed his hands on their heads and blessed them.

Mary hugged the children as they returned. Peter said nothing, but directed a scowl at the woman disciple he saw as impertinent, yet who seemed to understand Jesus better than he did.

☙

In the ensuing months Mary stayed close to Jesus, eager to take in his words. One day some wealthy men joined the group. Their smug looks betrayed their thoughts: *Let's see what he has to say to those of us whom the gods have already chosen to bless!"*

One of the wealthy men called out to Jesus, "You spoke earlier of eternal life. What must we do to receive this eternal life?"

Jesus replied, "Remember the ancient precepts. Love your neighbor as yourself. Treat others as you would want them to treat you. Do not murder or steal, do not commit adultery, do not accuse others falsely."[3]

Mary's eyes widened on hearing this latter commandment; it struck a personal chord. Anger welled up as the painful memories of her trip to Nazareth and the ensuing accusations came flooding back. She was also confused, for hadn't Jesus cured her of her anger?

Later, after their midday meal, Jesus approached Mary. She was pleased but nervous, as this was the first time he had spoken individually with her. The apostles were both surprised and upset, for men conversing privately with women was deemed improper and was never done.[4]

Jesus sat down beside Mary and said, "Once, not long before we met, I stopped briefly in Magdala to speak to the people there, and paid a short visit to your synagogue.[5] From Magdala, I went to Capernaum, where I met the first of my twelve Apostles, Peter and Andrew. I thought you might be interested to know that."

"Oh, yes, but I wish I'd known of your visit, so I might have met you then."

"I wish so too. However, I wanted to ask you something else. I saw your reaction when I spoke today of false accusations. Did this have special meaning for you?"

"Yes, Master, for I, too, have been falsely accused of terrible things."

"I know, of being a prostitute. I assure you, Mary, the truth of your virtue will prevail. The ninth commandment is frequently broken, and for this, many will have to answer for their false accusations, according to the magnitude of their sins."

Mary was grateful to hear this and felt honored he had chosen to speak privately with her, social conventions and the Apostles' stares notwithstanding.

She also had a question. "Master, may I ask why I still have out-pourings of anger? I hoped I was saved from such demons when we first met in Nazareth.[6] Was that not the case?"

Jesus replied, "I rewarded your faith in me by attending to your physical needs, such as your ankle. I saw in you a person of great potential, one requiring only greater confidence and self-discipline. I left it to you to conquer internal demons on your own. When you have done that, you will have gained the strength, patience, and wisdom needed to achieve great goals."

Mary stared at him as he departed. *Is it possible he really thinks that highly of me?*

❧

Jesus, seated on a donkey and surrounded by his Apostles and other devoted disciples, had entered Jerusalem through the northern gate. They were not alone; both behind and ahead of them were hundreds of townspeople, cheering his arrival. As he proceeded, they spread branches and palm fronds before him, shouting, "Praise him who comes in the name of the Lord!"[7]

Over the past two years, Jesus and his message had become widely known throughout Palestine, though not always favorably. Jesus knew this, and unlike his Apostles, he understood and accepted that this was to be the last week of his ministry.

As they proceeded through the jubilant throng, Peter asked, "Where are we going first, Master? Should we seek a place large enough for a sermon?"

"No," Jesus responded. "We shall go to the Temple. I would like to see what is happening there as Passover approaches."

On arriving at the temple, Jesus approached its main entrance. His eyes narrowed at what he saw. The entrance plaza more resembled a marketplace than a temple. Merchants were selling a variety of goods, including cattle, sheep, and birds, many intended for sacrifices. Farm animals are not fastidious, and their odor lent a nauseating addition to the commercial desecration.

To facilitate the marketing, numerous tables had been set up to exchange money, for the requirement at the temple was that purchases and donations had to be made in Jewish currency. The exchange rate was quite favorable to the money changers.

With anger etched on his face, Jesus accosted the men at the exchange tables. "God said his temple would be a house of prayer, but you have made it a den of thieves!" To the apostles' astonishment, Jesus began overturning the tables of the money-changers and driving the sheep and cattle onto the street.[8] As he did, the shocked merchants shouted obscenities and lunged at him. With difficulty, the disciples were able to intervene and maneuver Jesus away from the furious shopkeepers. Once on the road, they found safety among the milling pedestrians.

The Apostles were bewildered and astonished by Jesus' surprising behavior. Peter asked, "Master, I do not understand. Is it wise to anger these people so? And at the Temple? Might not some seek retaliation, or even revenge?"

Jesus showed no concern about reprisals. "Should we do nothing when the Temple is defiled? We have entered Jerusalem, and what will happen here, including the fall of the Temple, was foretold by the ancient prophets. The Son of Man will be betrayed, arrested, and crucified, but on the third day shall arise again. This has been prophesied and must be.[9] It is God's will."

The many disciples, including Mary, stared at Jesus in bewilderment and disbelief. They understood that by "the Son of Man" he meant himself, and what he was saying frightened them. Were these terrible things imminent? But meaningful questions eluded them, and they continued in silence down the road to the field where they would spend the night.

☙

Under a cloudy sky, Jesus and his closest disciples arrived at Bethany, a town not far from Jerusalem. There, they would dine at the home of Martha, a devoted follower of Jesus. Martha, in her early twenties, was by nature quiet though not shy, wanting to assess how she might be of help in any situation. She was practical and responsible, and after the loss of their parents had cared for her brother and sister, becoming the glue that held the family together.

Her younger sister Mary, an attractive young lady in her late teens, was also a sincere follower but did not hesitate to enjoy life when she could. Since "Mary" was a common name, she was often referred to as "Mary of Bethany".

Their older brother, Lazarus, was likewise an ardent follower of Jesus, but earlier had been in poor health for years. However, there was much more to his story than that. Most of those present did not know of it, but the ones who did wasted no time in sharing it with others.

Mary heard it from Mary of Bethany, who was more social and loquacious than her older siblings. At an opportune moment, she said, "My brother is quiet by nature and never talks about the miraculous thing Jesus did for him, but as you are Jesus' disciples, I think you should know."

"Before a previous visit by Jesus, Lazarus' health was failing, and Martha hoped our Savior could help him. She pleaded, 'Master, I am so happy to see you, but you are too late. Our beloved Lazarus has already passed away! Why has such misfortune befallen us? First, mother died, then father was killed at the quarry, and now Lazarus. Why is all this happening?' "

"Jesus replied, 'Martha, you've heard me say that he who believes in me shall live, even though he has died. Do you believe this?' Martha replied, 'Yes, you know I do.' "

"Then, an amazing thing happened. Jesus asked, 'Please show me the tomb.' He approached it and said, 'Lazarus, arise and depart from this tomb.' To everyone's astonishment, he did! Jesus had given him new life.[10] I swear this is true." Mary Magdalene and the other listeners could only stare in astonishment at Jesus and Lazarus.

Later, as Martha began preparing the evening meal, Mary offered to assist her. Martha, unfamiliar with her new helper, said, "Thank you. Have we met before?"

"My name is Mary, from Magdala. I am one of those who have been traveling with Jesus. I hope I'm not intruding. I just want to help Jesus any way I can."

"In that case, Mary, you will always be welcome in our house."

As they ate, everyone pondered Lazarus' history. Several Apostles looked at Peter for further explanation, but Peter was as perplexed as his companions.

Mary Magdalene, on the other hand, was more accepting of events beyond her comprehension. When asked if she could explain what had happened, she simply said, "I am unable to understand this either, but does it matter? I'm certain Jesus knows the reasons for everything that has happened and will happen, which for me is sufficient."

She did not know that Jesus had overheard her words – and had smiled.

CHAPTER 13

Jesus realized his most influential opponents were the Pharisees. These conservative religious leaders were responsible for enforcing the longstanding laws and conventions of their Jewish faith. They could not tolerate Jesus suggesting that any of those venerated customs be superseded by the message he was sent to deliver. Jesus understood this, but he also knew that his ministry was nearing its end. His work was being made difficult by the ongoing efforts of the Pharisees to confront and denigrate him.

The day after the temple incident, Jesus faced an angry group of Pharisees. All of them knew what had happened at the Temple, and demanded an audience with him to castigate his teachings. Jesus knew they would try to entrap him, perhaps even find reasons to arrest him.

The Pharisees' heated interrogation was interrupted when a woman arrived, being dragged by her arms behind a group of men that included Pharisees. They threw her to the ground in front of Jesus. Bruised and bleeding, she trembled with fear and dared not look up.

In a calm voice Jesus inquired, "What is this?"

"This wretch was caught in the act of committing adultery," a Pharisee exclaimed. "Our laws are clear: they say she must be stoned to death. Tell us, what do *you* say, teacher?"

Jesus saw the trap. This was a situation where his teachings defied traditional practice. The Pharisees had cornered him into either disavowing their laws in public, or concurring with the brutal execution of the woman. With glares and smirks, they awaited his choice.

After only a moment's pause Jesus replied. "Your laws say she must be stoned? I say, whoever among you has committed no sins, let him cast the first stone."[1]

The accusers stared at Jesus with blank faces. He had not only avoided their trap, but had forced them to reflect on their own short-comings. One by one, those who had dragged the woman before Jesus retreated, casting surly looks at him as they departed.

Jesus turned to the adulteress. "Your accusers no longer condemn you. Nor do I. Go, but sin no more." The woman, still wide-eyed with fright, bowed to Jesus and headed home.

Mary walked over to Jesus. "Thank you for that. I sometimes wonder, though, why all those who participate in acts of adultery are not held equally punishable."

Her implication was obvious, and Peter could not let it pass. "So, it seems Mary feels her personal ideas of right and wrong are more valid than the laws of the faith that have guided us for centuries." To Jesus he asked, "Master, tell us, are the ancient laws wrong?"

Both Peter and nearby Pharisees awaited the answer with eager eyes. Jesus, undisturbed, replied, "The laws should be obeyed, but there will be judgment on Pharisees and others who appear good, but inside are full of hypocrisy and sin.[2] Do not ignore the mandates of mercy and justice. Remember, the ancient writings also state, 'What does God require of you but to seek justice, love mercy, and walk humbly with your God?' "[3]

Andrew looked at Peter in confusion. "What does this mean? Is he saying the ancient laws are not eternal? That, over time, they can be interpreted in different ways? And he's the one to tell us how to do that? The Pharisees will never accept that."

Andrew was right; Jesus' defense of the sinful woman only further infuriated the Pharisees. One, wanting to see Jesus squirm, asked the trickiest question he could device. "Sir, your knowledge of theology is impressive, considering you are not a Pharisee. Tell us, in your learned opinion, which is the foremost commandment in the Law?"

Jesus responded to his sarcasm with soft-spoken counsel. "You shall love the Lord God with all your heart, soul, and mind. The second most important commandment is similar: you shall love your neighbor as yourself." For emphasis he added, "The whole Law of Moses and the teachings of the prophets are based upon these two commandments."[4]

Mary asked, "Teacher, when you say to love your neighbor as yourself, does "neighbor" mean just the people around you, or do you mean everyone throughout the world?"

Peter was quick to upbraid her. "Mary, must you always insert yourself into our conversations and question what Jesus says? Could you not show proper restraint and respect?"

Annoyed, Mary replied, "I believe I asked our Teacher a question, not you."

Jesus smiled at them. "It's a valid question. The words of God should be preached throughout the world.[5] In God's eyes, everyone is equal, and everyone is our neighbor."[6] To both he added, "All people should love and respect their neighbor."

Peter and Mary understood that he was talking to them.

Another Pharisee called out, "You speak of a judgment day. But how will we know when it is upon us? Some say it will be soon. What do you, the prophet, say?"

"I am not a prophet. No one can know when that day will come. You must be prepared, for the kingdom of God lies within each of you."[7]

A younger man, not a Pharisee, arose. "I have heard many men claim to speak the truth about religious matters, but they say different things. How are we to know what is true?"

Jesus saw this as a critical question, not an attempt to entrap him. "I have selected trusted Apostles who you see here today. They can be believed. It is true that false prophets will appear and tell you lies.

Pay them no heed. Though the earth may pass away, my words will endure."[8]

After Jesus responded to further questions, the Apostles gathered around him and began to depart. The women disciples, as was the custom, assembled a respectful distance behind the men and followed them down the road. The Pharisees, frustrated at their inability to entrap Jesus, had also dispersed. But their private conversations were focusing more on a single theme: *How can the teachings of this man be stopped?*

⌒

As they departed from the Pharisees, Peter overheard Mary say to a friend, "Could that be why I met Jesus in Nazareth, to help his words endure by letting others know of them?"

Peter replied, "We hope you will, Mary, and in a manner appropriate for women."

Mary understood his message: *Any preaching to men by women is, of course, forbidden.*

As Mary resumed talking with other women disciples, Peter turned to his brother and gave voice to a thought that had puzzled him for some time.

"Andrew, have you ever wondered why Mary Magdalene is identified by the town she is from? Why doesn't she carry the name of her husband or father to honor them, as other women do? Why isn't she known as 'Mary, wife of …' or 'Mary, daughter of …'? Has she no family? Has she never married? If not, why? Everyone knows a woman her age should be married."

Andrew agreed. "Yes, it is strange. I asked once if she had a husband, and she said no. I inquired why not, and she replied, 'It was God's will.' I, too, wonder what she might be hiding."

"Exactly. We need to know more about this Mary of Magdala. Much about her is odd."

CHAPTER 14

As the twelve Apostles walked from where Jesus had been speaking, they were quieter than usual. They feared the possible consequences of the Pharisees' increasing hostility, as well as the troubling predictions that Jesus had made concerning his own fate.

Peter, seeking a different topic, inquired about the forthcoming religious days. "Master, what preparations do you wish us to make for the Passover supper?"

Jesus replied, "Go to an address I will give you in the city, and say to the owner, 'The Master said his hour has come, and he wishes to celebrate the Passover in the upstairs room of your house with his disciples.' He will understand your request."[1] Peter, though concerned about the phrase "his hour has come," nodded his concurrence.

Jesus and the twelve Apostles had assembled in the upper room of the house visited by Peter. The wealthy Jewish owner was neither Roman nor an overt opponent of the empire and was comfortable hosting Jesus and his disciples.

The thirteen men were seated on one side of a long table, made from imported hardwood with inlaid mosaic patterns. Works of art and frescoes adorned the walls, and oil lamps provided light. A hired cook had prepared the supper, since Jews, unlike wealthy Romans, did not acquire slaves for such duties. A few women disciples helped serve dinner, and one of those was Mary Magdalene. As she served, she listened to the talk at the table but was careful to be discreet.

At the conclusion of the meal, Peter asked a question that concerned them all. "You have said, Master, that your hour has come.

Surely you don't mean you will soon depart from us?"

Jesus patiently reiterated what he had said many times. "I have not spoken on my own authority, but the Father who sent me has told me what I must say and do, and what will happen, even today."

A worried Peter asked, "Today, Master? What is it that will happen today?"

"All of you but one are loyal followers. Today, as prophesied, that one will betray me."

All the Apostles, with a single exception, looked at each other in disbelief. Several protested with words such as "Master, it could never be me. I will stand with you until the end!"

Mary, equally astounded, scanned the row of Apostles. Her eyes eventually reached Judas Iscariot who was directing a surprised look towards Jesus.

"Surely, Teacher, you cannot mean me?" Judas protested, feigning ignorance but in reality acknowledging himself as the traitor.

"So you say." replied Jesus. "Do as you must."[2]

The Apostles stared at Judas, then back at Jesus. When their attention was no longer on him, Judas arose and exited through the nearest door.

Jesus addressed the others. "You who remain are my devoted disciples, and for that I am thankful. Let us give praise and show evidence of our eternal commitment to God." He moved certain items on the table closer to him. "Here before you are bread and wine, which you ate and drank as part of your meal. But today they are more than food, for they have symbolic value, representing my body and blood. Take and eat, in remembrance of me."[3]

The eleven remaining Apostles did as asked, then bowed their heads in prayer. Peter was the first to break the silence. The exposure of Judas as a traitor made him want to reaffirm his devotion to Jesus, and in a strong voice he asserted, "Lord, I am ready to go to prison with you, and die with you if necessary."

The response by Jesus disturbed everyone. "I tell you, Peter, that before morning you will deny me three times. And the rest will run and leave me."

All the Apostles looked at Jesus in amazement, and in overlapping voices protested they would never show such disloyalty. Jesus calmly replied, "I know that is your intent, but although the spirit is willing, the flesh is weak. To you, Peter, I say that in time you will be bound and taken away against your will, and you will suffer in my name's sake, but at that time your faithfulness to me will be forever proven."[4]

All the Apostles looked astonished at what Jesus had just said, as did Mary, who was sweeping the floor in a corner of the room, facing away from the table but listening to every word coming from it.

"Please go to the Garden of Gethsemane and wait for me," Jesus instructed them. "I will join you shortly."

The eleven departed. It had been a long and emotional day, and they were tired. Once in the garden they soon fell asleep, which is how Jesus found them when he later arrived at the last place where they would be together, prior to his arrest.[5]

❧

The women who had been helping with the meal were finishing their various tasks. Soon, Mary was the last one remaining near the table, cleaning it with a cloth, as always wanting to be wherever Jesus was. The Apostles had all left.

Jesus turned to her and in a receptive manner said, "Mary, would you come and sit by me for a moment?"

Mary hesitated. *The Apostles were just there, is it right for me to be seated there too?* But it was Jesus who had invited her, and the question was answered.

Jesus spoke to her with straightforward sincerity. "Mary, my Mary of Magdala, no one has been more devoted to my teaching than you. In both good and troubled times you have remained my loyal disciple, and have always tried to understand my every word."

"How could I do otherwise? You have done so much for me, healed and comforted me, given my life new meaning and direction. Your words have inspired me and made me a changed person. All I am today I owe to you."

"I am pleased you feel I have helped you," Jesus replied. "To me, you are like a vessel that has been filled to the top. I often sense that you have understood my message the best of anyone.[6] You are worthy to be my disciple."

"That's most kind. I've tried my best, and I hope that I do understand your message. In the future, I'd like nothing more than to help others know and appreciate your gospel as well, and teach them all you have taught me."

"You shall, Mary. Go wherever people will receive you, speak to them as the Holy Spirit inspires you, and fear nothing, for you know that I will always be with you."

In a confiding manner he added, "When I said that I thought you best understood my message, I meant it as more than a compliment. As you know, I did not write down my thoughts myself; there were always scribes present when I spoke, and they did that for me."

Jesus took a piece of papyrus from his robe and laid it in front of Mary. "But I have written this message for you alone."

Mary looked at him, not understanding. "For me?"

"I sometimes said things to the Apostles that I never said to those who came to hear my sermons, because those messages required a certain knowledge of my words to be fully understood. For the same reason, I haven't told even the Apostles everything. To you, Mary, because your mind has been receptive and you have learned well, I give you these further insights.[7] Do not speak of them in your sermons, as I have not, but use them to construct a more accurate message to deliver to your congregations."

"Should I ever let anyone see them?"

"Only those who you believe understand my message as well as you yourself do."

Mary nodded. She concealed the gift he had given her in her robe.

After a pause, Jesus concluded his words to Mary, "I must go now, to the Garden of Gethsemane to pray. I will soon be arrested, as has been prophesied."

Mary could only stare at her mentor; no words offered themselves. She had listened to him and understood what would occur after his arrest. Their eyes conveyed their final thoughts.

"Farewell, Mary, my faithful companion. I will remember you with great respect and admiration. We will see each other again."

Mary, confused by his last statement, silently watched him depart, then buried her head in her arms on the table.

CHAPTER 15

It was Friday, two days later. Although daytime, it more resembled night, with black clouds hiding the sky, accompanied by terrifying thunder and lightning. A disfigured hill near Jerusalem, known as Golgotha, was crowded with people. The scarred hillside had been made even more foreboding by the presence of three crosses. To each had been nailed a man, a living human being. On the taller central cross that man was Jesus of Nazareth.

Near the base of the cross two women – Mary, mother of Jesus, and Mary Magdalene – were seated on the ground.[1] They gently embraced one another; the latter was softly crying, the other's drained face merely stared blankly at the barren earth. They were silent. There were no words that would make sense in such a senseless situation.

Soldiers stood guard near the crosses. Their faces had mixed reactions to the events they were enforcing. Some were impassive, perhaps thinking, *I just do what they tell me.* Some with hardened faces seemed pleased, even smug: *So! Three more enemies of the Empire eliminated!*

A few soldiers, very few, looked nervous, almost scared, as though they knew a terrible wrong was taking place. They also knew they were helpless to do anything about it.

Jesus' robe, which had been removed by his executioners, lay on the ground. One Roman guard, having won a dice competition, picked it up and walked away with it.[2]

Mary looked for the Apostles in the crowd, but they were not to be seen. At first this upset her, but she reasoned, *Perhaps they are some of the men in the distance. They might not dare approach closer, for should they be arrested, who would spread the words of Jesus?*

She prayed for their safety as well.

⊙

It had been over an hour since the crosses were erected. The ground trembled under the blackened sky, accompanied by a growing crescendo of thunder and lightning. A few of the onlookers covered their eyes and ran to their homes in fear.

A tremendous lightning bolt caused the shadow of the central cross to appear on the ground near the two women. A sound, barely audible, slowly emanated from that cross.

"Father, into thy hands I commend my spirit."[3]

It was over.

⊙

As the lightning became more intimidating and the thunder grew louder, the two Marys continued to console one another as best they could. They were no doubt thinking with broken hearts about what might have been, about the enormity of their loss; indeed, the loss to the entire world. They hardly noticed the storm and the earth shaking. Perhaps those things to them were nothing more than God's way of saying, *I have seen what you have done here.*

After a few minutes, the thunder and lightning began to abate, and the two mourners slowly arose. They felt as though all purpose in life had been stolen from them.

Mary Magdalene glanced towards the base of the cross; she could not bear to look upward. As she stared at the ground, a small stone near the cross caught her attention. A small drop of blood had fallen on it.

Mary picked it up.

CHAPTER 16

Later that day the same women, Mary Magdalene and Mary the mother of Jesus, were seated in front of a large and newly constructed tomb. It belonged to Joseph of Arimathea, a wealthy and respected supporter of Jesus. Making use of his influential position, he had requested from the Roman governor, Pontius Pilate, the right to receive the body of Jesus and to provide a proper burial place for it. His request was granted.[1]

The two Marys watched as the body of Jesus was laid to rest inside the tomb. Joseph of Arimathea joined them and with tears all fell to their knees for a few moments of prayer. The door to the tomb was closed and Joseph, assisted by other men, rolled a large rock in front of the entrance to secure the tomb. When the rock was in place, a seal was placed on it, and a Roman military guard was stationed there to ensure no one would remove the body and then claim that Jesus had been resurrected.

When all the others except the guard had left, the two women remained by the tomb for some time. There was nowhere else they cared to be; this was where the source of all their hopes and dreams now lay. As the sun approached the horizon they offered final prayers, and departed.

As was the custom of their faith, on Sunday morning Mary Magdalene and two other women brought spices and perfumes to the tomb to anoint the body of Jesus. Mary, having been there before, led the way. She worried, however, whether it would even be possible to carry out their mission. "Will the guard be able to move the entrance rock by himself ?" she asked of the disciple beside her. "In fact, will he even agree to do so?"

When they arrived at the tomb, their mouths dropped in shock and foreboding. The rock had already been rolled away, and the tomb had been opened. The Roman guard was cowering in the distance, too frightened for words; it seemed clear he was not the one who had opened it. Mary entered the tomb with hesitation, unsure of what to expect but dreading what she might see. Her worst fear was realized. The tomb was empty.

"No! How can this be? Surely his body has not been stolen!"

Looking up in anguish, she observed a human figure, garbed in white and encircled by light, who addressed her. "Why do you look among the dead for one who is alive? Do not be disheartened. He is not here; he has been raised, as was prophesied."[2]

Mary stared at the figure, speechless, then ran from the tomb and signaled the other women to come and look also. Her companions peered into the tomb, and tiptoed in. Mary shouted, "Wait here; I must go and tell the others," and began running to where the Apostles were assembled.

She had not run far, however, when she was startled by a man standing only a few feet in front of her. It was Jesus. Mary was speechless; tears of joy were instantaneous.

"Why do you cry? Who is it you look for?"

Mary was astounded and exuberant. "Teacher!" She reached out to touch his garment.

Jesus raised his hand. "Do not touch me, for I have not yet ascended to be with the Father. Go and tell the others these things you have seen, that I have appeared to you."[3]

Mary replied, "Of course; you know I will always do as you ask."

Mary slowly tiptoed past Jesus, never taking her eyes off him, and then burst off to bring the jubilant news to the Apostles.

☙

In a field distant from the tomb the Apostles were seated under the shade of a massive oak tree, mourning, and talking among themselves. Distraught and confused, one question absorbed them: *what should we do now?* They had no ready answer, as they had never discussed a post-Jesus scenario. Their confused conversations were abruptly suspended by the sight of a woman rushing towards them.

While still some distance away, Mary shouted, "Peter! Everyone! Come, see!" She paused to catch her breath. "The tomb! It's been opened! Jesus isn't there!"

Peter, as usual, was skeptical. "Mary, please try to contain yourself. What are you talking about? How could he not be in the tomb? He was buried there just two days ago."

"No! He has risen, just as he prophesied! I speak only what my eyes have seen; you know I would never lie to you. He appeared to me; he told me to bring the good news of his resurrection to you."

The Apostles looked at one another, then at Mary, then at Peter. They were now even more perplexed, as well as unconvinced.[4]

The apostle Thomas was the most skeptical. "Are you sure you saw these things? Who opened the tomb? Why would Jesus have appeared to you, rather than us? What you say seems difficult to believe."

This was hardly the reaction Mary expected, but she would not be intimidated. "I'm quite certain of what I saw, Thomas. Go and ask the other women. The tomb was open when we arrived, I don't know how. Jesus was not there. Go look for yourself if you must!"

The Apostle Philip sought to mediate the issue. "Should we not at least inspect the tomb? I do recall Jesus saying that he would rise on the third day."

The disciple Matthew also defended her. "Mary is an honest woman and would not deceive us. We should go to the tomb."

The other Apostles looked at one another, confused, as they also recalled Jesus' words.

Peter sensed a need to take control. "I will go. John, come with me. It's necessary that we inspect the tomb and verify, if possible, the peculiar claims of this woman. John Mark, come along also, in case we need a scribe."

Andrew, eyes wide, sprang up to join them. Thomas, still skeptical, remained under the oak, as did some other Apostles.

They hurried towards the tomb. John, much younger than Peter, was in the lead, with Andrew and John Mark close behind. Other Apostles and Mary followed.

When they arrived at the tomb, the women who had been with Mary had left. Peter and John entered through the open doorway and saw that the tomb was empty, except for the linen burial cloths in which Jesus had been wrapped. The guard was gone. The other Apostles soon joined them. The men stared at each other, now aware they were witnessing the fulfillment of both ancient prophesy and Jesus' own pronouncements. No one spoke.

After a few moments they departed the tomb. Peter was now convinced. "Come, John. We must hurry back and announce to the others that Jesus has indeed risen!"

Mary, ignored, thought to herself, *Didn't I just do that?*

CHAPTER 17

The challenges facing the eleven remaining Apostles now overrode the emotional events of the previous week. They were assembled once again in the welcome shade of the giant oak, seeking an answer to the question that most perplexed them: *How can we be certain our words and actions will be what Jesus would have wanted?*

Other disciples, including Mary Magdalene, Martha, and Mary of Bethany sat behind them, observing. The women knew they could not participate in the men's deliberations, but were nonetheless curious about what was being said and the decisions that might be made. Mary Magdalene sat in the forefront of the women, listening to every word.

Peter led the discussions. "Then we agree; regardless of the risks involved, we must spread the words of Jesus across the lands, as he instructed. Since the world is large, should we go as individuals, visiting many regions, or would it be wiser to travel in pairs?"

"Jesus sent disciples in pairs," Matthew recalled. "I think we should do likewise."[1]

"I agree," responded Peter. "However, we are now only eleven, thus we could form at the most five groups. That will limit where we can preach."

Mary saw the opportunity here and was not afraid to address the Apostles. "There need not be just five groups. I traveled with Jesus for two years and know his message well. I would be willing to go with one of you, to make a sixth group."

Peter bristled at this impertinence and was quick to rebut her. "First of all, Mary, we do not all agree that you have mastered the words of our Savior. Some of your ideas seem strange.[2] Further, do you pretend ignorance of our laws, which forbid women to be teachers of men?"

Mary recalled the encouragement Jesus had given her and held her annoyance in check. She responded with a challenge of her own. "Then why did Jesus appear to me and instruct me to tell you he was risen, as he prophesied? In doing that, didn't he authorize me to convey his words to others as would a teacher, even unto you eleven men, his chosen ones?"

The Apostles looked at one another in confusion. They weren't used to anyone challenging Peter, much less a woman. More to the point, none of them could think of a suitable rebuttal to her question.

Mary, sensing a momentary edge, pushed her case. "In all our travels with Jesus, I never once heard him say that women were precluded from teaching his message. Indeed, he encouraged me to do so. I only ask that you concur with his guidance."

Peter wanted an end to this discussion. "Mary, to suggest you might travel with one of us shows the danger of your impetuousness. You know unmarried men and women cannot travel together. You would pretend to be married? You can't be serious. Suppose you were invited to stay overnight at the house of a believer, in the same room? What would you do then? You could both be imprisoned, or worse. Consider the fate of your companion, the scandal that would ensue and, most important, the harm to our mission. You should learn to think things through!"

Realizing the validity of Peter's scenario, Mary retreated to the point of being allowed to teach. "I spoke truthfully when I said Jesus encouraged me to spread his words. We must present Jesus' teachings exactly as he stated them. I can do that."

Peter sensed a need to make one point clear. "No. That is important, but secondary. What's essential now is to create a strong church hierarchy with a single voice directing the work of all disciples, so they will understand and obey the rules and practices of the church. That includes what women may or may not do. Such organization is now our primary task."

Andrew added, "As you know, Jesus assigned that leadership role to Peter, who he called the rock upon which his church would be built.[3] Therefore we are all obligated to listen to him."

"I don't question that at all," Mary replied. "My concern is only that the teachings of Jesus be accurately passed on."

Peter made clear his displeasure. "Without question they will be. Do you insult us by implying we wouldn't do so? If decisions are needed, we, the church leadership, will make them. That is our role, and it doesn't require your gratuitous help."

He turned to the other Apostles and asked, "Does anyone wish to support Mary's position?"

To no one's surprise, no hand went up. Mary, too, was at a loss for words she could say at this point that would make any difference.

With a piercing glower at Mary, Peter concluded, "It is clear our groups must consist exclusively of men. It is equally clear that women cannot teach our beliefs, here or anywhere else. You cannot be the new twelfth Apostle, if that is your ploy. In time, we'll select a suitable disciple, a man, to travel with us.[4] Please resume your proper place among the women, and accept your role there. This issue is settled!"

Peter hastened to move on. "Now we shall discuss where the five groups might go for their ministry."

Mary turned away from Peter and spoke to the other women sitting by her. "I'm frustrated by Peter's intransigence, but I must accept that my request is hopeless. I may have to find a way to convey the words of Jesus on my own."

After listening a while longer to the Apostles' discussions, she realized that nothing could be gained by remaining there, and she prepared to depart. As she did, a hand tapped her on the shoulder. It was John Mark, Peter's companion.

In an amicable voice he said, "Mary, unlike Peter, I admire your dedication to the teachings of Jesus and your desire to instruct others. Still, you must face reality; you can only teach to other women. Women are forbidden even to approach men, much less instruct them. I think you know that. I speak only in the interests of your personal safety. I wish you well."

After a pause, Mary replied, "Thank you. I appreciate your friendship and counsel."

Martha and her siblings watched John Mark depart, then rose and followed Mary down the path. Martha, walking beside Mary, broke the silence. "I hope they haven't persuaded you to be silent and abandon your desire to teach about Jesus."

Mary had a steely, resolute look in her eyes that her friends had never seen before.

"What do you think?"

Mary Magdalene, no less than the Apostles, had to consider her future. She had accepted an invitation to stay with her new friend, Martha, at their home in Bethany. Mary appreciated Martha's quiet but supportive personality, and her willingness to help others achieve their goals.

Martha spoke first. "We all realize our lives have changed and indeed are at risk, and that we now have to assess both immediate and future goals in that light. Mary, we know how difficult recent events have been for you. We all are concerned you may still be in danger."

"I have mixed emotions. I'm inspired to have witnessed the ancient prophesies become fulfilled, yet I feel frustrated and, yes, a little fearful too."

Mary of Bethany offered a personal endorsement. "The apostles were most unfair to you, Mary. You'd be a wonderful teacher of his message. Your words have helped me in many ways, made me more mature, and I want to learn still more from you. You're already my teacher!"

Mary smiled. "Thank you both; you're most kind. It appears I will have to make my own opportunities. Peter was right, though, I wouldn't be accepted anywhere in Judea. I and anyone with me would be in constant danger. I must find a place where I can proclaim Jesus safely."

Martha added, "Sadly, that might be far from here. All of us who are followers of Jesus may be in danger if we remain in Judea.[5] But where can we go?"

Mary's eyes brightened. "You could all come with me to Magdala! I'm eager to see my mother again, and our friends would welcome you. Magdala is far enough from Jerusalem that we should be safe there, at least for a while. I could tell my friends there about Jesus. Where better to start spreading his message than Magdala? Jesus taught there!"

Lazarus had been silent during this discussion. Of slight build, he was by nature taciturn, pensive, and deferential to others. Martha had heard him say, "You only learn when your eyes and ears are open, and your mouth shut." He was unsure of his role as he was revered by some, disliked by others. He had let his beard grow out to hide his face. Like Mary, he sensed danger.

"I appreciate your offer, Mary, as I have also received threats."

"Really? What threats? By whom?"

"It may be because Jesus, for reasons I don't understand, chose me to exemplify the power of God. Many chief priests are displeased that a number of followers are rejecting them and turning to Jesus. A friend has warned me there might be violence.[6] Like you, I wish to convey Jesus' words, but would prefer a place where I need not fear for my life."

"Then we will help you find that place," Mary replied. "We can discuss that in Magdala."

Martha added, "Furthermore, Lazarus, it would be helpful to have you with us as we travel, since you are my brother. That will make our journey safer. Without you, we would be three women traveling alone. I would be uncomfortable doing that."

Mary of Bethany's eyes sparkled with anticipation. "I've never been to Galilee. I'd welcome such a trip. How soon could we depart?"

Mary didn't hesitate. "As soon as possible. Can you be ready tomorrow morning?"

☙

The commanding officer of the Roman military garrison in Jerusalem entered the ornate office of Pontius Pilate, Rome's governor in Judea, who had summoned him.

"You wished to see me, Governor?"

"Yes. The recent demise of that agitator from Nazareth does not assure us peace in the region. His followers may still incite the naïve to call him their so-called "king" and ignore the Emperor. There could be uprisings. Rome would be displeased, with major consequences for us. Thus, you are charged with eliminating such threats, and those who cause them. You will enforce Roman law in Judea, and will tell Herod Antipas to do the same in Galilee. Is this understood?"

"Of course. I will convey your orders immediately."

CHAPTER 18

Despite Mary's two-year absence from Magdala, Rachel's modest house and the dried grass in the courtyard showed little change. The olive tree appeared healthy, and Rachel had added some flowers to her vegetable garden. Mary hurried to the door and gave it an enthusiastic knock. "She'll be here. She never goes anywhere."

In a few moments, Rachel, not expecting anyone, gave a cautious peer around the half-opened door. Her worried face changed to unrestrained elation.

"Mary! I can't believe it! I thought I'd never see you again!" She virtually flew into Mary's arms, her eyes overflowing with tears. Mary's were no different.

"Mother, these are three of my dearest friends, Lazarus, from Bethany, and his sisters, Martha and Mary, who have accompanied me back home to Magdala."

"If Mary has befriended you, you are most welcome. Please, come in. And I have almost as big a surprise for you, Mary. Guess who else is here!"

A booming voice reverberated from the rear room. "Am I really hearing words coming from my niece? I was certain she'd be in at least Babylon or Armenia by now!"

Mary was ecstatic at the happy coincidence. "David! You devious old sea dog! What are you doing here?"

David entered, wearing his customary smile. "For the most part, assuring your mother that you're perfectly alright, no matter where on earth you might be."

"Of course I knew you were fine!" After introducing Mary's

friends, Rachel said, "David, tell Mary the news about your boat!"

"With pleasure. The seafaring business can be rewarding to those who master its ways. The owner of the *Ikaría* retired last year, and for an arrangement I could afford, he turned the ship over to me. The fate of the *Ikaría* is in my hands now. Poor boat!" David laughed. "There's no need for you to salute the captain!"

Mary gave David a big hug. "How exciting! I always knew you'd be successful."

"Thank you, Mary, but enough about me. Tell us about your life the past two years. Did you get to Nazareth? Did you meet Jesus?"

"Yes! I traveled around Galilee with him for two years. It's an amazing story, but a sad one as well. You may have heard he was crucified. Did you know he was here in Magdala, at the synagogue, not long before I left for Nazareth? But only for a short time."

"I knew nothing of that," replied Rachel.

"Nor I," added David. "Speaking of Nazareth, what was your trip there like?"

Mary had to think only a moment before deciding how to answer, and most important, which details to omit. All of them, she concluded. "Well, David, after we separated, I, ah, made it to Nazareth with ... no difficulties, and began looking for Jesus."

A rather large little lie, she knew, but there are things daughters would just as soon their mothers not know.

❧

The next morning, Mary was at the village well getting the day's water supply. David went with her, so they could chat along the way. By chance, Sarah was there also, and exchanged smiles with David as she ran to Mary and threw her strong arms around her.

"My word, Mary! Welcome home! It's been years since we last saw you. Where have you been? What have you been doing all that time?"

Mary seized the opportunity. "I left Magdala to look for Jesus.

Sarah, you suggested I try to find him, and I did! In Nazareth! Let me tell you about all the wonderful things ..."

To Mary's surprise the irascible Tamar immediately interrupted her. "Stop! We've already heard more than enough about him. We know all about his tales, how he was captured and crucified with two other criminals. Even the Jewish leaders hated him. He never denied his crimes! Why would you associate with such a vile person?"

What on earth? Mary hardly knew how to respond but was determined to dispel such misconceptions. "No, you don't understand. You see, he ..."

Again, Tamar's gravelly voice cut her off. "Oh, we understand all right. The Pharisees have told us all about his blasphemies and ridiculous fantasies. If you call him a friend, please keep your distance from us!"

Mary tried to respond, but Tamar pressed on.

"Are you ignorant of the Roman soldiers in Magdala, sent here by Herod Antipas? We think the orders came from Rome, from the Emperor himself. We hear they arrest anyone who knew Jesus. Want my advice? Keep your Jesus stories to yourself. And your mouth shut!"

Sarah had to agree. "I'm sorry, Mary, but I fear Tamar is right. I also saw the soldiers and heard the rumors they might arrest followers of Jesus. For the time being, it would be best not to tell people you knew Jesus, much less that you traveled with him."

Tamar leaned over to Sarah. "You know, the Roman soldiers might appreciate news about Jesus sympathizers in the area. They might reward those who provide information about subversive people who boast of their allegiance to some other kingdom besides Rome."

Sarah, shocked, protested. "Tamar, what are you saying? Mary is our friend; none of us would ever turn her over to the Romans! How could you think such a thing?"

With a smirk Tamar replied, "Oh, none of us would, of course.

There are those, though, who might say it isn't betrayal, merely self-preservation. They'd say, to survive against the all-powerful Romans, you must cooperate, do what is necessary."

"Even betray a friend?"

"Even if none of us would betray Mary, I would recommend you think about the possible consequences if you plan to lie to the Romans because you want to protect their enemies."

Mary was dumbfounded. She stared at the other women, who were staring at her, and realized there was no point in trying to correct their opinion of Jesus. She pressed her lips together, picked up her bucket, and with a bewildered David headed back home.

So much for assuring my friends they'd be safe in Magdala!

A few days later David was shopping for dinner in Magdala, and was enjoying the fine art of bargaining with the proprietor of a fish stand. Nearby, two men were observing David. Mary would have had no difficulty recognizing them. They were Erascus and Phlegian.

Erascus pointed to David. "He looks like a local person; we need to tell him about the whore." Phlegian, bored, merely shrugged.

"What's the matter? Have you forgotten that Mary from Magdala was the cause of our demotion? The reason we've been reduced to buying stinking fish for the damned magistrate? We said we'd get even and we will. So, move!"

They approached David, and Erascus put on his slickest insincere smile. "You're right to bargain, sir. Very poor fish selection. We live in Tiberias; they have much better fish there."

"Then why aren't you shopping there?" David paid the fish seller and tried to walk away, but Erascus stayed right behind him.

"Oh, we work for the Regional Procurator in Tiberias. We've come to Magdala on highly important business." Phlegian hid the bag of fish behind him. "We enjoy coming here, because we might see *her*."

David unknowingly took the bait. "Her? 'Her' who?"

"Why, the famous 'working lady' who lives here, the legendary Mary of Magdala. You know, the crazy prostitute who claims she was a personal friend of that terrible Jesus person. Ask anybody, they'll tell you all about her."

David couldn't believe his ears. Grabbing Erascus by the collar, he roared, "What! What idiocy are you spouting? Who told you such preposterous lies? Speak!"

Erascus, unfortunately, had no idea who he was talking to. "No, it's true. Everyone knows about this Mary of Magdala, the famous prostitute."

David tightened his grip on Erascus' neck, leaving him just enough air for a croaking plea, "I beg you, sir; I'm having trouble breathing. Please stop choking me!"

"You know, I agree. A miserable piece of scum like you deserves something more than just being choked!"

David released his grip on Erascus and cocked his fist. A huge roundhouse to the head sent Erascus sprawling to the ground, his mouth bleeding, a rotten tooth nearby.

Phlegian tried to run, but his pudgy body was soon overtaken. David grabbed him by the shoulder, spun him around, and cocked his arm again.

"Please, sir! I said nothing!"

"Nor will you anytime soon!" A left to his ample belly followed by a right to the jaw left Phlegian equally as prone as Erascus, and equally bleeding. Neither man was inclined to move a muscle, and lay there quivering in the drizzle.

David stood over the fetal form of Erascus with a menacing glare. "Maybe now you'll keep your filthy mouth shut. I've no idea where you heard the lies you were spewing, but Mary of Magdala is a fine, honorable woman. Mark my words, if I ever hear of you saying such things again – well, getting up and walking away won't be an option!"

David gave a final glare at the two prone objects cowering on the street. Ignoring the gawking onlookers, he gave Erascus a farewell kick, picked up his purchases, and headed for home. As he walked at a furious pace energized by his rage, one thought was firmly embedded in his mind: *What I need to find out is a lot more details about what happened during Mary's journey to Nazareth!*

⌖

The centurion gave a suspicious glance at the obsequious woman before him. "What is this important news you seem to think you have?"

"Christians! In the little village two miles north of town. I've seen them, and heard them, talking their superstitious nonsense and trying to persuade others. As a good citizen, I recommend you search there first!"

Uncertain of the credibility of this report, the centurion simply replied, "Thank you."

"I just want to help this important mission, you can trust me. I know how essential it is to the Emperor. My name is Tamar. From the village. No one keeps secrets from me. I think one of the leaders is named Mary. Perhaps you're authorized to reward those who provide such valuable information?"

"Reward? Hah! Go away, greedy woman. I've no time to waste on scheming rumor spreaders like you."

As a soldier grabbed Tamar's arm and pushed her through the door, the centurion reached for a scrap of papyrus and jotted down the words *search all villages north of Magdala.*

CHAPTER 19

The next morning found Rachel, Mary, and her friends attending to outside chores, often laughing amid lively conversations. It was a much different Mary from the one who had berated her mother in the same yard two years earlier.

During their banter Martha asked, "Mary, you said you might try teaching about Jesus here in Magdala. I was wondering if you've had any success?"

Mary's face hardened. "It was more like total rejection. I tried to tell about Jesus to Sarah and the other women, but their reaction was shock. They were frightened and some, like Tamar, even hostile. They refused to talk about him."

"Really? Why?"

"They knew of the crucifixion, and some seemed to think he was just a common criminal. Some Pharisees had lectured them, always disparaging Jesus. Worse, the women warned me there were soldiers in the area, and I should keep quiet. I was crushed; I had no idea what to say. I just picked up my bucket of water and headed home."

"Unbelievable! And soldiers? Why would they come to a peaceful place like Magdala?"

Lazarus replied, "Maybe they knew Jesus spent much of his time near the Sea of Galilee, so this area would be a logical place to look for followers."

"At least one thing is clear," said a discouraged Mary. "Teaching here in Galilee is out of the question, but I don't know where else I could go."

"You'll need to be far from Palestine," advised David. "Women will never be allowed to teach anywhere in the eastern part of the Great Sea."

"I fear you are right." Mary thought about other choices. "I recall the disciples talking about going to Greece and Ephesus and Galatia, even Armenia.[1] I need somewhere different. Rome is too dangerous … drunken soldiers everywhere. Certainly not Gaza. Egypt, no. Thrace and Carthage are too much of an unknown, especially for a woman. Where else is there?"

Martha added, "More important, where else that is safe?"

"A nearby possibility might be a new city south of here called Petra," mused David. "It's a new cosmopolitan trade center. They say the city is carved out of stone cliffs – that would be worth seeing! It's isolated, though, so it might not be the best choice."

His eyes lit up. "I may have a better suggestion, although farther away. In the western part of the Roman Empire is a region called Gaul, on the north shore of the Great Sea. We sailed there once; I remember it being both beautiful and peaceful.[2] It's under Roman rule, like everywhere else, but Rome doesn't seem to have too heavy a hand there."

Rachel cast a skeptical look at David. "Where? 'Gowl'? I've never heard of this place!"

Mary hadn't either, but she was open to any credible offer. "It sounds like a possibility, David. But if it's far away, how would I ever get there?"

David smiled. "Maybe easier than you might think. My next trip around the Great Sea will be a long one, but I hope a profitable one. I have stops scheduled at Alexandria, Carthage, Rome, and Genoa. Gaul is only a short sail from Genoa. It might be possible to take you there after I depart Genoa."

Mary saw the distress growing in Rachel's face. "I understand your concern, Mother, but Jesus said his gospel should be preached to all nations.[3] For the first time, I feel I have a goal for my life. David has traveled all over and is knowledgeable. I trust him. The main consideration is to be somewhere safe; I know you want that. This Gaul region could be a possibility."

She turned her attention back to David. "How long before you leave?"

"Soon. I must be back in Caesarea, where my ship is docked, in a few days. I've already arranged with Joel to take me to the coast. He could take you too."

Martha directed a concerned look at the boat captain. "David, I know this might be a huge imposition, but is it possible you could take the three of us to Gaul as well?"

"I see no reason why not. The *Ikaría* is large enough, and I know the captain quite well." He laughed. "Of course, you might have to wash the pots and pans for him!"

Lazarus knew he was joking, but added, "We'll be happy to wash the whole boat for you every day, if you can get us to a place where we can live and preach freely."

David sought to reassure them. "Mary and Rachel know how much I love my family, as well as their friends. I'd never put any of you in danger. I know I can get you to Gaul safely, and I'm also certain you'd be more secure there than anywhere else I can think of, including here."

Rachel could no longer downplay her concern. "Mary, I do support your desire to be a disciple of Jesus, really I do, but I value your safety above all else. I fear that if you go to this Gaul place, wherever it is, I might never see you again. I love you, and you're all I have."

Mary hurried to Rachel and embraced her. "Mother, I must do this because it seems I have no choice. I promise you that I love you dearly as well, and will think of you every day. Also, if there's any possibility of returning to Galilee, I'll make every effort to do that."

Rachel quietly said a little prayer that Mary's promise would come true.

As Mary walked by David, he said to her in a loud voice, "Well, we'd better start your packing." He then leaned closer to Mary and whispered in her ear. "By the way, Mary, sometime during our sail to Gaul you can tell me what *really* happened on the way to Nazareth. And how you got that scar on your cheek!"

☙

The group was sitting outside the following morning, enjoying soft breezes and warm tea before the midday heat arrived. Their socializing ended when Mary noticed a distant figure rushing up the path towards them. She had no trouble identifying her; it was Sarah.

"Oh dear, this may not be good news."

Sarah arrived panting and ran straight to Mary. "It's as we feared. The soldiers have left the town and are headed in this direction! They stop and search every house, rich and poor alike, it makes no difference."

She paused to catch her breath. "That's good for us, though, as it will take a while before they get this far out. I came as fast as I could. I have no idea what the soldiers' orders are, but you need to leave Magdala as soon as you can. I'm so sorry, Mary."

They all stared at one another with trepidation, but mainly at David, who sensed they were looking to the experienced sea captain for counsel. There was no need for David to think at any length; he knew they had only one choice, and Sarah had already stated it.

"We need to get packed, my friends. Sarah is right – we must speed up our departure. We no longer have a few days; we need to be on the road to Caesarea as soon as possible. Can all of you be ready to depart in an hour or less? I'll go tell Joel we need him now."

Forty minutes later, they were at the door, embracing a distraught Rachel who realized events had now raced well beyond her control. Mary and her friends extended their most loving and apologetic farewells. Mary tried one more way to console Rachel.

"You know, mother, I still have your necklace, the amulet you gave me. It brought me back here this time. Maybe it will again." She gave silent thanks she had not left it in the dirt.

Rachel raised her eyes to Mary. "I have no other wish."

Sarah had remained, to bid them Godspeed. David gave Sarah an appreciative smile, one big enough to cause the modest Sarah to avert her eyes and conceal her own faint smile.

After exchanging a few last tearful waves, the four travelers headed out in Joel's wagon on the trail that led to the southwest, towards Caesarea. It was a familiar route to Mary; it was the sheep trail that led to Nazareth. She remembered it all too well.

Rachel watched until they crested the nearby rise and then disappeared behind it. She searched for hopeful thoughts to counter the salty stream running down her cheeks, but nothing worked.

She felt lonelier and far more anxious than she had when Mary left for Nazareth.

CHAPTER 20

Caesarea was a new seaport, built to help assure Rome's dominance in the eastern Great Sea region.[1] David had arranged for his friends to stay at the best inn in town, as they would need a day to get organized for the trip, and he had to supervise the loading of the *Ikaría*. In any seaport, the "best inn in town" meant one with no brothel and, with luck, no bedbugs. On their last full day in Caesarea, David joined them for breakfast.

"Good morning to you all! This looks like a fine group of sailors. How did you sleep?"

"Very well," they responded, almost in unison. In fact, this was the first time any of them had stayed at an inn. They felt like royalty.

"I'm pleased to hear that," David replied. "Not every inn in a port city can guarantee a good sleep; many allow gambling and can be rowdy long after midnight. You can be grateful you slept well last night, because you won't be able to sleep late tomorrow. We'll all need to be up before dawn as we have an early departure time, around sunrise."

Mary of Bethany was not by nature an early riser. "Why so early?"

"Because of the winds," David explained. "Most of the day the wind blows in from the sea. It would be hard to get a large boat away from the dock with a stiff breeze blowing at you. Earlier, before sunrise, the land is cooler, and often a light breeze blows from the land towards the sea. That's your window of opportunity to get your ship out of port and underway."

"So much to know," said Martha. "We're fortunate to have you as our captain."

"Now, if I can just remember where Gaul is," teased David. They'd all been around him long enough to know he was joking. They hoped.

David offered one last piece of advice. "You'll want to spend some time this morning buying food and other necessary supplies for the trip. Ships such as the *Ikaría* have no dining room, nor any arrangement to acquire provisions from the ship's larder. We can buy fresh food in the ports we visit, and we'll catch some fish you can share, but whatever else you might want to eat or use, you should bring on board today."

꩜

That afternoon Mary and her friends, having completed their shopping, were at the Caesarea harbor watching the *Ikaría* being loaded. The docks were bustling with activity. Several ships were in port, taking on cargo or transferring it from boat to dock. They watched from a distance, as waterfront areas were not the safest part of port cities. Men lingered around, hoping for a day's work for meager wages. Some might also be skilled at picking pockets. As they watched, overloaded carts and wagons rumbled past, while winches squeaked as they lifted their contents which included everything from wine and pigs to mail and statues.

David was a different person now – serious, focused, and the unquestioned captain of his ship. He and the new ship's master were inspecting everything as it arrived at the dock. A lull in the activity allowed David to join his friends.

For Mary, it was a whole new world. "This is fascinating! I've never been to the Great Sea, or even any seaport. So much going on!"

"Caesarea is Palestine's largest port," David explained. "It's always busy along the wharves. These boats will soon be headed for every part of the Roman Empire."

"For us, it will be twenty-five to thirty days to Genoa, depending on the weather, so there's much to load on board. Besides the cargo, we need to stock a supply of food and other necessities for the crew, except for items we can pick up along the way."

His attention was drawn to some men pushing a large cart towards the *Ikaría*. "What have we here?" he asked as he examined the cart and its contents. "All those items are ours; store them in the aft hold. Take care, some of the amphorae are expensive and breakable."

One of the workmen noticed the nearby women, an unusual sight at the Caesarea harbor. "Are those women going with you?" he asked David with a look of concern. "That's bad luck, you know." As they trudged off, they looked over their shoulders at the women, clearly worried about the *Ikaría's* impending doom.

David laughed. "A great many seamen are superstitious; I select ones who aren't. Many captains believe you must sacrifice an animal before you dock your ship, to thank the gods for a safe journey. What gods? I've never seen one. To me, such beliefs are silly. If your journey was safe, it was most likely because your boat had a good captain. Of course, it might not hurt to say thanks to Poseidon and Neptune now and then. Just in case!"

Lazarus chose to believe David was jesting about relying on Greek and Roman gods. Nonetheless he was curious. "Tell me, David, why did you decide to embrace a life on the sea?"

"Mary may not have mentioned this, but Rachel and I had an older brother, Jacob. When he turned twenty, he felt he should have his own source of income and signed on as a sailor on a small merchant vessel. That duty was uneventful for a couple of years, although he once expressed doubts about the navigational skills of the captain."

David became more somber. "Then, one November day, Jacob set out on a trip to Rome, and we never heard from him again. We assume the ship went down in a storm. Unfortunately, that's not uncommon; the floor of the Great Sea is littered with ill-fated ships. Maybe I felt that by becoming a successful sailor, mastering the sea so to speak, I might in some way even the score for his loss." He paused. "That's only a guess. Who knows?"

Mary of Bethany, wanting to talk of happier things and thrilled at her first foreign travel, had more romantic visions. "It's the thought of seeing Rome that excites me! Carthage and Genoa too! Since my childhood, it's been my dream to visit Rome."

"Don't count on it," David cautioned. "You may only see Rome from the boat, as the officials there don't let passengers go ashore. Without being part of a group, you wouldn't want to. As a foreigner, you could be abducted and made a slave. Carthage? It's infested by Roman soldiers. Trust me, you don't want to spend an evening with Roman soldiers."

After another hour or so, the boat was loaded. Mary noticed the crew was still on board and asked, "Will they spend the night there?"

"Oh yes," responded David. "The ship could not be left unattended overnight; you might as well put a sign on it that says in bold letters *Robbers Welcome*. The crew will sleep on board and take turns at guard duty, and they're well armed."

David made one final look around the boat and, satisfied with what he saw, gave final instructions to his crew, and rejoined his guests. Now he could relax. As they strolled back to the inn David aimed a big smile at his friends. "I know an excellent restaurant in Caesarea that has a room where women are permitted. You'll be my guests for dinner tonight – no arguments!"

❧.

Well before sunrise the next morning, Mary and her friends were back at the *Ikaría*, despite the sleepy complaints from Mary of Bethany. David had rejoined his crew even earlier, checking everything and making final preparations. Dawn's first light was breaking beyond the silhouetted hills to the east. As the travelers faced the Sea, a drowsy Martha could feel a gentle offshore breeze caressing her from behind. David knew what he was doing.

After a final check of the boat, David signaled that his companions could board. He helped them up the gangplank and through a maze of ropes, winches, barrels, and other paraphernalia on the main deck to their makeshift accommodations.

"Ships like the *Ikaría* were built for hauling cargo," David explained. "There are no guest rooms. I placed some beds in a storeroom on the main deck; this will be the ladies' bedroom. Lazarus can room with me. You can prepare your meals in the ship's kitchen, but only after the crew is finished eating." David had warned them there was only one facility for relieving oneself, and it was outdoors on the port side of the boat. A large red cloth signified it was in use.

The deck hands were scurrying about, setting the lines and securing loose items. David kept a watchful eye on it all and made a final check on the set of the sails. Satisfied, he shouted the decisive order: "Prepare to hoist anchor!"

They were on their way.

Mary was glued to the stern of the boat, fascinated by everything about her first sail. She watched the retreating image of the world she knew as it slowly faded away, as the people on the shore grew smaller, as the buildings turned to white dots, and as the entire coast was reduced to a hazy line on the horizon. And then disappeared.

She was entranced by it all; it seemed almost magical. At the same time she couldn't help wondering, *Will I ever see Galilee again? More importantly, will I ever see Rachel again?*

Figure 2: The Mediterranean Region

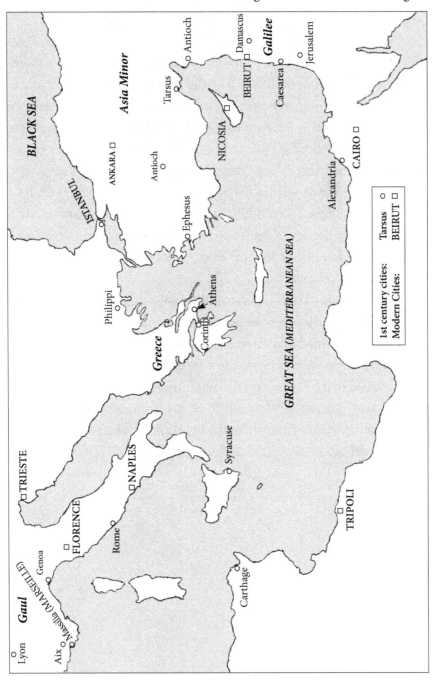

CHAPTER 21

The first week of their voyage on the Great Sea had been uneventful, and the four passengers had enjoyed their first stop, Alexandria. Fair weather, however, can mean light winds, and they had fallen behind schedule. There wasn't much scenery; only an occasional ship crossed the endless blue expanse before them. It had now been a week since they left Alexandria, and it would be at least another week before they reached the next port, Carthage.

David joined them. "It appears life on the sea appeals to you all."

"Now I understand why it was named the Great Sea," Mary observed.

Mary of Bethany grimaced. "I didn't care for the days with big waves!"

David replied, "You should be glad it's spring; the seas are calmer now. In winter, storms can be severe. Of course, even now an early spring storm is possible."

David shaded his eyes to study a ship on the horizon. "That vessel's no problem, just another merchantman. Pirates are rare, but a wise captain stays alert."

A worried Martha inquired, "Have you ever been attacked by pirates?"

"No, because they know this is a fast boat, and they'd lose the chase."

He continued, "Winter is when I can make money. The big Roman freighters don't like to set out in winter, due to storms and the difficulty of navigating when you can't see the stars.[1] I survive storms because I know the location of coves on the leeward side of islands, places where I can anchor the *Ikaría* safely and wait out bad weather. That allows me to deliver goods in winter when the bigger ships won't, and the customers are willing to pay more to get them. It all works out quite nicely."

He paused to scan the waves and check the set of the mainsail. "Slacken it a little," he called to the first mate. "The wind will shift around in a few minutes."

"Now, how can you possibly know that?" Mary of Bethany asked with a smile but also noticeable disbelief. "I had no idea you were clairvoyant!"

David smiled. "Look up ahead near the horizon. See how the water is darker in that area? That means the waves are higher there, which means the wind is blowing stronger ahead of us. We'll be in that darker water in about five minutes."

Mary of Bethany was satisfied, as well as quite impressed.

Lazarus asked, "What I can't understand is how you're able to navigate when the skies are cloudy, especially at night."

"It's not hard. You can gauge wind direction and maintain course by observing the angle at which swells approach the boat, and by watching your sails for changes in wind direction." He smiled. "It also helps to have a talent for making good guesses. The crew sometimes gives me funny looks, but we always get there. And they never complain when they get their pay."

"You certainly seem to like the sea," said Mary.

"I do. I understand the sea. Its laws are simple and unchanging. If you learn them, you can live and prosper. If you ignore them, you'll likely perish. The sea asks only for respect. I find that a reasonable request."

❧

For her part, Mary Magdalene was gaining a better perspective on the size of the world: substantially bigger than she had realized. "You're an excellent captain, David, and the trip has been fascinating.

I never imagined how far away Gaul is. I feel like I'm on my way to a whole new world, a distant and unknown one."

David replied, "In many ways you are, Mary. Back when you were a child and the Magi came to town, I recall your dash down the road to see them; you appeared to want adventure. It looks like your wish is being fulfilled."

Lazarus added, "Galilee to Gaul. It sounded simple back in Magdala. Now I understand Rachel's concerns. Galilee already seems a memory from the distant past. Gaul, and whatever it holds, is our future, whether we're ready for it or not."

Mary of Bethany's wish was simple. "I'd be happy if I could walk on solid ground again." She stared at the horizon. Nothing but water.

Mary Magdalene had more practical concerns. "I worry about after we get there. None of us know whatever language they speak in this Gaul region."

"Not the local language," David agreed. "But the Greeks were here long before the Romans, so some people in Gaul, especially in the coastal areas, should know a little Greek, like they do in Galilee. Greek is still the international language of commerce."

With a disgusted look, he added, "There's another reason. The Roman nobility, feeling themselves superior to the rest of humanity, naturally decided they needed slaves. They collected them everywhere they went, and many were kidnapped from Greece. You can find former slaves in any city where Rome entrenched itself, and most of them still speak their native language."

Lazarus agreed. "That's true. In school, we had to learn either Greek or Latin. Not liking the Romans, I chose Greek. I can still speak it a little. It might come in handy."

Mary envied his bilingual talents. "I'd feel more comfortable if I knew at least a little Greek, since we know nothing of the local language."

Lazarus' eyes lit up; he knew how to make the long hours aboard ship more interesting, and benefit everybody. He beckoned the three women and pointed to a nearby bench.

"Then, why not learn some? Ladies, please have a seat."

Mary gave him a confused look. "Why?"

Lazarus smiled. "You said you wanted a Greek lesson, Mary, so let's have one. Repeat after me: Where: *poo*. Find: *evrísko*. Road: *drómos*. Christian: *Cristianós* …"

⌒

The wind shift that David had noticed earlier was more than just a passing cloud. As sailors would phrase it, some heavy weather was headed their way. Hour by hour, the sky darkened and the wind gained force. David soon had all the larger sails dropped and securely furled; only a few small sails were left up to keep the boat on course.

The *Ikaría*, though of sturdy construction, was nonetheless now pitching and rolling at the pleasure of the waves. On extreme rolls, barrels on the deck would tip over like so many drunken soldiers, and the crew had to move fast to recover them and tie them down, all the while being careful to avoid the watery fate the barrels were rolling towards. The four passengers were becoming increasingly apprehensive.

Mary looked at David with anxious eyes and obvious concern in her voice. "Your boat is built to handle this kind of weather, I trust."

"Oh my, yes. The *Ikaría* was built by a master craftsman, one of the best. I assure you the crew has seen stronger storms than this." David felt his statement was probably true, but he was struggling to remember when.

Mary of Bethany stared at the dark clouds ahead. "This is scaring me too much to stay here on deck; I think I'll hide down below somewhere."

She headed toward the stairs, but David stopped her. "I wouldn't do that."

"Why not? The storm is frightening everyone out here!"

"That may be true, but going below when the ship is bouncing this much is a bad idea. Your stomach won't appreciate it. I doubt you want to revisit your last few meals. Trust me, the wind in your face is preferable."

She disliked her options, and already had doubts about her stomach. Nevertheless, she crouched down in the top of the stairwell, pulled her knees up to her chin, and directed a queasy scowl at the leaping waves.

As the storm progressed, their leaps got higher. When one particularly large wave caused the boat to come down hard into the ensuing trough, David knew corrective action was needed. He yelled at the helmsman, "Dominic, adjust course. Slow quarter-turn to starboard. Watch for rogue waves."

"What's happening?" asked a worried Martha.

"Merely standard procedure in a storm," David calmly replied. "When the waves reach a certain size, it's wise to stop going straight into them. If the ship keeps slamming down into the deep troughs between high waves, it can damage the hull, in a worst case even crack it. You can avoid this by sailing parallel to the oncoming waves."

He did a quick little dance to maintain his balance as the ship crested one of those unpredictable waves. "The good news is that this will eliminate the threat to the ship. The bad news for me is that it heads us in the wrong direction, so it may add a day or so to the length of the trip. The bad news for you is that it means the rolling is going to get worse."

This was hardly the news they wanted to hear. Since eating was out of the question, the four nervous passengers braced themselves together in the stairwell, pulled their hoods over their heads, and stared at their feet, which were getting wet. No better option seemed available. Except to Mary of Magdala, who closed her eyes and once again asked Jesus for a guiding hand.

Eventually the storm subsided and, as David had assured them, the sturdy *Ikaría* was none the worse. With calmer seas plus the extra miles added by the storm, boredom returned to the four travelers. The daily Greek lessons weren't all that exciting, even though Lazarus was discovering that he enjoyed teaching. Mary needed other ways to pass the hours at sea, and it occurred to her that handicrafts might be one of them. She had an idea.

One morning, when the sea was flat and the ship stable, Mary went to the *Ikaría's* workroom to examine the huge array of supplies stored there. After much searching she found the items she needed and sat down at a workbench. She would use the ship's tools and resins to attach the bloodstained stone she found at the cross to her mother's necklace. She looked at the necklace and smiled. *I was wrong; you do bring good luck. We made it safely through the storm. You are my amulet!*

Mary held the small stone up to the light, admiring it as she had many times previously. Although the stain had turned black with time, in her memory it would always be the color it was when she first saw it on Golgotha. It had come to mean a great deal to her, a lasting symbol of the transformation which had taken place in her life, and the man who had made it possible. In a short while, she would be able to wear it proudly, where all could see it.

The task of gluing it to the necklace was not as easy as Mary had imagined. The stone needed to be securely fastened, as Mary knew repairs would be difficult if the connection broke somewhere in Gaul. It was slow work, but she stuck with it. Eventually the task was completed, and Mary held it up for examination. *Not bad, and the stone appears to be tightly attached.* Rachel's humble necklace had been transformed into an eloquent adornment that had already taken on immense personal importance to Mary.

Chapter 22

Rome was now two days in the ship's wake, and all eyes were straight ahead as they approached a new harbor. A favorable breeze had allowed them to stay on a beam reach from Rome and make good time. The verdant hillsides welcomed them with a cover of oak and olive trees beneath a warm azure sky.

David came by to orient them. "The port straight ahead is Genoa. I much prefer it to Rome. Smaller. Nicer people. We'll be anchored a while, as I need to refill our water casks."

Mary, however, was becoming impatient. "Genoa looks pleasant enough, but our next stop interests me more. How long before we arrive in Gaul?"

"If the winds remain favorable, the morning after tomorrow."

"At last! I must admit, though, I still have concerns about what happens after we land."

"You needn't worry. The area enjoys a peaceful reputation. I expect the people to be friendly, perhaps even hospitable."

Mary's memory traveled back in time. "More so than in Tiberias, I hope." With a trace of ire she added, "I know we should forgive those who sin and wrong us, but I find it hard to forgive what Erascus and Phlegian did. Perhaps years from now …"

David put his arm around his niece and nodded. At his prodding, Mary had told him the history surrounding the scar, and all that led up to it. Martha likewise gave her an assuring hug; they all knew what had happened. They also knew they could never mention it to others, as many still thought that in such situations it was the woman who should be blamed and punished.

The stop in Genoa was successful and the next day uneventful. When they awoke the following morning, the ship was moving slowly in a gentle breeze, paralleling a much different coastline. The gentle hills of Genoa were behind them, and what they were now seeing was a low-lying plain, with extensive mudflats at low tide, occasional salt pans, and thick, reedy vegetation along the shore. Further inland, wooded areas were visible.

David was studying the shoreline as Mary approached him. A crewman was on the bow with a sounding line, measuring the depth of the water. Upon seeing his niece, he shouted out the happy news.

"Good morning, Mary. There it is ... Gaul!"

Mary examined the unfamiliar landscape. "This is different than I expected. It looks more like a swamp, just trees and marshy vegetation. No towns, or even houses. I envisioned something more inviting. How long before we arrive at the port?"

"There's only one port along here, Massalia.[1] Since we'd have to make an unscheduled stop, and Massalia isn't a port I usually visit, I have no permit to dock there. There might not even be a dock available. So, we'll try to anchor somewhere offshore from a fishing town."

"Really? Then what?"

"One of my crewmen can row you to shore in one of the ship's dinghies. The wind will assist him; it's from the south today, so it will help blow you in. You can hike from there. I don't expect any problems." *Of course, I said there wouldn't be any getting to Nazareth, either.*

By late afternoon, the *Ikaría* was anchored offshore from what appeared to be a well-used trail.[2] The crew had lowered a dinghy from the stern of the boat, and Lazarus and Martha were busy loading it with their personal belongings and other items they had bought in Genoa.

David scanned the shore. "This looks promising. See that trail straight ahead? It seems to get regular use. And those large trees nearby appear to have heavy ropes attached to them."

Mary strained to see what David's experienced eyes had spotted.

"The ropes could be used for securing small boats, most likely fishing boats. The trail might lead you to a fishing village, and from there, maybe to a road leading to the nearest town."

Mary wished he wasn't using words such as "could," "most likely," "might," and "maybe" quite so much. She had remained silent, wanting to avoid the inevitable words she knew had to be said. They were even harder to vocalize than she thought they would be.

"I guess this is it. David, you've been so helpful! How can we ever thank you?"

"Do you hear anyone asking for thanks? You're all family."

"Speaking of family, David, please send a message to my mother that we made it to Gaul safely. You know how she worries."

"You have my word."

David reached behind him and lifted a heavy leather bag off a bench. "Here is a modest going-away present. These might help make up for not knowing the local language."

Mary's eyes grew large as she looked inside the bag.

"Oh David, not again! Modest? There's so much here, even a few silver denarius! This is the second time you've been so generous."

"Yes, because it's the second time you've needed it."

In a more serious voice, he added, "Also, I said you'd be safe going to Nazareth, but I was horribly wrong. I can never apologize enough for that mistake. I beg you, please let me help you here."

"David, what happened wasn't in any way your fault! I went to Nazareth because I'm strong-willed – all right, stubborn, and wanted to seek out something new for my life. What happened couldn't have been predicted. You're to blame for nothing!"

"Thank you for that, but I'm bothered by guilt, nonetheless. Now, there's a variety of small bronze Roman coins in here, as well as a few silver ones; both should be accepted anywhere. Always keep just a few in your pocket. Never let anyone see the whole bag."

Mary needed no reminder of what had happened to the previous bag of coins David gave her. She searched for words to express her appreciation. "You're a good man, David. I'll pray for your safe travel always."

They exchanged one final lingering embrace. Mary slowly climbed down the rope ladder into the dinghy, turning her head so the tear couldn't be seen.

☙

The boatload of immigrants proceeded towards the unfamiliar coast, guided by David's crewman and the breeze. They studied the shoreline and its surrounding landscape, a landscape full of small trees and plants that were unknown to them, but would soon be their new home.

As they approached the shore, a breaking wave caused the leeward side of the dinghy to dip downwards. Martha slipped off the bench and tumbled down into the low side of the dinghy, tilting it still further. All four passengers then lost their balance and were thrown into the waist deep water. It was fortunate it was no deeper; none of them could swim.

As they regained their footing and the laughing oarsman handed them their belongings, Lazarus sought to reassure them. "We're fine; we can wade in from here. Try to locate all of your possessions. It will be hard to replace anything."

Mary clutched her bag with a relieved expression. Its weight assured her David's farewell present was still there. A quick hand to the neck confirmed that the necklace was safe, too. Of most importance, the papyrus with the message from Jesus rested unharmed in an inside pocket near the top of her robe. She had landed in the water on her feet, so it had remained dry.

Treading with care along the muddy bottom, they waddled ashore. Lazarus looked at his dripping colleagues, and asked, "That wasn't very graceful. Is anyone hurt? Do you still have everything?"

They nodded agreement. "Except we're soaking wet," complained Mary of Bethany.

Martha added, "I do pray there's a village nearby, and someone has a fire going."

"Then let's get underway," said Lazarus. "We don't know how long the hike ahead is."

Mary gave a farewell look back at the ship. They all had the same thought, *We're here, and for the moment we're safe. But we're on our own now.* Mary waved back to the *Ikaría* and uttered a parting thought, "If you can see us, David, we've made it to shore. We're in Gaul! Thank you so much for everything."

☙

From the railing of the *Ikaría*, David watched the group scramble ashore and saw Mary waving. He waved back, but his face was worried. She was in Gaul, and he was headed for Palestine. Like Rachel, he wondered if he would ever see her again. And this time, could she avoid harm?

He hadn't anticipated how emotional this moment would be for him. *Strange, how it's only at times like this, when caring words and loving embraces can no longer be exchanged, maybe not ever again, that you realize just how much someone means to you.*

He watched as the group who had become his best friends headed down the trail, rounded a bend, and disappeared from view. He stared at the empty shoreline for a few moments, unsure whether he just saved his friends, or for the second time made a terrible mistake trying to help his niece. Realizing that only time could answer that question, he turned and addressed the first mate in a voice much more subdued than his customary authoritative command.

"Prepare to hoist anchor."

PART TWO

Gaul

CHAPTER 23

The group headed up the trail at a quick pace, wet but anxious to make human contact. The landscape intrigued them. "Gaul certainly is different from Palestine," observed Martha. "Look at the trees, tall and shady, and even wildflowers along the trail."

Mary added, "Yes, and it sounds different too. Listen to the birds, singing songs I've never heard. Did you notice the horses in the fields we just passed? Do you suppose even common people can own horses here?"

Mary of Bethany was less captivated. "I think all these woods would be frightening at night. On the other hand, I appreciate the solid ground."

They followed the trail for some time, without encountering either people or houses. As the trail took a bend to the left, their spirits rose as some small buildings came into view. The first thing they observed was their wooden construction, rather than earthen. All of them had thriving gardens around them.

"It could be the fishing village David thought might be here," suggested Lazarus. "I see no signs of human activity, though."

With equal measure of excitement and caution they entered the village, which still looked almost empty. They saw only one elderly man, walking with a cane, who stared at them. Their eyes were drawn not to his wrinkled face but to his clothing; he was wearing a shirt and pants, rather than a robe.

Lazarus sensed the next step was up to him. He tried to hide his nervousness. "Let's hope this gentleman knows some Greek."

He said "hello" to the man. "Yáwsoo!"

The man stared at them, bewildered, and made no reply. After scrutinizing the strangers for a moment he spun around and headed toward into a nearby house.

Martha sighed, "That didn't work. Perhaps if we walked further around the village we might find someone."

They hadn't gotten far, though, when a taller man, more distinguished looking and sporting a thick mustache but no beard, appeared out of the same house, and said something in a language none of the travelers understood.

Lazarus smiled at the new man, bowed politely, and tried his Greek again.

"Yáwsoo!"

Both village men cast suspicious looks at Lazarus. After a moment, the taller one hesitantly replied, "Yáwsoo?"

Lazarus smiled and spoke slowly in his best Greek.

"Hello! Our boat overturned. We are wet. Have you a fire, where we can dry ourselves?"

The tall man scrutinized the group and concluded that three women and a wet gangly man probably posed little danger.

"Follow me," he responded in Greek, and led them into a nearby house. The main room had a large fireplace in which a most welcome wood fire was burning. He indicated to the women to sit close to the fire on some cushions he provided, and offered them some tea. He then pulled up chairs for himself and Lazarus, and offered Lazarus a libation as well. Following pleasantries, the two men commenced a rudimentary conversation in Greek, assisted by frequent gesticulation.

The women observed them with concern. "They don't seem to be having any trouble communicating," said Mary. "I think Lazarus understated his knowledge of Greek. I hope their discussion produces some useful directions."

After a few more minutes of conversation, the villager offered

Lazarus some wine, which he happily accepted. The two men arose, shook hands, and the villager pointed to something. Lazarus nodded, thanked him, and walked back to the women.

"Your talk seems to have gone well," observed Mary.

"Yes, he appears to be a village elder. David was right, some people here still know Greek. The fact that neither of us was fluent helped; we kept our sentences simple. And I must say, their wine is quite commendable." He finished off the rest of his drink. "The men of the village are all out fishing, so David's guess was correct."

"Do the people here speak Latin?"

"He knows a little, as it's the language of government in Gaul, but they avoid using it. It seems they hate Rome as much as we do, ever since Roman armies subjugated the area over a century ago. When I explained that we came here to escape Roman persecution, he immediately accepted us. As the saying goes, the enemy of my enemy is my friend."

"Did he know anything about Christians in the area?" asked Martha.

"A little. I was surprised to learn that Jesus is already known here. News of his teaching has been brought to Gaul over the past year by other merchant ships."

Mary's eyes brightened. "That's remarkable, and encouraging."

"Better still, he said he'd heard that some kind of Christian village exists inland, somewhere to the east, he thought. He had no details, however."

Martha was beaming too. "Was he able to suggest a general direction we should head?"

"Yes. He said we should follow this trail until we come to a large river. There's a city called Arelate nearby where we can cross the river on a barge. From there, we take the road east to a smaller city called Aix.[1] He thinks the Christian village is somewhere past there."

Mary looked hopeful. "That gives us a start, anyway."

Mary of Bethany was more focused. "Did he say anything about food?"

"He said for a small compensation, he'll prepare an evening meal for us. We can stay in the village tonight and be on our way in the morning."

Mary was elated. "God seems to be with us; the elder is very kind. I can manage the compensation."

After three days of walking since leaving the village, the roads seemed to be all uphill, and both their energy and enthusiasm were waning. The only break had been a welcome stretch during which one of David's coins had bought them a ride in a farm wagon every bit as bouncy as those in Galilee.

As they proceeded on their long march, Lazarus noticed something interesting. They had come from a region where male dominance was universal, and since Lazarus was the only man in their group, the three women tended to look to him for advice and decisions, as they had done with David on the boat. Plus, he was the only one with an adequate knowledge of Greek. This was the first time anyone had ever viewed him as their leader. *I may have to learn how to be more authoritative. How do I do that?*

The weather stayed fair, so at night they slept under the stars. They were used to this.

When they reached Aix and were hopeful their goal was nearby, they treated themselves to dinner at an inn. This was their first bit of luxury since wading ashore. To no one's surprise, Mary of Bethany had suggested spending the night at the inn as well, but was over-ruled by Lazarus in the interests of fiscal prudence. He was starting to enjoy making decisions.

After an hour of hiking the next morning, Mary was becoming weary and impatient. "We've come a long way from Aix. Could we ask someone if they know anything about Christians in the area? I worry the village elder could have been mistaken, and we might be on the wrong road."

"Very well," Lazarus responded. "I'll ask the next person we see."

After another twenty minutes of walking, they paused for a moment to rest. Lazarus stared down the road. His eyes lit up.

"Look, a short way ahead, on the left. I think I see some buildings behind the trees. Perhaps someone there can help."

In a few minutes, they arrived at a small settlement which bore little resemblance to a normal village. Before them was a collection of four buildings of varying sizes, all one story, built from earthen materials, and lacking any architectural imagination. The buildings and grounds seemed well-maintained, although most of the landscaping looked recently planted. Unlike the fishing village, numerous people were scattered about, all busily working in flower gardens near the buildings, or in nearby vegetable gardens and livestock pastures.

"It seems we have our choice of people to talk with," said Martha. "It's interesting that they all appear to be women, and most seem young. Look, even though they're outdoors, not all of them are wearing head scarves."

They approached the nearest person, a muscular-looking young woman working in a garden plot, digging holes for some newly acquired fruit trees.

Lazarus tried the only greeting he knew. "Yáwsoo!"

The young woman looked up, somewhat startled. She wasn't expecting visitors, much less ones speaking Greek.

"Yáwsoo?" she replied with a puzzled expression.

Lazarus tried out more of what he hoped would be a common language. "Do you speak Greek? I'm sorry, we are not familiar with your local language."

"I speak a little Greek. Who are you?"

"My name is Lazarus. We are Christians. We have come from Galilee, in Palestine, to escape Roman persecution. We are looking for a Christian community that might be somewhere nearby. Have you heard of it, or know where it is?"

Her reply was as welcome as it was unexpected. "We are a Christian community here. We try to live our lives as Jesus instructed. My name is Danielle, Sister Danielle." She looked at the three women, and then cast a quizzical look at Lazarus. "Men are not allowed here. There are only women living here."

Mary was intrigued at hearing this. She had learned enough Greek to ask, "Only women? Why only women?"

"Most of the women here have had a hard life. Many have been treated badly in some way," responded Sister Danielle. "We are able to give each other comfort and support, and take care of one another."

Lazarus translated the reply for Mary.

"That's most interesting. Lazarus, tell her it's late in the day, and ask if it would be possible for us to stay here tonight."

Lazarus conveyed Mary's request, which resulted in a frown from Sister Danielle.

"Oh. I'm not sure that's possible. Please wait a minute. I'll have to ask our Sister Superior. She decides such things."

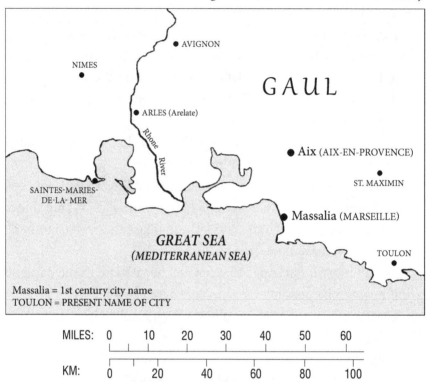

Figure 3: Southern Gaul in the First Century

CHAPTER 24

Sister Danielle led the group to a nearby building and opened the door. A muscular dog bolted through it, teeth bared and ears flattened, barking at his loudest intimidation level. The four strangers took a fast step backward, but the guard dog halted its charge in front of them, still growling at this new threat, but obediently awaiting instructions.

A few seconds later, a stern, heavy-set older woman emerged and approached the group. She was stiffly courteous with a skeptical, almost suspicious, edge to her demeanor. From the reaction of the young women nearby, she was the unquestioned authority here. No one spoke a word, and she had their full attention as soon as she appeared, and the dog's as well. It soon became apparent she had been listening to the group's conversation with Sister Danielle.

The older woman approached the strangers. In a strong voice and almost fluent Greek she said, "I am the Sister Superior at this priory. You say you are Christians?"

"In Jesus' name, I give you my assurance. My name is Lazarus, these two women are my sisters, and this is our friend, Mary. We've come to Gaul from Galilee to avoid Roman persecution, and walked here from the coast."

In a dubious tone the Sister Superior asked, "That far? Really? It seems odd that you carry almost no luggage."

Lazarus made a mental note that the Sister Superior was both astute and observant. "We had no choice but to depart Palestine as fast as possible, and we knew we'd have a long walk once we reached Gaul, so we chose to travel lightly."

"There are few towns along your route. Where did you stay at night?"

"We camped in wooded areas near the road."

"You were lucky."

"Lucky? Why?"

"You're new here, so it's possible you've never heard of the Druids. They're strange, mysterious people who are said to practice human sacrifice. Tiberias' armies drive them off, so there are few in this area. That's about the only good thing Tiberias has done for us."

"Thank you for warning us. We'll be more careful in the future."

The Sister Superior turned to the business at hand. "What do you want with us?"

"We've been traveling for weeks and are weary," Lazarus explained. "The hour is late, and we wonder if we might stay here for the night, where the women would be safe. We could compensate you, if that would assist your work here."

The Sister Superior trained her eyes on Lazarus. "It might, but you must understand that only the women could stay. No men are permitted here, ever. There can be no exceptions."

"We understand; that seems reasonable. I'd be happy to spend the night in the woods across the road, if that's allowed. From what you said it seems I should be safe enough there."

Martha looked concerned. "Lazarus, might we talk about this for a moment?"

"Certainly. Sister, would you excuse us?"

"Take your time."

The four travelers huddled together a short distance from the Sister Superior, and Martha spoke first. "We are strangers here, and know nothing about this area. I'm not comfortable with Lazarus sleeping alone in the woods. Even if the Druids aren't here, there might be robbers or other threats. Remember what happened to Mary!"

Mary said, "I agree, but there's something else. This little village intrigues me, as do the women who live here. I'd like to find out how much they know about Jesus, and if it's accurate. I want to tell them what I know about Jesus too. I'd like to spend some time here with them."

Mary of Bethany offered a different perspective. "Oh? I think I'd rather be in a larger town, where we could get settled. And take a bath!"

Lazarus agreed but for a different reason. "I'd also prefer a larger town, as that would be a better place for us to spread the teachings of Jesus. We could reach many more people."

Mary sighed. "I imagine we all knew that at some point we might need to travel down different roads. Although our goals are similar, the way we choose to implement them may not be. Right now, this little group of Christian women fascinates me. I would like to know more about them. I feel confident I'd be safe here for a few days."

"Oh, Mary! We'd like so much for you to remain with us. Really we would."

"And you know I feel the same. I love you all dearly. However, you three are family, and Lazarus is right. To spread the words of Jesus to the most people, you need to be in a larger town. I hate the thought of separating, but we must all do what is necessary to accomplish our goals."

Lazarus understood. "I think Mary is right. I'll be fine in the woods. We three can return to Aix tomorrow and decide if we wish to stay there or continue on."

Martha needed to make one small change to Lazarus' plan. "Very well, I agree. However, if you must sleep in the woods tonight, Lazarus, you will not be alone. I'll be there with you."

Mary of Bethany would have preferred a warm, comfortable bed. But that could wait. "Like Mary said, we're family. The sky is clear; I might enjoy looking at the stars tonight!"

Mary Magdalene smiled and said, "I'll make it a foursome."

The next morning, a golden sunrise filtering through the trees and the birds' enthusiastic chorus gave promise of a good day to travel. The four friends were at the village gate, three of them packed and ready to depart. Behind them, the sisters were starting their morning chores.

Lazarus said, "I think we're ready. It was kind of the Sister Superior to let us share their breakfast. Mary, I guess this is where we say good-bye." Lazarus was never one to show much emotion, but Mary thought she could see a glimmer of moisture in the corner of his eye. "So far, our great adventure has been blessed; I do pray it will continue that way. Most of all, I pray for Mary's safety, and that we'll all meet again soon."

Mary said nothing, but in a businesslike manner similar to David's she reached into her travel bag. "One last thing – let me give you some of this. I know David meant us to share it."

Martha put up a weak protest. "Oh, Mary, we could never …"

"You not only could, you must. You have to eat and find a place to stay while in Aix. Do you really plan to go into a strange city without a single coin in your pockets? I tried that; I don't recommend it." She divided up David's offering, giving her friends a little more than half, making sure they received an equal share of the silver denarius.

Lazarus would never ask for charity, but he understood what she was doing and accepted her gift. "Mary, you are most generous. We're fortunate in so many ways to have met you."

He rubbed his chin in thought and added, "It occurs to me, Mary, that your plans might change. In case you should have reason to depart the village sooner than you expected, we'll stay in Aix for at least a week. The town is large enough to contain a synagogue. We'll leave word there as to where we can be found, so you can rejoin us if you wish."

"Lazarus, that's most kind. If I haven't met you in a week, it will indicate my desire to stay here longer. Please follow your own goals without concern for me. I'll be fine here among the sisters." Laughing, she added, "Plus, I'll also have the guard dog!"

Turning serious again, she added, "And I will likewise pray for your safe journeys."

Martha went to Mary and gave her the most heartfelt hug she had ever given anyone. "Mary, I know God is with you, so I'll not worry about your safety. Like Lazarus, I hope our fates allow us to meet again soon."

Lazarus and his young sister exchanged their own final embraces with Mary and picked up their meager belongings. With farewell waves, they turned and started off.

Mary watched through moist eyes as the only friends she had in Gaul exited through the simple village gate and headed down the rutted road back to Aix.

As they disappeared behind the roadside foliage, it fully hit her.

She knew no Gaulish and little Greek.

She was on her own.

CHAPTER 25

A knock on her office door interrupted the thoughts of the Sister Superior. Without an upward glance, she said, "You may enter."

Mary, escorted by Sister Danielle, stepped through the doorway. Sister Danielle motioned to another young sister to wait outside.

"Sister, you said you wished to speak with Mary this morning."

The Sister Superior addressed Mary in Greek in an emotionless, curt manner. Mary strained to understand the rapid discourse, with frequent requests to have a phrase repeated.

"Be seated, Mary. You indicated you might wish to remain with us for some time. That is possible, but first we need to know more about you."

"Yes, Sister. I'll be happy to tell you all you wish."

"You say you come from Galilee. How is it that you know Greek?"

"A few people speak it in Galilee, so I knew a little. Lazarus taught us more on the way here. He thought we should know some common words and phrases, and he was right."

"I see. I teach Greek to the sisters here, because it's still spoken widely in the coastal region. In the cities Latin is taking hold; the infernal Romans insist on it being the official language. I fear someday it may supplant our native Gaulish. Do you know any Gaulish?"

"No, none."

The Sister Superior's look became more suspicious. "You said you lived in Galilee? Is that not where Jesus was from? Did you ever hear him speak?"

"Oh, yes! I traveled with him for about two years. We sometimes talked. I was even ..."

The Sister Superior cut her off and cocked an eyebrow, wondering if there might be some exaggeration taking place. As she questioned Mary further, the Sister Superior tapped her fingers, a habit she had whenever she was unhappy or annoyed. The sisters sometimes joked about it, in private of course.

"Really? You were a personal friend of our Savior? I must say that's very impressive!" She was not smiling.

"I assure you it's true. He spoke often near Magdala, so it was easy to …"

"Be that as it may, here no one is better than anyone else. We all live here communally, and we address everyone, even me, as 'sister.' Do you understand?"

"I understand. I meant no …"

"Never mind. You need to be aware that no one here ever brags or exaggerates the truth."

"Oh, no, I would never tell a falsehood. I really did … "

"Yes, yes, I heard you." The Sister Superior pointed to Sister Danielle who was standing near the door. "Please tell Sister Jeanette to come in."

She turned to Mary. "You have much to learn. I will assign someone to educate you in our ways and language. And everyone works here – maybe in the fields, or with the chickens or cows. Do you cook?"

"Yes, I do. My mother and I …"

"Very well. You are assigned to the kitchen. Report there every morning at five sharp to help prepare breakfast, and at the eleventh hour to assist with lunch. Tardiness is unacceptable. Sister Jeanette is also assigned to the kitchen, so she can instruct you there. We have fifteen sisters here who need three nourishing meals every day. Do not disappoint them."

"Oh, and by the way, you are now Sister Mary."

"Yes, Sister."

The Sister Superior made a hand gesture, and Sister Jeanette stepped forward out of the doorway. Sister Jeanette was about seventeen, quiet, courteous, and eager to please, yet rarely smiled. Her eyes remained fixed on the floor in front of her.

Sister Jeanette bowed and spoke hesitantly to the Sister Superior in Gaulish. "You wished to see me, Sister?"

"Yes, this is Sister Mary, from Galilee. She will stay here for a while. She speaks a little Greek. No Gaulish. Give her a tour of our village; show her where everything is located. It will be your responsibility to ensure she knows our rules and how we do things here. She must learn to fit in. Do you understand?"

"Yes, Sister."

Then, in Greek, the Sister Superior added, "Take her to the small empty room near yours. It will be hers. Get her a blanket and pillow from the storeroom. And when you have time teach her some Gaulish."

She gestured towards the door. "You may go now."

Mary and Jeanette replied, almost in chorus, "Yes, Sister."

<hr />

Mary was happy to have Sister Jeanette as her mentor; she found her interesting. Could her shyness reflect a lack of self-confidence? She also observed that Jeanette walked with a slight limp. And why was she at the village? Mary wondered if some darker memories were involved.

Mary and Sister Jeanette were walking along a winding, leaf-covered path that led towards a dormitory-style building. They found they could converse adequately in their rudimentary Greek. Sister Jeanette had learned basic Greek as part of the mandatory schooling for younger sisters. Having had no formal education as a child, she appreciated the opportunity to acquire any kind of knowledge and had proven herself a quick learner.

"Welcome to our little community, Sister Mary. Everyone here will be your friend. I'm sure you'll like it here."

"Thank you. If everyone is like you, I know I will."

Sister Jeanette, not used to compliments, blushed. After a few moments, she found enough courage to initiate a conversation with the intriguing foreigner. "Sister Mary, the Sister Superior said you came here from Galilee. I know nothing about Galilee. I'm not even sure where it is. Everything must be different there."

"In many ways, it is. I have found, though, that when those who follow Jesus come together, they seem to be more alike than different."

"I imagine so. You're the first person from another country I've ever met."

They entered the dormitory and walked to Mary's room. It wasn't really a room; the old dormitory had been sectioned off by makeshift partitions that went halfway to the roof. A tall person could have peered over them. Nonetheless, they afforded some semblance of privacy. The "room" contained only a wooden bed, chair, and small table with no drawers. Pegs for clothing stuck out of the wall amidst the random cracks.

"Here you are, Sister Mary. Our rooms aren't fancy; I hope you'll be all right."

"I have few possessions, so it will be adequate."

"We've all been here only a few months," Jeanette explained. "It used to be a barracks for some troops. Then somehow the Sister Superior got it turned over to her so it could be a home for young women who have had a difficult life. It was filled up in no time."

Mary lowered her travel bag to the floor and sat down in the hard, uncomfortable chair. Sister Jeanette sat on the bare bed, and looked at her first foreigner, fascinated.

"We have some time before lunch. We could talk now, if it would be all right with you. I want to learn about the rest of the world!"

Then, looking unnecessarily embarrassed, she asked, "Forgive me, but I could not help hearing you say you knew Jesus. That must have been wonderful! We have about an hour before we have to go to the kitchen; please tell me about Galilee, and how you came to know Jesus. Afterwards, if you'd like, I'll start to teach you our language."

"Sister Jeanette, I am so pleased you asked. I'll tell you what I can in my limited Greek. About two years ago …"

As Mary related her story, a wide-eyed Sister Jeanette hung on to every word. Mary concluded, "… and so, the day after we left Aix, we arrived here, tired but happy to have found other followers of Jesus. Then I met Sister Danielle, and the Sister Superior, and you!"

Sister Jeanette looked at Mary spellbound and captivated, but said nothing.

Mary smiled. "You look like I may have confused you with too much information."

"No, it's just that – I mean, you knew the disciples, and were even at the crucifixion, and saw Jesus after he died, and …"

"Yes, what I said is all true. It could be hard to accept, I know. I hope you believe me; I felt perhaps the Sister Superior did not."

"Oh, yes! I believe you. I really do. It's just all so, so … unbelievable!"

"It's all history now, as they say. Right now, it's time for me to become a humble kitchen worker. I'm sorry I talked so long; we'll have to postpone my Gaulish lesson. I can tell you'll be a great help to me." They headed off towards the kitchen, Sister Jeanette leading the way.

Mary entered the small but adequate kitchen and looked around. There were only two other sisters working there, aside from Sister Jeanette. They were expecting her and welcomed the additional help.

The kitchen wasn't fancy, but it had all the necessary utensils along with an assortment of pots and pans. Cooking was done on an outdoor fireplace; other food preparation took place inside. Most vegetables were eaten raw, as fuel to heat water was scarce, but today was an exception. The Sister Superior specified the daily menu, and the two other kitchen helpers were busy cutting up vegetables for a large pot of soup simmering outside the back door. The vegetable peelings would become dinner for the village's omnivorous goats.

Mary was soon being instructed as to how the daily meals were prepared and what her duties would be. She had never cooked for so many people before. It was good, hard work, and when she wiped her brow, it was with a smile. She felt comfortable and content, like she was already a part of this intriguing community.

CHAPTER 26

A few days later, Mary was relaxing on her bed after the last of her lunch duties – washing the pots and pans. Her rest was interrupted by a hesitant knock on her door.

"Come in."

Sister Jeanette entered, looking nervous and apprehensive.

"Welcome to my humble quarters, Sister Jeanette. How are you?"

Sister Jeanette did not return the greeting, and with an unsteady voice said, "Sister Superior wants to see you right away."

"Oh, all right. What about, did she say?"

"She said I should only say that she wants to see you right away. She seemed upset. Please come with me."

Mary cast a confused look at Sister Jeanette but got up and followed her out the door. Arriving at the Sister Superior's office, Mary's level of concern heightened. The Sister Superior continued to stare at something on her desk with an annoyed look, and neither glanced at Mary nor asked her to sit down.

Mary looked around. A few other sisters were in the room, including Sister Danielle. They all wore uncomfortable expressions; no one smiled, and all eyes were fixed on her. She sensed she must be in some kind of trouble.

"You wished to see me, Sister Superior?"

The Sister Superior still did not look up. "I understand you had a lengthy conversation with Sister Jeanette recently about your past in Galilee. May I inquire as to the topic?"

"Certainly. She asked me to tell her about Galilee, my home, and my travels with Jesus."

The Sister Superior raised her head and glared at Mary. "Which I gather included most everywhere he ever went?" There was little effort to conceal her skepticism.

"He had been teaching a while before I met him in Nazareth. After I heard him speak, and he ..." She paused. *Better keep it simple.* "... after I met him, I wanted to become part of his group and travel with him."

"And you went with him everywhere?"

"Yes, more or less everywhere."

"Which, according to Sister Jeanette, included being at his crucifixion. Is that correct?"

Mary bowed her head. "Yes, sadly, that is true."

The Sister Superior rose up, arms rigid, fists on the desk, and demanded, "I want you to look me in the eye and swear that you, a simple village girl from some insignificant town, were actually present at our Lord's crucifixion!"

Mary stared at the Sister Superior, shocked and at a loss for words. She was not expecting an interrogation, and felt the latent pool of anger within her trying to rise to the surface. She fought it, her face reflecting sadness at the memories she was being forced to recall, but also concealing a firm determination she would not be cowed.

"I have no need to swear anything. I have stated in God's presence that I wept at the foot of Jesus' cross, and I again affirm that what I said is a true statement."

"Oh, not just at the cross, but at the very base of it! Quite remarkable, since if anyone had been at the cross, it would have been his chosen Apostles, not some common village woman! Did you ever think of that?"

"No, that wasn't how it was. You see, the eleven disciples weren't at the cross, probably because they ..."

The Sister Superior's mouth was wide open in disbelief. She was not used to being contradicted, certainly not with other sisters present. Her voice was piercing, almost quavering.

"By what authority do you presume to correct me? You, Sister Mary, are the least senior among us, the least credible person here. Try to remember your place!"

She sat down and paused to regain her composure. After an energetic tapping of her fingers, she resumed in a calmer but still doubting voice.

"Your claim about the cross might be dismissed as mere fantasy or braggadocio. Your imagination hardly stops there, though. Sister Jeanette said you claimed to be the first person to whom the risen Christ appeared! I find it difficult, to say the least, to understand why you should merit such an extraordinary honor."

She looked at the other sisters in the room and addressed one, Sister Danielle.

"Perhaps I am unduly skeptical, so let us see what others think. Do you, Sister Danielle, accept these incredible claims? Do you believe this ordinary village woman was somehow chosen to be the first person to whom our risen Lord appeared?"

Sister Danielle stared at the floor, her heart pounding, not knowing what to say but certain she didn't want to cross paths with an agitated Sister Superior.

"I … I do find it … somewhat unusual. Maybe a little hard to believe."

The Sister Superior smiled the smirk of a cat that senses the mouse is trapped. With her fingers crossed, she looked at Mary out of the corner of her eyes.

"Tell me, Mary, could the young and naive Sister Jeanette have made that last part up?"

Mary was astonished. *You mean all I have to do is blame it all on Jeanette to save my own skin?* A distinct vision of Jesus came into her mind, reminding his followers of the ninth of the Ten Commandments, *Do not accuse anyone falsely.*

Without the slightest hesitation, Mary blurted, "No! She did not. To the best of my knowledge, everything I've said is true."

"Really! To the best of your knowledge? Then you admit what you said might not be true!" The Sister Superior, feeling she had won, adopted a quieter tone. "Is it possible, though, that you are merely delusional after your long journey?"

"No! Look, I have ..." Mary started to display her amulet, the necklace with the stone found at the cross, but stopped, realizing it might only reinforce the Sister's belief she was fantasizing. She removed her hand from the chain and left it unseen beneath her bodice.

"What? What did you want to say?"

Mary looked downward. "Nothing."

The Sister Superior tapped her fingers again, and then turned to the other sisters who were frozen in place along the wall, addressing them as a judge would a jury.

"Sisters, you have heard the strange claims of this foreigner, which demean our Savior for what I assume is the shameful purpose of enhancing her own image. You heard how she tried to implant these fantasies into the mind of our youngest sister. Now she cannot even look me the eye. Tell me, does anyone wish to speak in her defense?"

To no one's surprise, nobody made a sound. The other sisters merely stared at Mary or at the floor; one or two shook their heads. Mary glanced at Sister Danielle, who also dropped her head downward.

The Sister Superior rendered her judgment. "You can see that no one believes your blasphemous tales. I choose to conclude that you are not evil, merely delusional. We will pray for your return to sanity. Now hear me clearly, Sister Mary, you are absolutely forbidden to speak such nonsense here at the village ever again. Or anywhere else.

Do you understand me?"

"I understand." Mary's voice was barely audible.

"Good. Now return to your room. And pray for your forgiveness."

Mary couldn't understand any of this. Why didn't the Sister Superior believe her? Was there something she was failing to explain well enough? Could the Sister Superior be right; was it all just a dream, just her imagination? No, that was absurd. It was all far too real, and she had the scar on her cheek to prove it. She also remembered she still had the personal message from Jesus. *As if that would have impressed the Sister Superior.*

As a disheartened Mary departed the room, she passed by the other sisters, all of them looking at her with concern. The only one who spoke was Sister Danielle, who whispered in an earnest, almost pleading tone as Mary passed by. "Please do as she says, Sister Mary. Please don't cause any trouble."

Chapter 27

Mary sat on her rigid bed with hands clasped, eyes moist, face saddened. Sister Jeanette shared her distress but could find no suitable words to console her companion.

Mary looked up at her young friend. "Sister Jeanette, what is happening? This is not at all what I expected. I came here to praise Jesus, to make people happy by telling about him. I wanted to be friends with everyone. Now the Sister Superior thinks me delusional, and maybe the other sisters do as well. Why? I can't understand this." Mary stared at the floor. In a spiritless monotone she mumbled, "Maybe I should just leave, go somewhere else."

She cast an imploring look at her young mentor. "I need to know, Sister Jeanette. Please tell me in all honesty. Do you think of me as delusional too?"

Sister Jeanette was taken aback by the directness of the question. It was the first time anyone had ever requested her opinion about anything important. After a pause she responded. "No, I believe you're telling the truth. I want you to stay. Please don't say you'll leave!"

"Really? Why would you care if I left? Why do you believe the things I said about my travels with Jesus? No one else seems to."

"I want you to stay because you're the most interesting person I've ever met, and because you're like a mothe ... I mean, you're my friend. A good friend."

"Thank you for that. To be honest, it would be hard for me to leave here. My friends may have already left Aix. I have no idea where else I could go."

Mary also wanted an answer to her second question. "Why do you believe what I said about my travels with Jesus? Maybe I was making it all up."

Jeanette looked at Mary with concern, but with admiration as well. "My mother told me once that a person's eyes are the windows to their soul, and they reveal what is true. Your eyes … they seem very gentle and kind. I think they're the eyes of a person who speaks the truth."

Mary clasped Jeanette's hand between hers, fighting to hold back a tear. "That means more to me than you can imagine, Sister Jeanette. You're a wise and true friend, and I will treasure your faith in me always."

Mary thought for a moment. "I will remain here at your little village, at least for a while. I'm not a person who runs away from difficulties. If you believe in me, maybe in time others will too. At least, it will afford me practice at speaking truth to skeptics. Jesus wasn't afraid to do that, and I cannot give into fear and disappointment either."

Mary leaned closer to Sister Jeanette, smiled, and embraced her. She felt Jeanette's head softly rest against her cheek, a manifestation of the trust that defines enduring friendships.

Sister Jeanette wanted to know more about her fascinating new friend from that distant land, and inquired, "Could I ask you a personal question? Do you have a family in Galilee?"

As Mary pondered how to reply, repressed feelings of grief and despair welled up within her. Her face and voice changed, now reflecting sadness and pain. It was an innocent question, though, and deserved an answer. Maybe it would help her as well, if Jeanette knew her story.

"My mother still lives in Magdala." Mary paused for a moment, searching for words that would hurt the least.

"I had a family there once. My husband, Levi, was a fisherman, and had a small business salting a portion of the fish he caught to preserve them. I also had a young son, Nathan. I loved them both dearly." Another painful pause. "My father and my husband enjoyed taking Nathan – he was ten – out onto the Sea of Galilee, to teach him how to fish. Nathan seemed to enjoy it too. Then, one day …"

Mary paused again and stared at the floor. Her voice became quieter, a bit unsteady.

"One afternoon, they were out on the Sea of Galilee, and a sudden storm came up, very strong winds. That's not uncommon on the Sea. The boat must have capsized. My father and Levi probably tried to help Nathan. The boat may have been blown away from them, and they couldn't get back to it; no one knows. None of them swam well. The boat, missing its mast, was later found on the far shore. Levi and Nathan, and my father, were never found. They …"

Mary became silent, no longer able to hold back tears.

She hardly heard Jeanette as her stunned friend fumbled for words. "Oh, Sister Mary, I had no idea … What an awful … I'm terribly sorry."

Mary forced herself to regain her composure. "Please, do not concern yourself. All of that is now simply history. Life moves on, and we must learn to move on with it. The past can never be changed; only the future matters."

Mary wiped her tears and forced a smile. "Could I ask why an attractive young girl such as yourself is here at this community of unmarried women?"

Jeanette blushed at the word *attractive*, and Mary wondered if it could be because no one had ever paid her such a compliment before. Jeanette's face quickly became serious again, and Mary noticed she likewise hesitated before replying. She wondered, *Does she also have dark memories hidden from others?*

"My mother died about a year ago; she had been sick. I really loved her. My father never cared about me, and he didn't want any more children. I felt like he never even wanted me. He was not home much. After my mother died ..."

Mary observed it was now Sister Jeanette who was staring blankly at the floor. "... a few weeks later, my father started coming into my room at night, and ..." She paused, struggling for the right word, then almost in a whisper said, "... and began beating me."

"Why, that's horrible, absolutely inexcusable. Jeanette, I'm so sorry to hear that." Mary was about to ask why he beat her, and if that was the cause of her limp, but stopped.

Jeanette's appearance had changed. She seemed almost in pain. Her face was more than sad; it seemed almost tortured. Her eyes were pressed shut, as though a black void was all that her mind could handle. Her hands were so tightly clutched together they were almost white. Her tears were abundant and uncontrollable.

Mary was concerned for her young friend and wondered, *Is there more to this story? Why would he have come into her room at night just to beat her?*

After a few moments of increasingly uncomfortable thoughts, she felt she had to ask, "Jeanette, are you sure he only ... beat you?"

Sister Jeanette covered her eyes, dropped her head to her waist and, with her whole body visibly shaking, burst into spasms of uncontrollable sobbing.

Mary sat down beside Jeanette and embraced her. She understood only too well what had happened. It was not just beatings; it was far worse.

A tear rolled down Mary's cheek. They had way too much in common.

CHAPTER 28

Now that Mary and Sister Jeanette knew their pasts they had become even closer. Jeanette's slip of the tongue that she was starting to view Mary as a surrogate mother was becoming an understandable and accepted fact by both of them. Jeanette could discuss things with Mary that she would never mention to anyone else.

In between their kitchen duties, they enjoyed walking around the village grounds. In summer they could pick a variety of berries for future meals while enjoying the seasonal flowers. On one of those summer days that had just enough breeze to make the afternoon heat tolerable, Mary and Jeanette were enjoying such a walk.

"Jeanette, look at how the sunlight filters through the oak trees and creates dancing patterns of light and shadow. And the colorful array of flowers attract so many bees. I'm becoming impressed with the beauty of my new home."

That beauty wasn't accidental. The village's landscape architect was in fact the Sister Superior. Although she was a stern leader and disciplinarian, she also possessed a superb artistic sense. Designing the landscaping, including the new rose garden, was her relief from the onerous work of managing the village.

On strolls such as this one, their talks could encompass most anything, and today Mary was curious about her friend's childhood religious beliefs.

"May I ask you, Jeanette, before you came here to live with the sisters, did you know anything about Jesus, or his teachings?"

"No, not really."

"Was your family religious at all?"

"Certainly not my father," Jeanette responded with a scowl. "I think my mother and some of her friends sort of worshipped the forest, you know, the spirits in the trees and the animals and things. I think she liked deer and eagles the best."

"How about you?" Mary asked. "Did you worship the plants and animals too?"

"Sometimes. Maybe a little." Jeanette looked nervously at her tutor. "Oh, Sister Mary, did I sin when I did that?"

Mary smiled. "No, I don't think so. After all, you had not even heard of Jesus yet. The old writings tell us to respect God's creations, but only worship God the creator, not the creations."

"I understand."

A nearby pergola offered a convenient bench where they could rest and escape the sun for a few minutes and admire the surrounding beauty.

"Jeanette, you should remember that God made everything for a purpose. For example, those bees provide the honey that my mother uses in her baking, but there wouldn't be any honey if God hadn't provided flowers for the bees." She plucked a purple gentian blossom and tucked it into Jeanette's headscarf. "I think flowers are one of God's most beautiful gifts."

"They are," responded Jeanette. "But do you know what I like most? Birds. Maybe because my mother liked them so much. I enjoy watching them fly and soar. Wouldn't it be wonderful if we could fly? We could escape from all the world's troubles!"

Mary laughed. "Troubles seem to have a way of catching up with us."

"I guess so. How do they do it? Birds flying, I mean. Do the ancient writings tell us *how* they fly? If we knew, maybe we could fly too!"

"No, we don't know how birds are able to fly. Maybe someday we'll understand, if God wants us to."

Jeanette was deep in thought now. "You know, I've often wondered … everything we do, do we do it because God wants us to?"

"You have an inquiring mind, Jeanette, which is a good thing. Since God gave you an inquisitive mind, you honor Him by using it. Let me see, did we stop just now and look at those flowers because God wanted us to, or simply because we wanted to?"

Jeanette looked expectantly at Mary, awaiting her definitive answer.

Mary simply said, "Maybe that's a puzzle beyond our knowledge. I doubt we are meant to know everything God knows. A person would be arrogant to think they know as much as God does. And the ancient writings warn us not to be arrogant."[1]

"You know what bothers me? Why would God want wars to happen? All those people getting killed; it makes no sense. Or the awful storm that killed your family. Why would God want that to happen? Could it have been just horrible bad luck?"

"I choose to think the storm was just an unfortunate happening." She thought a moment. "You know, maybe there's a third possibility. Maybe God allows us to do as we choose, but every so often intervenes if it seems necessary. Do you think He intervened when He sent Jesus to us?"

Jeanette thought for a moment and nodded her head.

Mary cautioned her. "Maybe no one knows for sure. Thousands of years from now people may still wonder about the nature of God. Who knows?"

"I like your third possibility," said Jeanette. "It suggests God looks after us. Maybe that way God will keep me from doing something stupid some time."

"Believe me, we all do foolish things. I assure you I have. That is why He made you such an intelligent young lady, to figure such things out for yourself."

Jeanette paused and looked with surprise at her friend. "Do you know, Sister Mary, I think you're the first person who ever said I was intelligent."

Mary smiled at her. "That might be because I'm the first person who ever took the time to get to know you."

"Thank you so much, Sister Mary." Jeanette paused, searching for the right words.

"If you really think I'm intelligent, could I ask you one other question? It's somewhat embarrassing, but you're the only person I could ask."

"Certainly."

"Sister Mary, I'd like to be able to figure things out for myself, like you said. Perhaps you could help me do that."

"Of course. How can I help?"

"Could you teach me how to read and write?"

Mary put an arm around Jeanette's shoulder. "I would like nothing better. Shall we begin tomorrow?"

CHAPTER 29

Sister Jeanette had completed Mary's daily Gaulish lesson and was pleased. "You need to work on your pronunciation, but you're an excellent student. The sisters tell me they can understand you much better now."

"Thank you, but I still need your help. Could we practice a little longer, if you have time?

"I'd like to, but not today. Perhaps you heard that Sister Annette is returning from her trip to Rome. She should arrive before long."

Mary's ears perked up. "From Rome! How exciting! I hope she heard something about the disciples while she was there. Maybe even news from Galilee!"

Sister Annette arrived that afternoon and was welcomed with tea and biscuits in the dining room, which was also the village's only meeting room. She was one of the original sisters, but still in her twenties and dedicated to the village. She was a trusted assistant to the Sister Superior, though in no way her second-in-command. That position didn't exist. The Sister Superior had already briefed her about what she felt were Sister Mary's imaginary stories.

As she talked, Sister Annette captured Mary's attention for another reason. Her skin was pale by Palestinian standards, and when she removed her headscarf, her hair was golden! Being from a small town in Galilee, Mary had never encountered blonde hair before. She was fascinated by this unexpected addition to her knowledge of the world.

"Yes, I did learn a great deal while in Rome. Sadly, not all of it was good."

"That's to be expected when Rome is involved," replied an unimpressed Sister Superior. "Please start with the positive news."

"Yes, Sister. I learned that the Apostles are spreading the words of Jesus all around the eastern shores of the Great Sea. They've gone beyond the large cities and into smaller towns."

The Sister Superior already knew this. "And the bad news?"

Sister Annette's head drooped, and her tired eyes stared at the worn wooden floor. "Awful persecutions of our brethren continue, especially in Judea. It grieves me to report that a dedicated disciple, Stephen, has been killed – stoned to death – by a mob."[1]

Spontaneous sounds of disbelief and grief emanated from the sisters, especially from Mary, who had met him once. "Why? Who was responsible? What had he done?"

"No one was certain. Some said he was too outspoken and the Pharisees turned on him. Others blamed the Romans. In any event, I fear it may continue."

With a resigned expression, the Sister Superior said, "This tragic news is no surprise. We can only pray the persecutions do not reach here."

Mary recalled Lazarus' desire to come to Gaul. *He knew this would happen.*

☙

Another day, and another early morning in the kitchen for Mary. A different and delightful aroma was drifting about, for today the sisters would get a rare treat for breakfast: crepes. Sister Jeanette and an equally young Sister Arielle were helping her. As always, Sister Jeanette was prodding for more information about Jesus.

"Sister Mary, you once said you were concerned about what the disciples might be preaching. Why was that?"

"You see, it's wonderful so many disciples are spreading Jesus' words, but most of them never heard him speak. They rely on what others have taught, which reflects only a small part of what Jesus said. I'm sure they will speak words they believe to be true. I worry, though; will they reply to questions as Jesus would, or will they guess?[2] For example, you heard Sister Superior express her belief that the Apostles were at the cross, but that wasn't the case."

Sister Arielle, normally quiet and reserved, broke her silence. Her history was different from the other sisters, as she had been caught stealing a loaf of bread to help feed her family. She had stolen other things out of need, but until then had gotten away with it. Her unsympathetic father, unable to see anything but the crime, disowned her and threw her out of their home. His last words to his daughter were, "Don't you ever come back here!"

Her life changed when Sister Annette, running an errand in Aix, noticed her sitting under a tree, head buried in her arms, trying to survive a cold spring rain. She accepted Sister Annette's invitation to come to the newly established village. Arielle was happy there, but like many of the sisters she gave the appearance of harboring some dark secret, one she would as soon not share. Being shy and reclusive by nature, she had few close friends at the village.

She spoke in a low voice without looking at either Mary or Jeanette. "Sister Superior says we should never listen to Sister Mary when she says things about Jesus." She kept staring at the crepes she was making.

Mary became uneasy. *Is Sister Arielle going to report me to the Sister Superior?*

Jeanette jumped to Mary's defense. "Sister Arielle, since Sister Mary was there, what she is saying isn't just a guess or opinion. She actually heard what Jesus said!"

Sister Arielle made no reaction to Jeanette's comments, instead revealing some news Mary did not know. "Afterwards, one sister said maybe you should be shunned, that we should not speak to you at all. I was confused, so I said nothing."

Mary replied, "Here's a way to decide what's right. When you feel uncertain about what to do or say, ask yourself, 'What would Jesus have said or done in this situation?' For example, did Jesus ever instruct people to shun anyone? I can't recall him ever saying that."

Sister Jeanette was beaming at Mary. "See, you knew what Jesus would have said! You always do. Sister Mary, I can see a way to be sure the disciples are speaking the truth."

Mary, knowing that life rarely presents simple solutions, smiled at Sister Jeanette. "Tell me, please, I'm curious. What would this easy answer be?"

"You've said many times you wanted to teach about Jesus yourself. You would make a wonderful disciple. You know so much about Jesus! You talked with him personally and were friends with all the Apostles."

"I wish that were true, Jeanette, but the truth is that some of the twelve Apostles, including Peter and Andrew, who were the most influential, didn't think all that well of me.[3] I volunteered to be a teaching disciple but Peter wouldn't hear of it, and he had some valid reasons. Indeed, I was able to converse on occasions with only a few of the Apostles, such as Matthew, Philip, Bartholomew, and young John."

"Still, I'm certain you could go out and …"

Mary guessed what was coming next and hurried to object. "Thank you, Jeanette, for your faith in me, but I doubt I speak Gaulish well enough."

"The sisters tell me they can understand you, although you do have a strong accent. You have an impressive vocabulary. I think it's good enough."

"Would I be safe traveling around by myself?"

"Yes, it's safe here in Gaul. You saw Sister Annette return from Rome by herself."

Mary thought about it for a moment. "You know, I'd love to do that. I've never spoken in public, but Jesus told me I could help others understand his teachings and to fear nothing."

Sister Jeanette was ecstatic. "You see? It's been ordained! You must go out and tell others what you know!"

Sister Arielle's face changed from expressionless to consternation. She gave a quick disapproving glance in Mary's direction but said nothing.

Mary, however, was elated. "Maybe I should. I have to start some time." The thought was exhilarating. "Alright then, I will try! Where could I go? Certainly not here. Maybe Aix?"

"Yes, Aix!" Sister Jeanette began working out the timing. "Aix is less than two miles away. You could walk there after breakfast in an hour, talk to people for an hour, and be back here in time to help prepare lunch."

"Yes, that could work. At first, I will speak only with women. It will be easier for me, and I don't want to invite trouble on my first trip."

Sister Jeanette proclaimed, "Then it's settled! You can start tomorrow! Wonderful!"

"Yes, it is. Sister Jeanette, thank you for giving me the encouragement I needed."

Mary looked out the small kitchen window and glanced at the road leading away from the village to the west.

"Very well, it's settled. I will go to Aix. I will teach!"

CHAPTER 30

Mary was excited and confident, but also nervous, as she walked along a main street in Aix. When she arrived at the market area she studied the people around her, wondering who might be the best one to approach. It didn't look promising. *Everyone is scurrying around, in a hurry to get somewhere else.*

She entered an adjacent market area off the main street, where all the shoppers were women. Mary selected two she thought might be interested in talking and approached them. Trying to conceal her nervousness, she offered a simple "Good morning."

They paid her not the slightest heed.

She waited a few seconds and then backed away. *Maybe I should try women who are less busy shopping.* Looking around, Mary noticed two who seemed to be merely chatting and walked over to them. She decided to try a more conversational approach.

"Good morning." One turned her head and gave her an annoyed look.

"This seems to be a good market," she said in her heavy accent. "I have never been here before. Do they have apples this time of year?"

The one who had glanced at her gave a curt, "Sour ones, maybe" and turned away.

"Oh, thank you. I just arrived in Aix. Could I ask you a question?"

She received a cold stare. "If you're new here, perhaps you don't know it's rude for a stranger to interrupt others who are talking. We didn't intrude into your business."

The gruff response left Mary flustered. "Oh, I apologize. I didn't mean to disturb your conversation." She bowed slightly. "Good day."

The two women continued to ignore her as she backed away.

Mary sat down on a nearby bench, stared at the wind-blown leaves circling around her feet, and muttered, "This isn't going to be as easy as I imagined." Dejected but not disillusioned, she got up and walked the two miles back to the security of her village.

As she approached the dormitory building, an excited Sister Jeanette ran out with open arms. "Mary! Welcome back! How successful were you?"

"Not at all," replied a disheartened Mary. "I'm not ready for this yet. Teaching about Jesus sounded simple in Galilee. In reality, it's not so easy, as I just found out.

"What do you mean? You know so much about Jesus!"

"Perhaps, but I never got there. To them I was just an annoying foreigner, and they had no desire to talk with someone so different. I must learn more about your people and customs, and I need to speak your language better."

Her words became more determined. "From now on, I'll speak nothing but Gaulish here at the village. Jeanette, I need you to teach me all this, and improve how I speak your language."

"Of course. I'll be happy to help you any way I can. If you can teach me to write Gaulish, I can teach you to speak it!"

For the first time that day Mary laughed. "We're a perfect match!"

Then, more seriously, "It may take a while, but when I go back to Aix I want to be ready, to feel I can succeed. And I do intend to go back."

❧

After several months of language lessons, aided by daily conversations with the other sisters, Mary was back in Aix. She felt more confident than on her first trip, and approached two women about her own age and attempted a conversation.

"There seems to be an excellent selection of vegetables here today!"

As before, the reaction was annoyed disinterest without even a pause in their conversation. Mary again stepped back from the two shoppers and reconsidered her tactics. She wasn't discouraged but was at a loss as to what to do.

While she was thinking, Mary noticed a woman sitting nearby, her head down. *She looks worried; I wonder if she needs help.* Mary walked over to her.

"Pardon me, I don't wish to interrupt, but you look troubled. I hope you aren't ill."

"What? Oh, no. I was just thinking about my son, he's pale and hasn't been eating well lately."

"Oh, I'm so sorry. I hope he'll be better soon. I'm tired from walking; would it be all right if I shared your bench?"

She nodded, glancing sideways at this obvious foreigner.

"I've just arrived here in Aix. May I ask you a question?"

"I could spare a minute. You seem to have an accent. Where are you from?"

"Palestine. A small town called Magdala, near the Sea of Galilee. You've probably never heard of Magdala."

"I've barely heard of Palestine. What brought you such a long way?"

Mary saw the opening. "I follow the teachings of an inspiring man named Jesus. Sadly, his enemies killed him, and my friends and I feared for our own lives. We felt we would be safer if we came to Gaul."

She paused for a second and then asked, "Have you heard of Jesus?"

"As a matter of fact, I have. A merchant from Damascus was here a while back and mentioned the stir this preacher was creating in Palestine. A woman who overheard him later told me a few interesting things about Jesus' teachings. I would have liked to hear more."

Mary's face was a beaming sea of enthusiasm. "That's wonderful!

I'm so glad to meet someone who has heard of Jesus. My name is Mary. I met him while he was traveling and teaching near Magdala." Mary had learned that understatement was wise.

"Really! How exciting! In that case perhaps you can tell me more about him. My name is Isabelle."

"Might I ask, Isabelle, if you know of others who perhaps heard this merchant you mentioned? Do you think they might wish to learn more about Jesus' teaching?"

"Yes, I know a few."

Mary was ecstatic. "Isabelle, do you think … is there any way I could meet them?"

"Most of them were my relatives; one was a neighbor. They might enjoy meeting you. If you'd like, I could take you to my home sometime and introduce you."

"Oh, Isabelle, I would be so pleased. Would a week from today be convenient?"

Isabelle's house was the first private home in Gaul Mary had been to since the day she arrived. It was spacious, and a small but welcoming fire burned in the stone fireplace.

More than just Isabelle's family were present, all women. Mary was intrigued by the group's diversity. In the corner, a shy child clung to the robe of an elderly woman, perhaps her grandmother. A seated woman with a crippled leg could not take her expectant eyes off Mary, and a woman with darker skin who might have been from North Africa stared at her.

Following some social conversations Isabelle introduced her guest. "Welcome to our home, Mary. I recall you telling me the other day that you had met Jesus when you lived in Galilee. Please, tell us about it!"

"I would be delighted. Good morning, my friends. I've come here from a small town in Palestine called Magdala. One day about two years ago, in the nearby village of Nazareth, I had the good fortune to meet …"

Mary had them spellbound as she related key events in her travels with Jesus. After a while, though, she realized she may have talked too long and hastened to conclude.

"I must go now, but I will be in Aix again in a week, and I'll be happy to tell you more about Jesus then. If you can, please come, and bring a friend with you." Nodding heads assured Mary she'd have a return audience. Her own smile disappeared, however, as she whispered to Isabelle, "I fear I have talked far too long. Our Sister Superior will not tolerate tardiness."

"Then run along. We were all fascinated by everything you said, and I think more will come next time."

Mary clasped Isabelle's hand. "Thank you for your help. I will see you next week."

❧

She hurried the two miles back to the village. As she approached the kitchen door the imposing figure of the Sister Superior materialized in it. As Mary suspected, she was not happy.

"This must be our Sister Mary. I hope coming here to help prepare lunch today was not too much of an inconvenience?"

"I give you my most sincere apologizes, Sister. I realize I'm a little late. I was out walking and lost track of the time." She felt guilty at the necessity of a little lie.

"I thought I emphasized personal responsibility here. Did I not make that clear to you?"

"No, you have been very clear. I do understand the rules here, and respect them. I assure you I will never arrive late for any of my duties again."

The Sister Superior gave Mary a withering glare. "I'm quite sure you won't. Not in this community, anyway." She turned and strutted off.

PART TWO: GAUL

Mary had no doubts about her meaning. She dashed into the kitchen.

CHAPTER 31

On a crisp fall day, Mary headed down the now familiar road that led to Aix. This time she was not alone; Sister Jeanette was by her side.

"Sister Mary, I hope you're not upset. I know you'd prefer I not come with you, but ever since you began preaching in Aix I have wanted to be there and listen to you."

"It's not that I don't want you to come, Jeanette. I was only thinking of your welfare. When the Sister Superior finds out what I've been doing, and she will, there could be trouble. I only want to avoid her disliking you as much as she does me."

"I understand, but I want so much to learn how you talk to people, what kinds of things you say. I dream someday I might teach about Jesus the way you do, but I'm not a good speaker. To stand in front of a crowd would terrify me. I would just mumble nonsense."

"All you lack is experience. That will come with time."

They arrived at the field where Mary would give her talk. The number of attendees had already outgrown the capacity of Isabelle's comfortable home.

"Mary, I'm impressed. Look at all the people! And not just women, but men and children too. You are a huge success!"

"I believe it's Jesus who's the huge success," she replied.

As Sister Jeanette viewed the crowd, she noticed a young man with a scraggly beard, who smiled at her. She couldn't resist a modest smile back. Mary observed the exchange with an amused grin and quipped, "I thought young ladies under the tutelage of the stern Sister Superior were not supposed to notice beguiling smiles."

Sister Jeanette's reply was equally light-hearted, "Oh? What smile?"

As they scanned the audience, they observed a small group of men in the back who were not smiling; rather, they seemed to be glowering at them. Most of them were adult men, but Mary noticed one young boy, blond and slim with black eyebrows over narrow eyes, who had a determined look on his face. Jeanette and Mary looked at each other with concern.

"I can't recall seeing them here before," Mary said. "I have no idea who they are, but I need to get started. Let's hope they leave after a while."

Mary greeted the crowd as she passed by, made a slight bow, and began her talk.

Jeanette was impressed with how relaxed and confident Mary appeared now.

☙

Back in the village, a scene was taking place that would alter Mary's life forever. The Sister Superior was interrogating a nervous Sister Arielle. Every answer the young sister gave increased the Sister Superior's agitation. She glared at the frightened young girl.

"Sister Arielle, are you quite sure everything you have just told me is factual? I need to be absolutely certain of these things."

"Oh, yes. I would never tell you a lie."

"Aix, you say?"

"Yes, they said Aix."

"Right now?"

"Yes, I saw them leave here about an hour ago."

More calmly, she said, "I see. You may leave now. You will never tell anyone about this conversation. Is that clear?"

"Yes, Sister Superior."

"Likewise, you are not to talk with Sister Mary again. Is that also clear?"

"Yes, Sister Superior."

"Very well. You may go to your room." Sister Arielle wasted no time complying.

The Sister Superior stared at the ceiling, tapping her fingers with well above average vigor. When she had made her decision, she deemed it important enough to be proclaimed aloud.

"Such conduct is intolerable. I regret an example must be made of this."

☙

After about forty minutes, Mary finished her talk. Since her scolding and warning from the Sister Superior, she had her timing down to the minute.

"So please remember Jesus' words, to love God and all his creation, to love other people as much as ourselves, and to treat others the same as we want them to treat us."

She then asked, "Before I leave, are there any questions?"

An elderly man called out, "I have heard it said Jesus was called 'King of the Jews.'[1] If his message was for Jews, why should we be concerned? My family and I aren't Jews."

"That is an important question. As you may know, Jesus was a Jew, and initially much of what he said was directed at Jews and the rules of their religion.[2] Later on, it became evident he meant everyone. He spoke of taking his message to all nations so everyone could hear his words.[3] That is part of the reason I came to Gaul."

As Mary looked to see if there were more questions, she noticed on the ground nearby a thin, dirty man looking at her with hungry eyes, one of the many beggars in Aix. A filthy hand extended from his ragged sleeve. His dark complexion and facial features suggested he might be from North Africa. Mary walked over, bent down, and gave him her blessing and a coin.

A well-dressed man observed this, frowned, and confronted Mary. "Woman, why do you waste your money? This tramp is a nobody, an outcast. Look at his skin. He's not one of us!"

Mary listened patiently to her critic's complaints, then turned and addressed those around her, all of whom were curious to hear her reply.

"Jesus didn't care where anyone was from, the color of their skin, or how ragged their clothes. Remember, he said, 'In as much as you have done it unto one of the least of these, you have done it onto me.'[4] In God's eyes, the poor are as important as the rich. This is a key part of Jesus' message. I beg you never to forget that."[5]

Mary knew the customary response to a beggar, especially a foreigner, was at best to ignore him. She searched the crowd, hoping some would respond to the message she had just given them. Instead, the well-dressed man merely shook his head at what he considered Mary's ridiculous waste of money and strode off. One woman did go up to the hungry man and gave him a small coin, but she was the only one. Observing this, Mary commented to Jeanette, "It will take time, I suspect, to change the way people think about the less fortunate."

She asked, "Are there any other questions?"

She was startled as a young man in the rear, the slim, blond one she had noticed at the start of her talk, began berating her.

"Yes. I have a question for you. Why do you presume you have a right to teach here? You are a woman; you are forbidden to teach men. Go home and be silent! You violate public order by the illegal things you do here. Go back where you came from and stay there!"

Mary was taken aback but realized she must take control and make a firm response. She was upset at this public challenge to her legitimacy, and her reply was angrier and more personal than was perhaps intended. For a moment, the old Mary was in control.

"My authority to be here came from Jesus himself, as I explained at an earlier gathering. Perhaps you were not present then, or did not hear. You are young and of strong opinions. I suggest you study the words of Jesus yourself before speaking in so disrespectful a manner."

The young man was about to come back with an even stronger retort, but his colleagues restrained him. They began exiting, but the teenager continued the agitated conversation, accompanied by angry gestures back in the direction where Mary had been speaking.

Mary turned to the rest of the crowd, who appeared to support her. "Thank you for coming today, but I must head back to my village now. I hope to see you again soon."

❧

On their return Sister Annette was awaiting them. She looked worried, almost frightened.

"Sister Mary, the Sister Superior says she wants to see both of you immediately. Perhaps I shouldn't say this, but she looks quite angry."

"Really? Why? I'm not late for my lunch duties."

"I have an idea, but I shouldn't express opinions. Something has upset her."

Mary turned to Sister Jeanette. "We'd better go, my friend, and see what this is about."

She had a sickening feeling, though, that she already knew.

Her secret was out.

CHAPTER 32

The Sister Superior was sitting in her stiff wooden chair with her back to the visitors. Various papers were scattered around her desk. This time no other sisters were present. A cloudy day and the onset of drizzling rain made the meeting all the more foreboding.

"You wished to see us?"

The Sister Superior turned her chair and glared at Mary. "What I wish is that you had even the slightest respect for this community's Sister Superior."

"I do!" protested Mary. "You know I …"

"You were given strict orders not to go spreading your fantasies about Jesus. Where were you this morning? Don't lie! I know!"

"I never lie. I was in Aix. All I was doing was talking with people about Jesus. They're so eager to learn about him. I see no wrong in that."

"Really. Perhaps you also wish to plead ignorance of the strict prohibitions against women teaching their version of religion to men?"

Oh no, not again. Although her angry side was urging an indignant defense, her tactful side prevailed. She replied, "I know some hold that view, but Jesus never spoke such words."

The Sister Superior was in no mood for a discussion. "Still delusional! Disrespectful and disobedient as well. You therefore force me to take appropriate action. I have given you shelter and food only to see you repeatedly flout our rules. No longer!"

The Sister Superior picked up a sheet with the names of the sisters on it, turned it so Mary could see it, and drew a heavy line through the most recent name: "Mary of Magdala."

"Because of your persistent insolence, I regret that an example must be made of you. Therefore, you are no longer Sister Mary and are no longer welcome in our midst. You will gather your things and depart this community. Now!"

Mary was not expecting a reprimand this final. "Sister, I have nowhere to go! I know no one in all of Gaul well enough to stay with them."

"Perhaps you should have thought of that before you left for Aix."

An appalled Sister Jeanette attempted to help. "Please, Sister Superior, I know that Sister Mary truly does respect you ..."

"Silence! I did not ask for your opinion. I will get to you in a minute!"

The Sister Superior thought for a moment. "I have no idea why I'm so lenient. One of my weaknesses, I imagine. In a field across the road you'll find an old storage shed. No one uses it. It will keep the rain off you. You may sleep there until you find something better. However, you will not enter the grounds of our Christian community here ever again! Do you understand?"

Mary realized further protests would be futile. "I understand. I will obey your wishes."

The Sister Superior refocused her glare on Sister Jeanette.

"Now for you, young lady. Are you going to pretend you knew nothing about the prohibition against women teaching? Answer me!"

Sister Jeanette mustered up every bit of courage she could find. She looked straight at the Sister Superior and didn't hesitate. "I know of it."

"Yet not only did you disregard my instructions to be sure this Mary knew and obeyed the rules of our village, you even accompanied her while she mocked my instructions. Did she force you to go with her?"

Sister Jeanette paused, knowing she might have a life altering decision to make. Should she defend Mary further, or try to stay in the good graces of the Sister Superior? She stood ramrod straight, still looking the Sister Superior eye to eye. Inside, her heart was pounding, but she knew there was only one choice. She could not betray her friend.

"She did not force me to do anything. I went to meet the citizens of Aix who wanted to learn about Jesus. I went to hear what words Sister Mary used to win their hearts. My only desire was to learn how to be a better disciple of Jesus."

"I see. You acknowledge that your allegiance to this foreigner exceeds your loyalty to me, my work here, and my instructions. That was a poor decision, my dear former Sister Jeanette. For with that you have broken your vows, and your allegiance to this community. Therefore, like your friend, you may no longer be a member of it."

Jeanette blanched at the words "former Sister Jeanette." Mary as well couldn't believe what she just heard.

Mary's response was as passionate as it was impetuous. "No! Please do not punish this innocent young woman because of your displeasure with me. She does not deserve ..."

"Silence! What she deserves, and apparently desires, is to associate with you. Very well. I shall not deny her that wish. You may both follow whatever secular paths you wish, but not as members of this house of obedient disciples. Now get out of my sight, both of you!"

Mary and Jeanette cast blank stares at each other for a moment, then exited the Sister Superior's office and trudged through the drizzle to their former rooms to collect what few belongings they possessed. Then, for the last time, they headed down the familiar winding path that now seemed barren, hard, and unwelcoming.

❧

The drizzle had slackened but not gone away. As they reached the gate, they pulled their cloaks tighter against a bone-chilling autumn wind. As Mary did so, she felt her mother's necklace. With a sardonic smile she shook her head. *I can't tell if you bring me good luck or bad. It appears you are very good at both. But you're my mother's present to me, and now my physical connection with Jesus as well, so for better or worse you will always be my amulet.*

Jeanette's tearful eyes looked towards Mary, her face etched with anguish. "Oh, Sister Mary, I am so sorry. This is all my fault! The Sister Superior knew where we were because Sister Arielle heard me urging you to go to Aix. She probably mentioned it to some of the other sisters. It wouldn't take long for it to get to the Sister Superior. I beg you, please forgive me!"

"My dear, sweet Jeanette, you're being much too hard on yourself. I was part of that conversation too, you know. And you must have realized that the Sister Superior would find out sooner or later. Unfortunately, it was sooner." Mary put her arm around Jeanette. "It was I who disobeyed her orders, and as a result got you into trouble. I should apologize to you for making you share my penance."

Jeanette sighed. "I guess our fates are shared now."

She stopped and looked imploringly at Mary, grasping her arm. "I mean, I want them to be! I want to learn all I can from you, Sister Mary." She paused. "I guess you are just Mary now. May I call you that? I want to help you any way I can. Please say I can continue to be with you!"

Mary extended her soft, reassuring smile. "You've already been of great help to me. Of course you can stay with me. Right now, you're about the only friend I have. Please do call me Mary." She laughed. "Besides, I still need those Gaulish lessons!"

Mary felt Jeanette squeeze her arm tighter as she said, "Thank you so much, Mary."

With a forced smile Mary said, "The first thing you can do is help me find my new home, this no doubt luxurious tool shed. If the shed can be fixed up, I think I would be happy staying there. It would be peaceful and quiet, and I've always preferred the countryside to the city."

"It's only a short way down the road, but some trees hide it from view. I hope the roof is still solid. I know where there's a small spring up the hillside, so water is reliable. I'll stay with you tonight, and tomorrow go into Aix. I have friends there. They might have room for both of us. If not, I'll bring you blankets and all the food you need. If you choose to stay here, you'll be fine, I promise."

Mary gave her an appreciative embrace. It had become clear, and a little disconcerting, how dependent she would now be on Jeanette.

Chapter 33

Jeanette had been unable to find a place in Aix for the two of them, but a friend was willing to share a room with her. Jeanette accepted the invitation but spent her days at the shed. With effort and ingenuity they had turned the musty little spider sanctuary into passable living quarters. One blessing: the roof was sound. The sagging door was repaired, and they created something that could pass for a bed. Though primitive, Mary's new home would at least keep the winter wind and rain away.

Since water was available, they were hoeing an area that in the spring would become a vegetable garden. As they worked, Mary was alarmed to hear the distant voices of people approaching. Visitors? "That's odd. Who would know we're here?"

As they drew closer, she was surprised to recognize two acquaintances from the village, Sisters Danielle and Arielle. This was her first contact with any of the sisters since their eviction.

Mary's salutation reflected lingering bitterness. "Sisters Danielle and Arielle! What brings two dedicated followers of the Sister Superior to this terrible den of sinners?"

Sister Danielle's response, friendly but also challenging, surprised her. "Please, Mary, don't judge us in haste. Maybe it wasn't what it seemed."

"What do you mean?"

"I mean, the first time you were called in and chastised by the Sister Superior. I agreed with her because I was scared. When I said to you 'don't cause trouble' it wasn't to scold you, it was because I didn't want the Sister Superior to punish you. I admire you, Mary, and hoped you could stay with us and not be expelled. That was why I said 'don't cause trouble.'"

"Oh, I'm so sorry, Sister Danielle. I misunderstood. Then I apologize and welcome your friendship. I've always admired all of you at the village for overcoming your past hardships. It's good to see you, but aren't you taking a risk by coming here?"

"Not everyone at the village knows we're here, if you know what I mean. Tell me, how are you managing in this ancient shed?"

"Very well. In a way, I feel liberated. I can now go to Aix and teach about Jesus whenever I want, and in return I receive great happiness from conveying his words."

"I'm pleased to hear that. Most of the sisters feel terrible about what happened to you and Sister Jeanette, and they wanted you to know that. We volunteered to come and tell you, and we brought something for you from all the sisters."

Sister Arielle approached Mary with a bag she was carrying. With sorrowful eyes she said, "I confess that, at first, I thought you were lying, but not now. I'm truly sorry I told others about your trips to Aix. Please accept this from us and the other sisters." Mary opened the bag and was greeted by a generous assortment of fruit, fresh bread, figs, dried fish, olives, and even some handmade pastries. It had taken time and effort to prepare their gift.

"What a wonderful present! You've brightened my day. Thank you so much. There are really two gifts here, these marvelous treats, and the greater gift of your friendship, and knowing that you accept my truthfulness."

Mary thought a moment. "Does the Sister Superior know about your gift? I don't want you getting into trouble on my account."

"No, we dared not risk it," said Sister Danielle. "Like you, many of us have no other home. We all wish she were less strict, but we must live with that reality."

Mary's reply surprised them. "Please don't think too harshly of her. Any leader must maintain discipline, and the refuge she's created for troubled young women reflects Jesus' call to help others. She's worked hard to make a home for you and had nothing to model it after. She had to create her own rules of behavior. I rather admire her for that."

Then, with a sheepish smile, she said, "Besides, I've always had an independent streak. It sometimes gets me into trouble, as you can see."

"Maybe, but it also helped you meet Jesus and learn from him," enthused Sister Danielle. "Mary, your friends back in the village think you're special. They want you to keep teaching and travel more widely. To us, you're Jesus' apostle to Gaul!"

"That is quite exaggerated! But tell me, where do they think I should go to teach?"

"We thought about that," said Sister Danielle. "Maybe Massalia. It's not that far away. Sister Annette was there recently visiting her aunt and uncle and listened to a talk by the local bishop. She said he was quite friendly. He might suggest places where you could teach."

"Massalia! There's a bishop in Massalia? Interesting. Would it be safe to go there?"

"It's a larger, more varied city than Aix. The bishop could find a safe place for you."

"Oh, Sister Danielle, thank you. What do you think, Jeanette?"

"You know I want to be with you, so if you decide to go to Massalia, I'll go there, too. That is, if it's all right with you."

"Of course you can; your company would be a great pleasure. It does sound like an interesting possibility." Mary pondered it a bit more.

"Alright, perhaps a brief trip, to try to find this bishop and meet his disciples. I'll return here, though. This is where my friends and followers are."

They talked a while longer, and as Sister Danielle prepared to depart, Sister Arielle approached Mary and, with a sideways glance, addressed her in almost a whisper.

"Mary, I came here to give you our present, but I had another reason as well. There's something troubling me; maybe I'm a terrible sinner. You're the only one I feel I can talk to."

Mary was intrigued. "Of course I'll listen and not criticize. What concerns you?"

"Sometimes I think maybe I'm just an awful person, but I have to confess that I … I've never had any boyfriends. I just prefer to be with women, to be … well, very good friends with them, if you know what I mean. Especially with one particular sister. I don't want to say who."

Sister Danielle spoke up. "It's alright; Sister Arielle's confession is mine as well. We realized from the start we were … different from the other sisters. When my father guessed my secret, he beat me and threw me out of the house. That's how I came to be at the village." She looked at Mary. "I would also like to hear what you have to say, and what Jesus would have said."

Mary had to think. "I'm not certain how to answer. I don't recall Jesus ever speaking about such matters. However, three things come to mind."

"First, although I cannot remember Jesus discussing that subject, I also never heard him condemn such conduct, even though others did.[1] I should think if he were opposed, he would have said so."

"Second, I recall Jesus' words to 'judge not, that you be not judged.[2] Therefore, you have my assurance that I neither judge nor condemn you."

"Third, Jesus instructed his followers to love your neighbors as yourself, and if you love one another then you are his disciples."[3]

Mary's words were like loving hands lifting a burdensome weight off her friends' shoulders. Relieved, they expressed their appreciation for her willingness to hear their confession. Everyone agreed, though, that it would be best if this newly shared knowledge remained between them.

⊖

It was the kind of dim, smelly room which, by itself, suggests the people in it are up to no good. A group of scowling men were seated around a table talking and drinking, with curse words often thrown in. One of them was the slim, blond, grim-faced teenager who had been so incensed at Mary's recent gathering. He was the only sober one. He never drank, he explained to the others, as he didn't want anything clouding what he considered his superior senses.

The men were agitated about conduct they viewed as a serious threat to Aix. Their leader, a minor bureaucrat named Jacques, posed a question and a challenge.

"Why do we put up with this woman? The magistrate has told us it's wrong. It could give Aix a bad reputation. We hold respectable positions in the community. People look to us for leadership. We must do something!"

The blond teenager, whose name was Maurice, was quick to second the leader's sentiments. "Jacques is right. Women should stay home and remain silent. They can't be opinionated and order people around, like my stepmother did. The customs and traditions of our society are clear about this. We must not let such conduct continue!"

A third man, Claude, slim, squinty-eyed, and nervous, offered firsthand evidence. "Worse, she associates with filthy foreigners, even Africans, and gives them money. Can you believe that? I saw her with my own eyes! She's a foreigner herself, you know!"

The man next to him, a pudgy, squeaky-voiced merchant, had a pragmatic solution. "Perhaps it would please the magistrate if we ran her out of town."

A fifth conspirator, deep voiced and impatient, was happy to supply the details. "Yes! Give her twenty-four hours to get out of Aix, or we'll be happy to assist her departure."

Jacques added, "Or, much simpler, we could arrange for the magistrate to have her arrested. The charges are obvious."

All the men around the table nodded their heads in concurrence with these imaginative ideas for civic improvement, and all except one poured another round.

☙

The unhappy men, however, would seek Mary and Jeanette in vain, for the two women had already made their decision. They would visit Massalia, meet the Christians there, and look for the bishop Sister Annette had encountered. It would be a short trip, and then return to Aix.

Early the next morning they were on the well-used road leading south out of Aix. Mary handed a local farmer a coin, and she and Jeanette climbed into his farm wagon with their travel bags. A tap on the donkey, and they were on their way, the rising sun just beginning to warm the wagon's excited occupants. Their next stop was Massalia.

CHAPTER 34

Mary and Jeanette clung to one another in the strange, bustling city of Massalia, a larger city than either had been in before. Finding the bishop, or anyone who had heard of him, was a challenge. Only the largest streets had names, and those were often known only by memory.

When they came to yet another unnamed intersection, Mary peered down what appeared to be a major avenue. "Jeanette, up ahead, in that plaza. It appears someone is talking to a large crowd. Might it be a Christian disciple?"

"It could be anything, but someone there might know about this bishop."

The speaker was facing away from them, and as they got closer, Mary put her hand to her ear to hear better. "Odd, his voice sounds familiar."

"… and remember that through Jesus, forgiveness is always available. What you have done in the past is not as important as what you choose to do in the future."

Mary was ecstatic. She knew that voice. When he turned slightly, a lengthy beard came into view. "Jeanette, can you believe it? The speaker is Lazarus!"

They waited until he finished answering questions, then Mary's delighted voice rang out. "Lazarus! What good fortune! You said you preferred a large city, and here you are!"

"Mary! How wonderful to see you! God has answered our prayers! We stayed in Aix for a while as we agreed and then came here. Did you just arrive?"

"Yes. I've been at the little Christian village ever since you left." Mary decided the recent problems could wait. "This is my good friend, Jeanette, who I met there. I've been teaching about Jesus in Aix, but someone told me there was a bishop in Massalia. Do you know him?"

Lazarus' normally serious face took on an unexpected light-hearted grin. "Yes, I do know the Bishop of Massalia quite well. He happens to be me."

Mary was amazed. "Lazarus, congratulations! How did that come about?"

"You needn't be too impressed; there was no one else available for the task. Not long ago, a young disciple asked to create another congregation on the other side of the city, so I took on the organizing, ceremonial, and coordinating duties of a bishop. It seemed probable that additional congregations would emerge in other parts of the city. Also, having a bishop in Massalia would be a way to indicate the growth of the Christian faith in the region."

"I'm still impressed. Are Martha and Mary here also?"

"Yes, Martha is a huge help with our work. We had to spend the first few months learning Gaulish, as no doubt you did also. As for our young sister, her current calling seems to be seeking out the most eligible bachelors in Massalia."

Mary laughed. "I certainly wish her success."

"As do Martha and I. We hope her success will involve a man of good morals and gentle disposition. We worry that our young sister isn't as mature and discriminating as she might be. Come, let's go to my modest home. Martha will be delighted to see you."

Lazarus' home was indeed modest. It was nothing more than the second floor of a worshiper's house. It consisted of a bedroom used by the two women and a modest adjacent room with only a small table and bed – Lazarus' study and bedroom. Their kitchen was their benefactor's stove in the yard, and they shared bathroom facilities.

Mary and Jeanette were somehow squeezed in with the other two women; they slept on the floor. The travelers were sufficiently weary that the cramped quarters didn't inhibit their sleep in the least.

Breakfast the next morning was an appropriate time for exchanging each other's recent histories, including Mary and Jeanette's expulsion from the village. Martha's reunion breakfast featured a delicious omelet utilizing donated eggs, but its simplicity and the meager portions told Mary her friends were something less than rich.

Mary smiled at Mary of Bethany. "I know Martha assists Lazarus in his work here; how do you keep busy?"

"I've also tried to learn Gaulish. I enjoy asking people if they've heard of Jesus. I admire you, Mary, and want to be more like you. I'm only beginning, though." She grinned at her sister. "Martha thinks I'm too forward around men. She might be right. I should try to act more like you and my sister do."

"I'm delighted you're telling others about Jesus. If I can help you, please ask me questions at any time." Mary made a mental note: *There may be hidden potential here.*

Turning to Lazarus she asked, "I'm curious about something. To what extent do you discuss the return from the tomb in your sermons?"

"I've thought about that, Mary. In Bethany people avoided me, unsure what to make of me. Others wanted me eliminated. So I don't mention that miraculous day in Bethany here. Many wouldn't believe it; others might want to venerate me. That's the last thing I want. I'm still a little insecure when I talk, so I don't complicate things with my personal history."

"You have no need to feel insecure," Mary replied. "I heard you preaching yesterday; your Gaulish is excellent, and everyone was paying close attention to your inspiring words."

He laughed. "Maybe they were just struggling to cope with my accent. We're delighted you and Jeanette are here. Please stay as long as you wish."

"It can only be a short while. We've already found you and Martha, and the bishop! We'd enjoy hearing you preach and meeting your followers. Then I need to return to Aix."

"I understand," Lazarus replied. "Our congregation is growing, and my vision is of a small building to house our followers. At present we must cancel services in bad weather. Such a structure would also be a visible symbol of our mission to spread the words of Jesus."

"It sounds like a wonderful idea. Would you call it a synagogue?"

"No, that would imply Judaism was taught here. Like you, I wish only to spread Jesus' teachings. I will call it simply a church, a place where Jesus' followers can worship."

"Your goal sounds like it might be a lot of work."

"True, but less so if you were here to help. Will you think about staying for a while?"

Mary pondered that. "Your vision of a church is intriguing. Very well, if you can acquire a building, I'll help ready it for use. I can delay my return to Aix."

❧

Over the next few weeks Mary met several of Lazarus' followers. One of them, a successful businessman named Bernard, had heard of Lazarus' hope of finding a building suitable to hold his services. He had invited Lazarus to a residential area of town, where they were looking at an attractive house, enhanced by multicolored tufa around the entrance.

"This is it, Lazarus, the house where my mother used to live. Our old family home. She enjoyed hearing you speak, and before she died, she said she had become a disciple of Jesus and asked me to help you and your congregation in any way I could."

"I recall her well," said Lazarus, "It was a privilege to assist with her remembrance service. She was a very kind and humble woman."

"Very much so. With her passing, this house became mine. I have a fine home of my own and no need for this one. I could sell it, but I don't need the money. So I ask you, would you care to have this modest building as a home for your congregation?"

Lazarus could hardly believe what he was hearing. "Really? I pray my ears do not deceive me. Bernard, I would be overwhelmed with joy!"

"Then it is yours, my friend."

A few days later, Mary was resting in Lazarus' apartment, safe from the drizzling rain outside. Jeanette stopped at the door, as though hesitant to speak.

"I'm sorry to bother you, Mary, but I need to go to Aix right away. It's a personal matter."

Mary looked confused and concerned. "Oh, alright. I hope nothing serious?"

"No, not at all. I'm not ill or anything like that. I just need to … sort something out. I can tell you about it when you return to Aix."

Mary was troubled by the secrecy but replied, "Very well, then. I will pray for your safe journey and look forward to seeing you when I return." Jeanette gave Mary a fond hug and hurried out into the drizzle.

As Mary watched her fade away down the road, another missing person came to mind. For unknown reasons, none of them had seen Mary of Bethany for several days. She had just disappeared.

Chapter 35

A frenzy of activity engulfed the newly acquired house. Lazarus and Bernard had torn down an interior wall to create a larger meeting room, while others were enlarging the entrance. The multitude of tasks was exceeded only by the enthusiasm of the workers.

Lazarus and Martha had one more reason to be excited about the renovation – the second floor of the house would soon become their new parsonage. At last Martha would have a kitchen, and Lazarus a respectable study.

Two weeks later, Mary, Lazarus, Martha, and Bernard stood in front of their new church. Just one final task was required. Lazarus ascended a ladder and enthusiastically called out, "I'm ready! Hand it up!" He positioned a large, handcrafted cross at the top of the roof, nailed it into place, and descended. Everyone looked up to admire the new symbol of their faith gleaming in the sun, the finishing and defining touch on their now completed church.

Mary was ecstatic. "Such an inspiration! The first Christian house of worship in Gaul, and it will not be the last! We can't thank you enough, Bernard, for your generous gift."

He smiled. "It was my pleasure."

One person, however, was missing from the celebration. In her search for an eligible bachelor, Mary of Bethany had become enamored of a handsome centurion in the local Roman regiment, Marcus Achelias. His athletic physique, clean-shaven face, and valor were irresistible. After a brief courtship, they had become engaged. As she told Martha, "Marcus is a brave and dedicated soldier; I'm sure he'll be promoted quickly, maybe even become a general someday."

For her part, Martha had serious concerns about the centurion, and the extent to which Mary really knew him. Her concerns were valid.

Mary of Bethany and Marcus were socializing with some of his military friends, who were enjoying numerous strong wines while they discussed the next day's activities. One of the friends had what he considered a splendid idea.

"You may have heard, Marcus, tomorrow in the arena there will be a fight to the finish, matching some runaway Ethiopian slaves against wild bears captured in the Alps. They keep the bears hungry. It should be a most entertaining afternoon!"

Marcus' eyes lit up. "An excellent suggestion. Mary and I would be pleased to join you. Since they give slaves rather small swords, I'll be betting on the bears!" They all laughed.

Mary looked at her fiancé, appalled. She had attended violent martial arts contests where the loser often limped away more than a little bloodied. Never anything like this, though, where she might have to watch several human beings die horrible deaths. The thought of such a spectacle repulsed her, and she had no difficulty envisioning what Mary of Magdala would think of this kind of depravity.

Although nervous about disagreeing with her fiancé, she knew she could never look her mentor in the eye again if she did not find the courage to protest.

"Oh, my dear Marcus, must I go? I really do not savor such events; I wouldn't enjoy watching it. Please, you and your friends go, and I will wait for you at home."

Her plea was answered by a contorted face and outraged glare, followed by a strong hand grabbing her by the neck and another hand smashing her across the face. Blood ran freely from her broken nose. She tried to break away from his grasp but couldn't.

"How dare you contradict me!" he roared, his chin almost touching her bloodied face. "I am an officer in the imperial Roman army, a centurion who has fought in the great arena at Trier and never known defeat! You have the impudence to question my decisions in front of the other officers? You not only display your cowardice, but insult me by questioning the decision of a Roman centurion! Your behavior is unacceptable!" Inching even closer to her disfigured face, he bellowed, "You *will* be with me at the games tomorrow! Do you understand?"

His muscular arms pushed her away, sending her tumbling to the floor. "You are young and a foreigner and unschooled in the proud traditions of the Roman Empire, so I'll refrain from severely punishing you this time. But I warn you, never make such a serious mistake again!" He poured the rest of his wine in her face.

As Mary tried to deal with the insults and pain, Marcus leaned over her and in a muted and hypocritically loving tone whispered in her ear, "Sorry, I had to do that. The other officers were watching. You understand."

As Mary trembled and tried to crawl away from him, Marcus turned to the officer next to him and said in whispered tones, "You know, she may not be a suitable wife for a person of my position and authority. I may have to do something about her."

"She's a nobody, and an ignorant foreigner to boot," replied his compatriot, looking bored. "Surely you can make up some suitable charges to have her jailed."

Marcus glanced at Mary out of the corner of his eye. "She's hardly worth the bother. You cannot achieve greatness by wasting time on cowardly, worthless failures such as this Mary from Bethany. You just get rid of them, like you would an old rag." He cast an evil grin in his friend's direction. "If you know what I mean."

"In that case, I have experience making people, especially foreigners, 'disappear,' either by 'accident' or by selling them into slavery. After a night of delightful romance, of course."

"Yes, I had forgotten. I might be inclined to make use of your skills."

Mary of Bethany, bloody of face but much clearer of mind, saved him the bother. Awash in tears and pressing a scarf to her bleeding nose, she ran from her attacker, clearly recalling David's warning about Roman soldiers. She used a stream's cool waters to stop the bleeding.

Her focus was on the immediate future, and she had a plan. Experience suggested her fiancé would have imbibed a generous amount of drink over the course of the evening, and would fall asleep soon after staggering through the front door.

Since departing Massalia, her home had been an extra room at Marcus' house. Mary had agreed on the condition that there would be no intimacy, since she assumed they'd be married soon. The agreement was still intact, but hadn't stopped Marcus from implying that no such condition existed. Mary often suspected she might be the only one avoiding intimacy.

She tip-toed back to his house later that evening, and her guess was correct. As Marcus snored, Mary gathered up her few personal items, leaving behind anything Marcus had given her. She appropriated a handful of money from a table, as well as a supply of bread, dried fish, and fruit from the pantry. With a glance over her shoulder she tip-toed towards the door.

There remained the matter of Marcus' personal slave. He slept on a cot in the entry room to guard against intruders. *He thinks of me as the personal property of his master, so he won't question me. But what if I'm leaving with a travel bag?* Mary hoped he wouldn't be a problem.

To make certain, as she departed, she pressed a silver coin of Marcus' into his hand. "This is for your silence. You never saw me tonight. Do you understand?"

The slave, bewildered, stared at the coin and Mary's bloody face.

Being bribed was a new experience. He looked back at the coin, and after a minimum of thought put it into his pocket and nodded his assent. Mary nodded back, satisfied her coin was well spent.

Mary departed Massalia that same night. She was too ashamed to face Martha and Lazarus, and also worried that Marcus might search for her. Rather than stay in Massalia, she headed north towards the city of Lugdunum to seek a more anonymous future there.[1]

At the games the next day, Marcus boasted to his military colleagues about how he had just "gotten rid" of that unworthy foreigner, Mary.

Lazarus was happy to have Mary Magdalene speaking at his services. Her command of Gaulish was improved, and the new church inspired her. As much as she was enjoying this, however, she had a growing urge to get back to her own followers in Aix. She was also anxious to learn the reason for Jeanette's abrupt departure.

A few days later, Mary stood in the doorway of Lazarus' parsonage, travel bag in hand, bidding all farewell. Lazarus said, "You know how we'll miss you, Mary. Your help has been invaluable. Please, come back whenever you can."

"You know I'll try. However, my congregation is dear to me, so that's where I must be."

Mary thought of one other thing for which to thank Lazarus. "You have given me a new vision. I want to duplicate in Aix what you have accomplished here."

Chapter 36

Mary was back in her old familiar shed, focused on something she was writing. Her printing was neat but tiny, as she had only a single sheet of papyrus Lazarus had given her.

A knock at the door broke her concentration. Before she could ask "Who is it?", a familiar face peered around the door. "Hello, Mary. Oh, excuse me – you look busy."

"Jeanette! What a surprise! Come in! How has life been in Aix the last few weeks?"

"Not much has changed. I'm thrilled you're back; our congregation misses you. A friend said she thought she'd seen you, so I hoped I would find you here."

"Yes, my castle in the weeds. I plan to go into Aix tomorrow and greet my friends, but I'm delighted you stopped by today."

Jeanette gazed at the crude rock table in front of Mary. "What are you writing?"

"Oh, just putting down a few thoughts. Nothing important."

"A few thoughts? I hope you're writing your memoirs. You should, you know."

"I'm not much of a writer. It's merely a few things I'd like to remember."

"That's good, but what's that other piece of papyrus? The writing on it looks different."

"It's something very precious to me. It contains a message Jesus gave me on the evening of his last supper with his disciples."

"Really! He gave it only to you?"

"Yes."

Jeanette sensed its importance. "Does that mean you have some sort of special knowledge from Jesus, something no one else knows?"

"Not entirely. Jesus said I might convey its message to anyone who truly understands his teachings. At Peter's request, I shared it with the apostles."[1]

Mary appreciated Jeanette's curiosity, but to preclude her asking further questions she added, "I believe that someday I'll be able to share its contents with you."

Jeanette was flattered, but changed the subject to the real reason she was there. "There's something I need to tell you, as well." Her expression turned from curious to troubled.

"First, I've developed a friendship with a young man in our congregation. He's quite intelligent and polite; I think you'd like him."

"Jeanette, you hardly need my approval. I have complete faith in your good judgement. May I ask who the lucky young man is?"

"A follower of Jesus in Aix, named Eduard. He's the one who smiled at me at your talk that day. You remember, you kidded me about that. We started talking together and we began to really like each other. He's very talented; he sings, and he's teaching me to play the kithara."

"Kithara?"

"It's a Greek instrument, somewhat like a lyre. I'm not very good at it yet."

"I'm intrigued and quite eager to meet your young man."

"Yes. As you can guess, he's the reason I left Massalia. He had sent me a note indicating he might be in trouble. I apologize for leaving so suddenly."

"Trouble? I'm concerned for you, Jeanette. What trouble?"

"I'll tell you, but first there's something else I need to explain about Eduard. I'm sorry; I should have told you earlier. His name isn't really Eduard."

"Didn't you just say – I mean, what is it?"

"Dimitrios."

"Dimitrios? That sounds like something other than Gaulish."

"It is. He was born in Thessalonica, in Macedonia. He's not here in Aix because he wants to be, but because he's an escaped slave. He uses Eduard as his name to avoid being found."

"An escaped slave! That is quite remarkable!"

"Yes. His pompous Roman owner, Gavius Septavion, kidnapped him in Macedonia. Gavius was a centurion, the arrogant son of noble Romans, and commanded the occupying brigade in Thessalonica. No one had warned Dimitrios about drunken Roman soldiers. One night, on a dark street, he was abducted. His fate was to be a gift, meaning a slave, for the centurion. Gavius burned an "S" into Dimitrios' upper arm to show he was now owned by the Septavion family. The pain eventually went away, but the scar is still there. Later, Gavius was assigned to command the garrison in Massalia. During one drunken celebration, Dimitrios risked everything and made a run for his freedom. By some miracle, he wasn't captured and came here to Aix, where he thought he'd be safe. If caught, he would have been killed, of course."

"Oh, Jeanette, that's just appalling."

"Yes, and that's why Eduard never wears sleeveless garments, and why he grew that bushy beard."

"I can understand. Tell me, what is this trouble he might be in?"

"Roman soldiers have recently been seen in Aix; no one knows why. While in the city one day, Eduard overheard two men talking about the soldiers, and he thought he heard one of them mention the name 'Septavion'. Eduard thought I should know."

"No wonder you were in a hurry to get back to Aix."

"Yes. Eduard wanted to find out if the rumor about Gavius was true, and if so, should we leave Aix? Eduard felt as long as no actual search was taking place he would be safe."

"God willing. On a happier subject, I'll be in Aix for services starting tomorrow, so please join us. I'll enjoy meeting Eduard."

Mary had been preaching in Aix since her return several weeks earlier, and found it to be both satisfying and challenging to be in charge of her growing congregation. She didn't yet have a building for them as Lazarus had, and still met her followers in a field on the edge of town.

Before an appreciative crowd, Mary was finishing her weekly sermon. Today, though, something was different. In the rear of the crowd, she noticed a group of agitated men and one blond teenager huddled together, frowning and pointing in Mary's direction. She sighed. "Jeanette, I have a bad feeling we have seen those men before, and a worse feeling we may see them again before long." They both took note of the men's appearance for future reference, especially the one wearing a cloak with an unusual maroon pattern on the hood.

"I fear I must agree," replied Jeanette. "They were definitely looking at you."

"Yes, and I can guess what they want."

"So can I. Only for you to stop preaching, leave Gaul, and never come back."

Mary looked in the direction of the departing crowd.

"I will never agree to that."

CHAPTER 37

It was the same dark, smelly room as before, with the same group of scowling conspirators, and the topic of discussion had not changed. Jacques, their leader, set the tone.

"Like I predicted, the troublemaker has returned! She's nothing but a blight on the city of Aix, still trying to preach to men. Thinks she knows more than we do and mingles with the scum of the earth." He turned to the man next to him. "Claude, you said you had something to tell us?"

"Yes. Somebody had to do something besides just talk, so I followed her home the other night. She never saw me; I was too clever. She headed in the direction of that little community of disreputable women to the east. She probably lives there, or somewhere nearby."

The brawny man leaned over the table, slammed his fist on it, glared at his comrades, and roared, "Then what are we waiting for? Why are we afraid and indecisive? Talk is useless; we need to act. She must be made to shut up and leave town. Forever!"

The pudgy, squeaky-voiced merchant wanted more. "Maybe we could demand she be put in jail, have her charged with some kind of crime, and exiled from Aix or maybe all of Gaul?"

Maurice, the humorless teenager, added, "I've heard the new Roman Emperor, Caligula, hates Christians, so no local official would dare oppose our arresting her. So why not take action tonight? Let's meet here again in an hour. We can be at that village a little before midnight. She should be asleep by then, the better to surprise her."

Jacques concurred. "Yes! It's settled! Be back here in an hour. The magistrate will be pleased if we do this. Maybe I'll get a higher government position! Maybe all of you, too!

They nodded approval and poured another round of drinks, everyone except Maurice.

☙

Jeanette was in Aix, walking home at dusk after visiting friends. As she turned a corner, her thoughts were interrupted at the sight of a half dozen men departing a nearby house. The first one out looked around as if to be sure no one was watching. The last was carrying a torch which he lit as soon as he had closed the door. Jeanette retreated around the corner.

Something about the group bothered her. She scanned the group again. Then she saw it – one man wearing a cloak with a maroon pattern on the hood. *Those are the men who were at Mary's talk!* She waited until they rounded a corner, then followed them a few blocks.

"Dear God! They turned east, towards the village!"

Jeanette ran down a side road and onto a path that paralleled the main road but wasn't visible from it. She was running faster than she ever thought she could.

Mary, resting in bed and almost asleep, was jolted awake by Jeanette's frenzied shouting. "Mary! Get up! Now! A mob is coming, get dressed. Hurry!"

She leapt out of bed and looked out the one small window. She couldn't see anything out of the ordinary. "Jeanette! What's the matter?"

"Those men at your talk! I saw them, by pure chance, in Aix." She paused to catch her breath. "They're on their way here right now. One of them has a torch. I think they're planning to do something awful! Put some clothes on. You need to get away from here. Fast!"

Mary threw her robe on, grabbed her travel bag, and put the two pieces of papyrus and other important items into it. They bolted outside and ran from the shed as fast as they could.

Mary hoped Jeanette had a plan. "Where are we headed? I doubt those men know I live in the shed, but if they do, where else can we hide?"

"I suggest we head to the sisters' village," responded Jeanette.

"The village! Why? We would never be welcome there."

"I know, but the Sister Superior would have to protect us. She couldn't just sit there and let them attack us. Do you agree?"

"I worry about that. She was most emphatic we should never return to the village."

"We have to try. We only have a few minutes, and I can't think of anywhere else we could get to fast enough that would be safe."

Mary followed her to the village, hoping the Sister Superior was in a forgiving mood.

❧

They arrived at the Sister Superior's room and hastily knocked on the door. She was still working at her desk, certainly not expecting visitors at that hour. She opened the door part way, assuming it was one of the sisters. Her jaw dropped at the sight of her two banished visitors.

"You two! How dare you come here? Get out! Now!"

Jeanette, desperate, squeezed through the half open door. "Please, you must understand – a mob is coming to attack Mary. She's in danger of physical harm! You must hide us. Please!"

If the Sister Superior was sympathetic, she hid it well. "Oh, really? A danger of physical harm, I'd guess, she brought upon herself. You seem to forget you were dismissed from our company and forbidden to return. That decision was final. Get out!"

Mary sighed. *So much for a forgiving mood.*

As Jeanette desperately tried to think of somewhere else to go, a ruckus arose outside, not far away. The Sister Superior ran to a window and saw a group of men, their path illuminated by a flaming torch, approaching her office. She realized the gravity of the situation.

"Dear Lord! This is an outrage!"

She looked again at the advancing mob and turned to Mary. "All right. I have no choice." She pointed to a nearby door. "Get in that closet, both of you, and don't make a sound!"

Mary and Jeanette darted into the closet and closed the door.

A few seconds later, the men burst through the front door. The Sister's guard dog began protesting their presence at full volume in the next room. Jacques stood rigid in front of the Sister Superior's desk and, doing his best to ignore the dog's cacophony, stared down at her.

"Sister, I am a high city official from Aix. We know she's come back – you know who I mean – and we know she's somewhere around here. Something has to be done. She's a threat to the civic order of our good city, preaching in public to men and all that."

He placed his fists on her desk and leaned forward. "You must hand this criminal over to us so we can arrest her! The magistrate will be most pleased if you do."

The Sister Superior raised her eyebrows at that last statement and rose from her chair. She threw a scathing glower at Jacques and easily out-glared him.

"I have to do no such thing. I don't take orders from the likes of you! This Mary you seek was discharged from here many months ago and is no longer associated with this community in any way. I assure you, I neither know nor care where she lives now. You have no business here. What you and your undisciplined associates need to do is leave. Immediately!"

Jacques kept pressing. "You don't understand; I work for the magistrate. The magistrate himself! We want to obey his wishes. I should think you'd want to stay in his good graces too."

The Sister Superior, normally a humorless woman, suddenly broke out laughing. Poking her finger in the leader's face, she replied, "Thank you for providing me with such unintended merriment. Do you think I'm unfamiliar with the officials in Aix? Who do you think gave me money to build this village, and buy furniture for it? You wish to tell me how to please the magistrate? You idiot! The magistrate of Aix is my father!"

The men looked at each other, confused as to what to do next. Maurice glared at the Sister Superior, tight-lipped and brimming with contempt, but said nothing.

"My father and I have similar views on women preaching to men; we agree on that point. I have already acted regarding the Mary of Magdala problem and will do so again if necessary. I need no help from the likes of you. Now get out."

"Very well, we'll leave. But if you ever do see this Mary, remember, we want …"

"Out! Leave! NOW!"

The men, lacking any new strategies, reluctantly proceeded towards the door and out into the night, silent and infuriated. At the road they turned right, back towards Aix.

A few seconds later, Mary and Jeanette emerged from the closet, much relieved. "Sister, how can we ever thank you enough? You are truly a kind and considerate …"

"Don't try to flatter me. Nothing has changed. You're still unwelcome here, and I meant what I said about taking further action. I'll let you give those men five minutes' head start, and then I want you out the door and out of Aix as well. I would like to get a little sleep tonight!"

❧

Mary and Jeanette headed back into the moonless night, walking slowly along the path to the road. Jeanette, still shaken by their narrow escape, kept a tight grip on Mary's arm. "That was much too close," she said. "Those horrible men headed towards Aix, so I guess we'll be safe at the shed. At least now we know why the Sister Superior dislikes your teaching so much."

"She's doing what she believes in, and needs to maintain a good relationship with her father. We threaten that. I can understand the reasons for her displeasure."

"Mary, I've always been impressed by your ability to see things through the eyes of others. I can see why that's important."

"It's something I learned from Jesus. Even when he expressed displeasure with what others were doing, I always felt he understood why they were doing it. That was what made it possible for him to forgive them."

"I need to work on that."

Mary, however, was focused on a more urgent concern. "I never like to run from problems, but after what just happened, it's clear we both face a significant danger here. Worse, I may be placing the other Christians in Aix in danger. I could never do that."

Mary had to think only a few moments. "I need to return to Massalia. I'll put things in order here and train a successor, then rejoin Martha and Lazarus and devote myself to their church. I hope you and Eduard might come to Massalia too. I'd love for us to remain together."

"If it's true that Gavius Septavion is now in Aix, I think he will agree to go. If Massalia is to become your new home, then it will be ours too."

CHAPTER 38

Jacques, Maurice, and their fellow conspirators were back in the dingy room at the tavern, still smarting over their humiliating expulsion by the Sister Superior. Over copious glasses of cheap wine they pondered what to try next.

Jacques, not much of a strategic thinker, was at a loss for ideas. Most of the others were content to fling curse words at the Sister Superior, Mary Magdalene, and women in general.

Maurice, on the other hand, unencumbered by the side effects of mediocre wine, was never hesitant to think on a bigger scale.

"You know, we waste our time chasing this Mary all over the countryside. What we need is more influence in Aix, some position of power, so that more people will listen to us. If there were six hundred of us instead of just six, she couldn't hide; she'd have to flee the city. Perhaps we could even get her thrown in jail."

"More influence?" Jacques asked. "How? You mean like getting into politics?"

"Too slow, and people have no respect for politicians. No, what I'm thinking of is the ministry. Not Judaism, those people are too stodgy and rigid. Maybe this new group that calls themselves Christians. They seem to be growing fast and may need new leaders. Why not? I speak well, and people respect and obey priests. Once I'm ordained as a priest, it won't be long before I'm promoted. Then I'll have the power I need."

They all looked at Maurice, amazed. Claude mumbled to himself, "Is he serious? Great Jove, he has way more ambition than the rest of us."

Maurice's lips managed a rare smile, perhaps more resembling a smirk.

○.

A few days later Martha and Lazarus were spending a stormy evening at home in Massalia discussing various items of church business. Occasional bursts of lightning augmented their flickering candles, as they could not afford oil lamps.

Martha was relaying some news of interest to Lazarus. "One of our young parishioners, Gerard, said today he might like to become a priest. I imagine you inspired him. He seemed very eager, and we know several nearby towns that would like to have a priest."

Lazarus looked at his sister in surprise. "What a coincidence; then we might have two people in need of instruction. I just received a letter from a young man in Aix saying the same thing. He said a woman preacher there had motivated him to become a priest. Could he have meant Mary? He said he taught himself Latin and mentioned that he was particularly interested in learning about the social traditions, organization, and fundamental beliefs of the church."

"I suppose I could write to Mary and ask if she knows him. Do you remember his name?

"He said his name was Maurice."

○.

It had taken Mary longer than expected to complete her business in Aix, for she hadn't anticipated how many details she would have to teach those who were about to assume her duties. These included instructions on how to respond to questions about Jesus, as well as advice on how to handle sensitive political topics.

After months of training, she was standing on a windy hillside on the edge of the city, addressing her parishioners. It was a larger group than normal, but today the mood was different. Their faces were drawn, some almost in tears. Mary Magdalene was bidding them goodbye.

To Mary's left stood Isabelle, and as Mary talked she occasionally extended a hand in her direction. To her right stood one of her most earnest students, Alexander, who she felt could be relied on to convey Jesus' message accurately. At some point in the future she could ask about his interest in become a priest. For the time being, he would deliver the weekly sermons.

Mary and Isabelle both understood the necessity of this arrangement. Although Isabelle was as qualified as Alexander, Mary would never place her friend in the precarious position of trying to be a woman preacher in Aix. As Mary well knew, that was the reason she was leaving.

Isabelle had agreed and was philosophical about the situation, "Sometimes a small retreat is necessary in order to win the battle. I trust it won't be long before women are allowed to be priests and teach the words of Jesus."

When Mary was through speaking and explaining the reason for her departure, she, Isabelle, and Alexander stood together before her congregation. Mary had introduced her successors to them, and she felt confident they would be accepted and prove capable. Most of those present came forward to express their appreciation for all she had done and to wish her well. Many were in tears, as was Mary.

❧

In Massalia, however, Lazarus and Martha were happy. After months of training, they had just graduated their first class of new priests. Lazarus, in his position as Bishop of Massalia, had performed the ordinations of the two young men, and was watching them depart.

"Well, Martha, there they go. The first two new priests we have created. They both seemed very dedicated. I bid them Godspeed and wish them success in all their future evangelical endeavors."

"Where will they be going?"

"I examined all the towns in the province and found two that seemed to have good potential for increasing the number of follow-ers. In both towns that number is at present small, so the new priests shouldn't feel overwhelmed by their new responsibilities. Later, they can move to a bigger city if they'd like. I think they're both capable of doing so."

Martha agreed. "They were enthusiastic and committed, to be sure. That Maurice, though, seemed almost too serious. I can't recall him ever smiling. I wrote to Mary; she said she didn't know anyone by that name. He said he'd prefer a small town where he could gain confidence and ensure that church doctrines would be observed. He said he'd like to return to Aix someday. I only hope that in time he'll learn humility and appreciation for the views of others."

"I hope so too," said Lazarus. "He was a fast learner; he knew little about Jesus when he arrived. One thing bothered me, though. I noticed that he seemed to use the phrase 'the words of official church doctrine' as much, if not more, than he did 'the words of Jesus'. In any event, he was focused and resolute, and I would guess he'll be successful in life."

CHAPTER 39

David's commercial business had grown more profitable in the decade since he brought his friends to Gaul. This necessitated frequent trips to all parts of the Great Sea. His present voyage had taken him to Greece, to the city of Corinth, where he needed to have some halyards replaced at the boatyard where the *Ikaría* had been built.

While David waited for this to be done, he took advantage of a warm day to explore Corinth, enjoy some souvlaki, and examine the diversity of people and scenery that differentiate port cities. He had improved his knowledge of the Greek language and enjoyed roaming around Corinth more than Athens. It was smaller, cleaner, and less crowded.

As he wandered down a main street, he heard ahead of him a man's voice giving a spirited talk to a small gathering. David's knowledge of Greek was enough to identify him as a Christian preacher, as well as a person whose native tongue was likely something other than Greek. Having no pressing obligations, he joined the group.

The speaker, tall and thin, appeared to be in his late forties. By his authoritative bearing, obvious self-confidence, and the rapt attention of his audience, David surmised he was an eloquent orator. *Interesting, a Christian missionary here in Greece.* He walked over to where he could hear him better.

"Therefore, I appeal to you, my brothers, in the name of our Lord, that you all speak the same message so that there will be no divisions among you. Be united in the same mind and with the same purpose. Do not listen to false apostles. Do not let your minds be corrupted and turned away from the simplicity which is in Christ's teaching"[1]

As the missionary continued his talk, David looked at the group of men standing by him, who he assumed were his closest followers, and noticed there were no women among them. David recalled what Mary had said back in Magdala: *Anywhere in the eastern part of the Great /Sea might not be a good place for a woman to try to preach.* Maybe, he thought, not even to be a close associate.

After the preacher concluded his remarks, he spoke informally with his listeners. David waited for a pause and then asked a question of his own.

"Excuse me, but I am just starting to learn about the beliefs of those who are called Christians. I am curious. In your religion, are both men and women allowed to be priests?" David was certain he knew the answer, but he wanted to see how this missionary would respond.

The speaker retained his authoritative demeanor and gave a firm reply to David. "Women have been honored by being allowed the great privilege of bearing children, being mothers, and doing those things that are needed to make a home a proper place for a family. To men falls the responsibility of moral authority over society; of deciding right from wrong. This includes all religious teaching. Women are to be subservient to their husbands, and thus it is not their place to instruct men in moral precepts.[2] That has been the manner of civilized society for thousands of years. It remains so today, and will be so in the future. I hope that answers your question."

"Yes sir, it does. Thank you," David politely responded. Then he added, "I arrived after the start of your talk. If I may, could I ask your name? You appear to be very knowledgeable."

"My name is Paul, and I am a chosen and devoted disciple of our Lord. The risen Christ appeared to me personally on my way to Damascus to save me from my sins, and commissioned me to convey his message to Jews and Gentiles everywhere."[3]

Interesting. A conversation with this Paul might be much more interesting than dining alone tonight.

"Sir, I'm interested in what you are saying and would like to avail myself further of your knowledge about Christianity. Would it be possible for me to continue this conversation with you at supper this evening?"

Paul scrutinized David, concluding he appeared to be an intelligent and worldly person. "I enjoy the company of those who follow Jesus' teachings, if they are willing to help advance our mission by conveying those teachings to others. If you would support my evangelical efforts in this manner, you would be welcome to join us."

"It will be my pleasure to accept your offer."

❧

The supper provided for Paul and his associates was simple but adequate. There were six others at the meal, all men. They were all dedicated disciples, but not viewed by Paul as equals. David had noticed that in public Paul did all the talking and answered all questions. His manner of speaking radiated both insight and confidence, and his followers gave him due deference.

David wasted no time in resuming the earlier conversation. "I've heard there are numerous Christian disciples speaking in many lands about Jesus. Who decides what they will say?" Again, David was certain Mary had already provided him with the answer, but as with his earlier inquiry he was curious to hear Paul's response.

"The words I speak are words given me by God. There needs to be one person who makes any decisions needed, and who all agree is the earthly, temporal leader of the church. That person is the Apostle Peter. He is presently in Rome."

"Rome! Isn't that a dangerous place for him to be?"

"It certainly was when the madman Caligula was emperor, but we all go where God instructs us to go, in order to carry out His message. We will continue do so, and He will continue to protect us, so long as it is His will."

"I gather you travel a great deal. Where are you from, and what brings you to Greece?"

"I was born in Tarsus. After the risen Christ empowered me to spread his word to the world, it was clear I must travel widely. These are my associates in Christ who are with me on this trip. Next to you are Silas and Timothy, two of my most devoted disciples. Beside me are Tertius and Luke, who serve as my scribes. Luke is compiling a record of my current journey."[4]

David nodded to each disciple. They in turn viewed him intently but said nothing.

Paul paused to take a drink, and then continued. "This is my second extensive journey. On this voyage, I have already been to Antioch, Lystra, Troas, Neapolis, Philippi, Thessalonica, Athens, and many other cities, always preaching the word of God.[5] Sometimes we are well-received, sometimes we are thrown into prison."

David marveled at the matter-of-fact way Paul said the last part of that sentence.

"This trip is nearing its end; Corinth is the last city I will visit. Our followers here seem unsure what to believe or how to behave. I must prepare a letter to them providing guidance and reassurance. I may have to do something similar for our friends in Thessalonica, and maybe for the Galatians too. Now, however, it is time for me to return to Judea. I need to convey to my colleagues what I have learned on this trip and begin preparations for my next journey."

David's eyes lit up as he recognized a possible opportunity to spend much more time with Paul. "If I may ask, what arrangements do you have for returning to Judea?"

"I am usually able to find a believer in Jesus who has a suitable vessel I can utilize for my travels. God always provides for me."

"Perhaps He has again. I am a sea captain myself by trade, and have a most reliable ship in which I will be returning to Caesarea in a few days. Might you be interested in sailing with me? I'd be happy to offer you and your friends a safe passage at no charge. I need only to make a stop in Ephesus to deliver some goods."

"As I said, God has always provided. Your offer is most welcome and agreeable. I have followers in Ephesus that I would be happy to meet with while you are there."

"Then it's settled. I expect to depart Corinth in about two days."

The conversation continued for a while, with other topics relating to the teachings of Jesus being deliberated. Since David could contribute little to these discussions, he bid goodnight to his new acquaintances and headed towards the door to commence his walk back to the *Ikaría*.

After only a few steps, though, he was intercepted by the young scribe Luke, who indicated he would like a word with him.

"I sense, David, that you are a man who travels a great deal and might talk with many people about your visit here with the Apostle Paul. Therefore, I feel I should tell you more about this extraordinary man. He noted that the risen Christ appeared to him to save him from his sins, but he did not tell you how terrible were those sins. Under his prior name of Saul of Tarsus, he was not just a common sinner, but was in fact himself a zealous persecutor of the early Christians. He even participated in the execution of the Christian martyr, Stephen."[6]

"Thus, the reason for his conversion by our risen Savior was as a symbol that even the worst sinners can be saved if they devote themselves to the work of the Lord. For this reason, many consider Paul second only to Peter within the Church. Paul feels, and I agree, that he has worked harder to spread the words of Jesus than any other apostle.[7] I hope you will remember this when you talk to others about what has happened since the time of Jesus' crucifixion."

David was amazed by what he had just heard, and could only say, "I thank you, Luke, for telling me this. I assure you I'll not forget it, and will convey your words to others as well."

PART TWO: GAUL

Their trip back to Palestine was uneventful, and in a few days David's ship was safely berthed in the Caesarea harbor. Now that he was on land, his thoughts turned to his sister.

Over the years, David had often recalled the joy in Rachel's eyes each time he arrived to visit, how she enjoyed the treats he would bring, and how she went out of her way to cook for him. Each time he assured her he would return as soon as possible. But if a remunerative business opportunity presented itself, the business venture won out. With only rare exceptions, the assurances went unfulfilled.

Once David had his business matters in Caesarea completed, he arranged with a merchant for transportation and headed eastward for a long-delayed visit with his sister.

Chapter 40

His trips to Magdala were as close as David ever got to reuniting with what remained of his family. He had decided years ago that a sea captain would make a poor husband and an even worse absentee father. As a result, he never married. He loved the challenges of the sea and was an expert at meeting them. Even more, he loved the profit they provided. There had also been a few short-term romances in ports far from Galilee. No one in Magdala ever knew of these, as he valued both professional discretion and his niece's doting image of him.

He also hoped to see someone in Magdala other than Rachel. On his sporadic visits, he often encountered Sarah at the well. They were just friends, as Sarah was married. On his last visit to Magdala, however, he learned that Sarah was now a widow, and thought he might like to become closer to her. It had been years, though, since he had last seen her.

His infrequent visits notwithstanding, David called Magdala home. Rachel's humble house was smaller than David would have liked, but she was happy there and rejected his repeated offers to move her to larger accommodations.

As David approached the house, he smiled at her small but diverse vegetable garden and the now mature olive tree in the yard. Like Mary, David had enjoyed watching it grow. It was the most prized bit of greenery in the neighborhood.

Rachel was overjoyed at seeing her brother. She was now in her sixties and her pace had slowed but her health remained good. They were outside enjoying the sun and a late breakfast.

"You cannot imagine what a pleasure it is to have a few days off, Rachel. Coming here is my only form of vacation."

"David, you know that your every visit is the highlight of the year for me. What other excitement do I have to look forward to?"

"I apologize for coming so seldom. The problem is I have many regular customers who expect me to deliver goods whenever they want. Their business is profitable, and if I want to keep it, I must sail at their demand. After all, there are many other ships they could use." He lifted a small pastry with honey that Rachel had made for him.

As soon as his chewing permitted, he continued. "On top of that, I have a contract now to deliver official documents and letters from city to city, and even transport a few arrogant Roman officials on occasion. That meant adding a stateroom on the main deck, but it provides a good, steady income. Roman officials, as you might guess, can afford an overpriced stateroom."

"So, you deliver letters. I wondered how letters got delivered – it's you! When you get a letter to a city, what happens then? How does it get to the proper person?"

"Ah, a good question, Rachel. In many cities there are couriers that wait for ships to come in and make their living delivering letters and documents. I thought, 'Why take a chance on them?' So I select one of my crew members as the courier for the letters and documents the *Ikaría* carries. This assignment is highly prized, as the courier keeps half the delivery fees."

"You *are* busy. There's no need to apologize for not getting to Magdala more often, David, I understand how demanding being the captain of a ship must be."

"My sailing schedule is tight, but that's a poor excuse. In the future I'll try harder."

Feeling uncomfortable about his chances of fulfilling that promise, he changed the subject. "I do worry about you, Rachel, living here by yourself. You seem in good health, but what if something should happen? Do you have friends who could assist you?"

"Oh, yes. I go to the synagogue every Sabbath and have friends there. Sarah would be happy to assist me if necessary. I'm quite comfortable here. You needn't worry about me."

David was relieved and hoped she wasn't glossing over anything. She looked healthy and in good spirits, and that relieved his sense of guilt a little.

Perhaps more eagerly than intended, he asked "How is Sarah doing? Fine, I trust."

"Yes, fine. You know, I might need you to bring me more water from the well," Rachel said with a knowing smile.

An even bigger smile crossed David's face. "Speaking of bringing, you know I always enjoy finding a few things for you. In Greece, I found some fine olive oil, delicious apples and figs, and different kinds of dried fish. And of course a few sweets as well. Enjoy!"

"David, you're so good to me. Thank you for remembering what kind of treats I like. My own memory has slowed down, I fear."

He laughed. "I assure you, you're in good company."

She gave David an impish smile. "The only way you could be nicer to me would be to have Mary with you on one of your trips here."

David sighed. "That would be a little harder. As far as I know, Mary is still in Gaul, but I regret to say that I have had no contact with her since I dropped her off there years ago. The port of Massalia isn't on my normal routes."

"Tell your captain to give you more time off! He sounds like a shamefully mean man."

David jested back, "Only when he fails to visit his sister. Other than that, he's fairly nice." Then, more seriously, "I could reduce my schedule a bit. I promise I'll make every effort to get here more often." He dropped his eyes, recalling it had been years since his last visit.

Rachel's face showed no emotion, but her thoughts did. *Oh dear.*

That's almost the same thing Mary said when she departed for Gaul. And I've not seen her again. Please, let it not be the same with David.

"I know you will, David, I know you will."

In a small town not far from Massalia, a village priest was saying farewell to his parishioners after completing his last service there. To the side, others were critiquing his tenure. "I hope we'll receive a new priest before long. Father Maurice was a good speaker, but he was hard to get to know. Did you notice how seldom he smiled? He seemed distant and not inclined to mix much with his congregation."

"I know," said his friend. "I never understood why he insisted all the women sit in the back of the church. What would be wrong if they sat with their husbands?"

"I never understood that either. It seemed strange. He just said 'It's a requirement of the church.' I hope his replacement will be more sociable."

As Maurice was walking back to his cottage, on this day at least there was a hint of a smile on his face. *Well done. My apprenticeship in this boring little backwater is completed, and now I go to a larger city. A few years to get established there, and I'll return to Aix. Then we shall see what manner of higher position and greater influence I might be able to obtain!*

CHAPTER 41

The initial Christian church in Massalia, under the care and direction of Lazarus and Martha, had grown with time and prospered. Mary was comfortable teaching there, and Jeanette and Eduard, now married, were happy to be full-time workers there as well.

Neither Jeanette nor Eduard had any reason to be other than cheerful as they left the church one autumn day to visit the nearby market. They could not have heard about a military deployment made a few weeks earlier, one reassigning a company of Roman soldiers to a tour of duty in Massalia. Nor could they have known that the new commanding officer of the company was none other than the widely known and feared centurion, Gavius Septavion.

Worse, Eduard could never have guessed that Gavius Septavion, accompanied by his personal slave, would choose that day to visit a store in that same market where the finest wines could be procured by the rich to impress their friends. Nor could Eduard have anticipated that the centurion had a good memory, and as he emerged from the store would pause because he thought he saw something familiar about the man, despite his sprawling beard, who was entering the produce market next door with a woman.

Gavius suspected the young man bore a strong resemblance to his former slave, the one who had committed the capital offense of deserting him a decade earlier. There is no forgetting or forgiving a crime such as that. Gavius decided to accost the stranger to satisfy his curiosity. As Eduard spun around to see who had grabbed his shoulder, the centurion bellowed, "It is! It is you, the cowardly deserter Dimitrios!" With one swing of his muscular arm he ripped the sleeve off Eduard's tunic, revealing the telltale "S."

Gavius pointed a finger at Jeanette, which his slave knew was an order to seize her. He then drew his sword and pointed it, not at Eduard, but at Jeanette. With a menacing snarl he gave Eduard his ultimatum: "Surrender yourself to me this instant, craven traitor, to receive your just punishment. Your woman, too. She is a mere commoner but looks intelligent and will make a passable household servant. Resist, and you will watch your lady bleed to death!"

Eduard put his left arm up in the air as if to surrender, but his concealed right hand had already grasped the short dagger he kept hidden in a pocket for just such an emergency. With a sudden spin of his body he thrust the dagger into the wrist of Gavius' sword-wielding arm in an attempt to disarm him. His aim was true, but Gavius was able to grab the falling sword with his other arm. With the roar of a wounded lion, he plunged it deep into Eduard's torso.

Jeanette's horrified scream was the only sound as Eduard intentionally staggered one step forward, knowing that his small dagger could never penetrate Gavius' thick breastplate. His goal was to get close enough to the wild-eyed but triumphant centurion so that with his last reserve of energy he could slash his dagger diagonally across his adversary's neck. This he did with a vengeance, achieving his goal of severing Gavius' carotid artery. Both bleeding men slumped to the ground, each knowing his fate was sealed and irreversible.

With his next-to-last breath, Eduard gasped, "Run, slave, you're free now!" The slave, noting the state of his now immobile and terrorized owner, had already released his grip on Jeanette and was headed full speed for the docks.

Eduard's last breath was a quiet, "Jeanette, I will always love you."

Jeanette, overcome with shock, horror, and anguish, forced herself to neither faint nor scream, but instead ran as fast as trembling legs would permit to seek the help of her friends.

☙

Martha, Lazarus, and Jeanette, making no effort to stem the flow of tears but unable to utter any manner of words, transported the shrouded Eduard back to the church in the only conveyance available, a garden cart.

Bad news travels fast, terrible news even faster. Within an hour a host of church members were excavating a gravesite in the backyard of the church, since no money was available for a formal tomb. Following the most emotional funeral service that Lazarus ever had the onerous duty to perform, a large rock was maneuvered over the grave which would bear the simple wording, carved by an artistic parishioner, "Dimitrios of Macedonia, honored by all, gave his life for those he loved."

Through her tears, Jeanette held her head high and said, "My loss can never be replaced, but my future is now clear. I will devote my life to our church, to Mary, and to the message she has committed to proclaim."

CHAPTER 42

At the busy harbor in Caesarea a gray-haired man with weathered hands and wrinkled face stood on one of the docks, in serious conversation with a younger man. The older man was David, now past eighty. His sailing days had ended; his eyes were no longer sharp, his arms not so strong, his memory not as keen. In his prime he could memorize every item of cargo he had on any sail, but no longer. His journey to Gaul with his niece and his chance meeting with the Apostle Paul so long ago were distant memories.

The man he was talking to, a friend of long standing, was in the process of buying his boat. With a heavy heart, David handed the other man a set of formal transfer papers, and a letter of introduction. "Well, Simon, I believe everything is completed. The *Ikaría* is now yours."

"Thank you, David. I know you hate to give her up." He thought he could almost see a tear in David's eye.

"I'm getting a little old to be a boat captain. The *Ikaría* is a sturdy ship and has taken me safely all around the Great Sea for over fifty years. If you treat her well, she'll treat you well."

"Oh, I know she's an excellent ship; I'm delighted to have her. That's why I let you overcharge me." He laughed. "Rest assured, I'll take good care of her."

"I know you will, Simon. I would never have sold it to you otherwise."

"What about you, David? What are your plans now? You look too old to be chasing women, but still young enough to enjoy a good bottle of wine."

David laughed, then turned serious. "I have some business matters to conclude. Then I intend to re-connect with my family. I am guilty of ignoring them far too long."

He paused for a second and then concluded, "There are two people who are special to me that I need to find. My sister lives in Magdala. Sadly, I haven't visited her for many years. I've heard rumors of an insurrection there, and I worry about her safety."

David cursed the fact that he had not kept his promise to Rachel. In truth, he had only seen her a few times since the visit at the end of his sail with Paul, and not at all in the last several years. He slowly shook his head and looked downward. *You've always considered yourself an honorable man. Maybe you've forgotten that honorable men keep their promises. And now there's been fighting there!* He swore he would get to Magdala as fast as he could and had already arranged with a local merchant for a ride from Caesarea to Tiberias.

To add to his feelings of guilt, there was also his niece, the only other person he truly loved. He couldn't escape the reality that he had no idea where Mary might be, nor in what condition.

Chapter 43

In the lives of those people who were special to David, some forty years had passed since he conveyed Mary and her friends to the coast of Gaul. He had seen none of them since.

For Mary Magdalene, those years had passed quickly. Now well into her seventies, she had found a safe haven in Massalia. Mary still felt well in general and continued to preach every week, but had less energy and more of the memory problems that speak to one's age. She was also bothered by occasional coughing spells.

Since Lazarus was the head of the church in Massalia, Mary's right to teach had not been an issue. In such a large city, with bustling commerce and copious taxes to collect, the town fathers had more lucrative matters to attend to than a woman preacher. As for the local Roman overseers, so long as their generous share of the taxes arrived regularly, they could ignore a minor new religion. Even the Emperor Nero, prior to his suicide in 68 c.e., paid little attention to southern Gaul. His main problems lay further north.

The summer of 70 c.e. was drawing to an end. In the years since Mary's return, Lazarus' church had enjoyed impressive growth, and Bernard's old house had been replaced with a larger building. Whole families now attended the services, and Mary's greatest joy was teaching the children. Like David, Mary had seen her hair turn gray, but she still retained her pleasant, soft-spoken manner which reflected the love, admiration and respect the parishioners felt for her.

Lazarus, in his late sixties, had remained devoted to his church and growing congregation. His confidence and eloquence had grown in like measure. He had never married; the church was his life. Martha and Jeanette, as promised, had found their calling there as well.

The immigrants from Palestine were happier than they might have been if news from distant lands wasn't so slow in reaching Gaul. They had heard nothing yet of the Jewish uprising in Palestine, nor of the disastrous fighting that had recently occurred in Galilee and Jerusalem.

Martha and Lazarus still had not heard from Mary of Bethany, and efforts to find her in Massalia had been unproductive. They worried she had gone to some distant land with her arrogant centurion. Many a restless night they lay awake, wondering if she were even alive.

☙

Following a weekly service, Mary was chatting with some of the worshipers. When they departed, two women who had been waiting approached Mary with broad smiles and enthusiastic greetings. At first glance, Mary did not recognize them.

"Mary! I am Sister Isabelle, from Aix. Do you remember me?"

"Isabelle! Of course I remember you. How could I forget? You enabled me to begin teaching about Jesus and took charge of our little congregation when I left. How wonderful to see you again! What brings you to Massalia?"

Pointing to her companion, she replied, "My friend, Hélène, is visiting relatives, and I just had to come with her to see if we could find you. I'm overjoyed to have succeeded!"

Hélène added, "Sister Isabelle said such wonderful things about you that I felt I had to attend the service today and meet you. Everyone at our church remembers you and admires you so much. I think of you as my friend, too, even though I've never met you."

Isabelle touched Mary's arm. "Hélène is right, all our friends in Aix feel the same. Because of their great respect for you, I wonder if I might ask an immense favor? Could you come to Aix and talk at our church once more? Those terrible men who opposed you are no longer there. The younger people in the church only know you as a name, or maybe more like a legend. They would be thrilled and fascinated to have you visit them."

Mary laughed. "I appreciate your compliments, but I doubt I've been dead long enough to be a legend!"

As they all laughed, Mary thought about Isabelle's offer. "You know, it would be nice to pay a short visit and see old friends again. I'll consider your kind invitation."

After further reminiscing, Mary rejoined her friends.

"Jeanette, that was Isabelle, from our church in Aix. They want me to visit them and speak to the congregation there. I think I might like that."

Martha, however, had concerns. "That would be wonderful, but you know you lack the strength you once enjoyed. Are you sure you're capable of such an arduous trip?"

"Oh yes. Many wagons daily go to Aix; I wouldn't have to walk much. I'll be fine." A cough escaped her lips. She had tried to keep her coughing to herself but others had noticed.

"You are right that I am not so young anymore, and some days I tire easily." She looked at Martha. "Perhaps I should think about turning my duties here at the church over to someone younger, someone with more energy."

"No, no, Mary, you do just fine. Besides, who would replace you?"

"That's easy. Lazarus would deliver the sermons, and Jeanette can do everything else I do. I have no doubt Jeanette can carry out my responsibilities admirably."

Jeanette protested as well. "Mary, you have many years of ministry left in you, and everyone here loves you. There's no need to replace you. If you really want to go to Aix, I'll contact someone there you can stay with."

"You don't have to trouble anyone in Aix. If my comfortable old shed is still available, it will do fine."

Martha raised an eyebrow, wondering if she was joking. "Mary, that's absurd. You're famous and no longer a young woman! You deserve better than a dilapidated shed, which might not even be there. In addition, you'd have to walk an hour each way to church!"

"Thank you for your concern, but you needn't impose on anyone. A manger was adequate for Jesus. He walked everywhere; I can too. The weather's still warm. When I was with Jesus, many nights we slept under the stars. The shed would be almost a luxury."

Resisting the urge to remind her that Jesus wasn't seventy, Lazarus replied, "As always, Mary will do it her way. You know we will support whatever you wish to do, and God will be with you. I agree that Jeanette can carry out your duties here most ably."

Jeanette turned to Mary and added, "Mary, if you're going to Aix, I'll go with you. First, we need to be sure the shed is still there and make other plans if it isn't. If you're determined to sleep there, I'll make you a much better bed. I insist on going with you to help you get settled."

She thought about it some more. "Also, since local attitudes are slow to change, I'll visit you often. There could be a new group of people in Aix who might see you as a threat."

CHAPTER 44

As David headed east from Caesarea, he wished he had heard of the fighting in Galilee sooner. Other ship captains had told him of the Jewish uprising, but they had no details. He forced himself to believe that Rachel was safe and refused to even think about the worst case.

There was little evidence of the uprising in Caesarea. It was an important seaport, so a Roman military garrison was there, and the busy city wasn't a center of Jewish unrest.

As the merchant's wagon moved east across the upland plateau, David's optimism left him unprepared for the scene he encountered. There was heavy destruction in Nazareth, and David estimated half the houses were damaged or destroyed. As they descended toward the Sea of Galilee, the carnage grew worse. The town of Arbela, just a few miles from Magdala, lay in total ruins. All structures had been leveled, some appearing intentionally burned. There was no sign of life. His worst nightmare was becoming reality.

At least he was mentally steeled for whatever he might find in Magdala, and it was necessary. The center of Magdala had likewise been destroyed, including its iconic tower. The fighting here had been merciless, and almost no people were visible. Of more concern, the small villages on the southern outskirts of Magdala, similar to those farther north where Rachel lived, also lay in ruins. He searched his agitated brain for an optimistic thought. *Perhaps the razed villages I just passed through resulted from this being the route the Roman forces used to approach the center of Magdala. Perhaps the more outlying villages were spared.*

He knew full well that what follows the word *perhaps* might differ from reality.

He walked eastward to the Sea of Galilee. The waters were calm and small waves lapped gently along the shore. He took a few steps into the cool water. The quiet sea below and azure sky above briefly comforted him.

The sea, however, was too quiet. Although fishing boats rested along the shore, there were no fishermen. Not along the shore, not on the sea. The ruined city behind him returned to his mind's eye, and he retraced his steps back to Magdala's reality.

David gave the wagon driver another coin to take him the two miles to Rachel's village. Along the way, he examined every clump of bushes for damage that might have been caused by marching troops. His spirits were boosted as he detected none.

As the wagon crested the final ridgeline, David threw his arms high and gave thanks to every deity he could think of. The village homes were still standing.

Although it had been years since his last visit, David had no trouble finding his sister's house, which looked little changed. The path still led to the well, and sheep still looked for a few blades of grass in the courtyard. There were also differences. The flower garden seemed smaller, and where were the vegetables? Rachel loved vegetables. As he got closer, he observed attractive new curtains on the windows. *That seems odd. How could Rachel afford those?*

There was one major difference – the beloved olive tree was gone. Had it died, or been used for firewood? The missing olive tree not only saddened him, it seemed a premonition.

David approached the door, hesitated a moment, and knocked. After what seemed an eternity the door opened and an elderly woman peered cautiously around it.

It wasn't Rachel. He had never seen this person before, and the woman likewise didn't recognize David. She squinted at him through the half-opened door, and in a gravelly voice asked, "Who are you? What do you want here?"

"I apologize for bothering you. I am seeking my sister, named Rachel. Is she here?"

"There is no Rachel here." She started to shut the door, then paused. "Wait … that may have been the name of the woman who used to live here. She died a few years ago, I think, before the fighting started. I'm sorry if you hadn't heard. We own the house now."

David stared at her, mouth agape, stunned. Had he misheard what she said? *Died? Died!*

"Oh, I – I see. I didn't know. I'm sorry to have bothered you. Good day."

He started down the path, his mind a confused muddle, but still alert enough to turn and ask, "Wait, would you happen to know where she was buried?"

"No, sorry. Maybe in Tiberias someone would know. They keep records there."

"Thank you. I'll inquire there."

David, still stunned, turned, and walked down the path in a trance. He shook his head, half despondent, half furious at himself. *You selfish fool! You could have come to Magdala more often, and you know it. So, my punishment is that I will never see my sister again. Such a penance is what I deserve, but not what Rachel deserved.*

He soon realized that feeling sorry for himself, or Rachel, wouldn't help anything. He began to focus on the challenges at hand and had no trouble establishing his priorities. *Now I must do whatever is necessary to find Mary, no matter how difficult.*

First, however, he needed information about Rachel. He thought of looking for Sarah, who might know something, but he was so depressed and saddened that he just wanted to get out of Magdala and go where he was most likely to obtain information about his sister's burial. He gave his wagon driver another coin for the trip to Tiberias.

The growing congregation of Christians in Aix had acquired a church building too. It was smaller than Lazarus' church in Massalia, but the congregation was equally dedicated. They had been able to afford floor-length curtains and comfortable chairs instead of benches. Isabelle had realized the need to utilize only male preachers and had continued that practice. The desired result had been achieved; there had been no further attacks by outraged townsmen.

Being back in Aix, even if only for a brief visit, had energized Mary, and she was delighted with their new church building. Isabelle had urged her parishioners to spread the word to followers around the city that the speaker next Sunday would be none other than Mary Magdalene herself.

They had done so with enthusiasm, and as a result the church was packed, with more sitting on the ground outside. The windows and door were open to help them hear. Following a glowing introduction by Isabelle, Mary began speaking to the fascinated gathering with an authoritative, confident voice, one that could now converse in almost fluent Gaulish.

"… now you understand why I had to leave Aix so abruptly. Again, I apologize. It wasn't my choice. But today, I wish to talk about the present, not the past. Today is special, for it has now been forty years since our Savior's death. The events of the crucifixion are well known, but the resurrection is the real reason we are here."

While Mary talked, an imposing, serious-looking man wearing liturgical robes was seated in a place of prominence on the side. The robe was impressive, made of fine silk with elaborate gold and royal purple embroidering. Around his neck hung a finely crafted cross. He was the Bishop of Aix. He was slim and of serious demeanor. His hair was graying, but some of its original blond color was still visible. His dark eyebrows gave his face a striking appearance that commanded attention. His name was Maurice. Although Mary had seen this man before, it was far in the past and in a different context. Now he was universally addressed as Your Eminence, the Bishop of Aix. His narrowed eyes reflected displeasure, but he remained silent.

Mary could not help but notice him, and guessed he might be the bishop for the Aix region. She wondered if she should introduce herself after the service, and decided she might if he lingered a while.

Another man was seated beside him. This second man was elderly, with a flowing white beard. He had more the appearance of a scholar, and every so often would make a note of something. Both men showed an interest in Mary and what she was saying about her history with Jesus. On occasion they would exchange glances, but said nothing.

◦.

David had arrived in Tiberias, whose buildings weren't very impressive for a new regional capital. He noted there was no evidence of fighting there. "Roman administrative center," he mumbled. "No doubt hundreds of troops were stationed here." He regained his focus on where Rachel might be buried and realized he needed help. He approached a man wearing a plain brown robe, perhaps a priest, who was about to enter a nearby Christian church.

"Excuse me sir, but I'm hopeful you can help me, as I'm not familiar with Tiberias. I would like to learn where my sister, who lived in Magdala, might be buried."

"God extends his blessings to you, sir. I am a priest at this church. Are you yourself a Christian, by any chance?"

David paused for a second, somewhat taken aback. "Do you know, I believe you're the first person who ever asked me that."

He had to think for a moment before responding. "Based on my experiences with my niece, who traveled with Jesus in Galilee, yes, I believe I am."

"Then you must be as fascinated as we are about the new writings," replied the priest.

"What writings are those? I'm not familiar with church documents."

The priest could barely contain his excitement. "Why, the new gospel about Jesus, by a disciple named Mark. It's unfortunate it took so long for someone to write it. We recently received a copy here, and the scroll is kept at our church. It tells all about Jesus' life, his disciples, even about his crucifixion."

"Really! His disciples?"

"Yes. The scroll is right inside. It was written in Greek. If you know Greek you should be able to read it. Would you like to see it?"

"You know, I believe I would! Very much! I do know a little Greek."

David followed the priest into the church with great anticipation, not minding at all this temporary diversion from his main task in Tiberias.

Chapter 45

Time stood still as David, completely engrossed, spent hours studying Mark's history of Jesus. He had obtained papyrus from the priest, and was copying down the most pertinent passages. His whole face was a smile as he stood up and stretched, unable to believe his good fortune and the wonderful news he had for Mary.

As he reached the door, however, David heard the priest say something that stopped him in his tracks: "Can you help me here for a minute, Phlegian?"

Phlegian! That was a name David had not thought about, nor wanted to think about, for the past forty years. "It couldn't possibly be the same Phlegian," he assured himself. Still, he was in Tiberias, and Phlegian was not a common name.

He stopped and looked back into the church. In a few seconds, a stooped, aged man, his thin face a bag of wrinkles, entered the room where the priest was working. This person was not the pudgy Phlegian David remembered; this man was thin, hunched, and gaunt. *I'm sure the name's just a coincidence.*

David was about to turn and leave, when he realized he had only seen a side view of the man's face in dim light. Curiosity drove him back to the door of the room. He addressed the priest, feigning forgetfulness. "Excuse me, but did I leave a letter in here?"

Both men paused and looked at David as he spoke. The face of the stooped man was slimmer, discolored, and wrinkled, but contained the same round eyes and bore the same simple and uncomprehending expression.

I cannot believe it! It is Phlegian!

David ignored the priest's response, "I don't see a letter here," and stared at the other man. After a few seconds of thought, he addressed him.

"Excuse me, but you look familiar. By any chance, many years ago, did you ever work for the regional procurator?"

Phlegian was delighted at this modicum of recognition. "Yes indeed, I did," he replied with a silly self-congratulatory smile, not recognizing this gray-haired old man standing before him, much less the unfortunate circumstances involved.

"And did you ever know a man named Erascus?" David pursued, not smiling at all.

The happy grin on Phlegian's face was transformed into a contortion of frightened anxiety, bordering on outright panic.

"Uh ... maybe. Why do you ask?"

David decided not to be confrontational, at least not right now. After all, almost forty years had passed, Phlegian hadn't instigated the attack, and they were in a church.

"You might not remember me. My name is David. We may have met once before, in Magdala. Two men named Erascus and Phlegian were making false statements about a fine Christian woman named Mary. Do you recall that?"

Phlegian's face was now pure terror. He moved closer to the priest, as though to use him as a shield. His foggy memory had no difficulty recalling the fist.

"No ... please, let me explain. I'm not like that anymore. What I mean is ..."

To David's surprise the priest sprang to Phlegian's defense. "I have no idea what took place many years ago, but I can tell you that this man has worked here as our custodian for several decades now, and I assure you he has been a faithful and responsible helper for us."

The priest looked at his janitor. "I think I remember you talking about a man named Erascus when you first arrived here. I've forgotten the details, though, so please, tell both of us about your past, and how you happened to wind up almost dead on our church steps." He pointed to a chair. "You may sit down."

David was more than a little skeptical, but quite curious as well. "All right, go ahead. Tell us your story."

Phlegian sat down, never taking his eyes off David, and began his story.

"Yes, I could hardly forget David. He beat me up pretty good back there in Magdala. You know what? I deserved it. Erascus insisted that anywhere we traveled in Galilee, we should tell everyone about a prostitute named Mary of Magdala. I never figured out why this was so important to him. Maybe he wanted revenge, or wanted to blame all our troubles on this Mary. I thought it was funny at the time. I know, I've never been very bright."

David interjected, "What you couldn't have known on that day was that I happen to be Mary's uncle. Just so you know why I became annoyed."

Phlegian blanched at learning this and moved closer to the priest. "Oh, I'm truly sorry, sir. You see, I'm not that person anymore. Please, let me tell you what happened next."

David was still skeptical. "I'm listening. What happened next?"

"After you left us lying on the ground, when we were sure you were gone, we got up, and as soon as we got our mouths to stop bleeding, we went back to Tiberias. We had to report to our superior, even though we looked a mess. Naturally, he wanted to know what happened, why we were all bloody. I looked at Erascus. I always let him explain the problems we got into because, you know, I don't talk so good."

"I couldn't believe what happened next. I always thought Erascus was my friend. Partners, you might say, who would help each other. Hah! He looked straight at the procurator and said, 'I'm terribly sorry, your honor, but we did get into a bit of trouble. It was all Phlegian's fault. You see, Phlegian likes to go around telling people about this prostitute we met named Mary, who lived there. I never understood why. I tried to stop him, but he kept doing it. So today the man we were talking to seemed to know this harlot Mary and got real mad and starting hitting us. As soon as he left, we hurried right back here'. That's what he said!"

Phlegian looked almost deserving of sympathy as he continued. "How could he say that? It was always Erascus who started it. I tried to think of something to say, but before I could the procurator fired me on the spot. Said I embarrassed him once too often. I thought Erascus might help me, you know, ask him not to take away my job or something, but you know what he did? He said to the procurator, 'Good riddance to that imbecile'. That's exactly what he said!"

At this point David was starting to feel sorry for him. At the least, he was eager to hear the rest of the story.

"I mean, he threw me to the lions, just to save his own skin. I never thought he'd do that."

"Sadly, some people are like that," David said. "What did you do next?"

"Do? What could I do? I have no education, no skills, no friends or relatives in the area. I had no money, no home, no nothing. I tried to find food in trash piles. I went around looking for garbage outside rich people's homes in the middle of the night. You remember how fat I was? That went away fast. I got weak, probably sick with something. I'd pass out a lot. I tried begging, but I learned real quick people just ignore beggars. Especially filthy ones. I thought pretty soon I'd be dead, but I figured, what difference did it make? I had no future anyway."

"What happened then?" David couldn't believe it, but he was on Phlegian's side.

"All I know is, one day I passed out again, from hunger maybe. I had no idea where I was, but it must have been near the old church that used to be here. When I woke up, a priest was giving me water. When he saw me open my eyes, he asked how I was. I think I said, 'You should have just let me die.' Why should I care? What did I have to live for?"

"But the priest, this man here, said, 'You're still alive, my brother, so God didn't want to see you just yet. Maybe the Lord wants to give you another chance.' I thought, who, me?"

"I said something like, 'A chance for what? I'm starving. I'd be willing to work, but I've got no education, no skills. I don't know how to do nothing. Nobody's going to give me a job. That means no food. If this Lord you talk about wants to give me a chance, he can give me a job. Or some food. Maybe just more brains.' I didn't think there was any hope."

"Then the priest said, 'You know what, we need a janitor to help clean up around here. If you would be willing to do that, you can sleep here and we can give you something to eat. You see, maybe God is willing to give you both a chance and some food.' "

"I didn't understand why he'd do that for a lice-infested nobody like me. At least I was smart enough to say, 'All right, I can help clean up if you'd like'. I felt a little bit of hope."

The priest, fascinated by his story, explained, "I helped you because Jesus said, 'In as much as you have done it unto one of the least of these, you have done it unto me.' "

Phlegian added, "I've been here ever since. They treat me good. Now I understand a little what this Jesus was talking about."

The priest added, "This reminds me of Saul, a terrible sinner, but he became the apostle Paul after the Savior forgave him. If a person like Saul can be forgiven, so can Phlegian."

David's mouth was open, but he couldn't believe the words that were coming out. "In that case, I guess I can forgive you too. What happened was a long time ago." With a self-conscious smile he added, "I probably hit you a little harder than I needed to."

Then another thought occurred to David. "Your story is interesting, but only one side of the coin. Do you know what happened to Erascus?"

"Yes. That miserable backstabber just got worse and worse. One day, the procurator caught him stealing tax money. That was it for Erascus. The procurator had him jailed, and he got sentenced to a hard labor camp for the rest of his life. I saw one of those camps once. They're worse than horrible. They whip you and everything. You don't expect to live very long there."

With an almost expressionless face, he concluded, "Who cares? I say good riddance to that worthless troublemaker. He was no friend of mine."

David nodded his head but said nothing. The priest did not need to know how delighted he was at what Phlegian had just said.

David rose from his seat. "Thank you, Phlegian, for sharing your story. I'm happy you found the Church here and have a new life. It appears that Jesus came into your life, too."

"Is that possible? I mean, for a stupid, worthless person like me?"

"Maybe God didn't think of you as worthless," said the priest.

"I agree," David added. "If Jesus can convert Saul, he can convert Phlegian. It seems that sometimes this happens quickly, as with Saul and my niece, Mary, and other times he comes to you slowly, over a long period of time, as with me and now you."

The priest thought about how to respond. "Yes, at some point Jesus reaches out to each of us, and we make the choice to accept or reject him. If we accept him, his words live within us.[1]

Remembering his quest, David thanked the priest for his help and asked him for directions to the official records building. As he picked up his travel bag, he made a slight nod in Phlegian's direction. "My visit here today has been an unexpected education."

David's gaze dropped to the floor. "I need to be on my way. I have an unpleasant task in Tiberias I must attend to as soon as possible."

CHAPTER 46

Mary had been escorted into an elegant room, and observed with interest its tiled floors, bronze lamps, floor length curtains, wall paintings, and other embellishments.

This, however, was not a social visit; Mary had been summoned. She stood in front of a polished oaken desk, behind which an artistically carved Christian cross adorned the wall.

At the desk sat the imposing man who had frowned at her in the church, the Bishop of Aix. The bishop had left the church before the service ended; thus he and Mary had not met. The décor in his office and the lapis ring on his finger suggested he enjoyed influential friends and supporters. The same elderly man was with him, but as before said nothing.

The bishop did not ask Mary to sit down. He leaned forward and cast an intimidating glare into her eyes. "Tell me, Mary from Magdala, do you know why I have summoned you?"

Mary had a strong hunch but responded, "No, I do not."

"I think you do. I heard you when you when you first tried to preach in Aix over thirty years ago. I know all about your unsavory history. I know how the Sister Superior at the Christian village ordered you to cease preaching, which was the proper thing to do, and then was forced to discharge you for disobeying her."

He leaned back in his chair and cast a smug look at Mary. "It seems you've spent a lifetime disobeying authority and embracing your own rules regarding how Christians should behave. Tell me, are you by any chance one of those Gnostic heretics?"

Mary responded quietly but firmly. "I know nothing about these

'Gnostics', whoever they are.[1] I am simply a devout Christian who always obeys the ultimate Christian authority, Jesus."

"Yes, we're familiar with your curious claim to be the Mary Magdalene who was at the crucifixion, and who by pure chance now happens to be living in Gaul. Quite a coincidence! Even if that were true, which I doubt, it hardly permits you to disobey Christian doctrine."

"What 'doctrine'?" She paused to stifle a cough. "Christian doctrine to me means everything Jesus said. Jesus himself told me I should help spread his message."

"Then it seems you do know why you are here!" He looked out the corner of his eyes at Mary. "Do you have any proof that Jesus actually said those words to you?"

Mary still had lingering traces of her anger problem and was finding it hard to conceal her annoyance. In a determined tone she replied, "I was there. With all due respect, sir, you were not. I know what he said."

The bishop leaned forward and played his trump card. "So you claim. The letters of Paul, however, are clear that women are forbidden to teach."

Confused, Mary asked, "Who is this Paul? And what letters are you talking about?"

"Paul, together with Peter, are the main apostles who conveyed the message of Jesus. Paul wrote to a disciple, Timothy, that women should learn in silence. They may not teach or have authority over men, and must keep silent in church."[2]

"I never heard Jesus say that. Further, none of Jesus' twelve apostles were named Paul."

"Paul, my pretentious Mary, is merely the foremost writer of Christian beliefs. What he wrote is official church doctrine and will remain so whether you like it or not."

Glowering at Mary, he continued. "You must and will obey the decisions of the church leaders! The Apostle Peter was chosen by Jesus to lead the church. He decides what is to be said and who will say it. He warned us against false prophets such as yourself.[3] Do you understand?"

With a look that was part annoyance, part resignation, and part defiance, Mary responded simply, "I have never claimed to be a prophet. I listened to the words of Jesus, and regardless of what you may choose to believe, he did encourage me to teach."

The bishop was not impressed in the slightest. "What Paul's instructions mean is that you may talk with other women in private, in order to instruct them to be submissive to their husbands.[4] As Paul directed, you may never teach men, or attempt to teach at any gatherings at which both men and women are present. Is that quite clear?"

Mary was not about to back off, either. "You seem quite sure what Jesus meant, but how would you know? Unlike you, I heard Jesus' words. I will obey Jesus who, you might be surprised to learn, often talked with women, even though some of the apostles disapproved.[5] I was one of those women. I always felt Jesus considered men and women equal in God's eyes."

The bishop was not familiar with Mary's references to Jesus conversing with women, but had no intention of letting Mary know that. He was done with polite verbal sparring.

He arose, fists clenched on the desk, and cast his most intimidating glare at Mary. "It appears you are as insolent as you are ignorant! I strongly advise you to do as Paul directed and cease preaching. Serious consequences will result if you do not. Do you understand? Serious consequences! Those are my final words. You have been duly warned!"

Mary opened her mouth to respond but realized the likely futility of it. Without bothering to reply to his question, she turned and departed the room.

After Mary had closed the door behind her, the bishop snapped his finger at a man standing nearby, a trusted assistant.

"Follow her. I want to know where she goes."

⌖

The bishop then turned to the other man, the scholarly looking gentleman who had been with him at the church service. He was elderly and of thin build, with a long, flowing beard. His face was wrinkled, but his eyes were sharp. He was indeed a scribe, a writer David would have recognized. His name was Luke.

The bishop asked, "Well, what do you think?"

Without hesitation Luke replied, "I am inclined to agree with your conclusion."

"That her words are not credible? That this imposter seeks only to promote herself?"

"For the most part, yes."

"Excellent. Then, that is what you'll state in your history of the life of Jesus?"

"I will not credit her with anything that seems questionable without additional proof she was actually present." He thought for a moment, then added a clarification.

"It is true that on the third day a female disciple named Mary Magdalene went to the tomb with anointing oils. She saw the empty tomb and reported this to the apostles. However, I have seen no compelling evidence that the risen Jesus appeared first to this woman who we saw before us today, who claims to be Mary Magdalene. Therefore, that is the way I will depict the situation in my writings."[6]

The bishop then asked Luke, "Is it known what became of the real Mary Magdalene following the crucifixion?"

"I am aware of no credible record of what happened to the well-known disciple Mary Magdalene after the death of Jesus," he replied.[7]

"Is there any convincing evidence that she ever traveled outside Palestine, or to Gaul?"

"I am not aware of any."

The bishop leaned back in his chair. "Good. I am pleased to hear you say that. My main concern is that there are misguided elements among the followers of Christ, the Gnostics, who wish to give this Mary Magdalene a higher position among the disciples than even Peter. This is unacceptable, and we must work to discredit those who espouse this point of view."

The bishop replied, "I assure you that I disparage those heretical Gnostics at every opportunity. I fully support your recommendation that Mary Magdalene should be mentioned as little as possible in church writings, and the deluded impersonator who was just before us, this so-called Mary from Magdala, not at all."

Luke had one final thing to add. "I applaud your insistence that the teachings of Paul, with whom I traveled for many years and whose words I have put into writing, be obeyed. You are correct; the writings and instructions of the church leaders must be honored at all times."

"We are in complete agreement on this," the bishop assured him. "You may count on my enforcing this. We are most fortunate, Luke, that your travels to gather information for your new gospel have brought you here to Gaul. You may be sure I will acquaint my parishioners with all the insights you have given me."

CHAPTER 47

The next morning found David feeling both elated and despondent. He was thrilled with the writings of Mark and anxious to show them to Mary, if he could find her.

On the other hand, there was Rachel. He was ashamed of the visits he had failed to make. The loving times he might have had with his sister, but forfeited. Now, most depressing, the impending search for her grave. He kicked a stone in the path with all the force he could muster.

David had to knock on several doors before locating the building where the official records of the prefecture were kept. As he made his way into the building, he amused himself with the thought, *At least the Romans are useful for one thing; they keep good civic records ... for taxation purposes.*

The cavernous building appeared empty. After peering into several unoccupied rooms that were full of records, David approached the only person who seemed to be working there.

"Excuse me, am I in the right place to ask about cemetery records?"

"Yes sir, I can help you. Please tell me the name of the deceased, the town of residence, and the year of death."

The last of the three requests posed a problem. Together they perused various lists of all the people who had been buried in local cemeteries over the past ten years. Then David went back through the records for another ten years, with the same result. The name *Rachel* coupled with *Magdala* appeared nowhere.

"What does this mean?" a frustrated David asked the clerk. "I thought you kept all these records here. Is there somewhere else she could have been buried?"

"Perhaps at home?"

David pondered that. "Unlikely. She had only a small yard, and it was open to other yards and to animals grazing and digging. Not at all private or secure."

"There is one other possibility. On the edge of town, there's an unofficial cemetery where people are buried who … who do not have sufficient money to construct a private tomb or to afford a burial plot in the major cemeteries. You might look there."

David's first reaction was relief that he now had another location where Rachel might be buried. Then he realized the unsettling implications of what the clerk had said.

"You mean, only the poorest people are buried there? It's a cemetery for paupers?"

"Yes, sir. People who are either poor or who have no relatives."

David stared at him with mouth ajar. The clerk's words reverberated like thunder through his brain: *who have no relatives*. He wished this whole depressing scene could somehow disappear. Or perhaps that he could.

Finally, with a drooping head and heavy sigh he said to the clerk, "Please give me directions to this unofficial cemetery."

Following the clerk's instructions, David found the unmarked collection of graves on a weed-covered hillside along a little used farm road. The site was steep and devoid of trees or even wildflowers, and there appeared to be no provisions for maintaining it. After a lengthy search among its deteriorated and sometimes nameless headstones half hidden in the grasses, he stood with bowed head in front of an uncarved granite rock, lying on its side and almost hidden by weeds, that marked a gravesite. At the base of the rock was a rough piece of split wood, weathered by time, which bore the barely decipherable words, "Rachel, Magdala."

The thoughts going through David's head were tortured and choked with curses, all directed at himself. Tears rolled down his cheeks in greater volume than ever before.

You miserable scum. You liked to tell everyone how much you loved your sister, and here she lies in a pauper's grave. For people who have no relatives! Well, that's appropriate; you ignored her for years. Unforgivable! I hope you enjoyed all the money you made in your fancy boat. You are surely the most despicable of all greedy, self-centered hypocrites!

He searched desperately for some way to make this right, but his mind was so cluttered with self-condemnation that rational thought was impossible. Worst-case scenarios surged to the forefront. *Oh God, it could be worse! Suppose something has happened to Mary, too?*

David fell on his knees to the ground, his head buried in his chest. He lifted his eyes upward and pleaded, "Lord, I'm not good at prayers, so this is the only thing I'll ever ask for in my entire life. If I can find Mary alive – please let her be alive – I'll do whatever I possibly can to help her. Then I swear to you, I'll return here and give this wonderful person, my beloved sister Rachel, a proper resting place."

☙

Jeanette entered Lazarus' office at the church in Massalia, carrying her travel bag. Martha was working there as well.

Lazarus looked up with surprise, not having any idea she was planning a trip. "Jeanette! Where are you headed?"

"Aix. I'll only be gone a few days, but I feel I should go. When I went there initially with Mary, I promised I'd visit now and then to make sure she was feeling well and didn't need anything. I feel ashamed. I've only gone there once. I didn't keep my word."

"Go; don't worry about things here. Martha can cover for you while you're away."

Martha agreed. "Everything will be fine here. Try to convince

Mary to hurry back. She has been away longer than expected. We miss her, and I think she'd be safer here."

"You're right. I'd like her back in Massalia too, for many reasons. I'll urge her to return."

☙

David hired a wagon in Tiberias, as he had a few more tasks to carry out before leaving the depressing ruins of Magdala. As a courtesy, he wanted to tell the woman in Rachel's house he had located his sister's grave. He also wanted to check some of the other homes in the area, particularly Sarah's.

After visiting Rachel's old home, David went to Sarah's neighborhood. He noticed one thing right away: although the houses were intact they were empty, as was the entire village. He looked at the orchard, the one that Sarah had planted and cultivated so carefully. It looked abandoned, and although it was autumn, the trees contained little, if any, fruit.

Then he saw a faint movement. He told the driver to stop and wait for him.

In the shadows of a tree, someone was seated on the ground, staring at the dirt. David started running in the hope it might be Sarah, but realizing it was more likely someone else. As he got closer, he could see it was a woman, one tall enough to be Sarah. After a few more paces, the woman turned to see what new threat might be approaching. David's eyes grew wide.

"Sarah! Is that you?"

The face staring back at him hardly looked like Sarah. It was gaunt and wrinkled, unable to smile, and the body below it was painfully thin. Her blank face just looked at the old man standing near her, and with no emotion at all she muttered, "David?"

David hardly knew what to say. "Sarah, are you hurt? Where is everyone?"

She turned and stared at the ground in front of her. It was several seconds before she could say anything. When she did, it lacked any feeling.

"We had only a few minutes before they came. Some families grabbed important possessions and started running, mostly to the north. The ones that stayed … the men were all killed. The women and children were taken prisoner, most likely to … to become slaves of the officers. I ran, too, but not with the others. I knew of a steep ravine not far to the west. It had some dense bushes where I could hide. I took a chance the soldiers wouldn't come that way."

David could likewise only stare at the ground and shake his head.

"The families that had run off returned a few days later. They buried the bodies of the men who had tried to fight the Romans. I helped them. I was beyond tears. Then they gathered anything else they could find and left. I think they couldn't bear to live here any longer. I had nowhere else to go, so I stayed behind and ate what little fruit was left in the orchard." With no change in expression she offered one final memory: "I caught a lizard for supper once."

Sarah kept staring at the ground, and David at her. David then leapt up and shouted, "Well, I'm not going to let you lie here and starve!" He offered her some of the limited food he had available. "Get up, Sarah. I'll take you along with me, and we'll look for Mary together."

At the word "Mary", Sarah showed a semblance of a smile. With large hopeful eyes she gazed up at David and with a faint trace of emotion in her voice said, "All right."

❧

David had now completed his various tasks in Galilee, including some inquiries as to where the most reliable burial services were located. He was ready and eager to retrace his journey of long ago to the distant shores of Gaul. This time there were two differences: he no longer owned a boat, and the only person with him was Sarah.

Following a tiring trip across the plateau in his hired wagon, a trip that because of his age and its urgency seemed interminable, he was once again at the port in Caesarea. He was talking to an official there with the hope of finding a quick solution to his transportation problem.

"Sir, as the Caesarea Harbormaster, I believe you have the schedules of all the vessels here. I need passage for two persons on the first ship sailing to Massalia. It's quite important."

The harbormaster tried to sound as disinterested as he could. "I'll try, when I get a chance. This has been a busy day. I can't make any promises."

"I see," replied David. "Perhaps there are expenses associated with finding me passage to so distant a place?" He reached into his travel bag and pulled out something round and silvery. "Maybe this will help to cover some of those, ah, expenses. What do you think?"

The harbormaster eyed his newly created bank account. "You know, now that I think about it, I believe there's a ship heading that direction in a day or two."

David nodded and smiled. "I thought there might be."

CHAPTER 48

A few days after receiving the bishop's ultimatum, Mary was about to address a late afternoon gathering in a field on the outskirts of Aix. She didn't dare preach in the church; she worried that informants of the bishop might be sent there. As she walked to the front of the parishioners, she noticed a group of men in the rear whose displeasure was transparent. Their presence made Mary nervous, but she tried to ignore them as she began speaking.

"I welcome you all here today to hear more of the words of Jesus. I've been told I'm no longer allowed to preach in the city, so I greet you here in this church of trees and flowers, an inspiring temple created for us by God . . ."

After an hour, Mary ended her message so she could depart while it was still daylight. After a few final questions, she started to exit when from the crowd came a familiar voice.

"Mary! Over here!"

"Jeanette! How wonderful to see you! What brings you back to Aix?"

"You. I promised I would visit you regularly, but I fear I haven't kept my word."

"It hasn't been so long, and there's no need to worry. I feel fine." A cough she was unable to suppress belied that. "I'm about to head back to my little shed. It's a quite satisfactory place to stay, once you fix it up a little. I imagine you have friends here in Aix to stay with?"

"I do, but I have other plans this evening. I'll spend the night with you at the shed."

Mary looked puzzled. "Why would you . . . ?"

"I saw them, and I'm sure you did too. The angry men, standing in the back of the crowd, pointing accusing fingers at you, just like before. Did you notice some of them were nodding, like they had agreed on something? Whatever the agreement, I suspect it was not good. I'll go back with you. You need a second person at that shed."

"Very well, if you wish. I always welcome your company, but I think it unnecessary."

As they started walking in the direction of the little Christian community, a light rain began falling. They covered up as best they could and quickened their pace. Jeanette initiated a conversation to take their minds off the drizzle.

"I've wondered, Mary, why some people dislike you? You're a friend to everyone!"

"It's not a lot of people, only a few who oppose my teaching. It used to be townspeople, but now the opposition seems to be from the church itself. That puzzles and saddens me."

Mary looked up at the rain and pulled the hood of her cloak tightly around her head. "Some seem to find it difficult to believe that I really knew Jesus. I only wish to speak the truth, of course, but there is a wise saying: 'If you want to make people dislike you, lie to them. If you want to make them truly hate you, tell the truth.' Jesus told the truth, and look what happened."

"Yes, and you spoke the truth to the Sister Superior, and look what happened."

"I think most people, like the Sister Superior, do try to help people," Mary observed. "There are others, though, who claim to do good, but only wish to serve themselves. It's sad how many of them wind up in positions of power."

Jeanette sighed, "I wonder if it will always be that way."

❧

Mary and Jeanette had settled into the shed for the night. Mary was asleep. The rain had stopped, and an owl was serenading the night not far away. Jeanette got up and looked through the window to see if she could locate the owl, and her senses tensed.

"Mary! Did you hear that? I thought I heard men's voices off in the distance!"

Mary sprang to attention. "What? I heard nothing. Are you sure?"

"Yes! Get up! Look over here."

Jeanette continued to peer out the window with Mary beside her. Beneath dark clouds in the western sky they could see a faint, flickering glow on the horizon.

Jeanette gave voice to what they were both thinking. "Even though it was thirty years ago, I remember what that glow means. Someone is carrying a torch! Worse, I suspect they're headed this way."

"Oh, please, not again!" Mary stifled a cough. "I'm getting too old for this."

Jeanette handed Mary's travel bag to her. "Gather up anything important, your clothes, anything else you might need, and hurry. We need to get out of here!"

There was a flurry of arms as they threw their few belongings into the travel bags. At the last moment, Jeanette grabbed Mary's blanket and stuffed it under her arm, knowing Mary would need it at night. They bolted out of the shed and hurried up the hillside.

"Where are we going?" asked Mary between panted breaths.

Jeanette was familiar with the area. She often walked up this hill when she was new at the Christian village. She had few friends then and often just wanted to be alone.

"About halfway up the hillside are some rock outcrops. It will be a good place to hide. We can make it that far before they get close enough to see the shed."

The little shed now stood deserted. Almost. On the floor beside the bed lay a collection of handwritten papyrus sheets. The blanket had fallen over them when Mary arose from the bed, and Jeanette hadn't seen them when she snapped up the blanket.

A few minutes later, several men arrived at the shed, two with torches. They differed from the men who had sought Mary before. These acted like men of civic authority.

Their leader, Henri, shouted in the direction of the shed. "Mary of Magdala! We know where you stay! Are you in there? Hiding will avail you nothing."

He paused for a reply. Only the owl responded.

"If you are in there, come out now! We are here on orders from the Bishop of Aix. You have been found to be blasphemous. You must leave the region and never return to Aix again."

Jeanette tried to break the tension with sarcasm. "Thoughtful of him to shout so we can hear everything."

At the shed, Henri was tired of waiting and beckoned to one of the torchbearers. "She isn't answering. Let's go inside and see what we can find."

The two entered the shed while the others peered through the windows. Henri spoke first. "It seems obvious from the disarray that one or more persons departed not long ago, and in a hurry." He then noticed a woman's headscarf on the floor.

"This is where she stays. See the cheap headscarf? What decent woman would live in a wretched place like this?" With palpable contempt he added, "This proves she lies! If she were as important as she claims, she would live in a nice home like the bishop, not a filthy shed."

"If she's gone, how can we order her out of Aix like the bishop ordered?"

Henri thought for a moment and then began stroking his chin with a malevolent grin.

"She stays here because she has nowhere else to go. It would be too dangerous to live in Aix, and the nearby village wouldn't dare take her in. If this shed were no longer here, she would be homeless.

She'd have to go somewhere else."

"You mean we should tear the shed down?"

"Too obvious. It would take too long. On the other hand, if you were to trip ..."

"Trip?"

"Yes, trip."

Henri put his foot in front of the other man's leg and gave him a hard shove from behind, causing him to fall forward. The torch flew out of his hand and landed in the hay that had been Mary's bed. The flames began consuming everything in the vicinity, including papyrus.

"My, what a clumsy oaf you are! Get up! I suggest we get out of here, fast."

They ran from the shed, and the entire group watched as the fire intensified and raced through the wooden structure. Soon the entire shed was engulfed in a gyrating pillar of flames.

As the flames began to die down, Henri stood up and looked into the darkness. Nothing appeared to be moving. He shouted into the emptiness at maximum volume.

"Mary of Magdala! If you are in range of my voice, take heed. The bishop gave you explicit warning, which you chose to ignore. Because of your continued heresy, you are hereby ordered to leave the municipality of Aix immediately and never return. If you do not do this, you will be apprehended, jailed, and put on trial. Your punishment will be far greater than this!"

Mary and Jeanette stared at the conflagration, wide-eyed with despair and foreboding.

"Can you believe they did that? Jeanette, what can I do?" Another pause for a coughing spell. "I'm banned from Aix, and they will certainly look around the village."

"Right now it would be best to plan for tonight. I have an idea. I used to wander through these hills when I sought solitude. Farther up there's a cave large enough for two people to sleep in. Trees hide the entrance, so almost no one knows it exists. You would be safe there."

"That's good, but I have no bed … nothing."

Jeanette sought an optimistic reply. "Don't worry. I'll take you to the cave, and we can gather grass for a bed. Tomorrow I'll go to Aix and ask friends for a blanket and some food … "

Jeanette's assurances were abruptly terminated by Mary's sudden change of expression from slight hope to a combination of surprise and terror, as she looked beyond Jeanette and saw one of the men from Aix standing there.

"Oh, dear God! Jeanette!"

Jeanette whirled around to see what was frightening Mary.

The man couldn't suppress a grin of evil delight as he approached them, pointing a large hunting knife at Mary's head.

"Stay right where you are! Do not move! Did you think you could avoid capture so easily? My name is François, so you can remember your captor, and I have excellent eyesight. I saw you running up the hill, and circled around behind you. Your scofflaw days are over!"

He advanced closer to Mary and pointed the knife directly at her neck. With a haughty snarl he proclaimed, "So you think you can ignore the bishop's order to stop preaching to men? We will see about that. I hereby place you under arrest on the directive of his eminence, the Bishop of Aix!"

Jeanette got up and looked at the steep terrain around her and Mary, weighing the wisdom of trying to run. Mary again coughed heavily. *Running would be futile, maybe fatal.* Furious at her helplessness, Jeanette was reduced to insults.

"How brave of you, threatening an old, infirm woman with a knife! Perhaps I should find you a starving little girl, so you could poke a knife in her neck too!"

Jeanette's mockery infuriated François. He swung around and

sent the handle end of the knife crashing into her forehead, drawing blood, and causing her to fall on top of Mary. "Don't play games with me, woman. I think you know what crimes this Mary has committed. What's more, I would guess you assisted her. It seems I need to arrest both of you!"

He grabbed Mary by the arm and with a painful yank, pulled her to her feet. "Get up! You will both come with me." He glowered at Jeanette. "If you don't want a bad accident to happen to the old woman, you'll do as I say. Now start moving."

He led Mary and a bleeding Jeanette down the hill to where the rest of the mob was gathered, all the while directing further threats towards his captives.

When they reached the others, Henri, realizing that an actual arrest would be far better than merely shouting out a warning, greeted their arrival with a huge self-satisfied smile.

Both women could only stare at the ground and pray. At this point they had no other options.

CHAPTER 49

David had once again crossed the Great Sea, and once again with conflicted feelings. He was excited by the prospect of reuniting with his niece, but burdened by the news he must convey concerning her mother. It was also the first time in forty years he was not in command of the ship on which he sailed, and this trip reminded him of how much he missed that. He was amused at how hard it was not to offer gratuitous advice to the ship's real captain. After a few days, he decided the captain could probably get them to Gaul without his assistance.

Once David and Sarah reached Massalia, they began seeking information that might lead them to Mary. Although David had once docked in the city's harbor, he had no familiarity with its maze of unnamed streets. After hours of fruitless searching they found a man who was both familiar with the city and knew a little Greek as well.

"A church? At the top of the hill take the road to the left. In the distance you'll see a white building with a cross. That's the only church I know of."

They did as instructed and arrived at the church with its iconic cross. David paused to admire it, wondering if Mary had a hand in building it. Recalling the urgency of his search, he hurried to the door and knocked. An elderly man appeared.

"God bless you, sir. What brings you to our humble church?"

"I'm looking for my niece, a Christian woman. I thought I might start by asking here."

"Please come in. I merely work here, but I'll find someone who can help you."

David and Sarah entered and glanced around the entry room. It was austere, poorly lit, with only a few chairs and a small table to call furniture. Soon the figure of a woman appeared at a door on the far side of the room, but as she was backlighted by the window behind her, David was unable to discern any facial features.

"I bid you welcome to our church, sir. How may I be of service to you?"

"I'm hopeful you might help me find someone. You see, ..." David squinted at the silhouetted person before him. *Have I heard that voice somewhere before?* His eyes grew large with curiosity, and he took a couple of steps forward.

"Do I know you? Are you – Martha! Is that you?"

Martha leaned forward, trying to get a better look at this unfamiliar gray-haired man. "That is my name. How is it you know me?"

"Martha! I'm David. Mary's uncle! I brought you here, on the *Ikaría.*"

"David? Oh, my word, David!" She ran to the almost forgotten man who had made her present life possible. Smiles and embraces were exchanged with uninhibited joy.

"What a blessing to have found you so quickly. Such an impressive church!" Turning to his companion, he said, "Martha, you may remember Sarah, the friend of Rachel's who you met in Magdala. Perhaps you've heard that Magdala was destroyed in the recent fighting there, including Sarah's home. Sarah was starving, had no family, and no way to sustain herself. I was determined to help her, so I offered to bring her here."

"Sarah, yes," Martha replied, "Of course I remember you! It was you who warned us to leave Magdala. You may have saved our lives! Welcome to Gaul; you are now a refugee here too, like the rest of us."

David was not interested in small talk. "You can guess what brought us here. Please tell me that you or Lazarus knows where Mary is. Is she in Massalia?"

Martha's sudden apprehensive look and clenched fists were not at all what David expected, and he felt his heart beat faster.

"David, Lazarus isn't here. He left this morning to go to Aix. I'm so sorry, but I must relay bad news. We have received word that Mary is in jail in Aix."

His instantaneous relief that she was at least still alive changed for the worse as the import of Martha's words struck him like lightning. "What? In jail? What on earth do you mean? How can that be? Why?"

"I have no further information. All I know is she was arrested a few days ago on orders from the Bishop of Aix. I would guess the reason was most likely for preaching in public. Her friend, Isabelle, was able to get a message to us. Lazarus has gone to Aix to see if he can help her. That's all I know."

David stared at her, unable to make sense of this devastating news. Why was preaching in public a crime, and why would a Christian bishop, of all people, want her arrested? Questions aside, he knew what his only course of action was.

"It appears our hopes for a pleasant visit with you and Lazarus are not to be. Under the circumstances, I feel I should head for Aix as well. I'll try to find Lazarus and see what we might do to help Mary. It's getting late. May I stay here with you tonight, and leave for Aix early in the morning?"

"Of course, David. I appreciate your offer of help. I know Lazarus will welcome any assistance you can provide. I fear he may need it."

David turned to Sarah. "Do you feel well enough to travel to Aix with us, or would you rather stay here? I must tell you, I can't guarantee safety for any of us in Aix."

"I'd like nothing more than to go with you, but the trip was hard on me and I did not eat well. I still feel weak. And I know nothing of the local language. I'll stay here, assist at the church, and pray you can return with Mary."

Martha replied, "I appreciate that, Sarah; you're most kind." She thought about the situation, then added, "David, wait. I suspect that Mary needs all the help she can get. I can have others look after things here. Would you mind if I accompany you to Aix tomorrow?"

"Mind? I'd be delighted. We'll leave at first light."

CHAPTER 50

The assembly hall in Aix had been filled since mid-afternoon, with more people crammed outside the door. In the back of the room, a small group of frightened women clustered together; one of them was Jeanette. Some distance away sat a woman in a brown robe, her face almost entirely hidden by a gray hood. The trial of Mary Magdalene, presided over by the Bishop of Aix, was concluding.

Mary had been speaking for two hours, with periodic coughing spells, relating the story of her association with Jesus and her life in Gaul. The crowd paid rapt attention, while displaying a wide array of reactions. No one was paying more attention than Jeanette.

Mary concluded her story. "This man then forced us down the hillside, with his knife at my throat. After that we were made to walk back to Aix, where I was placed under arrest. That is how I happen to be here today."

Mary paused for a moment, then decided she had nothing to lose at this point.

"I have one final piece of evidence to present. On the terrible day of the crucifixion, as I was rising to depart, I noticed at the base of the cross a small stone. Onto that stone, by chance, had fallen a drop of our Savior's blood. I have kept and treasured it ever since. I secured it to a chain so it wouldn't get lost, and wear it always as a simple amulet, a remembrance of Jesus' sacrifice for us all."

Mary pulled the necklace from beneath her robe and held it up so the sun's last rays could illuminate it. All faces were fixed on the small stone, some in awe, many others skeptical. After displaying it for a few seconds Mary replaced the necklace around her neck.

"That, Reverend Bishop, concludes my remarks. I trust that as an official of the Christian church, you will honor the words Jesus spoke to me and agree that he authorized me to help spread his message to others."

Mary made a slight bow to her listeners. "Thank you for hearing my story."

As she returned to her seat, murmurs from the assembled throng escalated in volume. Some women nodded their heads in agreement, while most men shook theirs with angry eyes. Mary allowed herself the optimistic thought that her narrative had been persuasive. However, she knew that the crowd mattered not at all, only the bishop mattered.

His Eminence arose and faced the audience. "Before rendering my judgment, does anyone present wish to make any manner of statement regarding the subject of these proceedings?"

One of the women in the back of the room stood up. It was Sister Annette. All eyes focused on her.

"You may speak."

"Your Excellency, I have been the Sister Superior at the Christian village outside Aix for the past six years. I have known Mary Magdalene for almost forty years and do truly believe her to be an honest and devout Christian. In my prayerful opinion, what she has said here today may be accepted as the truth."

The bishop looked down his nose at her. "I see. I'm sure you believe your words to be true, but I question their objectivity. I think you would agree that if the accused is exonerated and her claims accepted, your little village, where she lived for a while, would gain greatly in stature. This, of course, would be of considerable personal benefit to you."

Sister Annette, stunned, couldn't believe what he said. "No! That is not true! The sisters and I seek no personal gain!" The bishop presented not to hear her.

"Further, do you really wish to position your community, which you call a Christian one, as condoning her sordid history of violating church doctrine? I doubt it; that would be very foolish. I think it prudent for your sake, and for the reputation of your village, that your remarks be excluded from the trial record. I shall grant you that favor."

Sister Annette and her companions, shocked by their first exposure to the base political arts of dissembling and deliberate misinterpretation, could only stare at one another, mouths agape. Mary was not at all surprised by what she heard and directed a disgusted glance at the bishop, who ignored her.

The bishop turned to the crowd again and asked, more as a challenge than a question, "Does anyone else wish to speak?"

Only one person was brave enough to volunteer. A thin, serious-looking man stood up. It was Lazarus. He was seated far enough from the stage that it did not occur to him he might have seen this man many years before.

"Your Grace, my name is Lazarus; I am the Bishop of Massalia. I would like to speak in defense of ..."

"Excuse me!" the bishop shouted, eyebrows raised.

"Excuse me, but I must correct the record. The speaker has lied. He is not the Bishop of Massalia; he is merely a priest at a church there."

Lazarus was astounded by this unexpected personal attack. "What do you mean? How can you say that? I have been the Bishop in Massalia for over thirty years!"

"By whose authority? Only your own, I believe. Do you have any evidence that the authorities in Rome ever sanctioned such an appointment?"

"Your Grace, I do not understand. All large cities have bishoprics. When I arrived in Massalia, no other priest was there. Nor at that time were there any authorities in Rome. Massalia is a large city and now has more than one church. The duties of a bishop needed to be performed, and I accepted those responsibilities."

"Yes, and gave yourself an impressive title in the process, without any official approval. That is unacceptable. Furthermore, there are too few followers of Jesus in this part of Gaul to require two bishops."

He turned and spoke directly to the audience. "I have reviewed this matter with the proper church authorities in Rome, who agree that two bishoprics in this small province cannot be justified. Therefore, they have directed that the two be combined into one, with its primary office located here in Aix."

He looked back at Lazarus with a smug air of victory and concluded his public demotion, which he had been rehearsing for years. "It's obvious that since there is no bishopric in Massalia, therefore there can be no Bishop of Massalia!"

Lazarus stared back at the bishop, searching for the right words. He was not a person given to anger, and after a moment replied, "Very well. You have proven you have power and influence and are willing to use them however and whenever you wish. I congratulate you. Nonetheless, the fact remains that the disciple Mary Magdalene did nothing more than what our Savior authorized her to do. I would like to know how you consider that improper, and how your opinion overrides the words of Jesus."

The bishop, pretending to be reading, did not even bother to look up. "Thank you, Priest Lazarus, for your opinions. They are duly noted."

It was clear to Lazarus that his testimony would have no effect on the bishop, or on his ultimate verdict. He said nothing further and, with a final glare at the bishop, sat down.

The bishop, feigning sincerity, asked, "Would anyone else care to make a comment?"

No one so much as moved a muscle. He then turned and addressed Mary.

"We have listened patiently to your detailed remarks. We have been entertained by your theatrical exhibit of a stone with a stain on it which you assert was found at the foot of the cross, but have offered no proof to validate such a claim. Even if you did, it would in no way excuse your many deliberate violations of official church policy."

Murmurs again arose from the crowd. They could sense which way the bishop was leaning. The sergeant-at-arms tilted his lance towards the audience, and the bishop raised his arm to quiet them. He now directed his words at Mary.

" We are the Church of Jesus. Being faithful to his teachings can be difficult, for he wrote nothing himself; others did. If certain writings do not agree, Church leaders decide what is correct. As to women, the Apostle Paul was clear: women will remain silent in church matters. Yet you chose to preach anyway, even to men, knowing that as a woman you are forbidden to do so. You were warned on many occasions to cease your heresies, but you refused."

He pointed a thin finger at Mary. "Further, we must think of the example being set. What if other irresponsible women were to follow the heretical path that this Mary, whoever she is, has chosen to tread? The traditions that stabilize our society would be jeopardized. No, this threat must be terminated now, before it spreads." A drone of agreement again rose from then men.

The bishop turned towards Mary, and now his demeanor softened. "Jesus, though, always spoke of repentance, and therefore so will I."

"Mary of Magdala, I am prepared to offer you a full pardon for your sins, if you will confess your blasphemy, openly repent, and agree that you will never again attempt to teach anything about Jesus in public, and absolutely never before men."

He paused for effect, and then directed a piercing glare straight at Mary. "This is your last chance to redeem your eternal soul. Do you so confess, and so repent? Speak!"

Every eye was on Mary, every ear turned in her direction. If a pin had fallen, it would have sounded like an anvil. Mary looked straight at the bishop and gave her response, which she knew would seal her fate.

"I will not confess to a crime of which I am not guilty, nor repent a sin which I did not commit. Jesus said, 'Let your light so shine before men that they may see your good works, and glorify your father in heaven.'[1] I am guilty only of complying with those words. On what grounds do you think Jesus' instructions are wrong?"

Ignoring Mary's question, the bishop summarized the prosecution's case.

"Very well, then. You, Mary of Magdala, have often and willfully flaunted Church doctrine, despite numerous admonitions and warnings. Your conduct can neither be condoned nor ignored. The Church is bound to uphold its teachings and enforce its rules of conduct, and I assure you it will do so."

With raised voice, he rendered his verdict. "Therefore, I, the Bishop of Aix, find you guilty as charged, and do hereby banish you from the territory of Gaul. If you are ever again seen within Gaul, you will be arrested and imprisoned for the rest of your life. It is so ordered!"

The sentence produced both immediate sobbing and shouting from the crowd, including cries of "No, jail her now!" and "Stone her!" Sister Annette and her friends could only bow their heads and tearfully pray, in part giving thanks that the sentence wasn't far worse.

The bishop gestured to the sergeant-at-arms, who grabbed Mary by the arm. "Take her to the holding cell for the night. Arrange for a guard to be stationed there. In the morning, a centurion will escort her to the provincial border. Go!"

The sergeant-at-arms ordered Mary to stand, then half led and half dragged her out through the back door.

Jeanette, grim-faced, rose from her seat. *So this is what the Bishop of Aix calls justice! Well, I have another version, which I intend to carry out!* She forced her way through the crowd and out the main door, just as the sun was setting behind buildings across the square.

The woman in the brown robe and gray headscarf watched Jeanette depart, then also exited the building and proceeded in the same direction Mary's friend had taken.

CHAPTER 51

The bishop had returned to his comfortable offices and was being served an evening meal freshly prepared by his kitchen staff. Dining with him was the centurion who would command the exile detail for Mary of Magdala the next morning.

While scanning his plate to be sure everything was to his liking, the bishop said to his colleague, "You may have observed that many men at the trial apparently thought I was too lenient with that arrogant imposter. Some were shouting to have her executed. I understand how they felt, but there were two reasons I couldn't do that."

"First, being a bishop within the Christian church places certain constraints on me. I am expected to behave as Jesus would, and I am certain Jesus would not have condemned her to death. Second, even if that weren't the case, I doubt I would decree such a penalty myself. As a child I hated my stepmother who always ordered me around, but I certainly didn't want her executed. I just wanted her to shut up and behave in the subservient manner that women should. The same goes for this delusional Mary person. Exiling her forever from Gaul I feel is sufficient, and ought to eliminate the problem she has created within our jurisdictions."

The centurion replied, "I understand your position. You may be certain that I will proceed in an appropriate manner."

As soon as dinner was finished, the centurion went to the officer who was his second in-command, and said, "We will depart early in the morning. As you know, it is a march of several days to the border, and our prisoner is ill, so we will not be able to move quickly. In my opinion, this whole exile thing is a waste of our time and resources. I agree, however, that she should not be allowed to spread her heresies any further, including not into territories beyond our borders. Her criminal behavior needs to be stopped, forever."

His assistant responded in an almost bored tone, "Do you mean she should receive the traditional punishment, a public stoning?"

"No, our fainthearted bishop has said he will not condone public brutality."

The centurion's face now took on an insincere smile and sarcastic tone of voice. "But she is ill, so we must of course think about her safety. As I recall, several rivers we will cross tomorrow have treacherous currents. It is unlikely that our prisoner knows how to swim. It would be most unfortunate if she were to fall out of the boat while crossing one of those rivers, especially at night. No one might ever see her again."

His comrade gave a quick look to be certain his superior was still wearing his familiar insincere smile. He was. Seeing that to be the case, his subordinate simply nodded his head but said nothing.

He had no trouble recognizing an order when he heard one.

CHAPTER 52

The twilight had faded and the sky was overcast, rendering the town dark and somber. A guard, an ordinary foot soldier, sat by the only door of a diminutive jail, which consisted of a barren holding cell behind a small entrance room. It was used to temporarily confine a prisoner such as the one now in it, who was to be exiled in the morning.

A furtive figure approached the jail, scanning the surroundings to be sure no one else was present. The figure stopped by a narrow window on the side of the jail, which was too small for an average person to slip through. Through the window Mary could be seen sitting on the dusty floor, as the cell had no furniture. She was staring at the opposite blank wall.

The secretive person looked down the street one last time to be certain she was alone. The street was empty; the shops had long since been closed. She stuck her head in the window.

"Pssst! Mary!"

Mary spun around and peered at the window. Wide-eyed, she leapt up and ran to it. "Jeanette! How on earth did you know where I was?"

They were whispering, and a gusty head wind helped ensure the guard would not hear their words. "It was hardly difficult. I simply followed the sergeant-at-arms at a safe distance."

"What are you doing here? This is dangerous! If anyone sees you, you could find yourself in here too!"

"Dangerous? If you want danger, think about tomorrow. Suppose the soldiers decide the easiest thing is simply to turn you over to the mob, rather than hike all the way to the border. I'm sure you remember how a mob treated Jesus!"

Mary blanched at even the thought of it, but also at the chance she would have of staying alive if she had to march all the way to the border of Italy. The very thought produced another coughing spell. "All the alternatives are bad, but what can we do?"

In a whisper Jeanette replied, "I have an idea. If it works, you may be free. If it fails, then I'll gladly join you in there."

"You must be joking! Did you see the sentry out front? With a sword! How are you going to get rid of him?"

"He appears to be half asleep and may have had a few drinks; that will help, as will the fact that it's quite dark. Listen, I want you to stand in the corner on this side of the cell door. Squeeze yourself as close to the wall as possible so the guard won't be able to see you."

"I don't understand ..."

"You'll have to trust me, Mary. The little window in the door to the cell appears to be very small; I don't think it would be possible to see the entire cell through it. Is my contrivance risky? Yes, but it's our only chance. Pray that our Savior is watching over us tonight."

Mary did as asked and went to the corner of the cell. At this point, she was willing to try anything. Her main concern was what might happen to Jeanette if the plan failed.

Jeanette looked over the alignment of things inside the cell and said a little prayer. She then tiptoed to the corner of the building and peered around it at the guard. He was seated on the ground, legs apart, nodding, perhaps asleep.

Jeanette took a deep breath, looked skyward for courage, and then rounded the corner and ran straight at the sentry. She yelled loudly to gain the advantage of surprise and confusion.

"Guard! GUARD!"

The guard bolted upright, straining his eyes to make out who was yelling at him.

"Oh, honorable guard, I thought you should know – I just saw someone, a small woman, squeeze through the little window on the side of the jail and run off in that direction." She pointed behind her, at the road that led west, back towards the center of the city.

The guard, now wide-eyed, looked at Jeanette with suspicion, but also with no small amount of trepidation. "What? What the devil are you talking about, woman?"

He leapt up, pulled out a key, unlocked the front door of the jail, and ran to the door of the cell. Peering through the little window in the cell door, he could see only what appeared to be an empty cell. The window was too small for him to stick his head through, leaving him unable to see Mary squeezed into the corner.

Jeanette's hope rose as she watched panic engulf the guard. His eyes were wildly searching the walls, looking for a key to the cell. "Dammit! They didn't give me a key to the cell door, just the outside door. I don't see a key here anywhere!"

Jeanette, standing against the wall, wore a faint smile. Where she was standing was not accidental. Behind her head was a hook with two keys on it. The guard, between being terrified, having had a few drinks, not being the sharpest of thinkers, and Jeanette's innocent face, didn't think to look behind her.

"Holy Caesar! She's gone!" Wide-eyed, he turned and stared at Jeanette in disbelief and undisguised fear. "Why do these things always happen to me? I'm as good as dead!"

Jeanette, summoning every speck of actress within her, pointed to the far corner of the plaza and shouted, "Look! Over there! Someone just ran past that building with the fancy wooden door!"

The guard charged out of the jail without bothering to shut the outside door and ran in the direction Jeanette had pointed, waving his sword as if somehow that would help.

As soon as he was out of sight, she turned, grabbed the two keys, and ran to Mary's cell.

"One of these has to be the right key. Oh, dear God, please. It just has to be!"

Mary peered through the little window. Jeanette inserted the first key; it would not budge left or right. Her heart beating faster, she inserted the second key.

It turned.

A click. The lock opened. And then the door.

"Jeanette, you're a genius!"

She threw down the keys and helped Mary out. "Save your breath for running! Hurry!"

They exited the jail, checking first to be sure nobody was around to observe the jailbreak. Seeing no one, they started running off in the direction opposite that taken by the guard.

But unseen by them, someone was looking. From the shadows of a building a short distance away, the eyes of a person in a brown cape and gray headscarf watched their every move as the two women fled down the road.

CHAPTER 53

The centurion in charge of the detail raced around the holding jail as though deranged, shouting orders and organizing a search for the escaped prisoner. He had been embarrassed and was furious, but he was not alone. The Bishop of Aix had also arrived, having caught rumor of the escape. He was even more incensed than the centurion, who became the target of his anger.

"Centurion, hear me well, your highest obligation is to recapture the prisoner. Is that clear? You are authorized to do whatever is necessary to make it happen."

"Yes, your eminence."

The fact that a bishop had no authority over a military officer seemed to be irrelevant. The Bishop of Aix was not one who took embarrassment in silence, and he viewed himself as outranking a mere centurion. For his part, the centurion didn't mind someone else assuming responsibility for the present chaotic mess, since it was the bishop's trial that led to it.

The centurion had already sent the first detachment of soldiers into the city to search for Mary, but when they returned all they had captured was the terrified jail guard. A grim-faced soldier held a sword at his throat.

Dozens of soldiers were scurrying around the plaza in all directions. Everyone gave the appearance of having no idea what to do. Maybe no one had ever escaped from the jail before. And a frail old woman, no less, made it all the more humiliating.

⤙

After an exhausting day of travel David and Martha had arrived in Aix, and under a darkening sky headed for the center of town. They soon heard the noise of the bickering crowd outside the assembly building. The throng had swollen from being just the trial spectators. The whole town was aware of the verdict handed down to the now infamous Mary of Magdala and wanted to argue about it. Now they had something even more bizarre to argue about.

David and Martha hurried in that direction, and David approached the first man they saw. "Excuse me, sir, we just arrived in town. Can you tell us what's going on here?"

"You haven't heard? Only the trial of Mary Magdalene! Or at least someone who says she's Mary Magdalene. No one seems to know for sure. The bishop found her guilty of blasphemy and heresy and threw her in jail. She'll be exiled tomorrow."

"Exiled! What the … never mind. Where is this jail?"

"There's a small one down the street three or four blocks. They use it to jail prisoners overnight. That might be where she is. There's a lot of soldiers there."

"Thank you." David started to push his way through the crowd, with Martha close behind. Halfway through the masses, he noticed someone who looked familiar. "Martha, over there, could that be …"

Martha peered around his shoulder, and even through the darkness had no trouble identifying the slender elderly man with the long white beard. "Lazarus! Over here!"

As Lazarus hugged his sister he peered at her companion. "David? Is that you?"

"Yes. We are overjoyed to have found you, but right now our priority is locating Mary. I was told a small jail might be nearby. Do you know where it is?"

"I've never seen it, but I think it would be in that direction," Lazarus said, pointing down the road. "It looks like some kind of commotion there. If Mary is in that crowd, she may need our immediate help. Whatever that could be."

They dashed the few blocks to the jail, dodging the soldiers who were everywhere.

David approached the nearest spectator. "Pardon me, sir, what's happening here?"

"Someone said that Mary Magdalene just escaped from this jail. The bishop just convicted her, you know. I guess that explains why all the soldiers are here."

"Escaped? You must be kidding! How?"

"Who knows? Soldiers are all over looking for her, but no one has brought her back yet."

"Thank you, my friend."

For the first time that day, David's face had a smile on it. "Escaped! Amazing. Somehow that doesn't surprise me at all. It's no help to us, though; she could be anywhere."

Lazarus pondered David's statement. "I remember Mary once told me something about an old cabin where she lived for a while. She said it was not far from the village where we left her. Could she have headed there?"

"Possibly. She might want to get away from Aix, since they would assume she'd try to hide somewhere in town overnight. That cabin could be a good place for us to start looking. Do you think you can find it?"

"I think so, assuming it's even still standing."

David considered the threatening sky and his own heavy eyelids. "There is no point in looking for it in the dark. Let's find a place to get a few hours' sleep, then head out in the morning at first light."

☙

David didn't know, however, that the centurion had other sources of information. He was talking to the Bishop of Aix, who had established his right to be the leader of the search.

"Your Eminence, is it not possible this Mary has acquaintances here in Aix who could hide her? She's too frail to have gone far.

Perhaps she might be at the house of a friend?"

"She's cleverer than you think. Nothing so obvious. She knows we'll search the town first, so she'd want to hide farther away. I've had people following her; and I've learned she used to live at a community of Christian women a few miles down the road. Their Sister Superior tried to defend her at the trial, so I know she has friends there. That's the first place I'd look."

"Very good thinking, Your Eminence. I will assemble a full company of troops immediately. Since she's weak, we can overtake and capture her in no time. I assure you, this Mary criminal will soon be back in custody."

"You had better be right. Your career depends upon it. This time, I'll make certain there can be no escape. You will personally guard her!"

The centurion gave a questioning look at the overreaching bishop and shouted an order for his men to assemble. He began issuing detailed assignments so as to ensure that every road out of town would be inspected by one of his detachments.

Before he could order them to move out, however, he was interrupted by a person who had moved silently through the crowd and was standing at his side, a person of slight build wearing a tattered brown cape and gray headscarf. The new arrival looked at the centurion through barely visible eyes and addressed him with a feminine voice.

"Excuse me, sir, I know you're busy and I shouldn't interrupt, but I thought you might want to know something I heard. I only want to help if I can."

"Well, what is it?" snarled the centurion.

"A few moments ago, I was standing next to two women, and I heard one of them say, 'I think she should be safe enough tonight in the basement of the church.' The woman said something about a secret room in the basement. That was what I heard her say, sir."

"The basement of the church, of course! Hide there tonight, and then head out of town before dawn. That's her plan! Bishop, I will order my men to check there first, if you agree."

"Granted, but make it fast. She could have left town already."

The centurion gathered a small detachment and hurried to the church, which even at a quick pace was several minutes away. Upon arriving, he had his troops surround the building and ordered one of his largest men to pound vigorously on the door.

There was no response.

"Stop hammering at it, you're wasting time. Knock it down!"

One swift kick by the bulky soldier was adequate to break the flimsy bolt. Several men rushed in and initiated a thorough search of the church. They soon discovered two things. At night, no one is there, particularly no one named Mary Magdalene. Even more infuriating, they also learned the church had no basement.

After some vehement curses, the centurion raced back to the jail and reassembled his troops. He selected a few to remain in Aix and arrest any small woman in a brown cape and gray headscarf, and assigned the rest to the various roads leading out of town. He took command of the largest platoon, the one that would follow the road east towards the Christian village.

CHAPTER 54

With the aid of the overcast sky, Mary and Jeanette had made it to the outskirts of town. They were still running, though barely faster than a walk. The toll was obvious on Mary, who was panting and struggling to keep up. Jeanette was concerned and led Mary behind the next building they came to. Jeanette peered into the darkness to be sure they were alone. Satisfied, she said what Mary most wanted to hear, "We can pause here for a while; I think we'll be safe."

They both collapsed onto the ground, exhausted.

Mary tried to pull herself up against the side of the building, but to no avail. She dropped back down, all the while coughing and wheezing. Her face was pale and her heart was pounding. She had never felt so enervated in her life.

"Jeanette, I can't go on; I have no strength. It seems Aix wastes little money feeding prisoners once they're in jail."

"That's awful! Just relax. We can rest as long as you need." Jeanette searched her clothing for any remnant of food, finding only a small portion of a biscuit which she gave to Mary. She then closed her eyes, trying to think of what to do next.

She didn't get far with her thoughts, as she soon heard a distant clamor. As it grew louder, Jeanette peeked around the corner of the building.

"It's the centurion with his detachment! Crouch down and don't make any sound."

Ignoring her body's protests, she managed this. The centurion's obsession with finding Mary worked to her favor, since he was focused on getting to the village as fast as possible and wasn't inclined to investigate every building along the way.

When the entire column had passed, they crawled to the corner of the building and watched as the soldiers faded into the distance, obscured by their own cloud of dust.

Jeanette took a deep breath and glanced at Mary. "That was close. We can rest a little longer to let them get further down the road."

After a few minutes of merciful rest, an odd sound next to Jeanette broke her train of thought, and she glanced at her friend.

"Mary! You're crying!"

"I'm sorry, Jeanette. Look at me! Please tell me, what has happened? Here I am, a spent old woman. What do I have to show for my life? Nothing! When I was young, I dreamt of doing something significant to help people, something to make the world a better place." She stared at the ground with a blank look.

"Tell me, what do I have to show for my life? I'm old. Sick. Homeless. No money. No family. Eating crumbs. Reviled and dismissed by those from whom I most wanted respect. Condemned as a common criminal. Sentenced to be exiled. Chased by soldiers. My teacher and inspiration crucified. Now I'm running through the cold night like a frightened animal."

Mary raised her tear-filled eyes to her friend. "Jeanette, where did I go wrong? My life seems so meaningless. I've accomplished nothing. I've failed at everything I ever hoped to do."

Jeanette was taken aback, almost shocked. She had never seen Mary even a little depressed before and searched for words of reassurance.

"Mary, you never did anything wrong! What are you talking about? Your life has been admirable and a model for others. You know that Jesus respected few human beings more than you. No one could ask for anything greater than that!"

Mary cast a hopeful look at Jeanette and waited for more assurance.

"Believe me, all you've done for the Christians in Aix and Massalia will never be forgotten. You're an inspiration to thousands, both here and in Galilee. Think about how much you've inspired me! I've never met anyone with the fortitude and determination you display. You know I'll always be your friend and companion, and administer to your needs. You have my solemn promise!"

Mary looked at Jeanette for a few moments and slowly began to regain her composure. "Thank you, Jeanette. How silly to be feeling sorry for myself. Jesus would have expected more from me." She paused and wiped her eyes. "I feel better. Thank you for your kind words. You're a good and cherished friend." She took a deep breath. "I imagine we need to keep going."

Mary forced herself to stand, which produced more coughing. Jeanette cast a worried look at her friend. The day's physical strains and mental stress on the elderly woman were apparent. Nonetheless, Jeanette realized they had little choice, as spending the cold night lying in a field with no coverings was no better option. They headed off towards the village at a more measured pace.

Mary realized she was now entirely dependent on Jeanette, so with a perplexed look asked, "Where are we headed?"

"Right back to where they arrested us."

Jeanette's reply only confused Mary. "What? The hillside? The shed is nothing but ashes. What about the soldiers? What advantage would we have there?"

"Our advantage is that the hillside is the last place they'd expect us to go," Jeanette replied. "They'll first go to the Christian village and ask about us, and the sisters will tell them the truth, that we're not there and they haven't seen us. The sisters might tell them about the shed, but when the soldiers see the shed is just ashes, they'll head back to Aix."

"That seems to make sense. I pray it does. But with the shed gone where will we stay?"

"Do you remember the cave on the hillside I mentioned when we were arrested? The soldiers have no knowledge of that. It can serve as our home for a while."

"A cave on a hill. That's reassuring, Jeanette. I remember a psalm my mother used to recite to me when I was a child. *I will lift up my eyes unto the hills, from which cometh my help. My help cometh from the Lord, who made heaven and earth.*[1] I love that psalm. All my life, those words have always comforted me."

"The Sister Superior taught us that psalm too. Tonight the hills will be our shelter, and I do believe help will come." *Or at least I want you to think I believe that.*

Jeanette and Mary shared an embrace; they were both in need of reassurance.

"The sky is still cloudy and it's quite dark, so there's less chance of being seen. From here on, we can walk at a more comfortable pace. If the soldiers come back this way, we'll hear them at a distance, and we can hide in the nearby fields."

They proceeded down the road, Jeanette's arm around Mary, assisting her unsteady gait as they receded into the darkness.

CHAPTER 55

David, Martha, and Lazarus were pondering how Mary could have escaped and where she might be hiding, but without much success. They had noticed with concern the soldiers departing down every road. While scanning the remains of the crowd for some hint of Mary, they spotted the unmistakable robes of the Bishop of Aix.

Lazarus pointed him out to David, emphasizing that it was he who had denounced his niece as a heretic and condemned her to exile. He studied his nemesis as he directed the soldiers. "How can a bishop do that, David? His appetite for control seems boundless."

Martha, to her ultimate chagrin, was more observant. "Lazarus! Look at his thin face and dark eyebrows. He appears to bear some resemblance to the young man who came to us from Aix many years ago wanting to become a priest."

One studious look, and Lazarus realized his sister was right. The obvious implications almost made him gag, and he could only gasp through a tortured face, "I can't believe we actually ..." He was unable to finish the sentence. The two siblings could only stare at each other in agonized dismay and shake their heads.

David didn't understand the reasons for their dismay and said, "It might be that we can change the bishop's mind, for I have exciting new information that proves Mary is telling the truth. While in Tiberias I was shown the writings of a man named Mark, and I have some of his testimony with me. What he has written supports what Mary said at the trial."

Lazarus was skeptical about convincing the bishop of anything. He started to ask for the writings, but David was already approaching the domineering figure in the resplendent robes.

"Your Grace! I am Mary's uncle, from Palestine. May I have a moment of your time?"

The bishop gave David a dismissive glance and said nothing.

Undeterred, David continued. "Look, I have writings from a Christian writer named Mark who tells in detail about the life of Jesus. What he wrote proves that everything Mary said is true. Please, sir, I implore you, open the trial again, and let me present this new evidence!"

The bishop tilted his head back and looked down his nose at David. "Of course I know the writings of Mark. Do you think I am ignorant of what goes on in the Church? There is no evidence that this heretic Mary, who was properly on trial here today, is the Mary Magdalene about whom Mark wrote. In any event, what you ask is pointless. She isn't here."

Lazarus tried to back up David. "Sir, I assure you that the niece of this man truly is Mary Magdalene. David is her uncle and knows her history, including her travels with Jesus. Further, he was the captain of the ship that brought her here from Galilee, and he …"

Sensing that Lazarus might have a compelling point, the bishop cut him off. "I am sure you believe all that, but I have a criminal to find. I'm rather busy, so if you will excuse me …"

Lazarus could no longer keep his frustration to himself. His voice rose. "Bishop, I must protest that I do not understand your attitude. May I ask why you so relish denigrating Mary, who I can assure you is Mary Magdalene, and me as well, to such an unwarranted extent?"

The bishop looked at him as one would a child. "You know quite well that both of you have brought this upon yourselves by acting with disregard for Church authority. In the process, you have ignored the hierarchy of duly appointed Church leaders, arrogantly placed your opinions above theirs, and even given yourself a gratuitous promotion. Needless to say, none of this is tolerable. You and this

Mary must be, and have been, duly disciplined."

"Indeed, I recall your demoting me to, as you phrase it, 'a mere village priest'. I don't hold village priests in such low esteem as you appear to. I would ask, though, if I was never a bishop, does that mean that all who I ordained are, therefore, not legitimate Christian priests?"

The bishop had no difficulty spotting the trap, recalling full well who it was that had ordained him. With a smirk he replied, "If such men have proven their worth to the Church, I see no reason to question ordinations from long ago. I am only concerned about persons, such as this Mary from Magdala, who willfully disobey Church doctrine."

Lazarus protested, "She has taught nothing other than the words of Jesus."

"What you fail to grasp is that since the crucifixion such authorization must necessarily come from the recognized Church leaders."

"You mean such as yourself?"

The bishop ignored the sarcasm. "You appear incapable of understanding that the Church's foundation we are now building must last forever. What its leaders do today will influence millions of worshippers for centuries to come. What we do is most important. Your fantasies about being a bishop have no significance whatsoever."

Lazarus pressed his point. "Yes, but by 'Church' do you mean the human institution you seem intent on creating, or the eternal words of our Lord?"

"They are the same."

"In all instances?", asked Lazarus. "Those of us who traveled with Jesus and heard his words might have reason to disagree."

"Really?" the bishop replied. "It is fortunate, then, that your anti-Church views will soon be forgotten, while the true orthodoxy lives forever in official doctrines and Church history."

"Doctrines and history which you intend to help write, no doubt."

"Successful leaders write history, Lazarus. Village priests do not. You feel you know everything about the Church. Does it ever occur to you that you might be wrong?"

"Yes, often," countered Lazarus. "The difference between us is that I always consider that possibility whereas, apparently, you never do."

The bishop smirked again. "Did it ever occur to you that perhaps it is more appropriate for you to consider such failings and weaknesses than for me?"

"Could it be that I understand Jesus' instructions about humility better than you?"

As the two continued their verbal sparring, David again tried to intercede on behalf of Mary. "Sir, I implore you to consider …"

The bishop was tired of the debate. "I made it clear the trial is over. As of now, so is this conversation. I have no interest in anything either of you has to say. I must resume my work."

David was about to reply when Lazarus interrupted him. This time, Lazarus' voice was louder, more animated, and angrier than David had ever heard before. Gone was the hesitant, deferential man of the past. This was a new Lazarus, rising to the occasion.

"Sir, you should be ashamed of both your words and your attitude. You know full well that what David has to say about the writings of Mark is relevant. It is also a fact that he was the one who brought Mary Magdalene here from Palestine, and knows well her history with Jesus, as do I. You appear not to seek justice, only to advance your own image and your own power. Far worse, you violate the ninth of God's ten commandments by accusing Mary falsely!"

The bishop had never before heard such accusatory words directed at him. "How dare you? I demand you retract those impudent remarks and show me proper respect!"

Lazarus would not be intimidated, not this time. "Respect? It appears I must remind you that respect is the birthright of no man.

Do you not know how a person gains respect? It is earned day by day, word by word, act by act. People will respect you only if you respect them. It is not too late for you to begin earning the respect of those around you. Their respect, Bishop Maurice, not just their fear and enmity."

The bishop's jaw dropped. "What insolence! If you are too arrogant to respect an actual bishop of the Church, you must at least respect my vestments."

"Really? Perhaps no one has told you that Jesus wore no splendid vestments. He dressed the same as his followers. Vestments are unimportant; all that matters is the worth of the person within them."

Lazarus could sense the bishop becoming flustered. Pleased to have gained the offensive, he continued the attack.

"You, sir, may be an official Christian bishop, but then I ask, why do you not behave like one? The laws you pretend to uphold instruct us to seek justice, love mercy, and walk humbly before God. You do none of these things! Jesus told his followers not to criticize the speck in their neighbor's eye while ignoring the log in their own. That, sir, is good advice. I recommend you embrace it."

Lazarus maintained his glare at the bishop. He was finding it highly satisfying, almost therapeutic, to be dressing down his tormentor. "Do you believe, sir, that you are somehow immune from God's judgment?"

The bishop tried to glare back, but at this moment his face reflected more confusion and fear than confidence and authority, as did his wavering voice.

"You impudent … you … I don't have to take this impertinence from a mere village priest! Do you really hold church authority in such contempt? You think yourself very clever with your slanderous accusations, but I assure you my views are those of the Church, and therefore I will prevail. You and that pretentious Mary, whoever she is, will learn this to your sorrow in due time. You should pray for

God's forgiveness, lest you be damned for all eternity. Now be gone! I waste no more time with the likes of you."

With that final threat, he turned his back to his detractors, stormed off into the milling crowd, and disappeared from sight.

David, Martha, and Lazarus kept their eyes fixed on him as he withdrew, as one might track a venomous snake retreating into the underbrush. Martha gave her brother a silent but appreciative embrace. Then they began looking for somewhere to get a few hours of sleep before beginning their own search for Mary.

CHAPTER 56

The soldiers had returned to Aix via a different route, eliminating that immediate threat. Jeanette and Mary, exhausted and without a bed, nonetheless enjoyed a welcome night of undisturbed rest inside the hidden cave.

The rising sun was beginning to peek above a saddle in the eastern hills, and a few beams filtered their way through nearby trees. An enthusiastic nightingale let the cave's two occupants know they were missing a beautiful morning. Breakfast took up little time, as it consisted of sharing the few crumbs that were left from Jeanette's biscuit.

Lacking chairs but seeking the warmth of the rising sun, they were sitting on rocks outside their cave, talking. After Mary's second outburst of coughing, Jeanette decided it was time to address the topic that had long bothered her.

"Mary, I must confess, I worry about your health. The shed kept you warmer than this cave. We must find you a better place to live. You need more than a rock floor for a bed."

"Please don't worry, Jeanette. Remember, Jesus told his disciples not to be concerned about material things. Your friends have always kept me adequately provided."

Jeanette got straight to the point. "Mary, I do worry about your cough. That's not a material thing and I don't think we can ignore it. Also, you look thinner. Are you sure you feel all right? I'll go into Aix tomorrow and try to find a safe place for you to stay."

"As you wish, but it's not necessary. I'll be fine here. A decent meal would do much to resolve my looking thinner, and would give me some energy as well. As I mentioned, they feed prisoners poorly." Her confident tone was soon undermined by another coughing spell.

Jeanette had serious doubts she'd be fine in the cave, but unless she could find a secluded house in Aix, what other choice was there? She looked at her friend, bewildered. "So much hardship has befallen you, Mary, and I can't understand why. You're such a wonderful person."

"Perhaps it's the way God strengthens us and leads us to new opportunities. For a long while, I was angry and lonely because I lost my family. Viewed another way, though, had the horrible storm on the Sea not occurred, I imagine I would have continued to be a wife and mother in Magdala. I would never have met and learned so much from Jesus."

She placed her hand on Jeanette's arm. "If misfortune befalls us, we should never blame God. When adversity strikes, sometimes a great opportunity appears as well. All that's necessary is to recognize it."

Jeanette considered Mary's words. "I never thought of it that way. When I was a child, terrible things happened, and I thought my life had lost all meaning. Then you arrived at the village; and you were my opportunity!"

Mary smiled at her friend. "I believe the true measure of everyone's life is not what happened during their lifetime, but what happens in the future, in the lives of other people that knew them and were influenced by them."

"You have been the great influence in my life, Mary. To me, that's been the next best thing to meeting Jesus, which for me wasn't possible."

Mary took Jeanette's hand. "In many ways, you've already met Jesus. You truly have."

Jeanette had one other question, one that was of increasing interest to her. "Mary, I've always admired your determination to teach. Can you tell me why teaching is so important to you?"

"You see, all mortal beings eventually pass away, but words are eternal. Kings, ambitions, wars, and empires die when those who pursue them die, but words, like those of Jesus, are everlasting. Teaching is the pathway along which truths and good ideas are passed on to future generations and become eternal."

Jeanette had long felt a desire to teach, and this seemed like an opportune time to ask a favor. "I want to learn everything you know about teaching, Mary. You are so good at it; would you be my mentor? Teach me how to teach? To me, you're someone special."

Those words elicited a smile from Mary, as she recalled a conversation from long ago.

"When I was younger, Jeanette, my mother said to me that no one special ever came from Magdala. In one sense, she was right. I am no more special than Rachel or Sarah or anyone else in Magdala. I just had the good fortune to meet someone who *was* special, and that changed my life. It made me wiser and indebted, but not special. I only wish to repay that debt by carrying the words of Jesus to the world." Her smile faded. "Sadly, many people seem to think that's wrong."

"I'd say they're the misguided ones. No matter what you say, Mary, you'll always be special to me."

Mary smiled, then said, "Thank you. In return, I have a favor to ask of you. Do you remember those memoirs I was writing? I'd be grateful if you could look after them for me."

"Of course, Mary. Anything you ask. Where are they?"

Mary thought for a moment and started to look for them in her travel bag. They weren't there. Then the reality of the situation hit her, and her face turned to anguish. "Oh no, I think the last time I saw them was in the shed. In our hurry to escape did I leave them there? If I did Jeanette, they're gone! Just ashes! Even worse, that means the fire also destroyed ..."

There was no need to finish the sentence, Jeanette knew what she was referring to – the irreplaceable piece of papyrus she had been given by Jesus himself.

Jeanette and Mary could only stare at each other, perhaps having the same thought: *Arsonists not only destroy material matter, they also destroy ideas and even history.*

Jeanette put on an optimistic face. "The loss can be fixed, Mary. We'll start rewriting them tomorrow. I'll buy whatever you need in Aix."

"Thank you, Jeanette. I doubt my thoughts have any importance, but I would like to write down the teachings Jesus gave me. Those are …"

Jeanette touched Mary's arm. "I'm sorry to interrupt, but look off in the distance. Can you see them? Three people walking towards the ruins of the shed."

Both women shaded their eyes from the sun as they tried to make out the distant figures, without success. Jeanette, curious, offered to go down. "I'll say I live in the Christian village and ask them what they want."

"All right, but be careful. They may have been sent by the bishop, and might arrest you if they suspect you know me. Who knows what they might do to make you disclose where I'm hiding?"

CHAPTER 57

The three people they saw were not sent by the bishop; they were Lazarus, Martha, and David, all desperate to find any clue about Mary. David was the first to notice Jeanette's approach. Having never met, neither recognized the other.

"Good morning, sir," said Jeanette. "I'm from the Christian village down the road. I beg your pardon, but may I ask what you are seeking in these ruins? Can I help you find something?"

"We are merely trying to locate someone …"

Lazarus and Martha turned to see who was there. In unison they shouted "Jeanette!"

"Lazarus! Martha! What a wonderful surprise! What brings you here?"

"Exactly what you might guess. Do you know where she is! Is she all right?"

"Yes, nearby – follow me! Mary is fine, except for a bit of a cough from the cold weather." *At least, I pray it's nothing more.*

After Lazarus introduced Jeanette to David, they started up the hill as fast as their ages would permit. The next few moments were among the happiest of Mary's life. "Martha! Lazarus! David too! I can hardly believe it! Please say this isn't a dream!"

David and Mary shared a prolonged embrace, for which they had waited almost forty years. Mary was not the only one in tears, and David was incapable of words.

Beaming, Mary asked, "How on earth did you find us?"

"We thought they might know at the village where you were," Martha replied. "The Sister Superior knew nothing about you but told us about the shed, that it had been burned."

Jeanette blurted out, "Burned by henchmen of the Bishop of Aix!"

"Really?" Martha recalled the irony of the bishop's ordination. "Since we had no idea where you were, we started looking in the ashes for clues. Then Jeanette appeared."

Mary shook her head, "Yes, it seems I'm a fugitive from the law, or at least from the bishop's version of the law. Welcome to my new accommodations!" She pointed to some nearby rocks. "We can sit on my fancy marble furniture here." Another cough forced itself out.

David was shocked at Mary's situation. "You must be joking that you have to live here. You could freeze! And it's certainly not helping your cough. I'll find you a proper place in Aix first thing in the morning. No arguing!"

"I fear it's not that simple. I have no choice but to live here because, as Lazarus knows, the bishop has banned me from Aix. If I were caught living there, I'd be sentenced to prison for the rest of my life. Further, what would happen to the owner of the house?"

Jeanette added, "There's no one in Aix I'd place in such a fearful position. You should also know, David, the bishop demoted Lazarus from a bishop to, as he put it, 'a mere village priest.' That means nothing to us, Lazarus. You will always be our Bishop of Massalia."

"That's kind of you. What he did doesn't bother me that much. To me it's an honor to be a priest to the people. I need no fancier title. Now I can devote more time to my church, my congregation, and the needy people of Massalia. That is my calling."

David could see some humor in it. "Yes, and since you are no longer a bishop, you will have less work and ceremonies to take up your time, and the Bishop of Aix will have more. Maybe that will help keep him out of trouble!"

Lazarus joined in the laugh but felt a need to turn to more serious matters.

"Unfortunately, there's more tragic news. Peter and Paul are now dead, both martyred."

Mary could only stare at Lazarus, then bury her head in her hands. "How awful and discouraging. May they rest in peace with God. You know, Peter and I sometimes disagreed, but he was a devoted disciple, chosen by Jesus to lead his church. I have always respected that."

David's reply, however, was a surprise to all. "I'm appalled, too, at this news from Lazarus, but for a different reason. Mary, I actually met Paul."

She spun around, astonished. "Really! Where?"

"In Corinth, quite by accident. He was preaching there at a time when I was delivering artwork to a Corinthian merchant. We talked for a while, and it turned out Paul needed passage back to Caesarea. There I was with the *Ikaría*, about to head in the same direction in a few days."

"Amazing! Tell me, what was he like?"

"A compelling speaker, authoritative, self-confident. He said Jesus appeared to him after the resurrection, to rescue him from persecuting Christians. We had a pleasant conversation. A man named Luke was also there. He had traveled with Paul and was writing about his teachings. We talked more on the trip back to Caesarea. I'm saddened to hear of Paul's death."

"This is amazing," said Mary. "After the bishop chastised me for not knowing Paul, you not only met and talked with him, but even helped him on his journeys!"

Then, with more urgency she asked, "But tell me, David, did you happen to ask him whether women could be preachers of the gospel, and if they could instruct men?"

"I did. His response was similar to what Lazarus told me the bishop had said. Simply stated, women are forbidden to preach if men are present."

Lazarus added, "Our bishop, and others as well, will continue to exclude women from leadership roles. Regardless of how we feel, we haven't the power to change that."

Mary nodded but had another concern. "True, but we must all work to ensure the words of Jesus are accurately relayed. With each passing year, those who heard Jesus speak will be further outnumbered by those who didn't. In time, only the latter will be left. Will the Gospel they preach be that of Jesus, or will it be a version colored or even altered by their own beliefs?"

"I share your concerns," adds Lazarus. "Jesus warned repeatedly about false prophets and false teachers. I've been told Paul said similar things."[1]

As they contemplated the future, Mary wondered about the present. "Speaking of Palestine, David, please tell me anything more you might know about the situation in Galilee. Have you been to Magdala recently?" She tried to suppress a cough, without success.

David realized he could no longer postpone telling Mary the distressing events concerning Magdala. "Unfortunately, Mary, I must start with very sad news. I'm so sorry, but it grieves me to tell you that Rachel has passed away."

Mary stared at her uncle. "Oh, no! When? How?"

"As best as I could determine, a few years ago. I do not know the cause; perhaps just the afflictions of old age." He saw no wisdom in mentioning her burial right now.

As tears formed in her eyes, Mary recalled the years of shared joys and sorrows, now reduced to treasured memories. "Yes, she was elderly. She'd be over ninety by now."

She stared at the ground. "I feel terrible that I never returned to Galilee. I said I'd try, but it was too long a trip." She shook her head. "That's a pitiful excuse. I should have tried harder."

David put his arm on her shoulder. "It's just as well you didn't return, at least not in the last few years. You may not have heard, but the Jews in Palestine staged a revolt against Roman authority. Sadly, it didn't end well for them. Some of the worst fighting was in Galilee."

"How terrible! Is Magdala … do you know anything about my friend Sarah?"

"Unfortunately, Mary, there was heavy fighting around Magdala; many people died. The town of Magdala was destroyed, as were some nearby villages. No one was fishing on the Sea, and only a few from shore. Some outlying areas were spared, and your house is still standing. A different woman lives there now." He said nothing about the missing olive tree.

"What about Sarah?"

"There had been resistance in Sarah's neighborhood and most of the men were killed. I know nothing about Joel. The homes were empty, but I noticed someone in Sarah's orchard. To my great relief, it was Sarah. She was trying to live off the remaining rotting fruit, or anything else she could find. There was no future for her in Magdala, so I asked her to come to Gaul with me. Mary, here's some good news. She's in Massalia right now, helping out at the church!"

Mary's face was transformed with joy and relief. "Do you think we could go back there now? I might need to ride in a wagon, but …"

"First, Mary, we need to get you eating more, help you get stronger. Also remember that we'd have to elude both the bishop and the troops."

David's face became somber again. "I fear I have one other piece of tragic information. Much of Jerusalem was destroyed in the fighting, and the Temple was reduced to rubble. I was told that a single wall on the western side is all that remains. I'm sorry."

Martha buried her head into her hands. "How awful! What do you suppose will happen to the Palestinian Jews?"

Lazarus stared ahead but with a determined glint in his eyes. "They will survive. They'll find a way. They always have. If Rome could be rebuilt after the great fire, so can the Temple." [2]

Mary recalled the prophesy. "The temple destroyed, just as Jesus foretold."

Jeanette looked at Mary and asked, "Couldn't Jesus prevent wars?"

Mary replied, "If everyone accepted Jesus' teachings, wars would not exist. He did give us the most important kind of peace, though, the inner peace we have within ourselves. That gift sustained me during the trial, and in other dark times as well."

Mary's words were comforting to everyone present. That interlude came to an end when David's keen eyes noticed something of concern.

"Lazarus! Look down at the ruins of the shed. Am I not seeing someone there?"

Lazarus and Martha could indeed see a figure near the shed, but the person was hard for them to identify. The ashy ruins of the shed blended almost perfectly with the brown cape and gray headscarf of the person who was examining them.

CHAPTER 58

The two men ran down the hillside as fast as their aging legs would allow. David wondered who else might be interested in the shed's ashes? *Could it be someone sent by the bishop?*

Arriving at the shed, they found it odd that the figure in brown made no attempt to run. The gray headscarf obscured almost all facial features.

David shouted, "Who are you? What do you want here?"

A calm voice replied, "I am only seeking what you also sought."

Annoyed at the ambiguous response, David considered removing her headscarf himself to get at the truth. She saved him the decision and pulled it back herself.

David stared at her, not recognizing anyone familiar. What he saw was a frail and troubled-looking woman in her late fifties with a deformed nose. It didn't occur to him that she might be someone he had known years ago, when she looked far different.

Her identity, however, was apparent to his companion. Despite an absence of almost forty years, Lazarus had no trouble recognizing his own sister.

Lazarus gave his long-missing sister an emotional, tear-stained embrace. "Mary! God be praised! What ... how on earth did you find us? Where have you been?"

Mary of Bethany thought and, replied, "It's been so long, I don't know where to begin."

"When you mysteriously left Massalia would be a good start."

"Perhaps even better would be to tell you my name for the past thirty-eight years."

"What do you mean? Isn't it Mary? Did someone force you to change it?"

"No. When I left Massalia, after a long journey I settled in Lugdunum. When I met people, and said to them in my feeble Gaulish, 'My name is Mary,' they would respond 'Ah, Marie!' Before long, I just thought, *Mary, Marie, what's the difference?* Since I was living in Gaul, I might as well use the local version. Besides, 'Mary of Bethany' was useless; no one here ever heard of Bethany. As a result, for the last thirty-eight years I have been Marie."

"Would you like us to call you 'Marie'?" David asked.

"You might as well. At least that will avoid confusion with our dear Mary of Magdala."

Then reality hit her. Mary wasn't with them. "Is Mary alright? Where is she?"

"Yes, Mary is fine. Well, we hope she is," Lazarus responded. "She is weak and has a cough. The past few days have been hard on her. Right now she's up on the hillside, hiding from the authorities. She's in good hands, though, Jeanette is with her. Even better, Martha is there, too!"

"What? Really? How did – never mind. Why are we wasting time here? Please lead me to this cave, I want to see them!"

☙

Martha was equally thrilled to greet her long-lost sister, whose present appearance was almost as unfamiliar as her new name. Martha could see that the intervening decades had not been easy on the once beautiful Mary of Bethany.

Mary of Magdala likewise greeted her with a prolonged embrace. "What a joy to see you again! Can you imagine … almost forty years!" Another coughing spell.

"That is true, but what you have no way of knowing is that I've seen you much more recently and know all about those forty years in your life."

"What? How could you know that?"

"It's a long story. After I left Massalia, I went to Lugdunum; more about that later. A few weeks ago, I decided I was wasting my life in Lugdunum. More than anything, I wanted to locate my family. I went back to Massalia, and found the marvelous new church you created. A person there told me Lazarus and Martha had left for Aix a day earlier. I wondered, was it just coincidence, or had a premonition prompted my return to Massalia?"

"I arrived in Aix in time to hear about the trial and found the last empty seat in the hall. I listened to Mary tell about her life in Gaul and her capture by the bishop's men, and I was fascinated. Like you, I was furious at the verdict. The bishop had no intention of conducting a fair trial." Her friends nodded agreement.

"One thing puzzled me, though. Jeanette, why weren't you on trial as well?

"The bishop no doubt considered it," responded Jeanette. "I think he was so intent on punishing Mary and Lazarus that he felt I would be a distraction. Plus, I had done no teaching. I think he wanted everyone's attention focused on Mary's demise and his own power."

Marie agreed and continued. "After the so-called trial, I followed Jeanette to the jail and watched you escape. Brilliant! I was worried the soldiers would find you, so I gave some misdirection to the centurion. I hope my little lie can be forgiven, because it did what I wanted; it gave you additional time to make your escape."

"God bless you for that," said Jeanette. "I wondered why the soldiers were not right behind us when we were running away. It was you!"

"Then I walked to the little community where we left Mary. It was dark, so I slept in the nearby woods where we stayed that night long ago. In the morning, I went into the village and found Sister Annette. She told me about the shed, and there I was when you saw me."

They shared a little food that the sisters had given Marie, and eagerly pressed her to tell them what had happened to her over the past thirty years.

☙

As she began her story, she did not look happy. "You need to know, there are parts of it that are not so easy for me to talk about."

David seized the moment. "Might that include what happened to your nose?"

"Yes, it does. When I left Massalia, it was because I had made a fool of myself with that centurion Marcus. You were right, Martha; he was an egotistical brute; he cared nothing about me." She stared at the ground. "I felt so ashamed. How I could have been so blind?"

"The last straw was when he insisted I go to an event – a mass murder, really – in the arena. When I objected he hit me in the face and I fell bleeding to the ground. Then, incredibly, he leaned over and whispered, 'Sorry; I had to do that. You insulted me in front of the officers; you understand.' I thought, *Yes, finally, I understand. All too well, and much too late.*"

"I had endured enough. I packed my bag, helped myself to some of Marcus' money, and ran away. I was too ashamed to come back here with my freshly broken nose. Instead, I went north to Lugdunum, the regional capital, to seek work there."

"Oh, Marie," said Martha, "you know we would never have condemned you; we would have helped you any way we could."

"Of course I knew that, but I needed a new start somewhere far away. I wanted to do something worthwhile before seeing you again. So off I went."

"I found a small Christian church in Lugdunum, which was my home for a while. I swore there would be no more muscular military men. What I needed, I thought, was someone of means: educated, dignified, and well placed in society. I was still not very mature, now wanting a wealthy and attractive man to whom I could attach myself."

"Not too long after arriving in Lugdunum I found him, or so I thought. André was rich and handsome, no doubt about that, and influential politically. He seemed to be what I was looking for, and we were married much too soon. For a while we got along well, and before long we had a child, a charming little girl."

Martha beamed. "Marie, how wonderful! I'm delighted. What's her name?"

Marie was not smiling at all.

"Judith. I didn't like the name but André did, and André always got what he wanted. I devoted myself to raising my precious child, so much so that I paid little attention to what was going on around me. For example, when André stayed out late at night, it wasn't because he was working, like he said. No, he had a sizable collection of lady friends scattered around town."

"No! How awful for you!" Martha exclaimed.

"Oh, the story becomes worse, much worse. When I found out, André blamed it all on me. I spent too much time with Judith, he said, and ignored him. Did he want me to ignore Judith? He did nothing to help raise his child. I think he had wanted a boy. Anyway, he decided I should be punished. Perhaps he just wanted to be rid of me. He went to a magistrate, a close friend, and accused me of being a bad mother. A hearing to assess my guilt was arranged."

"Unbelievable!" protested Lazarus. "Surely the magistrate exonerated you?"

"As I said, it gets worse. Before the hearing I was quite nervous. André, pretending he wanted to be helpful, said, 'Here, have some wine. It will help calm your nerves.' Like a fool, I accepted a glass."

Marie stared at the floor. "Soon, the hearing began. André said I was an unfit mother. I expected that, but not what came next. The magistrate asked if he had proof. Helpful old André said, 'Well, for one thing, she drinks too much. All day sometimes.' I was stunned; you know how rarely I drink. I cried out, 'I do not!' André says,

'Really? Your Honor, just smell her breath; you decide.' Surprise – I smelled like wine. The case was closed; I was unfit. André was granted full custody of Judith and a divorce, which is what he really wanted. I was alone once again"

A tear came to her eye. "Since that day, I have never seen my little Judith. Not once."

Marie's listeners were aghast, their mouths open but unable to form words.

"I needed to find work. After a few days of searching I was hired as a housemaid for a rich lady, Madame Lesarde. She was kind to me and treated me better than a household servant, which is what I really was. She had a little girl named Bernadette, and over time she trusted me to become a part-time governess to her. That made up in a small way for the loss of Judith."

"I was so ashamed of it all that I couldn't find the courage to return to Massalia. I felt I had made a fool of myself and rubbish of my life, not once, but twice. I've lived with Madame Lesarde and worked for her all these years. Whenever I felt confused, I would ask myself what Mary would do. You were always there with me, Mary. Over time, I discovered that Jesus provides comfort for people who ruin their lives with stupid decisions. I'm grateful for that."

"And we're all grateful you're back with us," added Martha. "This is a day we'll long remember."

Chapter 59

David sensed his niece needed to hear some happier news. "Mary, here's something I believe you'll be gratified to hear. When I was talking with a priest in Tiberias, he called out to the custodian at his church. Mary, can you believe it, his custodian was Phlegian!"

Mary's jaw dropped. "You're joking! How could that be happier news?"

"Because of how it ends. As you might expect, Erascus blamed every cruel act of his own on Phlegian who, unable to defend himself, became a jobless beggar and almost starved to death. The priest I met saved him and made him church custodian. Over the years, Phlegian found Jesus and repented. In the end, even I said I could forgive him. An amazing story."

He paused. "Mary, I hope you're not upset that I told Phlegian I forgave him?"

"No, not at all. Jesus said to forgive those who wrong us. If Phlegian has accepted Jesus' words then I join you in forgiveness. I must ask, though, did he say anything about Erascus?"

"Yes, Phlegian said he stole money once too often, got caught, and was sent to a hard labor camp. He said criminals in those camps seldom live very long."

Mary reflected on this, and chose her words carefully. "Then God has administered justice. I will forgive Erascus as well, because Jesus would. I'm content with that."

"Well, I say good riddance to Erascus," added David, while thinking, *But I can never forgive him. I guess I'm not yet as good a Christian as Mary.*

David continued, "However, the priest had other information, much more important, that I'm sure you will like, Mary. He told me that a man named Mark had recently written the first account of the life and teachings of Jesus.[1] He even had a copy of it."

Mary's eyes lit up. "Really! I knew Mark, a friend of Peter's. I would love to see it."

Lazarus, who had also met Mark, said, "I've heard rumors of it, but nothing more."

David was unable to conceal his excitement. "I was amazed when I read the church's copy. It was more detailed than I anticipated, especially about Jesus' last days in Jerusalem."

"How detailed?" Mary asked. "Does it talk about the crucifixion?"

David was barely able to contain himself. "Mary, it talks about *you!*"

"What? No! Why me? I wish I could see it!" Her excitement induced a coughing spell.

"Indeed you can, for I copied down the four sections that mention you."

"That many? Thank you, David, how thoughtful. But how could he have known? I don't believe Mark, who was also called John Mark, was at either the crucifixion or the resurrection."

"We don't know Mark's sources, maybe the scrolls of others, or perhaps he talked with some of the Apostles," suggested Lazarus. "You said he was a friend of Peter's."

"Yes, and I believe I did speak once with John Mark after the resurrection."

David was impatient to see Mary's eyes light up. "Let me read from my notes. About the crucifixion, Mark says: 'Mary Magdalene, Salome, and Mary the mother of Joseph and James were watching from a distance, and later saw where the body of Jesus was placed.' "

"That's correct, except we did approach the cross when it seemed safe to do so."[2]

"And then you saw them roll the stone in front of the tomb. Later, you and two others brought spices to properly anoint his body and saw that the rock had been rolled away."[3]

"Yes, and a young man said that Jesus had risen, and we should tell this to the Apostles."

David frowned. "It also says you were afraid and ran away from the Apostles."

"That's not true!"

Lazarus supported Mary. "It sounds like Mark's source was ill informed. We can hope those words will be corrected in the future."[4]

After a moment of thought, Mary added, "Maybe Mark thought he was protecting me. I recall him warning me that women are forbidden to approach and talk to men."

David added, "Nevertheless, in time Christians everywhere will read Mark's writings and learn that Mary was the first to know the good news of the Resurrection!"

"Please, everyone, I beg you not to get carried away. I only did as I was asked. I just happened to be there at the right moment."

"Just happened to be?" Lazarus asked. "Maybe. If Jesus had wanted Peter to be the first to hear the good news, it would have happened that way. Instead, he chose you to be first and bring the news to the apostles. There must have been a reason."

Mary frowned slightly and said, "I don't wish to continue this speculation. I don't presume to know why Jesus acted as he did. We are not privy to know everything. Please, all this undue praise and conjecturing is making me weary." She coughed again, harder than usual. All four looked at Mary with concern. It was clear she needed to rest.

"Perhaps this would be a good time to have some supper, whatever we can find," suggested Martha. "I'm afraid it might not be much."

Then her eyes lit up. "You know, there might be a better solution. Perhaps if I went down to the village and asked the sisters, they might have some leftover food they could let us have. They would be happy to know we are all safe."

Smiles appeared on everyone's faces, as today's meals had been meager for those searching for Mary, and almost nonexistent for Mary and Jeanette.

As she arose, Martha said, "After we eat, David can give us more news."

"Yes," added Mary in a subdued voice. "I want to hear more about my dear mother. After that, I need to rest; I feel exhausted."

"I imagine we are all in need of a good night's rest," said David, wanting to delay any more detailed conversation about Rachel for as long as possible. "I suggest we eat and then get some rest. We can continue sharing stories in the morning."

❧

Martha had gone down to the sisters' village to inquire about getting some food. Her friends, expecting to see her return with a bag containing something edible, were dismayed to see Martha approaching with empty hands.

When she arrived at the cave, she was met by a silent group of associates with long faces and sad eyes, resigning themselves to going to bed hungry.

Martha, however, was beaming.

"Everyone, get up! Wonderful news! I talked with Sister Annette, and when I said we were all together at the cave and were wondering if they might have any leftover food, she got up and walked around with a resolute look on her face. You'll never guess what she said next."

Martha was bursting with joy. "Sister Annette, who is now the Sister Superior, said, 'This nonsense has gone on long enough. What happened forty years ago is irrelevant history. Jesus taught us forgiveness. Therefore, I hereby rescind the ban on sisters Mary and Jeanette from coming to our village.' Then she smiled and said,

'Furthermore, I invite all of you to come down here and have dinner with us tonight. This will be your last night in that musty hole on the hill. We'll find some space, and you can spend tomorrow night here at the village.' "

Martha took a breath and continued. "All the sisters erupted in a chorus of cheers. I doubt such euphoria had ever been seen at the village before. I gave Sister Annette a huge embrace. After the surprise wore off, she did the same for me. Then I ran back here as fast as I could."

David looked at Mary, who appeared half asleep. "Perhaps it might be best if we brought Mary's food back with us to save her the long walk. Mary, would that be all right?"

"Thank you," came a faint response. "I will be fine here. I would enjoy seeing the sisters again, but I'm weary and not all that hungry."

Jeanette looked at Martha and whispered, "Not all that hungry? She has had almost nothing to eat all day!" Martha just stared at the ground, expressionless.

Marie said, "I would like to do something to help. I'll stay here with Mary, and you can bring me something to eat when you return."

David donated his outer robe to help keep Mary warm, and Martha said, "Well, what are we waiting for? Dinner is being served!"

None of them thought they could move that fast.

Chapter 60

The combination of a warm night, a sufficient dinner, and the exhaustion of the day produced a sound night of sleep for all. With gratitude, they consumed the various items Sister Annette had provided for breakfast, which were adequate also to suffice as a midday meal.

The prospect of regular meals caused Marie to wonder, "If we asked, do you think she might let us stay at the village longer than just tomorrow?"

"We should only accept her hospitality for tonight," countered Lazarus. "It would be discourteous to ask for more. We are too many in number. Besides, the Bishop's obsession with Mary might result in more troops being sent there. We shouldn't risk endangering anyone."

Following their morning meal, Mary was napping. Long naps were frequent, and she hadn't left her bed since the previous day. To help her rest the others moved to a grassy area outside the cave, where wildflowers created a pleasant ambiance. Their conversation, however, was serious and focused on Mary.

Jeanette spoke first. "I think we need to discuss Mary's health. I'm concerned about her lack of energy, and especially her cough. She's had it for months, and it keeps getting worse."

"I must agree," said David. "What all of us are thinking needs to be said. Her health may be worse than just a cough, perhaps much worse. She seems so frail. I'm sure she wanted to see the sisters but had no energy. She ate little supper. Or breakfast."

David got right to the point. "I fear we must discuss unpleasant things. Mary will pass from us sooner or later. That's inevitable. As her closest relative, I've had to think about what will happen next and about her burial. First, I assure you I will take full responsibility for that."

Lazarus, not knowing of David's ulterior motive involving Rachel, thanked him for his generosity and asked, "What are your thoughts about where she should be buried?"

"Mary would have no desire for a fancy tomb, nor would she want to be buried in a public place where people might try to visit and venerate her. I think she would want to rest in private beside her mother."

Trying not to look embarrassed he continued, "I know where Rachel's grave is located; few others do, if any. When Mary passes from us, I will transport her back to Galilee and see to it that she is buried alongside her mother in an appropriate manner. I feel certain this is what she would want." David had decided the details of Rachel's initial burial could best be left unsaid. "No one but her family needs to know where she is buried."

Lazarus looked at David, puzzled. "Perhaps I'm wrong, but I thought she had no family now but you."

A faint smile appeared on David's face. "Then she will rest in peace."

David had one other worry on his mind, in the form of a favor to ask. "Lazarus, Martha – I am more and more reminded of my own advancing years. I have no relatives besides Mary, and no home of my own. I still have some money left. If I promised to work hard for you, might I come to Massalia to live and help out at your church?"

Martha replied without the slightest hesitation. "What on earth made you think you even needed to ask? Of course you can."

"Thank you so much. When the time comes, it will take two or three months to get Mary home and re-united with her mother, but after that I will return to Massalia. Furthermore, having a lot of money means nothing to me now; I've learned it's what you do with wealth that counts."

He smiled at Lazarus. "Your church looked like it could use additional seats and perhaps some repairs to the roof. I think that can be arranged. Also, I'll be happy to take care of Sarah's monetary needs."

A different topic occurred to Jeanette. "Did you know Mary had started to write some memoirs? Unfortunately, when the mob burned the shed they were destroyed." She started to mention also the message Jesus had given Mary but had second thoughts, and said nothing.

Lazarus understood the significance of her writings. "What a loss! The world should know about Jesus through Mary's eyes. Maybe she can dictate her thoughts to me. I would be delighted to be her scribe, if David could provide the papyrus."

"Consider it done."

Another thought came into Jeanette's mind. "She may never have mentioned this to you, but Mary once told me that Jesus had said he thought she understood his teachings as well as, or maybe better than, any of the other disciples."[1]

Lazarus responded, "Really? That is remarkable. I've often thought that Jesus' message was fairly simple. Some church leaders make it much more complex than I feel Jesus intended."

Lazarus' comment brought forth a memory to David. "You know, that reminds me, when I met Paul in Corinth he said the same thing. People should beware of being lured away from the simplicity of Jesus' teachings by self-serving false apostles."[2]

"This is why Mary's writings would be so important," said Jeanette. "They could help the basic truths of Jesus to be better understood."

"Perhaps, but I'm not optimistic," said Lazarus. "Mary has powerful opposition, even within the church. Even if she rewrites her memoirs, her enemies might try to destroy them."

Lazarus stared at the floor. "It's so sad; all Mary wanted to do was to teach about Jesus, but she couldn't, solely because she's a woman."

Mary's pupil was more optimistic. "I said a similar thing to Mary once, and she replied by saying, 'I feel sure it will happen, Jeanette. It may be a hundred years from now, or even a thousand, but I am confident women will teach about Jesus someday.' In any event, I'm certain that if people know about Mary and her faithfulness to Jesus and his message, and the respect that Jesus had for her, then the world will know the truth."

⬦

They took turns observing Mary as her nap extended well into the afternoon. When she finally awoke, Jeanette was alone watching over her. She gently reminded Mary that Sister Annette was expecting them to relocate to the village that afternoon.

In a barely audible voice Mary said, "Thank you for reminding me. It will depend on how much energy I have. Right now, Jeanette, I have something I wish to say to you."

"Yes, of course. What is it?"

"It's the special message that Jesus gave me. It isn't long, and I believe I still have a good memory of what it said. I would like you to hear it."

Jeanette's eyes grew wide as she sat down beside Mary. She said nothing, fully concentrating on hearing and memorizing what her mentor was saying.

When Mary finished relating Jesus' words, she added, "In due time, Jeanette, you may pass this message along. Do so only when you find someone in whom you have as much trust and confidence as I have in you."

Jeanette, unsure of what to say, replied, "Thank you. I understand."

Jeanette went outside and signaled to the others that Mary was awake. Martha knelt by Mary and repeated the reminder that Sister Annette was expecting them.

It took Mary a minute or so to recall the conversation. "Oh, yes, she offered us lodging. I have little energy right now and am comfortable here. Could we stay here tonight and move to the village in the morning? I usually have more energy ..." She pulled her headscarf over her mouth to contain a vigorous, body-shaking cough. Noticeably wincing, she whispered in a cracking voice, "... more energy in the morning."

Her friends exchanged concerned glances. After a pause resulting from no one knowing how to respond, Jeanette smiled at Mary and said, "Of course. I'm sure you will feel stronger after a good night of sleep. One of us will go to the village and tell Sister Annette our arrival will be delayed until morning."

Martha gently stroked Mary's hair. "Jeanette is right; you just rest as much as you need. The morning will be fine."

Jeanette, however, had ceased smiling. Her now frightened eyes were sharp enough to have noticed the small dots of blood that had newly appeared on Mary's headscarf.

CHAPTER 61

In a spacious and well-furnished room, an elderly man in re-splendent robes sat in a finely crafted chair made of pure Carrara marble. The chair was on a platform to emphasize the status of its occupant. An exquisite Persian carpet enhanced the stairway to the platform. Attendants stood on both sides of the elderly man seated on the marble chair. That elderly man was Linus, the Bishop of Rome, who had succeeded the martyred Peter as head of the church.[1]

Before him stood a tall, thin man almost as well-attired, his head respectfully bowed in deference to the position of the person before him. This was Maurice, the Bishop of Aix, who had been summoned to Rome to appear before Bishop Linus. The latter was concluding his remarks, while nearby scribes copied down every word with careful precision.

"I want you to know, Bishop Maurice, that as the successor to Peter, I constantly ponder the dilemma that faces us. On the one hand, I am delighted at the speed with which the word of God, given to us by our Savior Jesus, is spreading across the land. With the passage of time, however, it will become more difficult for those of us in Rome to be certain those words are being transmitted accurately. Yet it is essential that this be done."

He crossed his hands, and in a somber tone continued. "How can we deal with the likelihood that within the Christian realm there will arise ill-informed priests, or worse, insidious impostors? Such people could, either out of ignorance or arrogance, misrepresent the words of our Lord and the manner in which Christians are asked to live. The writings of Mark and others remind us that Jesus warned of this.[2] Are you familiar with those writings, Bishop Maurice?"

"Most assuredly, your Eminence. I have studied the passages you mention in detail."

Bishop Linus gave an almost imperceptible nod of approval, and then continued. "I have thought about this at great length, weighing various options for addressing the problem. I have concluded that an office needs to be established within the administration of the Church to address this compelling question. This new office will oversee the proper conduct of our priests, as well as the content of their teaching. Only in this manner can the Church's message remain forever consistent and orthodox wherever it is preached. This in turn will render the Church strong, united, and universally respected. I am convinced that such a department must be created and endowed with strong leadership as quickly as possible."

The Bishop of Rome looked intently at his subordinate. "Do you, Bishop Maurice, concur with what I am saying, or would you counsel some other course of action?"

"You have my assurance, I am in complete agreement with both your analysis of the problem and your proposed solution. I will support you in any manner I can."

"Excellent," replied Bishop Linus. "I have talked with numerous people, including my advisor Luke, who have commended you for your verdict in the unfortunate Mary of Magdala incident. They noted that the Bishop of Aix is a strong Church leader, one who understands Church orthodoxy, and who is energetic and resolute enough to oversee and enforce these matters."

He kept his eyes fixed on the Bishop of Aix. "Tell me, Bishop Maurice, if you agree with the importance to the Church of the problem I have presented, and with my proposal for addressing it, would you consider yourself capable of heading such a department?"

Maurice understood the huge import of the question, but was also conscious of the need to appear none too eager, nor too pleased.

He responded in a calm, measured manner.

"Your Eminence, I agree with all you have stated. I am deeply humbled and most grateful that you would consider me for such a position. If it is your will, I am prepared to assist you in every way possible to carry out your vision."

"Then it is so. I hereby appoint you to be the first director of the ecumenical Committee for the Doctrine of the Church, with the title of Conservator of Church Orthodoxy." He looked at his scribe who was recording every word with extreme care. "It is so ordered." The Bishop of Rome opened a drawer and removed his official seal.

Maurice was barely able to contain his elation. His childhood dreams of greatness had been achieved. He thought of his stepmother's orders and inwardly smirked. *Not learn Latin? Hah! Now she'd see how foolish her dictates were. I will live in Rome and wield power over millions! Where would I be had I listened to the whims of that silly woman? I have triumphed!*

He had sufficient discipline, however, to maintain an expressionless face.

Maurice stood erect and directed his most serious look at the Bishop of Rome.

"It is a high honor to be selected to head the Committee for the Doctrine of the Church. You may be assured that, under my administration and guided by your vision and counsel, all traditional practices of the Church will be perpetuated. I will give particular attention to the venerable rules governing the relationships between men and women, including the right to teach, and will ensure that they are adhered to everywhere throughout the Christian realm." [3]

"I will, with dedication and determination, enforce Church orthodoxy."

CHAPTER 62

That evening, after another welcome supper supplied by Sister Annette, the five friends sat outside the cave discussing a variety of topics. Mary had been quiet during supper except for another bad coughing spell, and had eaten almost nothing. Afterwards, she had said little more than that she was feeling weak and a little dizzy, and wished to get some sleep. Her friends had noticed that she appeared to be in pain as well. Nor could Jeanette forget the blood drops.

To provide the maximum quiet for Mary, her companions had taken their conversation outside. They had tired of all the worrisome subject matter, so Jeanette was entertaining her eager listeners with the details of Mary's first efforts at preaching in Aix, and of their life together as cooks and dishwashers at the little Christian village.

Following Jeanette's engaging vignettes, the conversation subsided and they relaxed in silence and private contemplation. Each was taking in the beauty of the earth and sky around them, lost in their own thoughts about it.

The sun was close to setting, covering the landscape with a soft, warm glow. The earth, the grass, and the trees seemed almost golden. A lark gave voice to its appreciation of the surrounding beauty. In the western sky, a dramatic cloud formation developed, and then slowly split into two sections, each with a luminescent white border around vivid gold, orange, and saffron clouds. A beam of sunlight radiated to earth from the bright center of the formation, illuminating the hillside.

Marie was enthralled by its color and elegance. "Look at that sunset! I think it's the most magnificent one I've ever seen."

Lazarus was equally taken by it. "It is quite remarkable. With a little imagination, you could think that the beam of sunlight coming from between the clouds resembles a pathway leading straight up into the heavens."

They sat for a few moments admiring the beauty before them, appreciating the gifts of clouds and color and sunlight. Before long, however, a troubling thought forced its way into each of their minds, and one by one they turned and looked quizzically at those nearest them.

It was as though Lazarus' interpretation had suddenly taken on another possible meaning, an infinitely more somber and disquieting one. Their pleasant expressions changed to concern, and then to something close to trepidation. They arose almost in unison and rushed towards the cave.

All was quiet there. There was no coughing to be heard.

Peace had descended, and their friend suffered no more.

Mary of Magdala had passed from this earth.

♒

The five friends stood frozen in silence, thinking their own thoughts while wiping away their tears. They all had vivid memories of the ways in which Mary had been a central transformative factor in their own lives.

Lazarus and Martha recalled Mary's years of help in making their church a success, but before that she had provided them, through David, a means to escape from the turmoil in Palestine. Lazarus thought, *Without Mary, not only might our local churches never have been built, we might not even be alive.* Each, in their own way, expressed silent words of thanks and gratitude.

David, for his part, thought about the invisible Mary that had always been beside him. *From that early visit with the magi, I knew Mary was somehow going to be special, both in my life and her own. In a sense she was always with me, being my better angel, prompting me to do the right thing, even though I was never aware of it. I was desperately in need of it, though, and eventually found it. God bless you, Mary.*

Marie's thoughts were simple. *I could have avoided making a mess of my life, for the guiding light I needed had always been right there, wanting to help me, but I was too blind to see it. At last, through Mary, I achieved a measure of both peace and wisdom. I assure you, Mary, I shall walk in your footsteps from now on.*

Innumerable thoughts were racing through Jeanette's mind, but one stood out. It was that poignant night when she and Mary revealed to one another the tragic experiences that had befallen them. *She was willing to share with me the most horrible events of her life, and in so doing gave me the strength to deal with mine and escape from the terrible memories of my childhood. She freed me from the prison in which I had been living and opened a whole new future for me, a wonderful future. In every way, she transformed my life.*

Jeanette then recalled a proverb Mary said Jesus used often. *'For what does God require of you but to seek justice, love mercy, and walk humbly before your God?'* That was how Mary lived her life. Jeanette closed her eyes and promised herself, *And that is how I'll lead mine.*

For a while they said nothing, looking at Mary one last time. Eventually Lazarus spoke. "Mary has departed. Her trials are over, and she rests in peace. Her legacy is for the ages now. The world has lost a wonderful person, but we can take comfort that the will of God, through the words of Jesus and then through the words of Mary and all who heard her, will triumph."

David's eyes were focused on Mary as well, but he was noticing something no one else had. "Look, in her hand. Is she clutching something?"

In Mary's hand was a small piece of papyrus. On it were written in shaky handwriting just two words, *For Jeanette.*

David gently picked it up and handed it to her.

Jeanette slowly unfolded it. What was inside was familiar to all of them. It was a simple ornamental chain with a small stone fastened to it. On one side of the stone was a slight discoloration.

Jeanette's eyes were huge, one hand pressed over her mouth. "It's – it's her mother's necklace, the one she called her amulet. And the stone that …"

Jeanette broke out in tears, overcome with emotion. Trembling, she slowly raised the necklace, and with unsteady hands fastened it around her own neck. She took a deep breath, as if summoning the courage to make a life-changing decision.

After a few seconds, Jeanette raised her head and looked toward the golden-hued sky. Through her tears, she spoke in a firm, resolute voice.

"I will go back to Massalia, perhaps even Aix. And with Mary always there to inspire and guide me – I will teach!"

The end

Epilogue

Almost 2000 years have passed since Mary Magdalene traveled through Galilee with Jesus, yet her vision of gender equality for Christian women has been little realized. The path is heading in the right direction, but there is still much ground to be covered.

During the Renaissance, many artists painted Mary, but almost always as either an active or repentant prostitute. In 1888, Czar Aleksander III of Russia built the Church of Saint Mary Magdalene in Jerusalem to honor his mother. Mary's reputation, though, remained the same.

That appears to be changing. Although the Roman Catholic Church still does not permit female priests, two significant events have taken place since the mid-20th century with regard to Mary Magdalene. First, in 1969, Pope Paul VI acknowledged that she was never a prostitute, and noted that the idea had been created around the year 591 c.e. by Pope Gregory I, who wanted a well-known person to serve as the model of a reformed and forgiven prostitute. Fourteen centuries passed before Mary was freed from this accusation.

More recently, and of even more significance, was what transpired in 2016. On June 10 of that year, the Congregation for Divine Worship and the Discipline of the Sacraments, an office of the Roman Catholic Church, made public a decree which elevated Mary's liturgical status to a feast day, the same status given to the Apostles selected by Jesus. Only Peter and Paul are honored with a higher status, known as a solemnity. For the first time, Mary Magdalene was referred to as the "apostle to the Apostles."

These and other recent events relating to efforts to advance gender equality within the Christian world are noted in Appendix B, which follows. While these are encouraging, in many other parts of the world, as well as in other religions, such progress has not yet been seen.

The majority of the world's population hopes the goal will be realized soon.

Appendix A:
Notes and References

<u>Introduction.</u>

[1]In this regard, there is an interesting passage in the Acts of the Apostles. In Acts 1:14 there is wording about "the women." This at least suggests that Mary Magdalene could have been with the apostles at some point, and possibly often, following the resurrection.

[2]Additional information about the Gnostics and the Gnostic Gospels can be found in Elaine Pagels, *The Gnostic Gospels*, Vantage Books, 1979.

[3]For a fuller description of this action by the Roman Catholic Church, see the Epilogue and the 2016 entries in Appendix B.

<u>Chapter 1</u>

[1] The abbreviation "c.e." stands for Current Era (or Common Era, or Christian Era), and has replaced the former term, *Anno Domini* (A.D.; the Year of Our Lord), as the international time scale terminology. It is also generally accepted, based on other historical events, that Jesus was probably born, not in 1 c.e., but more likely sometime between 4 and 7 b.c.e. (before current era). About 4 b.c.e. is commonly accepted.

<u>Chapter 3</u>

[1] The Sea of Galilee has been known by different names. In Biblical times it was also known periodically as the Sea of Chinnereth (or

Kinnereth), Lake Tiberias, and the Sea of Gennesaret. Its elevation (variable) is about 700 feet (213 meters) below ocean level.

² The Jewish exile to Babylon occurred in the 6th century b.c.e. The exile is described in the Old Testament in 2nd Kings, Chapter 25. Many Jews eventually returned to Palestine, but others remained in Babylon. Those that returned brought the Aramaic dialect with them. It is generally believed that Aramaic was the language Jesus spoke. Babylon (Babylonia) was the region where the Tigris and Euphrates Rivers come most closely together, located in what today is the nation of Iraq.

³ The place name "Magdala" may come from the word "migdal", meaning "tower". A reference in Matthew (15:39) to a town named "Magadan" might be using an alternate or older name for Magdala. Readers interested in knowing more about first century Magdala can find a detailed account in the work by Jane Schaberg cited in the bibliography. Chapter 2 in the book by Esther de Boar also discusses Magdala.

Chapter 4
¹ The Great Sea was the common name at that time for the Mediterranean Sea.

² The standard unit of distance in the Roman world was the (Roman) mile, or in Latin the *mille passus*. It was equal to .92 contemporary English miles, or about 1.48 kilometers. For simplicity the term "mile" is used herein; in all instances it will mean the Roman mile.

³ See the Gospel of Matthew 2:1-12. In the King James version of the Bible they are called "wise men"; other translations (*Living Bible, Good News Bible*) suggest their occupation was more akin to astrologers. Coming from "the East", they would quite likely have passed through, or near, Magdala as they rounded the north end of the Sea of Galilee. Matthew is the only one of the four gospels that mentions the three wise men.

Chapter 5

[1] Depending on how direct the trail they would be using was, it would be about 20 miles (32 kilometers) from Magdala to Nazareth.

[2] Tiberias was the administrative center of Galilee, founded by Herod Antipas about 18 c.e. to honor the emperor. It was the largest city on the Sea of Galilee, located about 5 miles (8 km) south of Magdala. For more about Tiberias, see the reference by Achtemeier (ed.).

Chapter 11

[1] Mark 6:1-5 and Luke 4:22-24.

[2] For a similar statement by Jesus concerning believing in him prior to seeing him, see John 20:29. Jesus said, "Your faith has made you whole" to a Samaritan in Luke 17:19, and similar wordings appear in Luke 7:50 and in Mark 5:34 and 10:52.

[3] A scene in the New Testament where Jesus shows he has knowledge of past events that, in theory, he couldn't know about is John 4:16-18.

Chapter 12

[1] Matthew 5:1-12, also Luke 6:17-26. This sermon by Jesus is commonly known as the Sermon on the Mount; the opening portion is termed the Beatitudes.

[2] Matthew 19:13-15; Mark 10:13-16; Luke 18:15-17.

[3] Matthew 7:12 (this is often referred to as "the Golden Rule"), and Matthew 19:16-19. Also Luke 18:18-20 and Mark 10: 18-19. The original wording of the Ten Commandments is found in Exodus 20:1-17.

[4] A scene where the apostles are surprised at Jesus talking with a woman is John 4:27-29.

[5] The possibility that Jesus may have preached in the Magdala synagogue is discussed in the 2016 article by Sabar in the references.

⁶ The Gospel of Luke (8:2) refers to "seven demons" (without indicating what they were) that inflicted Mary Magdalene. This term also appears in the alternate ending of Mark (16:9), which states they were driven from Mary by Jesus. Since it is unknown who wrote Mark 16:9, the repeat of the term "seven demons" has led to speculation it might have been written by Luke, or someone familiar with Luke's writings.

⁷ Matthew 21:1-9. In contemporary Christianity this is known as Palm Sunday. See also Mark 11:8-10, and John 12:12-15.

⁸ John 12:12-16; also Matthew 21:12-13 and Mark 11:15-17.

⁹ Matthew 20:17-19; Luke 18: 31-34; Mark 10: 32-34. See also Luke 21:5-6.

¹⁰ John 11:1-44. The story of Lazarus appears only in the Gospel of John; it is absent from the other three, although Matthew mentions Jesus visiting Bethany.

Chapter 13
¹ John 8:3-11. This passage is only in John, and is missing in some early translations.

² Jesus' strong condemnation of the Pharisees is in Matthew 23:13-36.

³ Micah 6:8. This passage, with slightly different wording, is in Matthew 23:23.

⁴ Matthew 22:34-40; also Mark 12:28-31and Luke 10:25-28.

⁵ Matthew 28:19; Luke 24:45-47; Acts 1:8.

⁶· Galatians 3:28. This is the main place where men and women are said to be equal.

⁷ Luke 17: 20-21. See also Matthew 24:36-44 and Mark 13:32-33.

⁸ Matthew 24: 23-24; Mark 13:21-31; Luke 21:32-33.

Chapter 14
¹ Matthew 26:17-19; Mark 14:13-16; Luke 22:8-13.

[2] Matthew 26:20-25; Mark 14:18-21; Luke 22:21-23; John 13:21-30. John is the only gospel in which the last four words ("Do as you must") are found.

[3] Matthew 26:26-28; Mark 14:22-24; Luke 22:17-20.

[4] Matthew 26:31-35; Mark 14:27-31, 37-40; Luke 22:33-34; John 13:37-38 and 21:18.

[5] Matthew 26:43; Mark 14:40; Luke 22:45.

[6] This specific statement does not appear in the Bible; however, some biblical scholars, in writing about the Jesus - Mary Magdalene relationship, suggest it might be an accurate assessment. See, for example, the reference by Karen King, 2003, p. 87. See also the entry for June 10, 2016, in Appendix B.

[7] The suggestion that some special knowledge had been given to Mary Magdalene comes from the Gnostic Gospel of Mary, 9:30 to 10:4. See the Karen King reference, p. 17, and also the Elaine Pagels reference (1979), p. 64.

Chapter 15

[1] Mark 15:40 and 15:47. The gospels of Matthew, Mark, and Luke state that the women watched the crucifixion "from afar"; only John (19:25) places the women close to the cross.

[2] Matthew 27:35; Mark 15:24; Luke 23:34. This passage was the basis for the book and motion picture "The Robe".

[3] Luke 23:46.

Chapter 16

[1] Matthew 27:57-66; also Luke 23:50-56 and John 19:38-42. In this chapter the role of Mary Magdalene in the events of the Resurrection combine elements of what appears in all four Gospels, as the Gospels differ in their descriptions of several key points, such as how many women went to the tomb or to whom Jesus appeared first.

² Mark 16:1-6; Luke 24:1-3. Matthew (28:1-7) states that an angel moves the rock. The four gospels are not in agreement on the names of the other women who were with Mary at the tomb. Mark names three women, Matthew names two, Luke names three but states that other women were also there. All three gospels list the name of Mary Magdalene first. The Gospel of John (20:1-2) has only Mary Magdalene going to the tomb. In John, Mary doesn't enter the tomb. The first three Gospels refer to a young man, an angel, or two men, in the tomb. John says "two angels".

³ John 20:14-18. Mark 16:9-11, is similar but many believe these verses may have been added later, perhaps by a different writer (see footnote 4 to Chapter 58). Mark 16:8 states the women told no one about the resurrection. Luke (24:5-10) has Mary and several other women reporting the news of the Resurrection to the Apostles, but does not indicate that Jesus appeared to any of them. Matthew's version (28:5-10) has Jesus appearing to Mary Magdalene and one other woman; he then instructed the two of them to deliver the news to the apostles. John 20:19 states that Jesus appeared to the Apostles on Sunday evening.

⁴ Luke 24:8-11; Mark 16:11.

Chapter 17

¹ Mark 6:7; Luke 10:1. Luke does not name the 72 disciples, nor specifically where they were sent, nor what they did subsequently, but they were given the power to heal.

² This opinion by Peter is found in the (Gnostic) Gospel of Mary, 10:2. The Gospel of Mary was not selected to be part of the New Testament. Mary was not the only disciple who had disagreements with Peter; Paul came out strongly against Peter at least once (Galatians 2: 11-14).

³ Matthew 16:18.

[4] Subsequently, Matthias was chosen as the new twelfth apostle (Acts 1:21-26).

[5] The concerns for the safety of Jesus in Judea, even from the Jewish authorities, are noted in John 11:53-54.

[6] John 12:9-11.

Chapter 19

[1] Galatia is one of several provinces in Asia Minor (now the country of Turkey) that were visited by Paul and other disciples. Ephesus is on the west coast of Turkey.

[2] At the time of Jesus the region now known as France was called "Gaul" by its inhabitants, but "Gallia" in Latin and Greek. The language was correspondingly "Gaulish" or "Gallic". "Gaul" and "Gaulish" are used here.

[3] Mark 16:15-16, Luke 24:46-47, and Matthew 24:14. See also Acts 1:8.

Chapter 20

[1] Caesarea was built by King Herod only a few decades before the birth of Christ, and it quickly became the major seaport of ancient Palestine. Almost all artifacts from that era, except an amphitheater and the footprints of some buildings, no longer exist. It is today being developed by Israel into a resort community.

Chapter 21

[1] Casson, L., *Travel in the Ancient World*. Toronto: Hakkert, 1974, p. 150.

Chapter 22

[1] Massalia (often spelled Massilia) is today known as Marseille.

[2] The dominant tradition in Provence is that Mary, together with

Martha, her sister, and Lazarus, landed at a spot on the south coast of France, a little west of the Rhone River delta, that is now called "Saintes-Maries-de-la-Mer". Today it is a coastal resort town. But there are other versions of how Mary Magdelene arrived in Gaul.

Chapter 23
[1] The 1st century town of Aix (pronounced 'ecks') is now the city of Aix-en-Provence. The large river they crossed was the lower Rhone, and the crossing point was at the present city of Arles, in Roman times known as Arelate. After Julius Caesar conquered Gaul in 58-51 b.c.e. this region was named Gallia Narbonensis, after the port city of Narbo, now known as Narbonne. Earlier the area around Massalia was known as Provincia Romana, the origin of the present name for the region, Provence.

Chapter 28
[1] Proverbs 8:13 and Isaiah 13:11. See also Micah 6:8.

Chapter 29
[1] Acts 7:54-60.
[2] The apostle Paul expressed such concerns at some length in 1 Timothy 1:3-7. Similar thoughts appear elsewhere in the New Testament.
[3] The suggestion that there was friction between Mary Magdalene and Peter and Andrew comes from the Gnostic Gospel of Mary, 10:1 to 10:4. See the Karen King work in the bibliography, p. 17.

Chapter 31
[1] Matthew 27:37; Mark 15:18; John 19:2-3.
[2] Matthew 10:5-6.
[3] Mark 13:10 and 16:15-16. See also Matthew 24:14, and Luke

24:46-47.

[4] Matthew 25:40. Regarding ethnicity, Peter states in Acts 10: 34-35 that God accepts all people who believe in his word. Slightly differing wording appears in various Bibles; the King James version says "in every nation", but the Good News Bible says "no matter what race".

[5] James 2:1-9. It is not clear exactly when the Letter from James was written.

Chapter 33

[1] According to Biblical concordances, the only reference to homosexuality in the New Testament is in Romans 1:24-32. These forceful passages were written by Paul, and in them there is no reference to any statements made by Jesus.

[2] Matthew 7:1-2.

[3] Matthew 22:39; Mark 12:30-31; Luke 10:27; and John 13:34-35.

Chapter 35

[1] Lugdunum was the original name of the present city of Lyon. For a time it was the capital of Roman Gaul.

Chapter 36

[1] That Mary may have received such knowledge and shared it with the apostles is suggested in the Gnostic *Gospel of Mary*, 6:1-3, as translated in the work cited in the bibliography by Karen King, 2003, p. 15. However, the author of the *Gospel of Mary* is unknown, and none of the Gnostic Gospels were chosen to be part of the New Testament.

Chapter 39

[1] 1 Corinthians 1:10 and 2 Corinthians 11:3 (King James translation).

[2] Titus 2:1-5. See also 1 Peter 3:1-2.

[3] Acts 9:3-20. At that time the Apostle Paul went by the name of Saul.

[4] This is inferred from the opening words in the Gospel of Luke (1:1-4) and in Acts of the Apostles (1:1). That Luke was with Paul on his second journey is assumed from the use of the word "we" in places such as Acts 16, verses 10-11, and elsewhere. See also Romans 16:22.

[5] Acts 15:36 to 18:22.

[6] Acts 7:54 to 8:1, 8:3, and 9:1-2, and. See also 1 Corinthians 15:9.

[7] 1 Corinthians 15:10-11.

Chapter 45

[1] For a statement by Jesus that is similar, see Luke 17:20-21.

Chapter 46

[1] For more information about the Gnostics and the Gnostic Gospels, see the work in the references by Elaine Pagels.

[2] 1 Timothy 2:11-14. See also 1 Corinthians 14:34-35.

[3] 2 Peter, chapter 2.

[4] Titus 2:1-5. See also 1 Peter 3:1-2.

[5] For example, see John 4:7-29.

[6] Luke 24:1-10. Although Luke, alone among the four gospel writers, does not say that the risen Christ appeared to Mary Magdalene, he does state that she and other women were the ones who delivered the news of the empty tomb to Peter and the other apostles. But he then goes on to say that they thought what Mary was saying was nonsense. (Luke 24: 11-12). The wording in verse 24:10 suggests that at least five women were in the group that went to the tomb.

[7] There is no mention of Mary Magdalene in the Acts of the Apostles, nor anywhere else in the New Testament following the four Gospels. As noted earlier, there is subsequent mention of her in the Gnostic Gospels.

Chapter 50
[1] Matthew 5:16 (King James version). This is part of the "Sermon on the Mount".

Chapter 54
[1] Psalm 121: 1-2 (Wording from the King James version).

Chapter 57
[1] Among the four Gospels, Matthew contains the most passages on the topic of false prophets and religious preachers who misrepresent Jesus' teachings. For example, see Matt. 7:15-20, Matt. 15:3-9, Matt. 24:11 and 23-24, and Mark 13:21-22. The Apostle Paul frequently voiced the same message, as in 1 Tim. 4:1-3, 1 Tim. 6:3-6, 2 Tim. 4:3-4, and 2 Cor. 11:3-4 and 11:12-15. Similar warnings appear in 2 John 7-11 and 2 Peter 2:1-3 and 10-21.

[2] The destruction of the Temple occurred in 70 c.e. The Great Fire of Rome that burned most of the city occurred in 64 c.e. There is disagreement as to how it started; some sources blame it on Nero himself.

Chapter 59
[1] It is generally accepted that Mark was the first of the four gospels to be written. Interested readers can find a concise history of the Gospel of Mark at www.religionfacts.com/gospel-of-mark
[2] See footnote 1 to Chapter 15.
[3] Mark 15:46-47 and 16:1-4.

[4] Mark 16:5-11. There are two accepted endings to the Gospel of Mark. The older one suggests that Mary might not have conveyed news of the resurrection to the apostles at all (verses 5-8). A later second version (Mark: 16:9-11, author unknown) says Jesus appeared first to Mary Magdalene, and that she did convey the news to the apostles. The author of the second ending might be Luke or someone familiar his writings, since it includes the phrase "seven demons" which otherwise occurs only in the Gospel of Luke. When the second ending was written isn't known.

For comparison, see also Matthew 28:5-10, Luke 24:8-10, and John 20:14-18.

Chapter 60
[1] Refer to Chapter 14, footnote 6.
[2] See footnote 1 to Chapter 39, especially 2 Corinthians 11:3 (King James translation).

Chapter 61
[1] Before the adoption of the term "Pope", the Bishop of Rome, a title first held by Peter, was considered to be the head of the Roman Catholic church. Peter's successor is generally believed to be Linus, although there is some debate regarding that.
[2] Mark 13: 5-6 and 13: 21-22. See also footnote 1 to Chapter 56.
[3] At the time of this writing (2020) there existed in the Vatican a "Congregation for the Doctrine of the Faith".

APPENDIX B:
ADDITIONAL INFORMATION
OF INTEREST, AND CHRONOLOGY OF EVENTS,
RELATING TO MARY MAGDALENE

• There are a great many variations to the tradition of Mary Magdalene's life in Provence. In this book, the part of her life in Gaul is based on some of the more possible segments from a number of these varying traditions, with fictional, but plausible, persons and events added for story continuity and completeness.

• Nothing is known of Mary Magdalene's life prior to when she met Jesus.

• There is no credible evidence that Mary Magdalene ever was, or was not, married.

• The Book of the Acts of the Apostles is believed to have been written about 65 c. e. It contains no mention of Mary Magdalene.

• The Gospel of Mark is believed to have been written about 70 c. e.

• The Temple in Jerusalem was destroyed in 70 c. e.

• The first version of *The Gospel of Mary* is believed to have been written in the early part of the 3rd century c. e. Who compiled it, and the sources used, are unknown.

• In 397 c. e., the Council of Carthage decided which writings would constitute the official Canon (Bible) of the Christian Church. Twenty-seven writings were chosen, which today are known as the New Testament. *The Gospel of Mary* was not among them, nor were any other Gnostic gospels.

• Both Mary Magdalene and Lazarus have received Sainthood status from the Roman Catholic Church.

• Pope Gregory I, about 591 c. e., issued a homily praising Mary Magdalene for seeking forgiveness for her prior sinful ways, which included accusations about weaknesses of the flesh and lust, thereby creating within the church the perception that she was a reformed prostitute. For elaboration, see the Karen L. King 2003 reference in the bibliography, p. 151. See also the 7th entry that follows, below.

• In 13th century France, church images showing Mary Magdalene preaching were widespread.

• In the period 1480-1590, a great many paintings of Mary Magdalene appeared, mostly by Italian painters but also by others. Some earlier ones are known as well (Donatelli, others).

• In the 17th and 18th centuries, many paintings appeared on the theme of "the penitent Mary Magdalene," including one by El Greco.

- In 1888, Czar Aleksander III of Russia built the Church of Saint Mary Magdalene in Jerusalem on the Mount of Olives in honor of his mother, because Mary Magdalene was her patroness saint.

- In 1896, the first known partial copy of *The Gospel of Mary* was purchased in Cairo. It wasn't published in a modern language until 1955.

- A partial copy of *The Gospel of Mary* was found at Nag Hammadi, Egypt, in 1945.

- In 1969, the Roman Catholic Church, then headed by Pope Paul VI, acknowledged that Mary Magdalene was not a prostitute.

- In 1977, the Vatican issued a declaration reaffirming the Roman Catholic Church's ban on female priests. (Source: *San Diego Union-Tribune*, January 27, 2019, p. B9)

- In a 1979 speech, Theresa Kane, president of the Leadership Conference of Women Religious, a United States organization of nuns, asked Pope John Paul II to permit the ordination of women. The Pope's response was reportedly to forbid the discussion of this topic (*Los Angeles Times*, April 27, 2015).

- On June 30, 1982, the effort to pass an Equal Rights (for women) Amendment to the U.S. Constitution was terminated, as the necessary number of states hadn't ratified it.

- On November 11, 1992, the General Synod of the Church of England approved the ordination of women as priests.

• On April 27, 2015, the *Los Angeles Times* stated, "Relations between the Vatican and the Leadership Conference of Women Religious grew uneasy in 2012 when the Congregation for the Doctrine of the Faith – the Vatican's enforcer of orthodoxy – issued a report saying the nuns in the Leadership Conference had deviated from Roman Catholic doctrine and had promoted 'radical feminist themes.'"

• On November 20, 2012, the General Synod of the Church of England voted not to allow women to become bishops.

• In November 2014, the General Synod of the Church of England voted to allow women to become bishops; the first female Bishop was ordained in January of 2015.

• On April 16, 2015, representatives from the American organization Leadership Conference of Women Religious met with Pope Francis in Rome to discuss their divergent views, and issued a joint report. To date, the ordination of women by the Roman Catholic Church has not been approved.

• On June 10, 2016, the Roman Catholic Church's Congregation for Divine Worship and the Discipline of the Sacraments issued a decree which elevated Mary's liturgical status from an obligatory memorial to a feast day, the same status as enjoyed by the Apostles selected by Jesus. (Peter and Paul are further honored with a solemnity). A preface was added to the Mass which for the first time explicitly referred to Mary as the "apostle to the Apostles."

• In June 2016, a leader of a Jewish group of women was detained by Israeli police for trying to exercise prayer rights equal to those of men at the Western Wall in Jerusalem.

• In 2018, a meeting of Catholic bishops called by Pope Francis discussed women's rights and issued a statement saying a place for women at the church's decision-making table was a "duty of justice" and that the church as a whole must recognize the urgency of "inescapable change." The nuns present were not allowed to vote. (Associated Press, October 28, 2018. See Appendix C for full report.)

APPENDIX C:
FULL TEXT OF THE REPORT
ON THE 2018 VATICAN CONFERENCE

ASSOCIATED PRESS, OCTOBER 28, 2018; VATICAN CITY

A month-long meeting of Catholic bishops marked by demands for women's rights wrapped up Saturday with delegates saying a place for women at the church's decision-making table was a "duty of justice" and the church as a whole must recognize the urgency of "inescapable change."

Pope Francis had called the summit of church leaders to debate ways to better minister to young people and help them find their vocations in life. But the synod was quickly taken over by debate about issues that are particularly dear to the young in many parts of the world: the clergy sex abuse scandal, respect for gays, and women's rights.

The issue of women was acute given only seven nuns were invited to participate in the synod alongside 267 cardinals, bishops, and priests. No women could vote on the final document.

A petition launched on the sidelines of the synod demanding women religious superiors be allowed to vote garnered some 9,000 signatures, but reference in a draft to the gender disparity at future synods was scrapped in the final document.

The language that was kept, however, was strong and included one of the few straight-forward recommendations in the entire 60-page document.

"The synod recommends that everyone be made aware of the urgency of an inescapable change," it said. It called for greater presence of women in church structures at all levels, including positions of responsibility, while respecting that the priesthood remains for men only.

"It's a duty of justice, that finds its inspiration in the way Jesus related to the men and women of his time, as well as the importance of the role of some female figures in the Bible, in the history of salvation and in the life of the church," the document read.

Church doctrine reserves the priesthood for men, given Christ's apostles were male. Women have often complained they have a second-class status in the church. History's first Latin American pope vowed to change that, but he has done little and counts no women among his own advisers.

Paragraphs referencing the role of women in the church were among the most contested during the final vote Saturday. But the full text passed with only the paragraph referencing homosexuality and "sexual inclinations" receiving enough no votes as to threaten passage. In the end it passed with 178 yes votes and 65 no votes.

On abuse, the bishops stopped short of issuing a straight-forward communal apology for the decades of sex abuse and cover-up committed by priests and their superiors against young people. While that section of the document was titled "Seek Pardon," the text voted

Appendix D:
The various Mary's in the
Four Gospels and The Acts

In John's description of the crucifixion, the author places four women at the cross, and three of them are named "Mary" (John 19:25). Thus, it is useful to try to separate the various Mary's that are mentioned in the first five books of the New Testament.

Mary Magdalene: Disciple of Jesus, from Magdala; details of her family are unknown. She was at the crucifixion, and all four Gospels say she was the first to see the empty tomb. In all Gospels except Luke, she is identified as the first person to whom the risen Christ appeared. There is no mention of Mary Magdalene in the New Testament following the end of the four gospels.

Mary (Virgin Mary): Mother of Jesus, wife of Joseph, daughter of Anna and Joachim; from Nazareth. Some sources also refer to her as the mother of James and Joseph, and other brothers of Jesus (see Mark 6:3). Others feel James (and the other brothers of Jesus) are half-brothers, by a previous wife of Joseph. There is a lack of agreement on this point. There is only one mention of her after the crucifixion (Acts 1:14).

Mary of Bethany: Lived in the town of Bethany with her sister Martha and brother Lazarus (John 11). Some Biblical scholars believe Mary Magdalene and Mary of Bethany are the same person, and thus Mary Magdalene is the sister of Martha and Lazarus. However, most Biblical scholars do not concur.

Some versions of the French Mary Magdalene tradition say that Mary of Bethany, Martha, and Lazarus went with Mary Magdalene to Provence after the Resurrection, along with (Saint) Maximin. However, the only known disciple named Maximin is one who lived in France in the 3rd century c. e.; there is no Maximin in the Bible. The "French tradition" appears not to have originated until perhaps the twelfth century c. e.

Mary [who lived in Jerusalem], mother of John Mark (Acts 12:12). John Mark was a close disciple of Peter, and is often referred to as the author of the Gospel of Mark.

Other Marys:
"Mary, the mother of the younger James and of Joseph [or Joses in the King James version]" (Mark 15:40 and 15:47; see also Mark 6:3);

"Mary, the mother of James and Joseph [or Joses in King James version]" (Matthew 27:56; see also Mark 6:3);

"Mary, the mother of James" (Mark 16:1; Luke 24:10)

It is generally assumed that all three of the above passages are referring to the same woman. See also the entry above for "Mary (Virgin Mary)."

"Mary, wife of Cleophas" (spelled "Clopas" in the *Good News Bible*). This Mary was present at the crucifixion (John 19:25). It is assumed that "Cleophas" and "Clopas" are two different spellings of the same name, not two different people. (Note: adding to the confusion, a

"Cleopas" is mentioned in Luke 24:13-18, but no one named Mary is mentioned there.)

" . . . the other Mary" (in Matthew 27:61 and 28:1). It is assumed that this refers to Mary the mother of James and Joseph, who Matthew mentions in 27:56.

The first 3 references to "Other Mary's" mentioned above refer to a woman or women, other than Mary Magdalene, who were present at the crucifixion and/or resurrection.

Sources: *The Harper Collins Bible Dictionary*, pp. 657-9; M. L. del Mastro, *All the Women of the Bible*, pp. 86-88; Richard Bauckham, *Gospel Women*, p. 298; *Guideposts Family Topical Concordance to the Bible*, pp. 437-8; and the four Gospels and the Acts of the Apostles, as indicated.

Appendix E:
References Consulted

(An * indicates this work was particularly helpful in the writing of *Mary's Vision*.)

* Achtemeier, Paul J. *The Harper-Collins Bible Dictionary*. San Francisco: Harper-Collins. 1996.

* American Bible Society. *Good News Bible*. New York: American Bible Society, 1976.

* Bauckham, Richard. *Gospel Women*. Grand Rapids, MI: Amazon, 2002

* Borowski, Oded. *Daily Life in Biblical Times*. Leiden and Boston: Brill, 2003.

Bourgeault, Cynthia. *The Meaning of Mary Magdalene*. Boston: Shambhala, 2010.

* Brock, Ann Graham. *Mary Magdalene, the First Apostle: The Struggle for Authority*. Cambridge, MA: Harvard University Press, 2003.

* Burstein, Dan, and de Keijzer, Arne. *Secrets of Mary Magdelene*. New York: CDS Books, 2006.

Casson, Lionel. *Everyday Life in Ancient Rome*. Baltimore: JHU Press, 1988.

Casson, Lionel. *Ships and Seafaring in Ancient Times*. Austin, Texas: University of Texas Press, 1994.

* Casson, Lionel. *Travel in the Ancient World*. Toronto: Hakkert, 1974.

Chilton, Bruce. *Mary Magdalen: A Biography*. New York: Doubleday, 2005.

* Cowell, F. R. *Everyday Life in Ancient Rome*. London: B. T. Batsford Ltd. , 1961.

* de Boer, Esther. *Mary Magdalen: Beyond the Myth*. Harrisburg, PA: Trinity Press, translated from the original Dutch, 1997.

del Mastro, M. L. *All the Women of the Bible*. Edison, NJ: Castle Books, 2004.

Ehrman, Bart. *The New Testament: A Historical Introduction to Early Christian Writings*. New York and Oxford: Oxford University Press, 1997.

* Ehrman, Bart. *Peter, Paul, and Mary Magdalene*. Oxford University Press, 2006.

* Fredriksen, Paula. *From Jesus to Christ* (2nd ed.). New Haven, CT: Yale University Press, 2000.

Good, Deirdre. *Mariam, the Magdalene, and the Mother.* Bloomington, IN: Indiana Univ. Press, 2005.

* *Guideposts Family Topical Concordance to the Bible.* Nashville and New York: Thomas Nelson Publishers, 1982.

* Haskins, Susan. *Mary Magdalen: Myth and Metaphor.* New York: Harcourt Brace & Co. , 1994.

Holy Bible (New Revised Standard Version). Grand Rapids, MI: Zondervan Bible Publishers, 1990.

* International Bible Press. *The Holy Bible (King James Version).* Philadelphia: John C. Winston, n. d.

Isbouts, Jean-Pierre. *In the Footsteps of Jesus.* Washington, DC: National Geographic Society, 2012.

Isbouts, Jean-Pierre. *The Biblical World: An Illustrated Atlas.* Washington DC: National Geographic Society, 2007.

* Isbouts, Jean-Pierre. *The Story of Christianity.* Washington, DC: National Geographic Society, 2012.

Jansen, Katherine L. *The Making of the Magdalen.* Princeton University Press, 2000.

* *Jesus and the Apostles: Christianity's Early Rise.* Washington, D. C. : National Geographic Society, 2017.

Keller, Werner. *The Bible as History in Pictures.* New York: William Morrow, 1964.

* King, Karen L. *The Gospel of Mary of Magdala: Jesus and the First Woman Apostle*. Santa Rosa, CA: Polebridge Press, 2003.

Koester, Helmut. *History and Literature of Early Christianity* (2nd ed.). Berlin: W. de Gruyter & Co. , 2000.

* Leloup, Jean-Yves. *The Gospel of Mary Magdalene*. Rochester, VT: Inner Traditions, 2002.

Markale, Jean. *The Church of Mary Magdalene*. 2003.

* Meyers, Carol (ed.). *Women in Scripture*. New York: Houghton Mifflin Co. , 2000.

* Moltmann-Wendel, Elisabeth. *The Women Around Jesus*. New York: Crossroad, 1982.

Oxford University Press. *The Gospels*. Norwalk, CT: The Easton Press, 1996.

* Pagels, Elaine. *The Gnostic Gospels*. New York: Vintage Books, 1979.

Picknett, Lynn. *Mary Magdalene: Christianity's Hidden Goddess*. New York: Carroll and Graf, 2003.

Ricci, Carla. *Marty Magdalene and Many Others*. Minneapolis: Fortress Press, 1994.

* Rogerson, John (ed.). *The New Atlas of the Bible*. London: MacDonald and Co. , 1985.

Sabar, Ariel, "The Gospel According to King", *Smithsonian*, November, 2012, pp. 74-83.

Sabar, Ariel, " Unearthing the World of Jesus" , *Smithsonian*, January-February, 2016, pp. 42-55 and 122-130.

Saunders, Ross. *She Has Washed My Feet with Her Tears.* Berkeley, CA: Seastone, 1998.

* Schaberg, Jane. *The Resurrection of Mary Magdalene Understood.* New York: Continuum, 2002.

Severy, Merle, ed. *Everyday Life in Bible Times.* Washington DC: National Geographic Society, 1967.

Starbird, Margaret. *Magdalene's Lost Legacy.* Rochester, VT: Bear & Company, 2003

Talbert, Richard J. A. (Ed.). *Barrington Atlas of the Greek and Roman World.* Princeton, NJ: Princeton University Press, 2000.

Thompson, Mary. *Mary of Magdala: Apostle and Leader.* New York: Paulist Press, 1995.

Todhunter, Andrew. "In the Footsteps of the Apostles," *National Geographic Society*, March 2012, pp. 38-65.

White, L. Michael. *From Jesus to Christianity.* San Francisco: Harper, 2004.

CPSIA information can be obtained
at www.ICGtesting.com
Printed in the USA
LVHW101456150822
725981LV00005B/73